gregory gargoyles

book 2

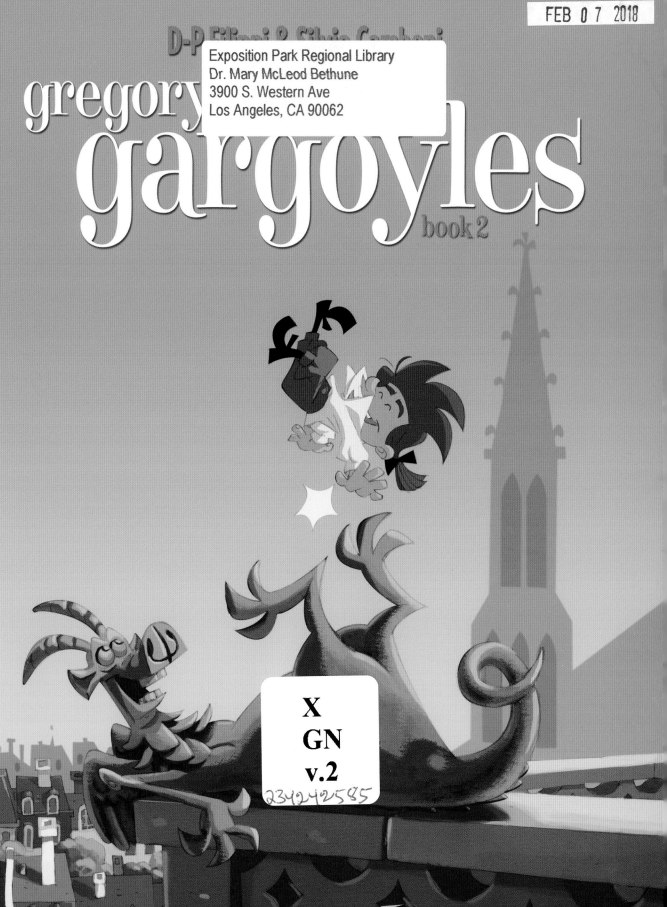

HUMANOIDS KIDS

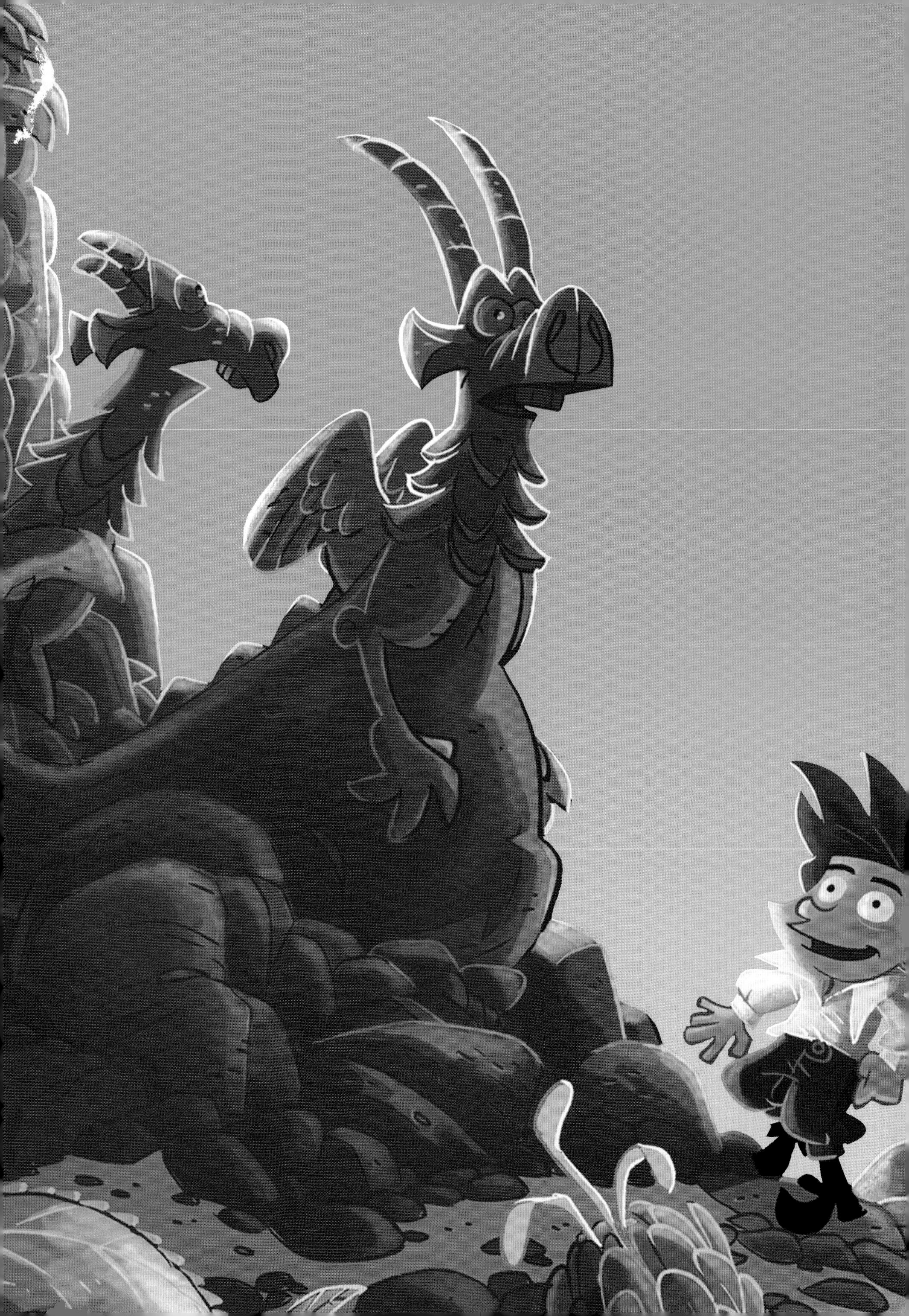

D-P FILIPPI
WRITER

SILVIO CAMBONI
ARTIST

CHRISTELLE MOULART
(PAGES 5 TO 58)
BRUNO OLIVIERI
(PAGES 59 TO 110)
COLORISTS

BLASE A. PROVITOLA
TRANSLATOR

JERRY FRISSEN
SENIOR ART DIRECTOR

TIM PILCHER
& ALEX DONOGHUE
U.S. EDITION EDITORS

FABRICE GIGER
PUBLISHER

Rights & Licensing - licensing@humanoids.com
Press and Social Media - pr@humanoids.com

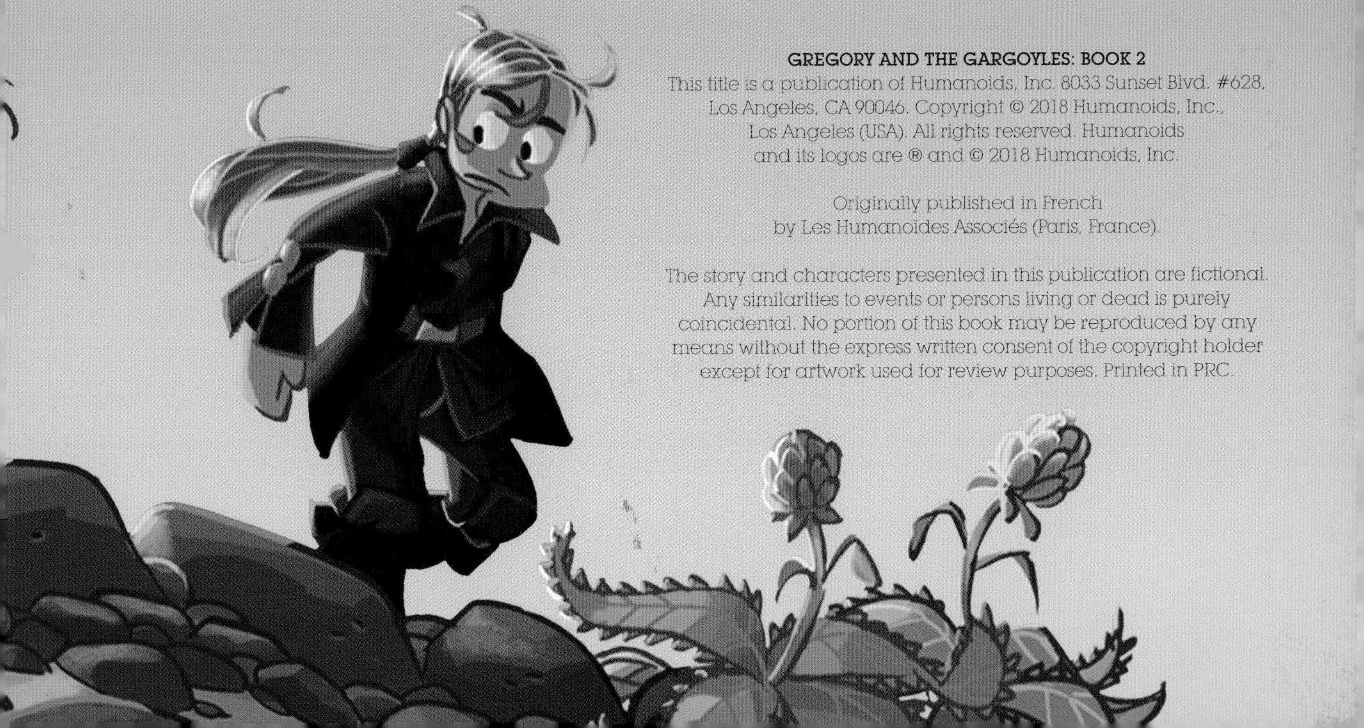

GREGORY AND THE GARGOYLES: BOOK 2
This title is a publication of Humanoids, Inc. 8033 Sunset Blvd. #628, Los Angeles, CA 90046.

Originally published in French by Les Humanoïdes Associés (Paris, France).

ALSO BY D-P FILIPPI:

GREGORY AND THE GARGOYLES: BOOK 1
ISBN: 978-1-59465-798-6

JOHN LORD
ISBN: 978-1-59465-183-0

MARSHALS
ISBN: 978-1-59465-140-3

MUSE
ISBN: 978-1-59465-038-3

OTHER HUMANOIDS KIDS TITLES:

HALLOWEEN TALES
ISBN: 978-159465-654-5

THE MAGICAL TWINS
ISBN: 978-1-59465-408-4

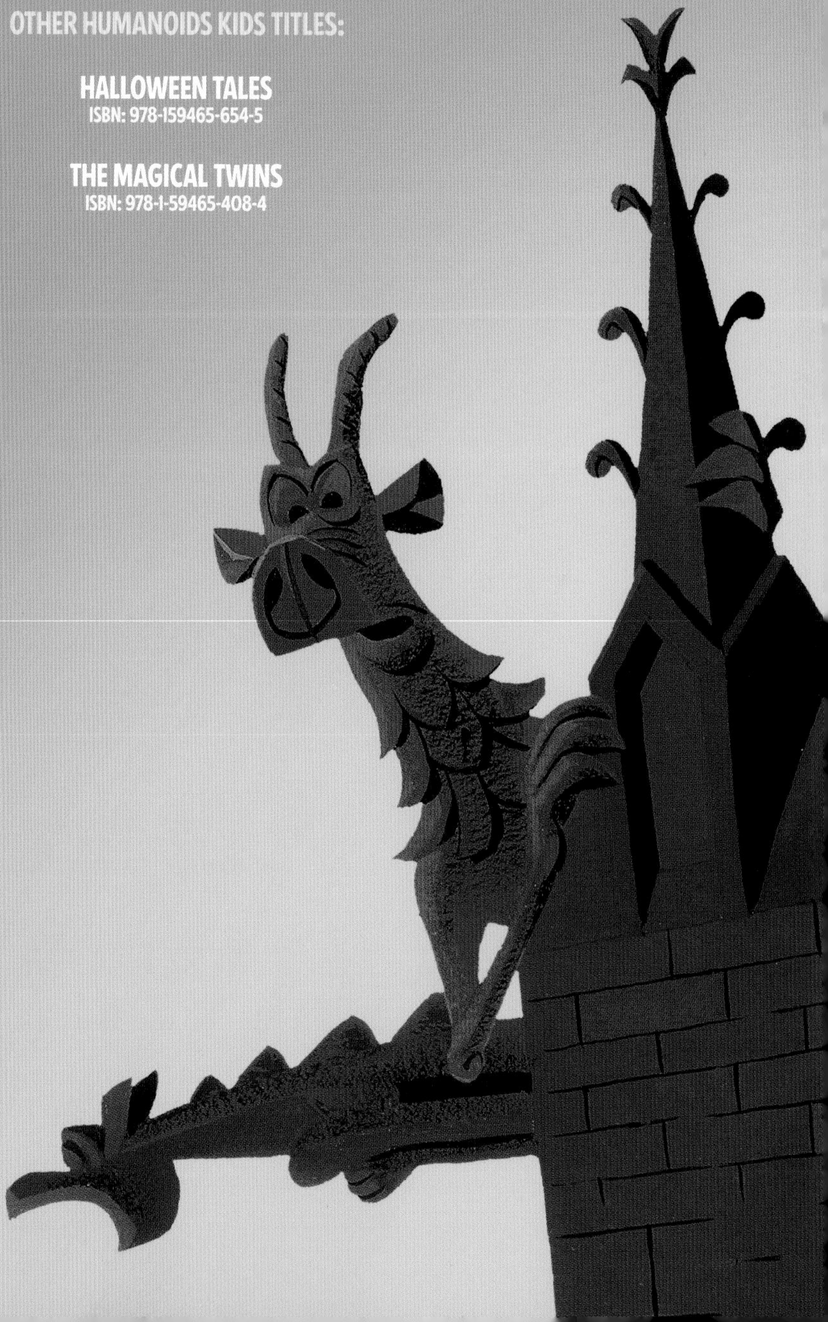

The Story so far...

Meet Gregory. He's pretty much normal, except that he's a tad lonelier and he daydreams a bit more than the average kid. He lives across from a cathedral with his parents and his annoying sister, whom he can't stand. One day, he finds a magical medallion under the floor in his bedroom that gives him the power to travel back to the 17th century, where an extraordinary destiny awaits him: becoming a magician!

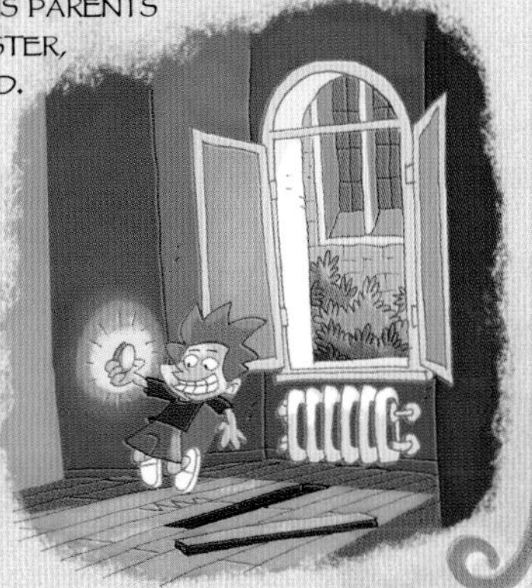

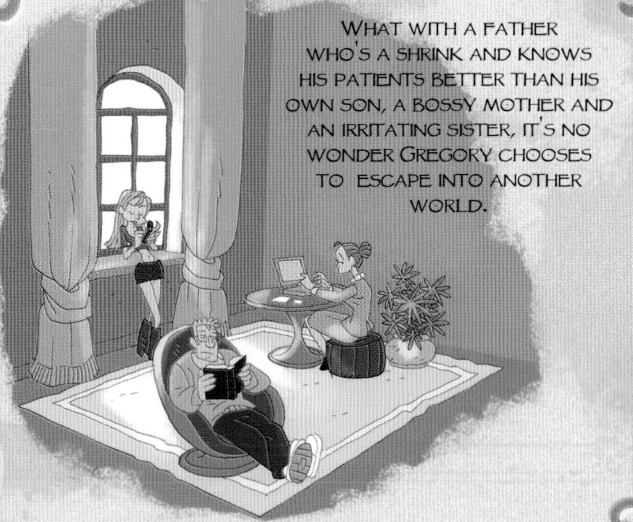

What with a father who's a shrink and knows his patients better than his own son, a bossy mother and an irritating sister, it's no wonder Gregory chooses to escape into another world.

Back in the 17th Century, his mom is nicer and more caring, his father is a blacksmith who takes him fishing and treats him like a man, and his sister is about to be married.

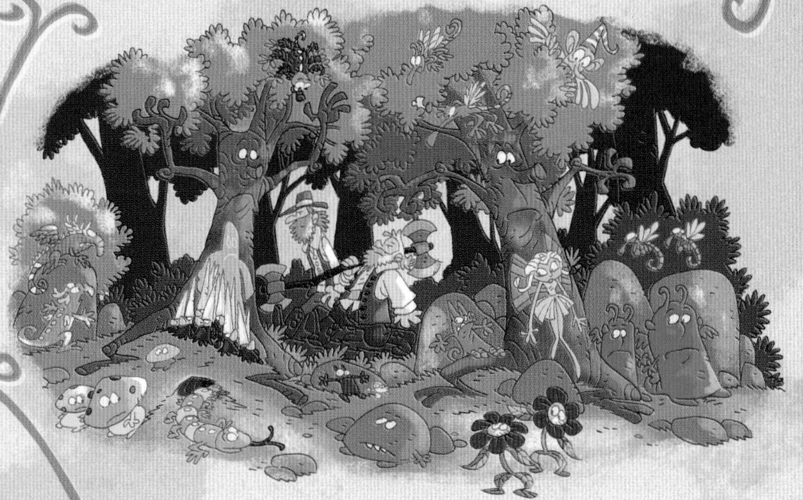

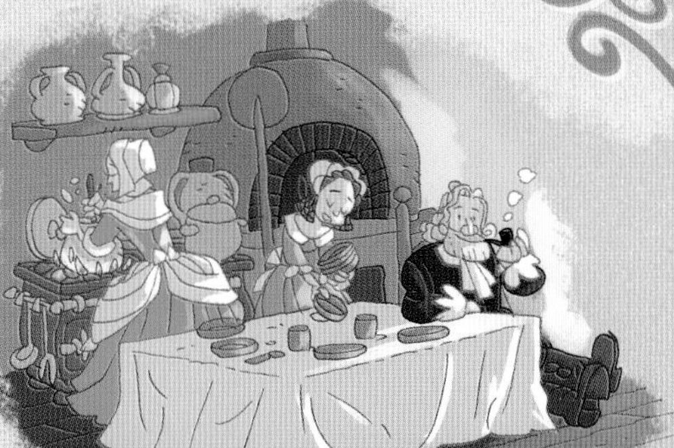

But that's not even the best part! Imagine, if you will, that in those days, magic and magical beings of all sorts are still real and they co-exist right alongside humans.

But, alas, not for much longer, as there are no magicians left to protect the two universes and keep them separate. They all perished during the great conflict with the terrible, fearsome Black magician.

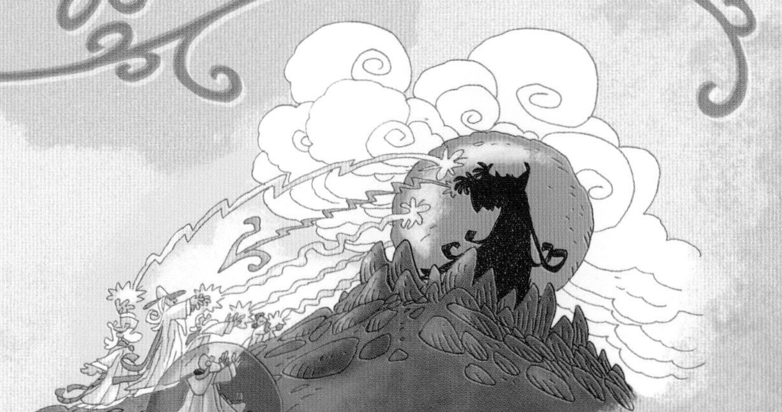

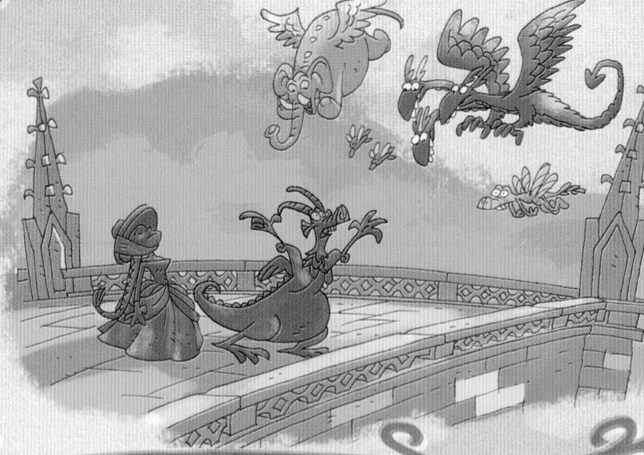

That weird-looking statue there, waving wildly, that's Phidias. He's Gregory's guide and instructor. Phidias and his friends all live on top of the cathedral. They are the guardians of the last magic door through which supernatural beings can escape. Phidias is the one who told Gregory he could become a magician and save them all.

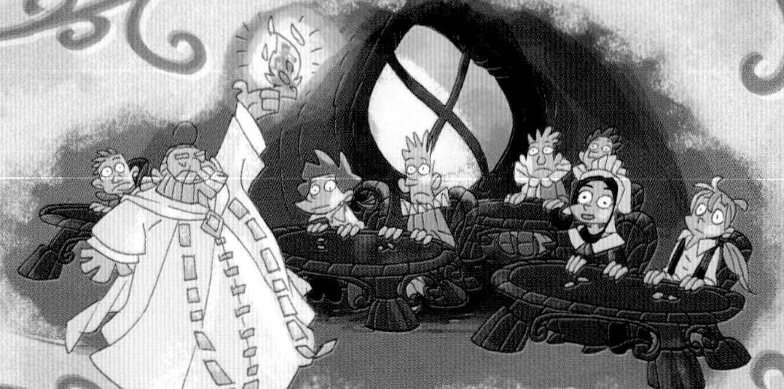

In order to do this, Gregory has to undergo intensive training. Thanks to the Key of Time, he travels back to the past where he and other apprentices from different time periods take lessons with Master Wilgur.

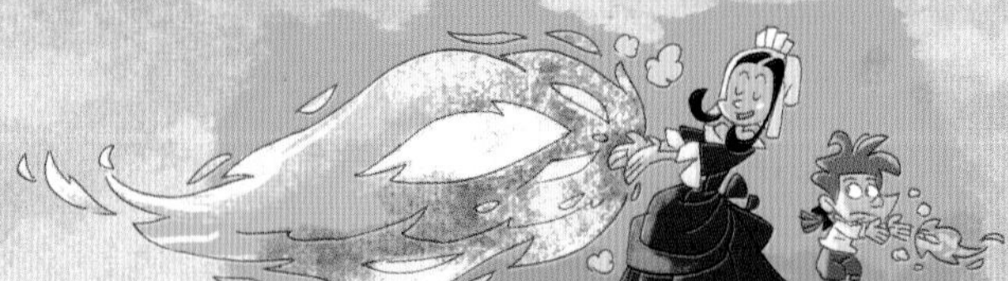

Gregory is especially close to his cousin Edna, a fellow student in Wilgur's class. She's awesome with spells. Maybe even a little too awesome, if you ask him.

Edna's mother, i.e. Gregory's aunt, is an evil being who, along with a mysterious man in a hood, seeks to bring the Black magician back to life, perhaps even using Edna's body for his reincarnation. To do this, she captures supernatural beings and steals their powers. Needless to say, Edna's aunt is the sworn enemy of Phidias and the guardians.

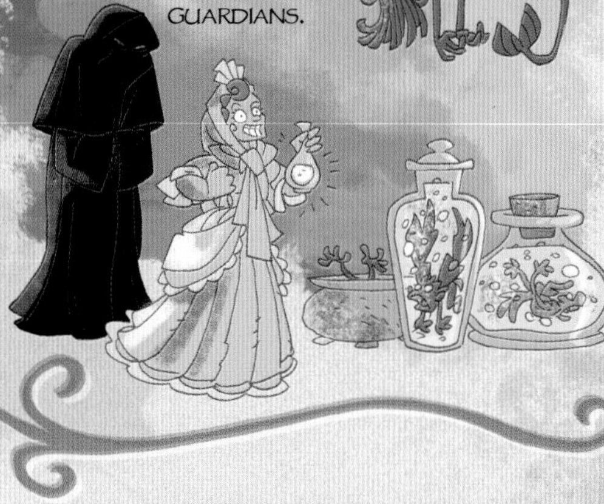

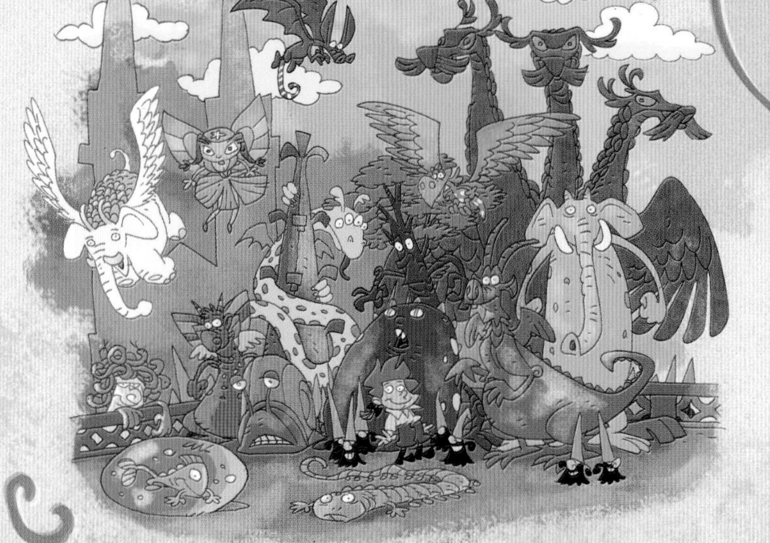

But Gregory intends to do everything in his power to reach his goal. Thanks to the medallion that allows him to come and go as he pleases between time periods, he gradually learns how to become the one who embodies all the hopes and dreams of the supernatural beings - the one who could bring magic back one day. But with all that said, Gregory is still just a boy, with confused feelings...

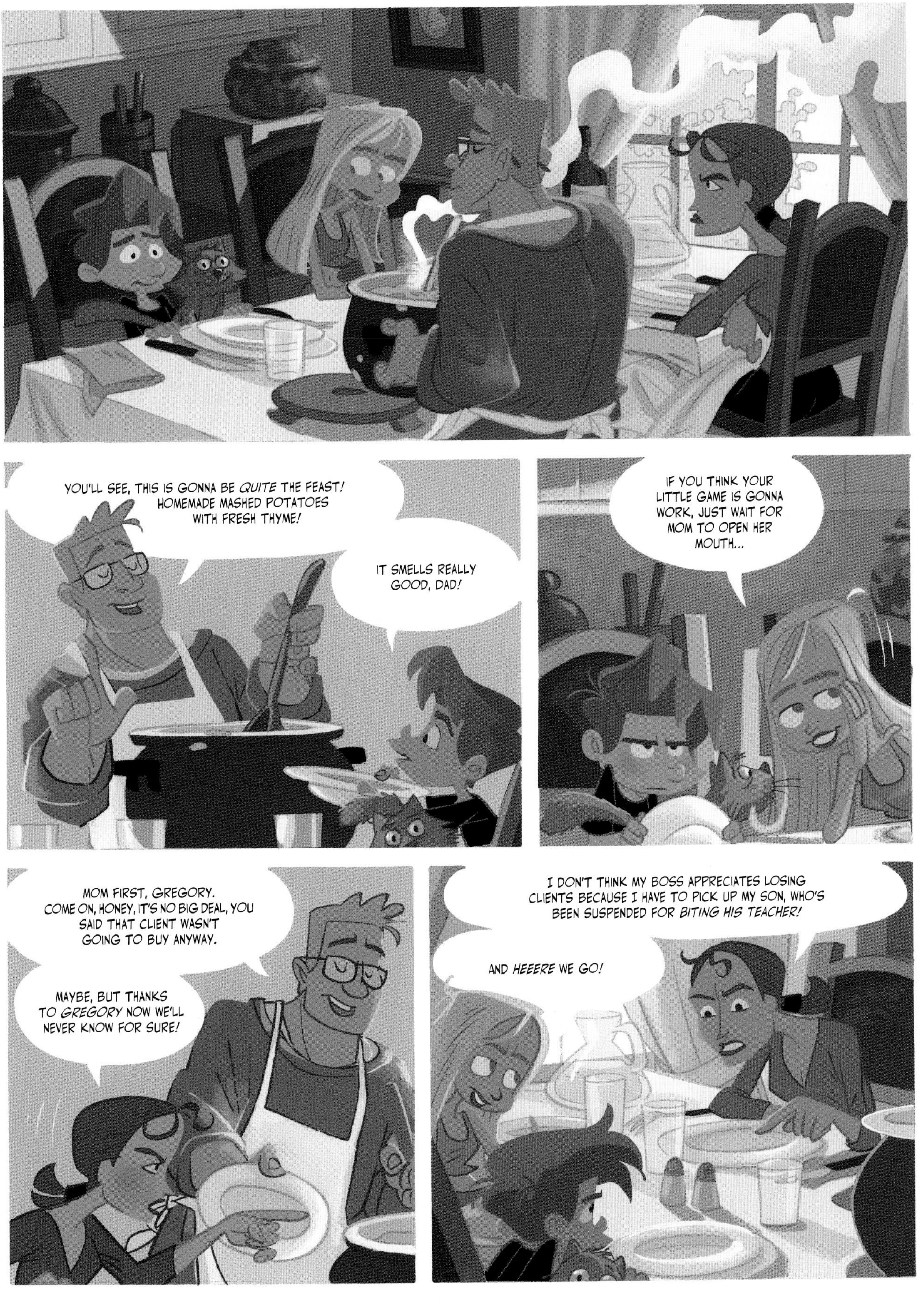
YOU'LL SEE, THIS IS GONNA BE *QUITE* THE FEAST! HOMEMADE MASHED POTATOES WITH FRESH THYME!
IT SMELLS REALLY GOOD, DAD!
IF YOU THINK YOUR LITTLE GAME IS GONNA WORK, JUST WAIT FOR MOM TO OPEN HER MOUTH...
MOM FIRST, GREGORY. COME ON, HONEY, IT'S NO BIG DEAL, YOU SAID THAT CLIENT WASN'T GOING TO BUY ANYWAY.
MAYBE, BUT THANKS TO *GREGORY* NOW WE'LL NEVER KNOW FOR SURE!
I DON'T THINK MY BOSS APPRECIATES LOSING CLIENTS BECAUSE I HAVE TO PICK UP MY SON, WHO'S BEEN SUSPENDED FOR *BITING HIS TEACHER!*
AND *HEEERE* WE GO!

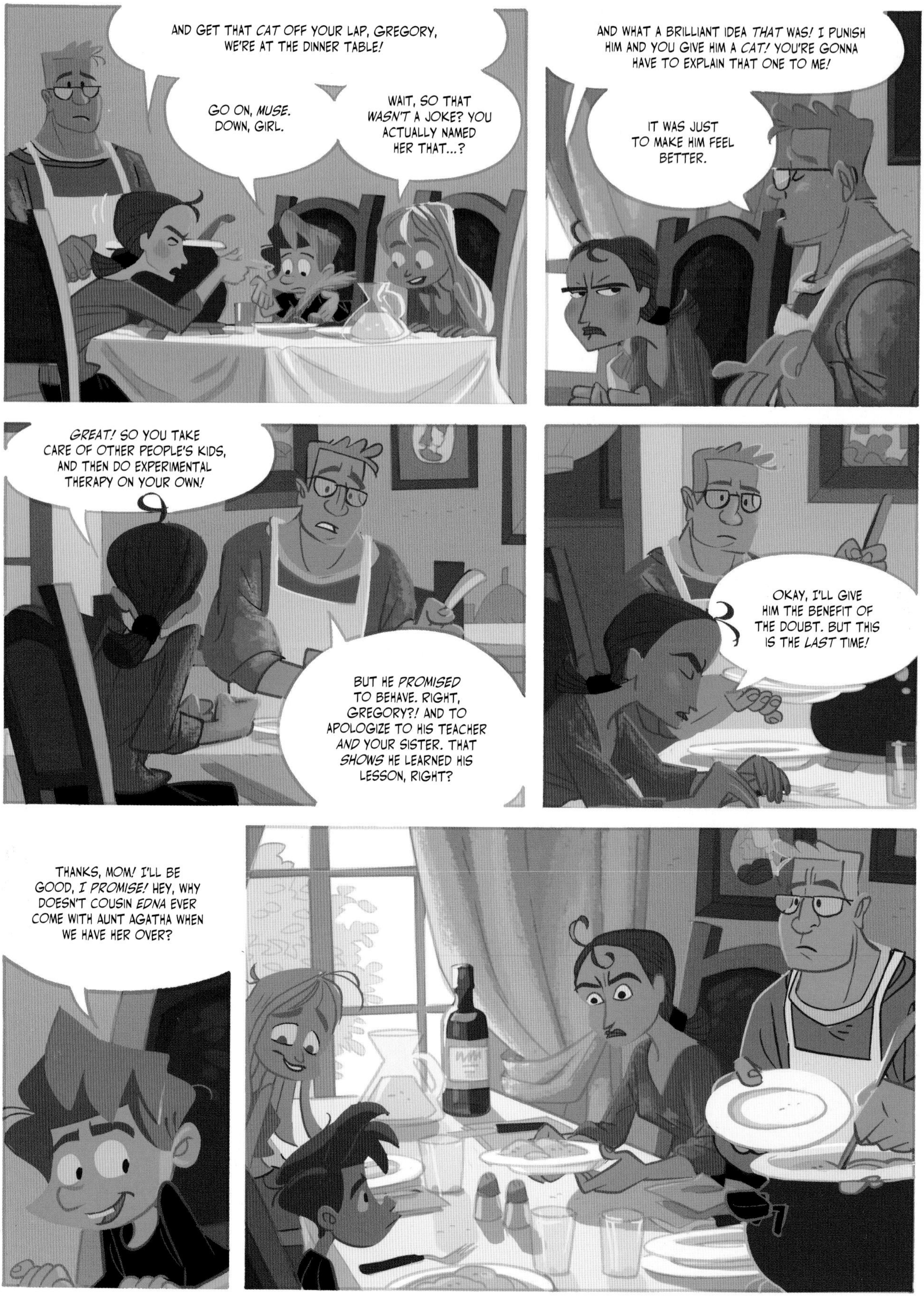

AND GET THAT *CAT* OFF YOUR LAP, GREGORY, WE'RE AT THE DINNER TABLE!
GO ON, *MUSE*. DOWN, GIRL.
WAIT, SO THAT *WASN'T* A JOKE? YOU ACTUALLY NAMED HER THAT...?
AND WHAT A BRILLIANT IDEA *THAT* WAS! I PUNISH HIM AND YOU GIVE HIM A *CAT!* YOU'RE GONNA HAVE TO EXPLAIN THAT ONE TO ME!
IT WAS JUST TO MAKE HIM FEEL BETTER.
GREAT! SO YOU TAKE CARE OF OTHER PEOPLE'S KIDS, AND THEN DO EXPERIMENTAL THERAPY ON YOUR OWN!
BUT HE *PROMISED* TO BEHAVE. RIGHT, GREGORY?! AND TO APOLOGIZE TO HIS TEACHER *AND* YOUR SISTER. THAT *SHOWS* HE LEARNED HIS LESSON, RIGHT?
OKAY, I'LL GIVE HIM THE BENEFIT OF THE DOUBT. BUT THIS IS THE *LAST* TIME!
THANKS, MOM! I'LL BE GOOD, *I PROMISE!* HEY, WHY DOESN'T COUSIN *EDNA* EVER COME WITH AUNT AGATHA WHEN WE HAVE HER OVER?

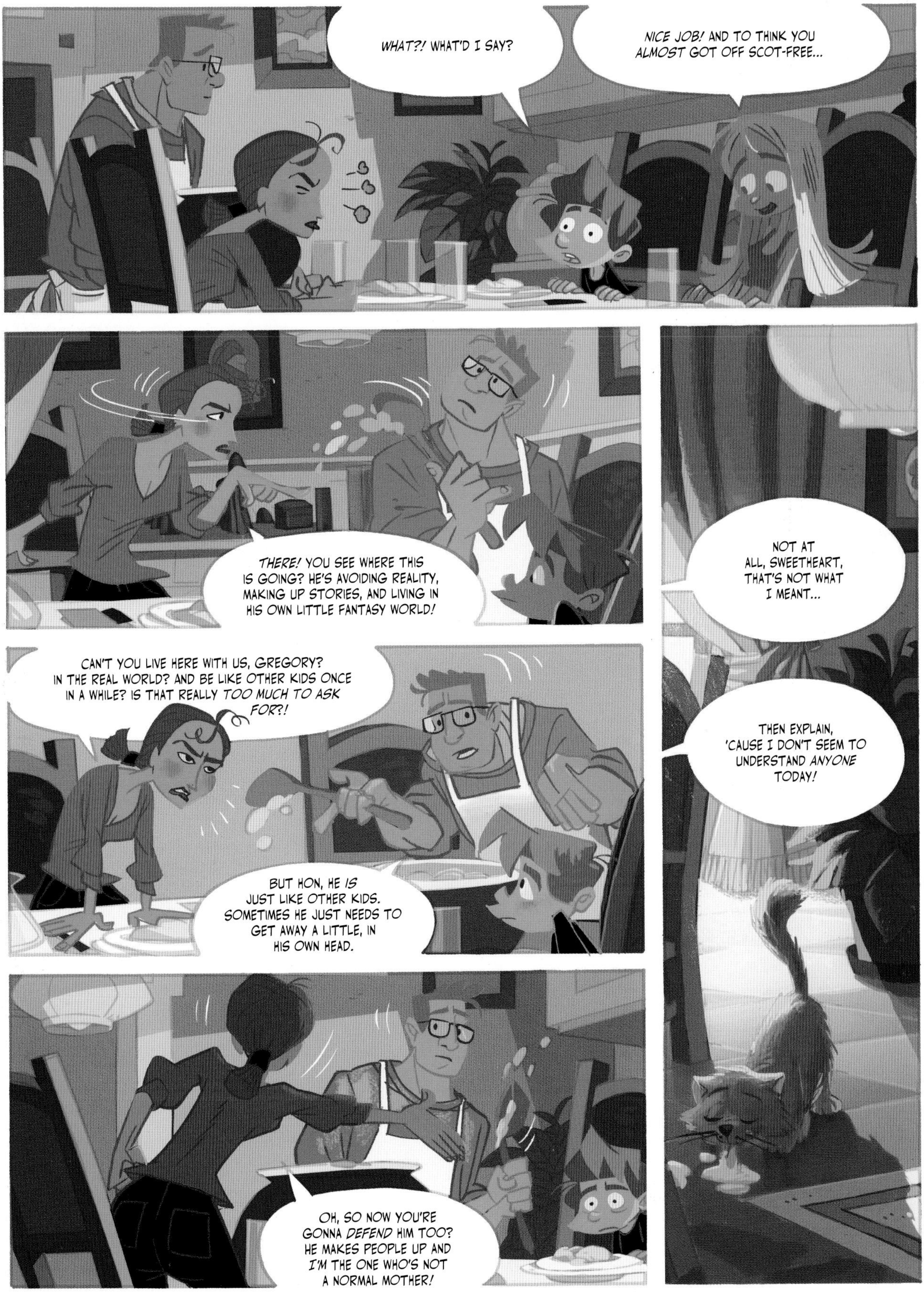

WHAT?! WHAT'D I SAY?
NICE JOB! AND TO THINK YOU *ALMOST* GOT OFF SCOT-FREE...
THERE! YOU SEE WHERE THIS IS GOING? HE'S AVOIDING REALITY, MAKING UP STORIES, AND LIVING IN HIS OWN LITTLE FANTASY WORLD!
CAN'T YOU LIVE HERE WITH US, GREGORY? IN THE REAL WORLD? AND BE LIKE OTHER KIDS ONCE IN A WHILE? IS THAT REALLY *TOO MUCH TO ASK FOR?!*
BUT HON, HE *IS* JUST LIKE OTHER KIDS. SOMETIMES HE JUST NEEDS TO GET AWAY A LITTLE, IN HIS OWN HEAD.
NOT AT ALL, SWEETHEART, THAT'S NOT WHAT I MEANT...
THEN EXPLAIN, 'CAUSE I DON'T SEEM TO UNDERSTAND *ANYONE* TODAY!
OH, SO NOW YOU'RE GONNA *DEFEND* HIM TOO? HE MAKES PEOPLE UP AND *I'M* THE ONE WHO'S NOT A NORMAL MOTHER!

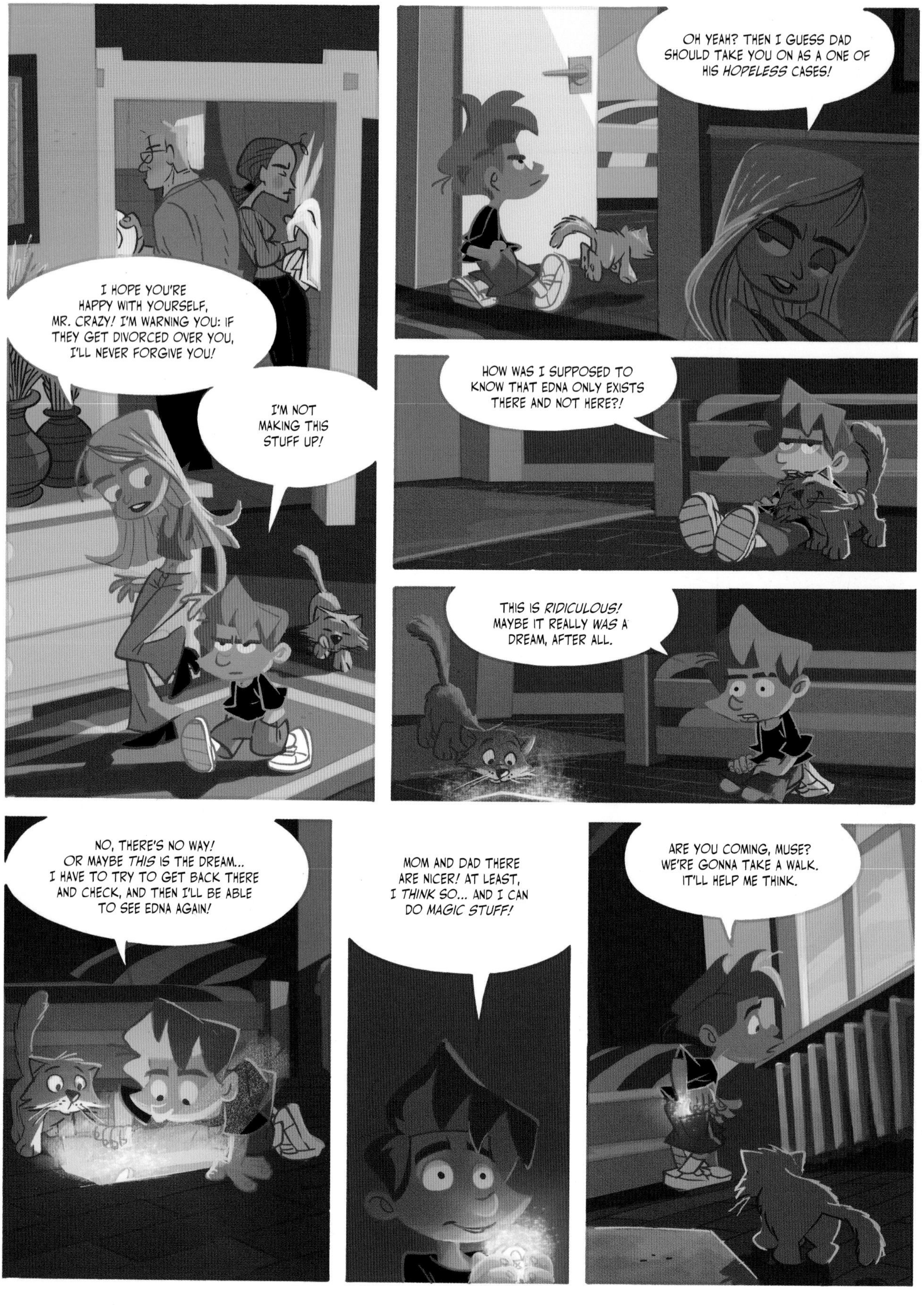
I HOPE YOU'RE HAPPY WITH YOURSELF, MR. CRAZY! I'M WARNING YOU: IF THEY GET DIVORCED OVER YOU, I'LL NEVER FORGIVE YOU!
I'M NOT MAKING THIS STUFF UP!
OH YEAH? THEN I GUESS DAD SHOULD TAKE YOU ON AS A ONE OF HIS HOPELESS CASES!
HOW WAS I SUPPOSED TO KNOW THAT EDNA ONLY EXISTS THERE AND NOT HERE?!
THIS IS RIDICULOUS! MAYBE IT REALLY WAS A DREAM, AFTER ALL.
NO, THERE'S NO WAY! OR MAYBE THIS IS THE DREAM... I HAVE TO TRY TO GET BACK THERE AND CHECK, AND THEN I'LL BE ABLE TO SEE EDNA AGAIN!
MOM AND DAD THERE ARE NICER! AT LEAST, I THINK SO... AND I CAN DO MAGIC STUFF!
ARE YOU COMING, MUSE? WE'RE GONNA TAKE A WALK. IT'LL HELP ME THINK.

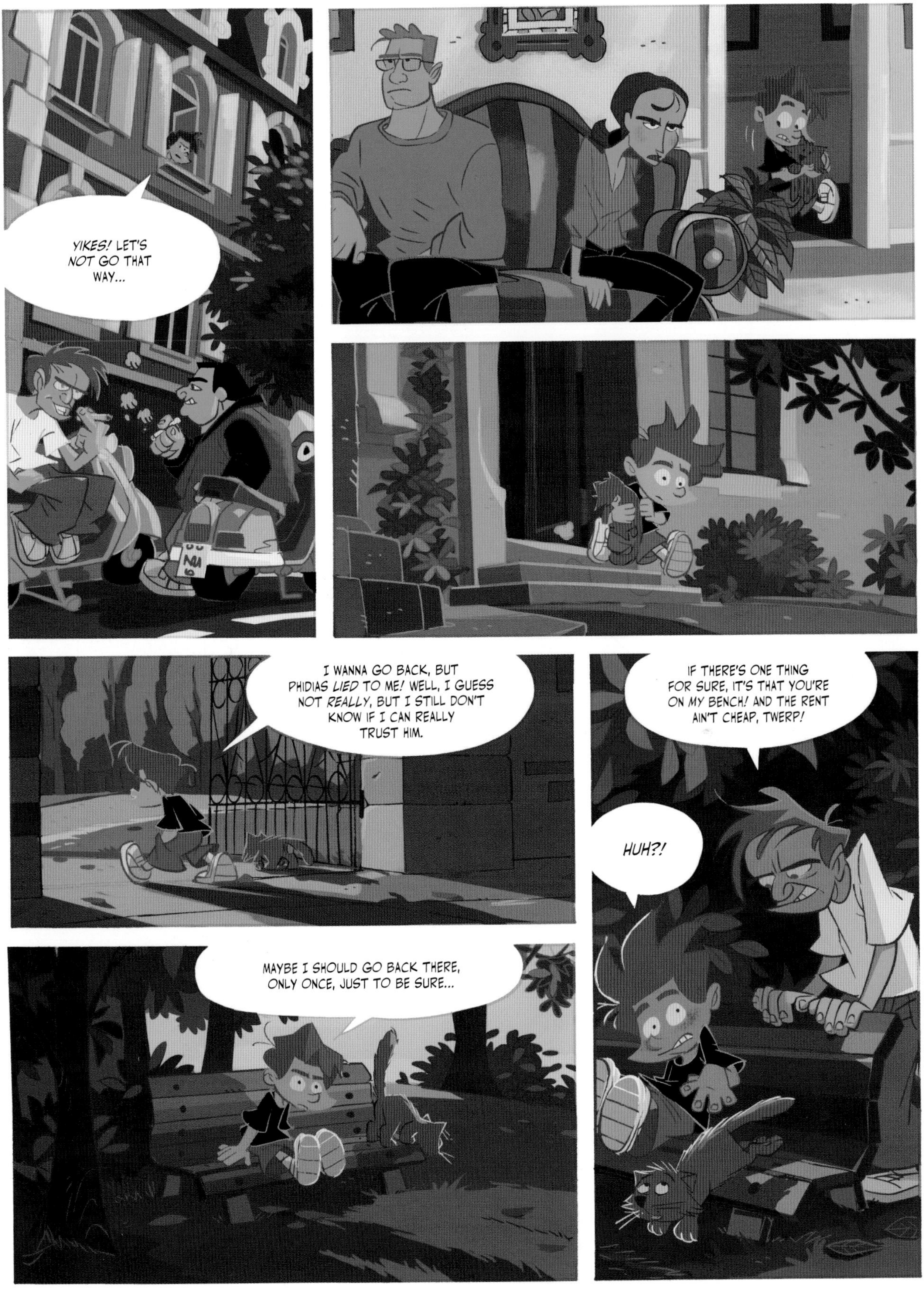
YIKES! LET'S NOT GO THAT WAY...
I WANNA GO BACK, BUT PHIDIAS LIED TO ME! WELL, I GUESS NOT REALLY, BUT I STILL DON'T KNOW IF I CAN REALLY TRUST HIM.
MAYBE I SHOULD GO BACK THERE, ONLY ONCE, JUST TO BE SURE...
IF THERE'S ONE THING FOR SURE, IT'S THAT YOU'RE ON MY BENCH! AND THE RENT AIN'T CHEAP, TWERP!
HUH?!

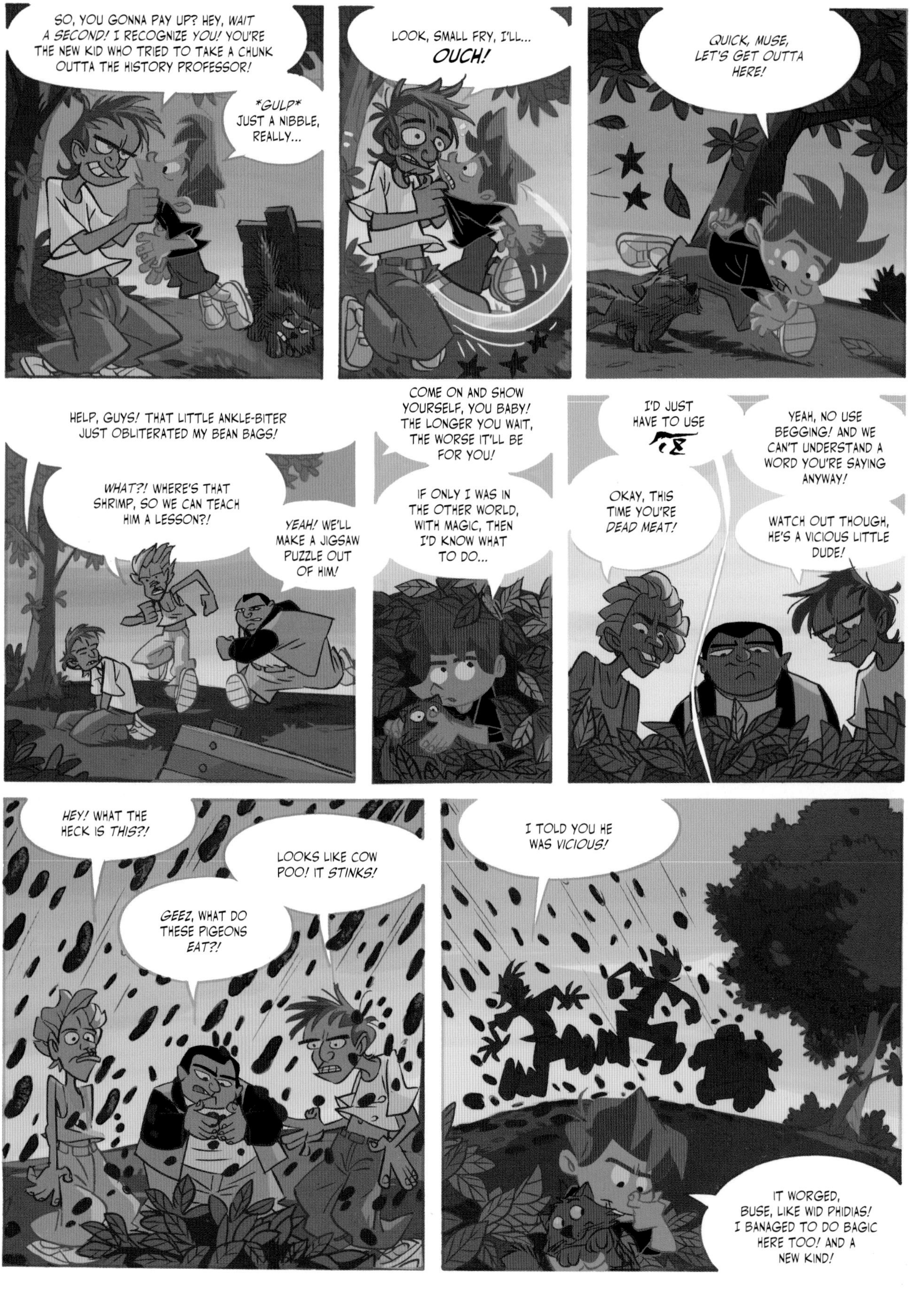
SO, YOU GONNA PAY UP? HEY, WAIT A SECOND! I RECOGNIZE YOU! YOU'RE THE NEW KID WHO TRIED TO TAKE A CHUNK OUTTA THE HISTORY PROFESSOR!
GULP JUST A NIBBLE, REALLY...
LOOK, SMALL FRY, I'LL... OUCH!
QUICK, MUSE, LET'S GET OUTTA HERE!
HELP, GUYS! THAT LITTLE ANKLE-BITER JUST OBLITERATED MY BEAN BAGS!
WHAT?! WHERE'S THAT SHRIMP, SO WE CAN TEACH HIM A LESSON?!
YEAH! WE'LL MAKE A JIGSAW PUZZLE OUT OF HIM!
COME ON AND SHOW YOURSELF, YOU BABY! THE LONGER YOU WAIT, THE WORSE IT'LL BE FOR YOU!
IF ONLY I WAS IN THE OTHER WORLD, WITH MAGIC, THEN I'D KNOW WHAT TO DO...
I'D JUST HAVE TO USE
YEAH, NO USE BEGGING! AND WE CAN'T UNDERSTAND A WORD YOU'RE SAYING ANYWAY!
OKAY, THIS TIME YOU'RE DEAD MEAT!
WATCH OUT THOUGH, HE'S A VICIOUS LITTLE DUDE!
HEY! WHAT THE HECK IS THIS?!
LOOKS LIKE COW POO! IT STINKS!
GEEZ, WHAT DO THESE PIGEONS EAT?!
I TOLD YOU HE WAS VICIOUS!
IT WORGED, BUSE, LIKE WID PHIDIAS! I BANAGED TO DO BAGIC HERE TOO! AND A NEW KIND!

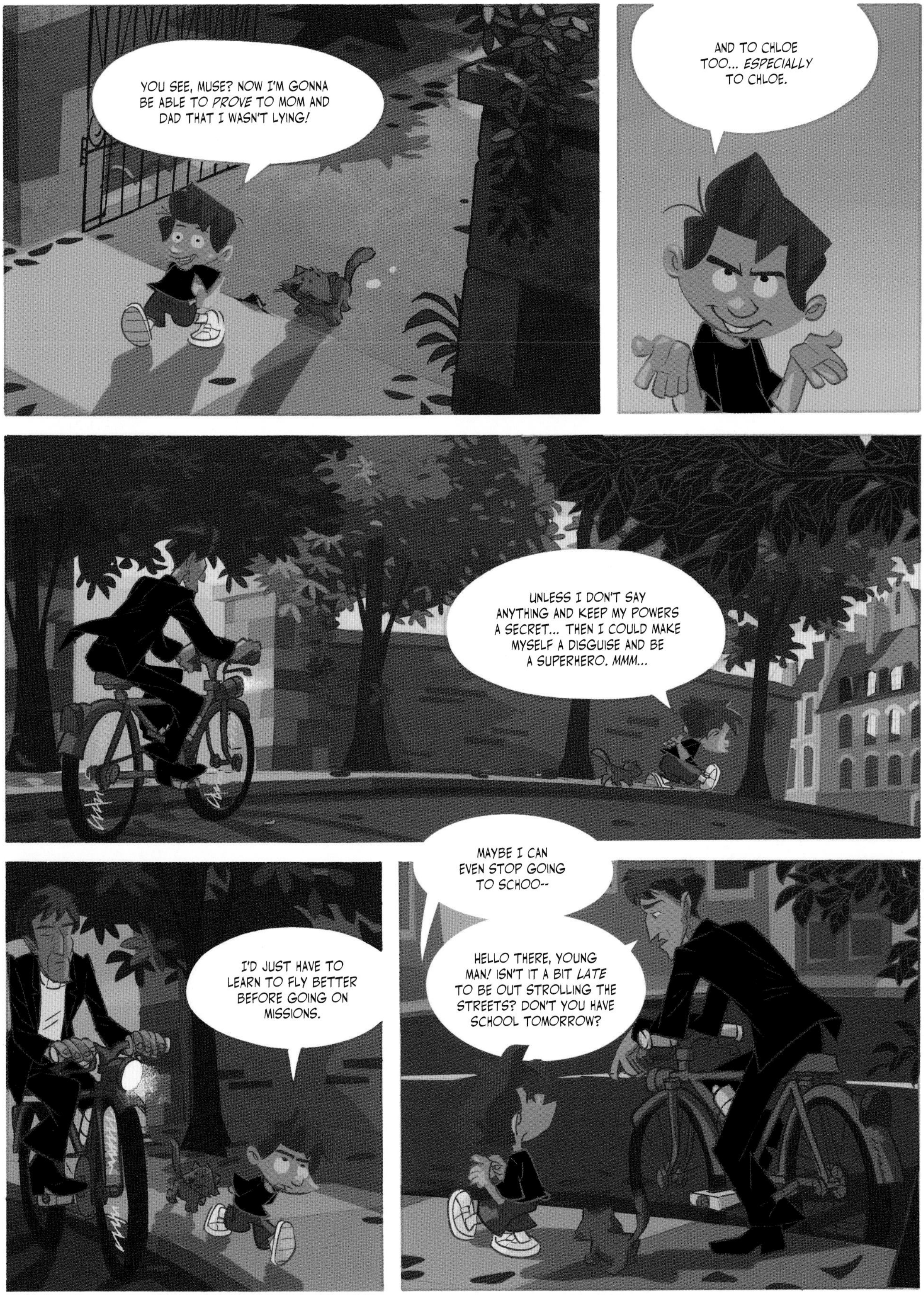
YOU SEE, MUSE? NOW I'M GONNA BE ABLE TO *PROVE* TO MOM AND DAD THAT I WASN'T LYING!
AND TO CHLOE TOO... *ESPECIALLY* TO CHLOE.
UNLESS I DON'T SAY ANYTHING AND KEEP MY POWERS A SECRET... THEN I COULD MAKE MYSELF A DISGUISE AND BE A SUPERHERO. MMM...
I'D JUST HAVE TO LEARN TO FLY BETTER BEFORE GOING ON MISSIONS.
MAYBE I CAN EVEN STOP GOING TO SCHOO--
HELLO THERE, YOUNG MAN! ISN'T IT A BIT *LATE* TO BE OUT STROLLING THE STREETS? DON'T YOU HAVE SCHOOL TOMORROW?

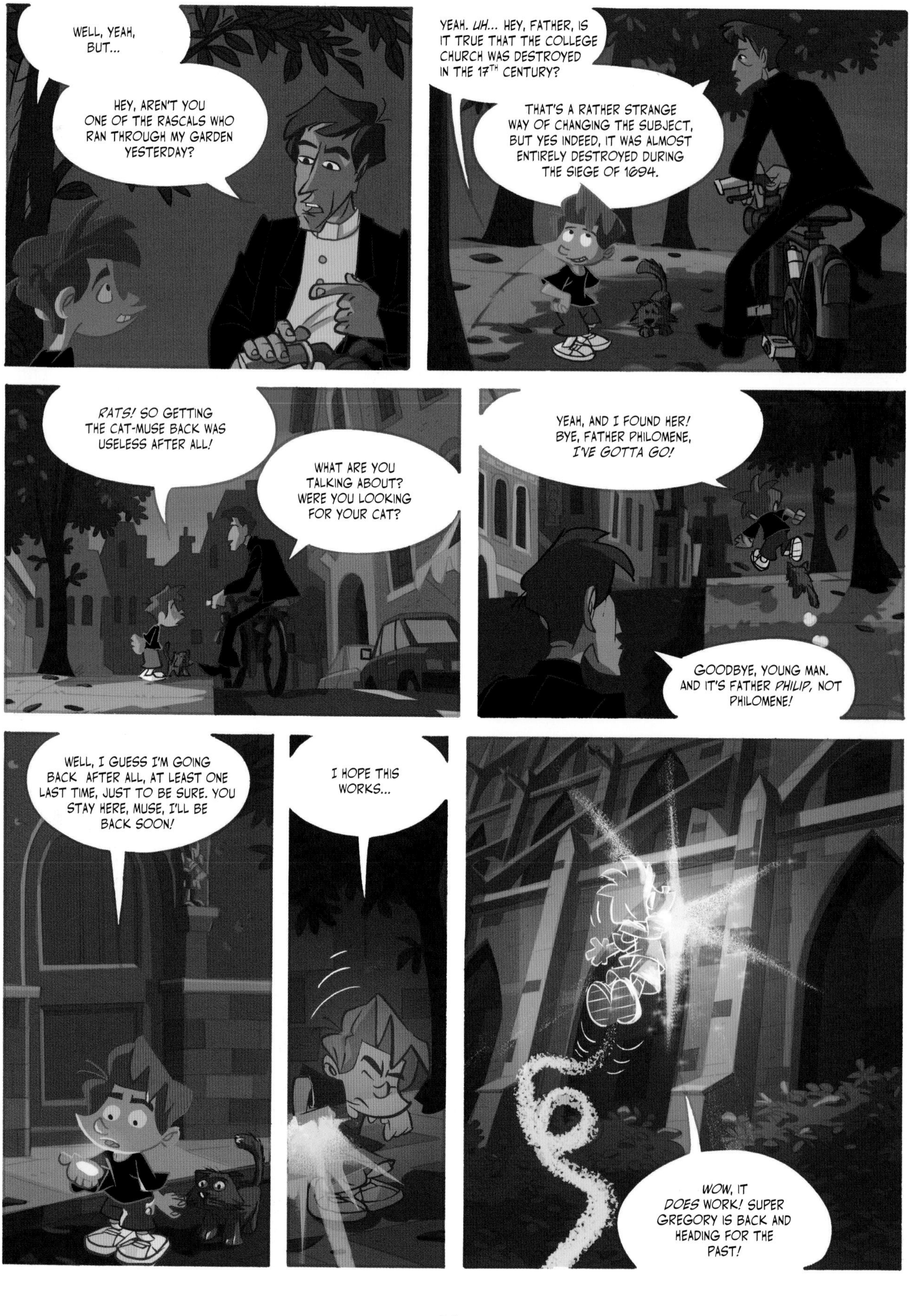
WELL, YEAH, BUT...
HEY, AREN'T YOU ONE OF THE RASCALS WHO RAN THROUGH MY GARDEN YESTERDAY?
YEAH. *UH...* HEY, FATHER, IS IT TRUE THAT THE COLLEGE CHURCH WAS DESTROYED IN THE 17TH CENTURY?
THAT'S A RATHER STRANGE WAY OF CHANGING THE SUBJECT, BUT YES INDEED, IT WAS ALMOST ENTIRELY DESTROYED DURING THE SIEGE OF 1694.
RATS! SO GETTING THE CAT-MUSE BACK WAS USELESS AFTER ALL!
WHAT ARE YOU TALKING ABOUT? WERE YOU LOOKING FOR YOUR CAT?
YEAH, AND I FOUND HER! BYE, FATHER PHILOMENE, *I'VE GOTTA GO!*
GOODBYE, YOUNG MAN. AND IT'S FATHER *PHILIP,* NOT PHILOMENE!
WELL, I GUESS I'M GOING BACK AFTER ALL, AT LEAST ONE LAST TIME, JUST TO BE SURE. YOU STAY HERE, MUSE, I'LL BE BACK SOON!
I HOPE THIS WORKS...
WOW, IT *DOES* WORK! SUPER GREGORY IS BACK AND HEADING FOR THE PAST!

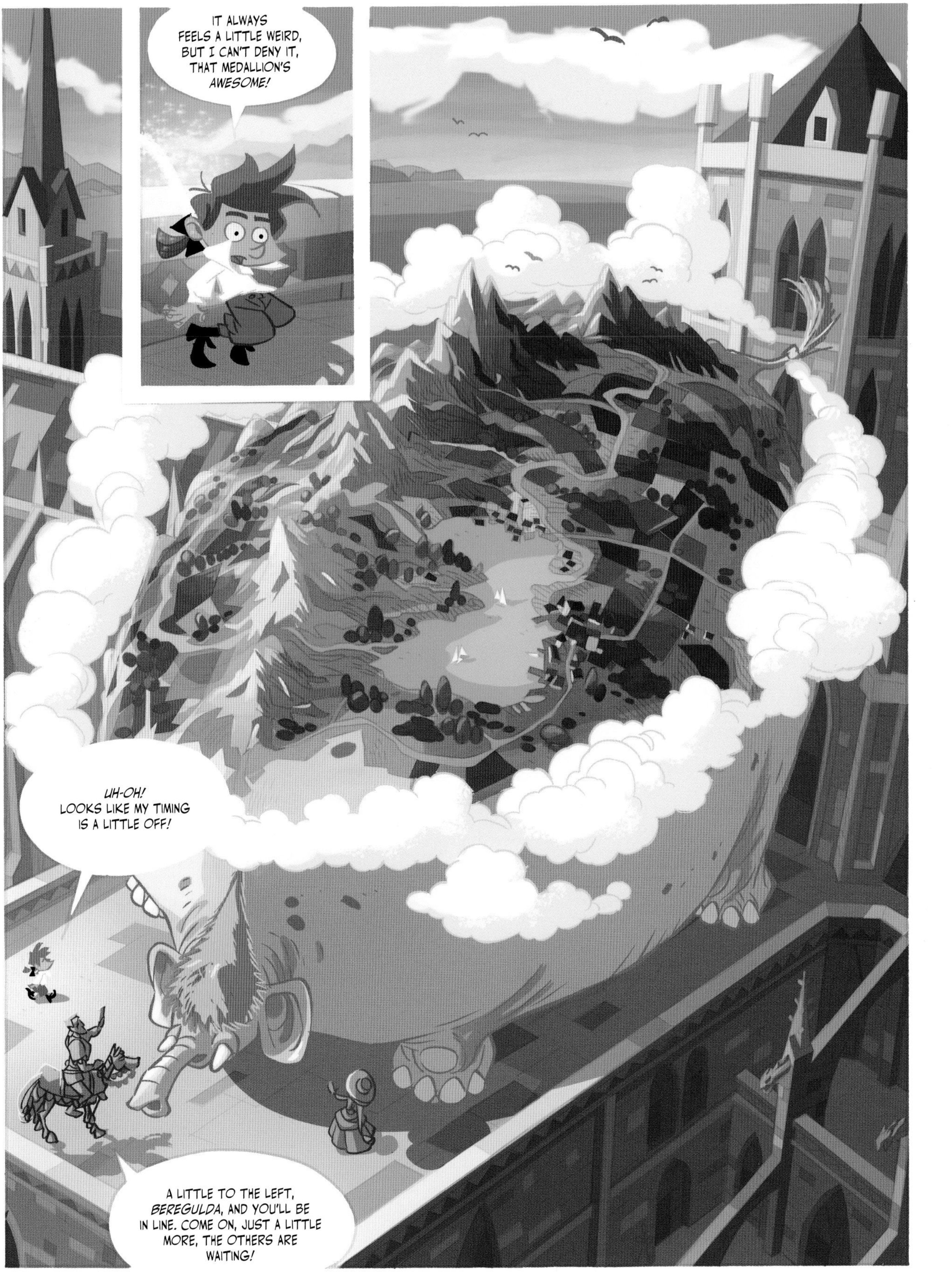
IT ALWAYS FEELS A LITTLE WEIRD, BUT I CAN'T DENY IT, THAT MEDALLION'S *AWESOME!*
UH-OH! LOOKS LIKE MY TIMING IS A LITTLE OFF!
A LITTLE TO THE LEFT, *BEREGULDA*, AND YOU'LL BE IN LINE. COME ON, JUST A LITTLE MORE, THE OTHERS ARE WAITING!

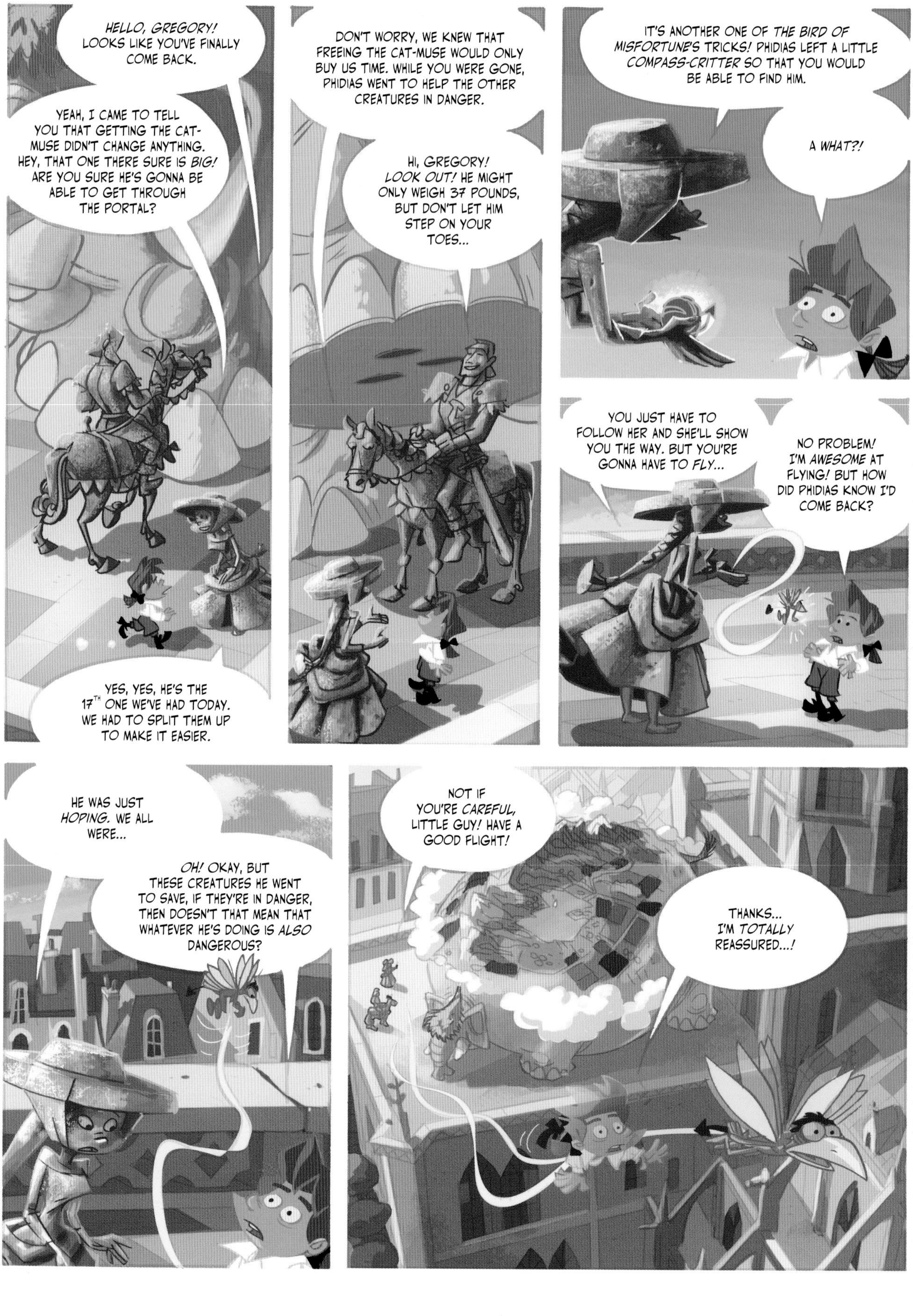

HELLO, GREGORY! LOOKS LIKE YOU'VE FINALLY COME BACK.
YEAH, I CAME TO TELL YOU THAT GETTING THE CAT-MUSE DIDN'T CHANGE ANYTHING. HEY, THAT ONE THERE SURE IS BIG! ARE YOU SURE HE'S GONNA BE ABLE TO GET THROUGH THE PORTAL?
YES, YES, HE'S THE 17TH ONE WE'VE HAD TODAY. WE HAD TO SPLIT THEM UP TO MAKE IT EASIER.
DON'T WORRY, WE KNEW THAT FREEING THE CAT-MUSE WOULD ONLY BUY US TIME. WHILE YOU WERE GONE, PHIDIAS WENT TO HELP THE OTHER CREATURES IN DANGER.
HI, GREGORY! LOOK OUT! HE MIGHT ONLY WEIGH 37 POUNDS, BUT DON'T LET HIM STEP ON YOUR TOES...
IT'S ANOTHER ONE OF THE BIRD OF MISFORTUNE'S TRICKS! PHIDIAS LEFT A LITTLE COMPASS-CRITTER SO THAT YOU WOULD BE ABLE TO FIND HIM.
A WHAT?!
YOU JUST HAVE TO FOLLOW HER AND SHE'LL SHOW YOU THE WAY. BUT YOU'RE GONNA HAVE TO FLY...
NO PROBLEM! I'M AWESOME AT FLYING! BUT HOW DID PHIDIAS KNOW I'D COME BACK?
HE WAS JUST HOPING. WE ALL WERE...
OH! OKAY, BUT THESE CREATURES HE WENT TO SAVE, IF THEY'RE IN DANGER, THEN DOESN'T THAT MEAN THAT WHATEVER HE'S DOING IS ALSO DANGEROUS?
NOT IF YOU'RE CAREFUL, LITTLE GUY! HAVE A GOOD FLIGHT!
THANKS... I'M TOTALLY REASSURED...!

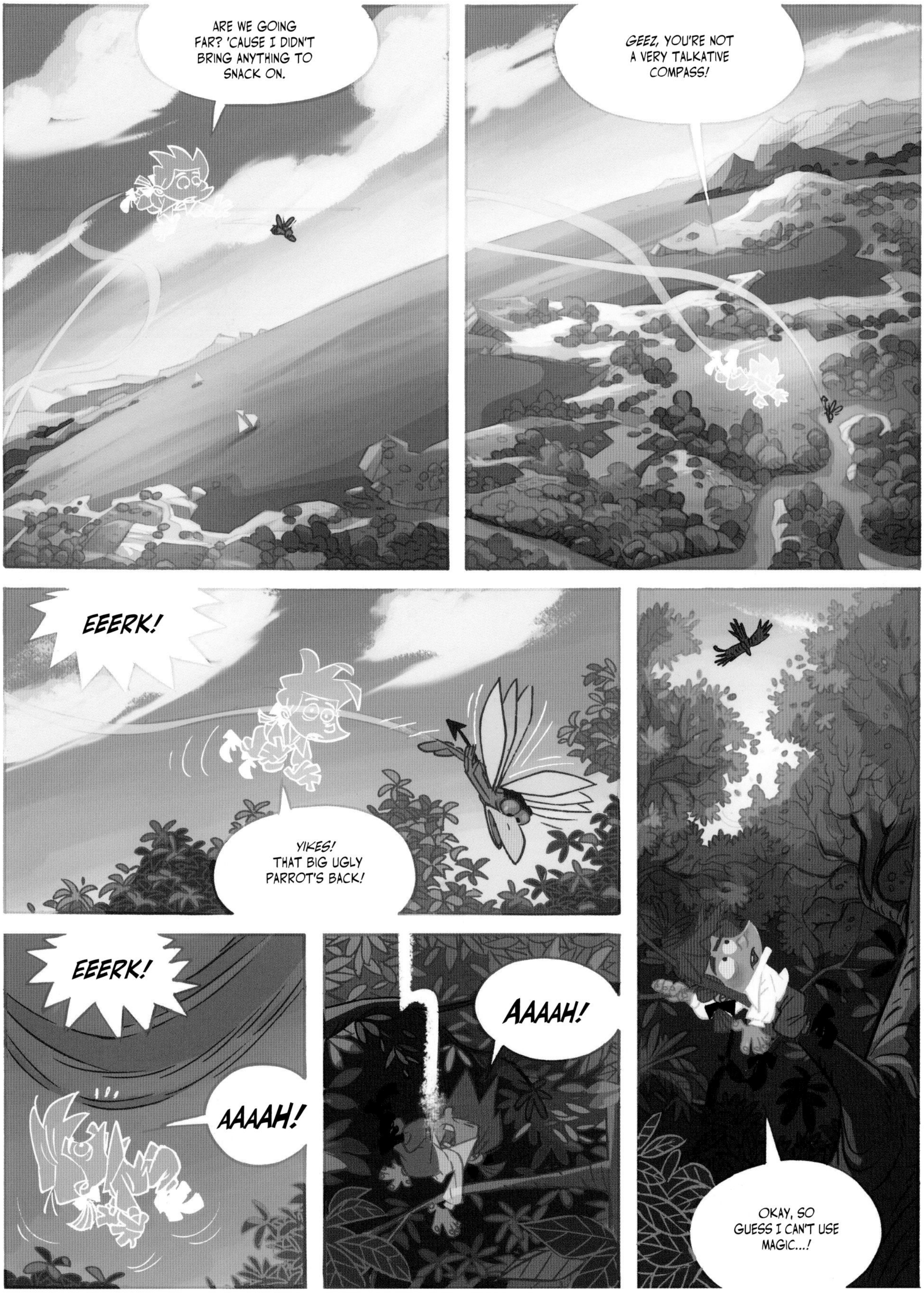
ARE WE GOING FAR? 'CAUSE I DIDN'T BRING ANYTHING TO SNACK ON.
GEEZ, YOU'RE NOT A VERY TALKATIVE COMPASS!
EEERK!
YIKES! THAT BIG UGLY PARROT'S BACK!
EEERK!
AAAAH!
AAAAH!
OKAY, SO GUESS I CAN'T USE MAGIC...!

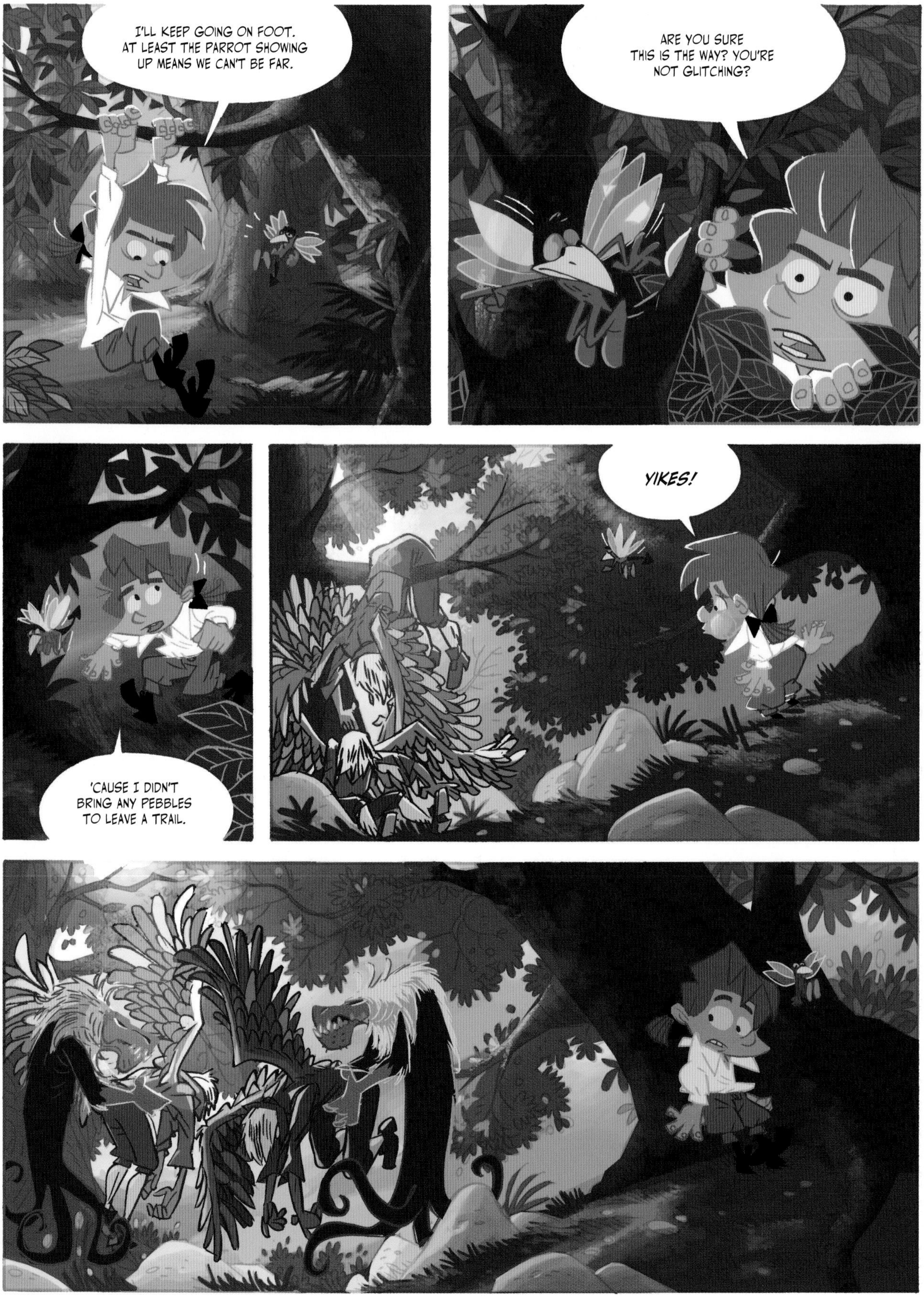
I'LL KEEP GOING ON FOOT. AT LEAST THE PARROT SHOWING UP MEANS WE CAN'T BE FAR.
ARE YOU SURE THIS IS THE WAY? YOU'RE NOT GLITCHING?
'CAUSE I DIDN'T BRING ANY PEBBLES TO LEAVE A TRAIL.
YIKES!

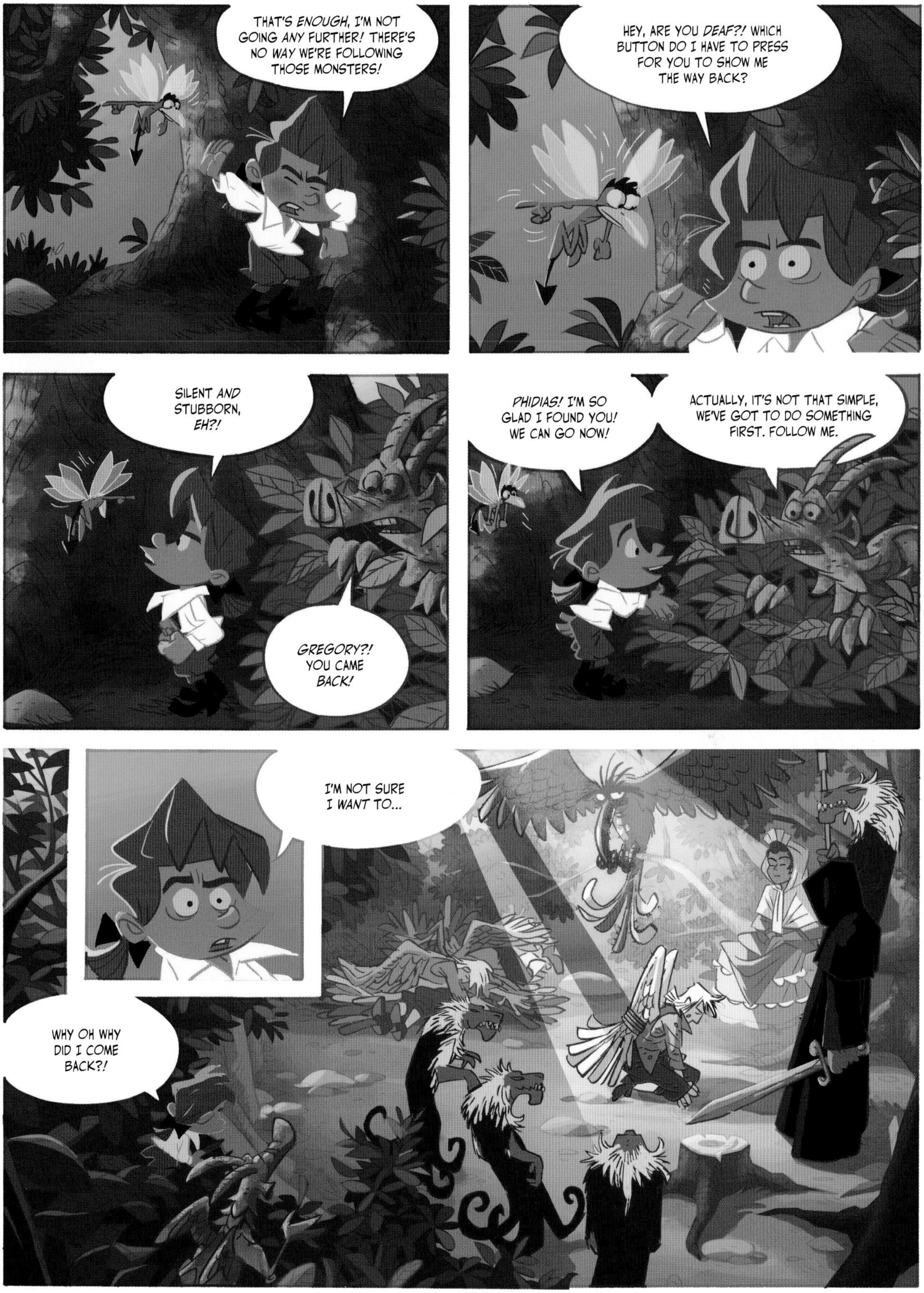
THAT'S ENOUGH, I'M NOT GOING ANY FURTHER! THERE'S NO WAY WE'RE FOLLOWING THOSE MONSTERS!
HEY, ARE YOU DEAF?! WHICH BUTTON DO I HAVE TO PRESS FOR YOU TO SHOW ME THE WAY BACK?
SILENT AND STUBBORN, EH?!
GREGORY?! YOU CAME BACK!
PHIDIAS! I'M SO GLAD I FOUND YOU! WE CAN GO NOW!
ACTUALLY, IT'S NOT THAT SIMPLE, WE'VE GOT TO DO SOMETHING FIRST. FOLLOW ME.
I'M NOT SURE I WANT TO...
WHY OH WHY DID I COME BACK?!

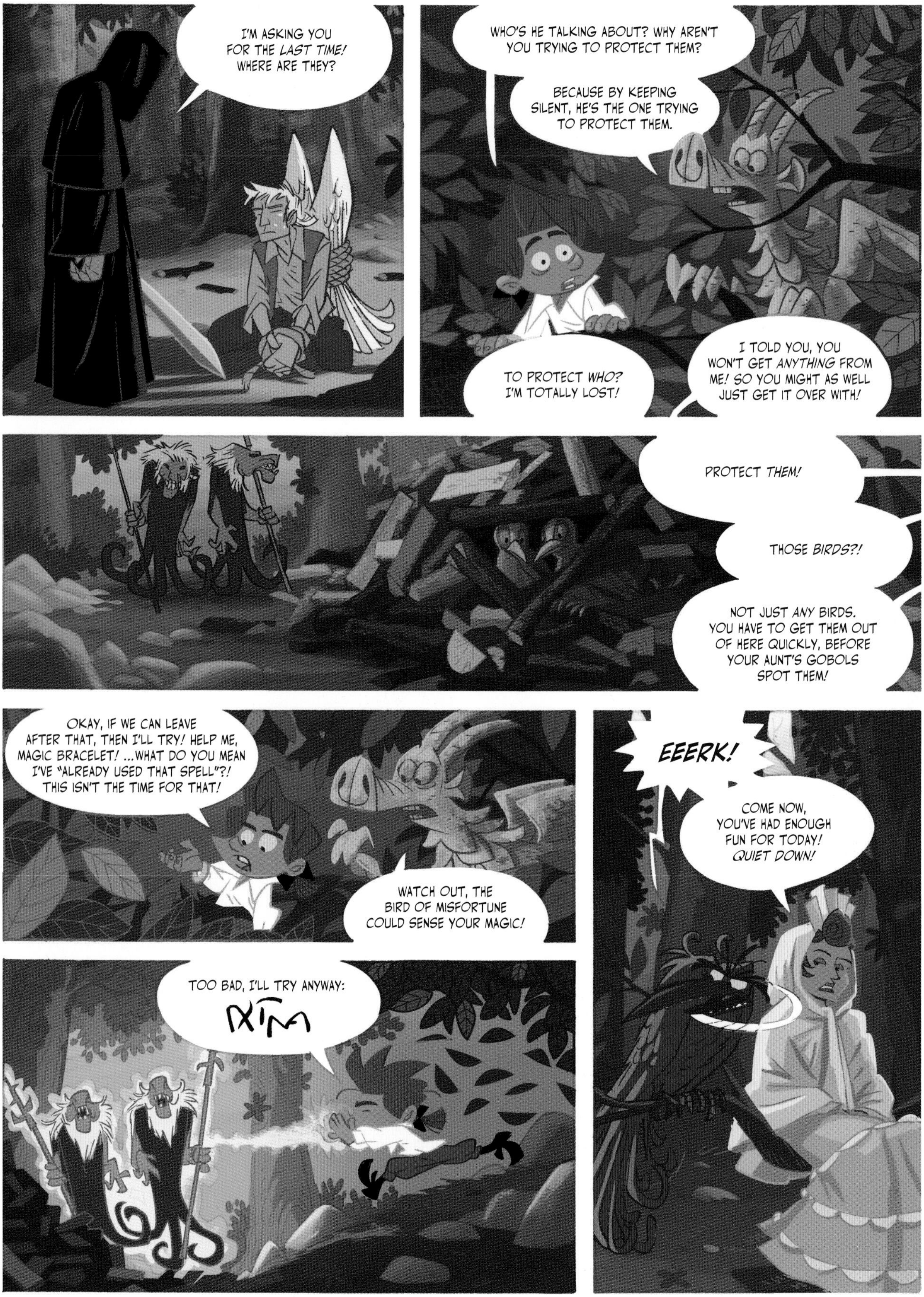
I'M ASKING YOU FOR THE *LAST TIME!* WHERE ARE THEY?
WHO'S HE TALKING ABOUT? WHY AREN'T YOU TRYING TO PROTECT THEM?
BECAUSE BY KEEPING SILENT, HE'S THE ONE TRYING TO PROTECT THEM.
TO PROTECT *WHO?* I'M TOTALLY LOST!
I TOLD YOU, YOU WON'T GET *ANYTHING* FROM ME! SO YOU MIGHT AS WELL JUST GET IT OVER WITH!
PROTECT *THEM!*
THOSE *BIRDS?!*
NOT JUST *ANY* BIRDS. YOU HAVE TO GET THEM OUT OF HERE QUICKLY, BEFORE YOUR AUNT'S GOBOLS SPOT THEM!
OKAY, IF WE CAN LEAVE AFTER THAT, THEN I'LL TRY! HELP ME, MAGIC BRACELET! ...WHAT DO YOU MEAN I'VE "ALREADY USED THAT SPELL"?! THIS ISN'T THE TIME FOR THAT!
WATCH OUT, THE BIRD OF MISFORTUNE COULD SENSE YOUR MAGIC!
TOO BAD, I'LL TRY ANYWAY:
EEERK!
COME NOW, YOU'VE HAD ENOUGH FUN FOR TODAY! *QUIET DOWN!*

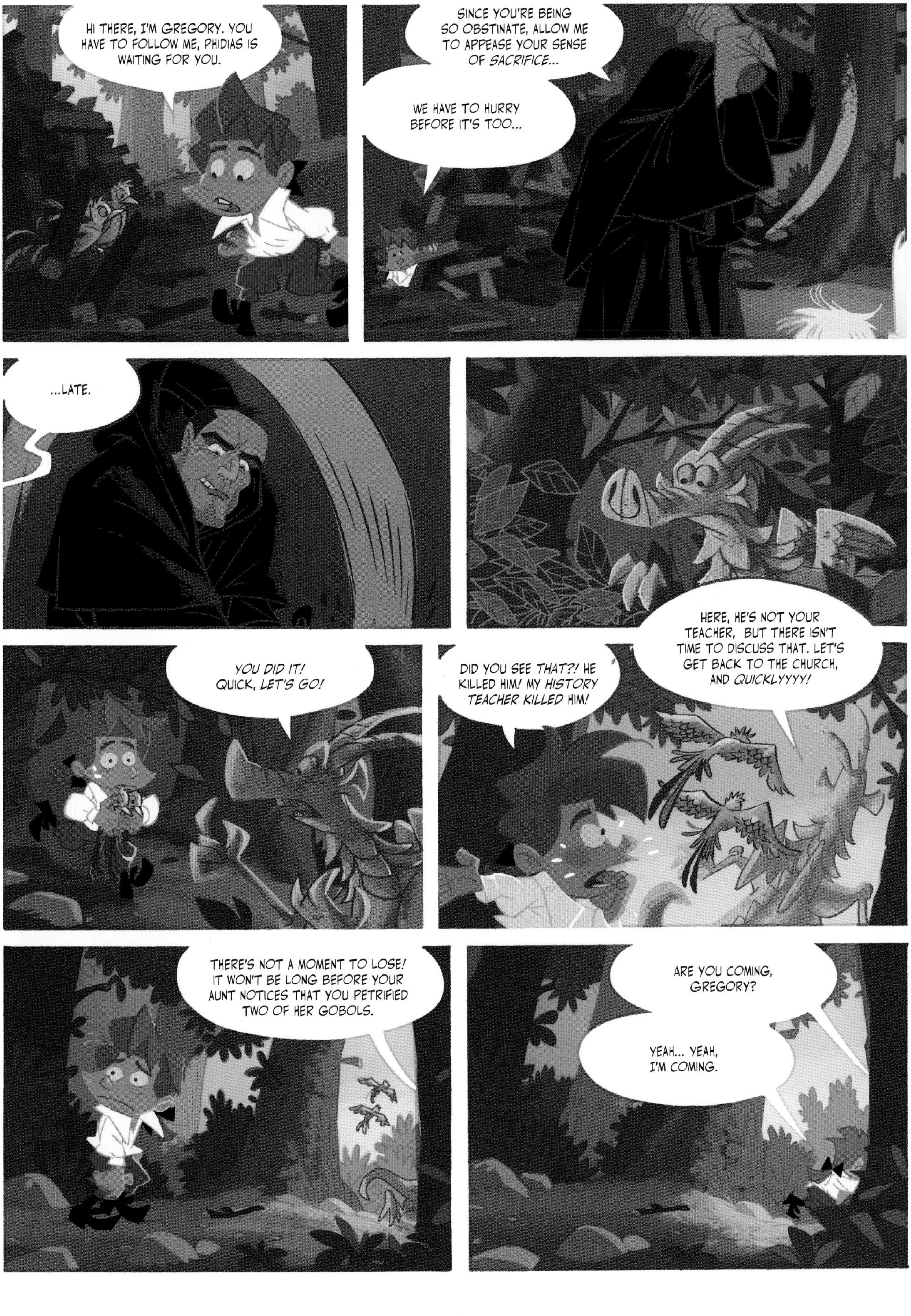
HI THERE, I'M GREGORY. YOU HAVE TO FOLLOW ME, PHIDIAS IS WAITING FOR YOU.
SINCE YOU'RE BEING SO OBSTINATE, ALLOW ME TO APPEASE YOUR SENSE OF *SACRIFICE*...
WE HAVE TO HURRY BEFORE IT'S TOO...
...LATE.
YOU DID IT! QUICK, *LET'S GO!*
DID YOU SEE *THAT?!* HE KILLED HIM! MY *HISTORY TEACHER* KILLED HIM!
HERE, HE'S NOT YOUR TEACHER, BUT THERE ISN'T TIME TO DISCUSS THAT. LET'S GET BACK TO THE CHURCH, AND *QUICKLYYYY!*
THERE'S NOT A MOMENT TO LOSE! IT WON'T BE LONG BEFORE YOUR AUNT NOTICES THAT YOU PETRIFIED TWO OF HER GOBOLS.
ARE YOU COMING, GREGORY?
YEAH... YEAH, I'M COMING.

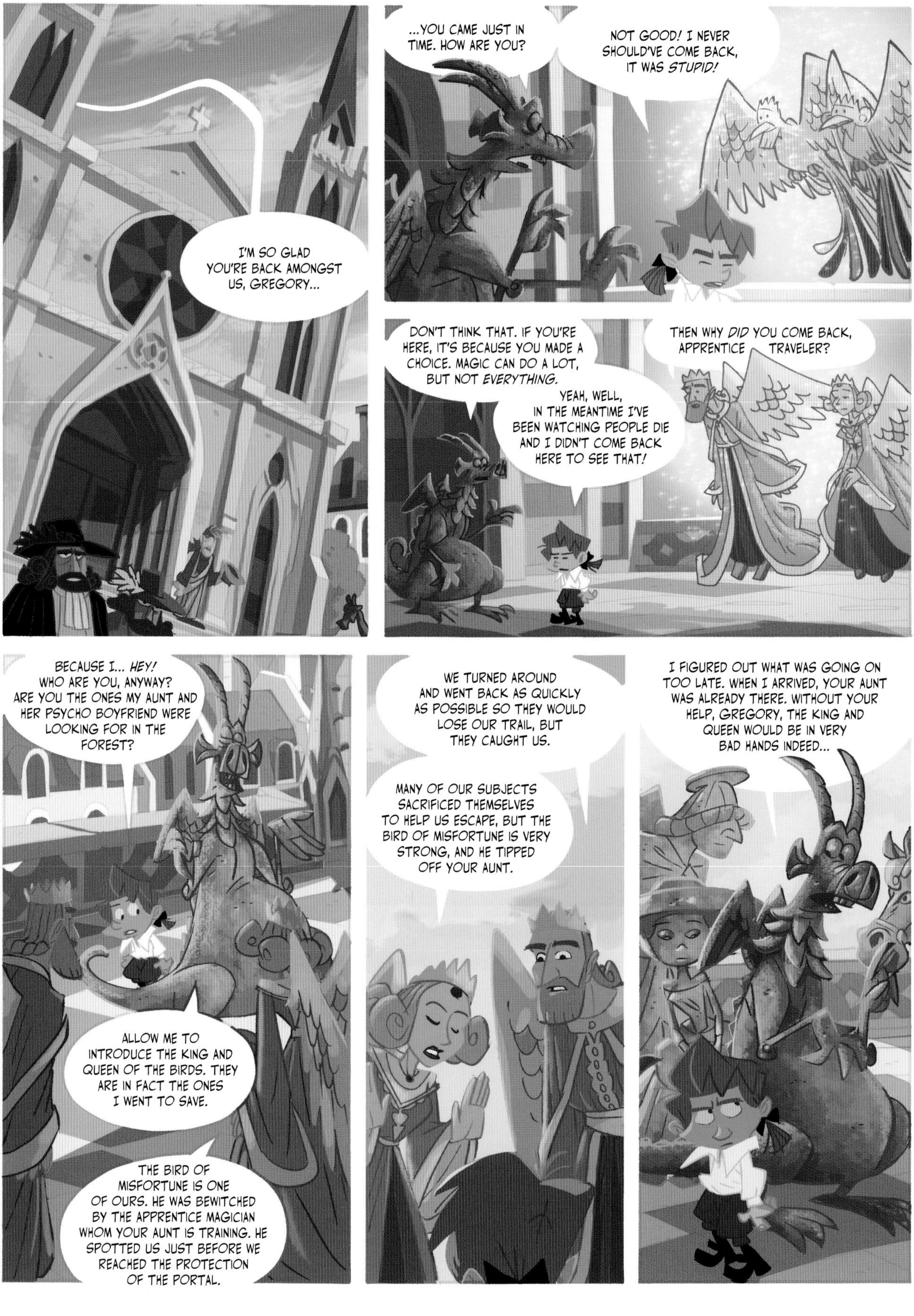
I'M SO GLAD YOU'RE BACK AMONGST US, GREGORY...
...YOU CAME JUST IN TIME. HOW ARE YOU?
NOT GOOD! I NEVER SHOULD'VE COME BACK, IT WAS STUPID!
DON'T THINK THAT. IF YOU'RE HERE, IT'S BECAUSE YOU MADE A CHOICE. MAGIC CAN DO A LOT, BUT NOT EVERYTHING.
YEAH, WELL, IN THE MEANTIME I'VE BEEN WATCHING PEOPLE DIE AND I DIDN'T COME BACK HERE TO SEE THAT!
THEN WHY DID YOU COME BACK, APPRENTICE TRAVELER?
BECAUSE I... HEY! WHO ARE YOU, ANYWAY? ARE YOU THE ONES MY AUNT AND HER PSYCHO BOYFRIEND WERE LOOKING FOR IN THE FOREST?
ALLOW ME TO INTRODUCE THE KING AND QUEEN OF THE BIRDS. THEY ARE IN FACT THE ONES I WENT TO SAVE.
THE BIRD OF MISFORTUNE IS ONE OF OURS. HE WAS BEWITCHED BY THE APPRENTICE MAGICIAN WHOM YOUR AUNT IS TRAINING. HE SPOTTED US JUST BEFORE WE REACHED THE PROTECTION OF THE PORTAL.
WE TURNED AROUND AND WENT BACK AS QUICKLY AS POSSIBLE SO THEY WOULD LOSE OUR TRAIL, BUT THEY CAUGHT US.
MANY OF OUR SUBJECTS SACRIFICED THEMSELVES TO HELP US ESCAPE, BUT THE BIRD OF MISFORTUNE IS VERY STRONG, AND HE TIPPED OFF YOUR AUNT.
I FIGURED OUT WHAT WAS GOING ON TOO LATE. WHEN I ARRIVED, YOUR AUNT WAS ALREADY THERE. WITHOUT YOUR HELP, GREGORY, THE KING AND QUEEN WOULD BE IN VERY BAD HANDS INDEED...

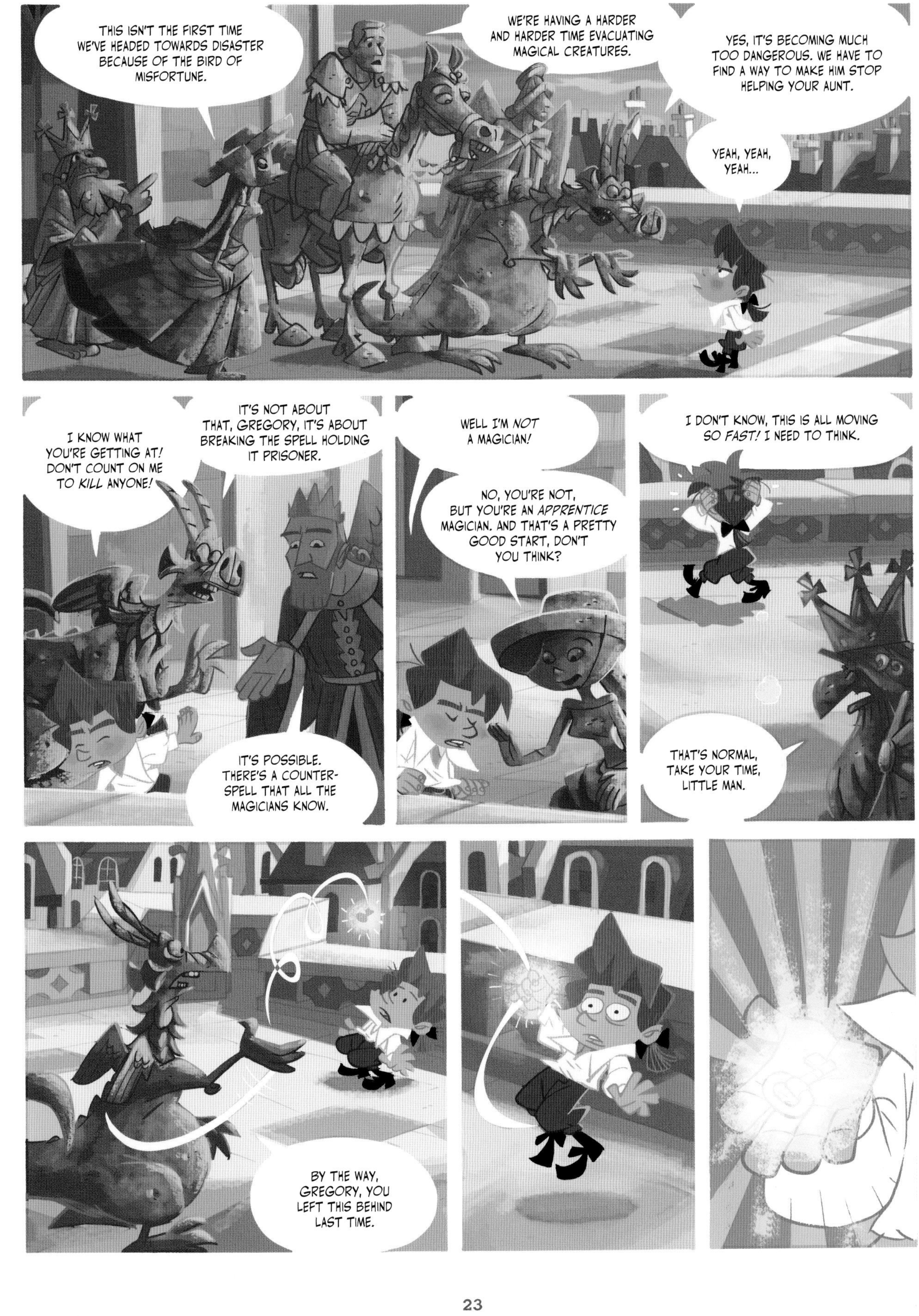
THIS ISN'T THE FIRST TIME WE'VE HEADED TOWARDS DISASTER BECAUSE OF THE BIRD OF MISFORTUNE.
WE'RE HAVING A HARDER AND HARDER TIME EVACUATING MAGICAL CREATURES.
YES, IT'S BECOMING MUCH TOO DANGEROUS. WE HAVE TO FIND A WAY TO MAKE HIM STOP HELPING YOUR AUNT.
YEAH, YEAH, YEAH...
I KNOW WHAT YOU'RE GETTING AT! DON'T COUNT ON ME TO *KILL* ANYONE!
IT'S NOT ABOUT THAT, GREGORY, IT'S ABOUT BREAKING THE SPELL HOLDING IT PRISONER.
IT'S POSSIBLE. THERE'S A COUNTER-SPELL THAT ALL THE MAGICIANS KNOW.
WELL I'M *NOT* A MAGICIAN!
NO, YOU'RE NOT, BUT YOU'RE AN *APPRENTICE* MAGICIAN. AND THAT'S A PRETTY GOOD START, DON'T YOU THINK?
I DON'T KNOW, THIS IS ALL MOVING SO *FAST!* I NEED TO THINK.
THAT'S NORMAL, TAKE YOUR TIME, LITTLE MAN.
BY THE WAY, GREGORY, YOU LEFT THIS BEHIND LAST TIME.

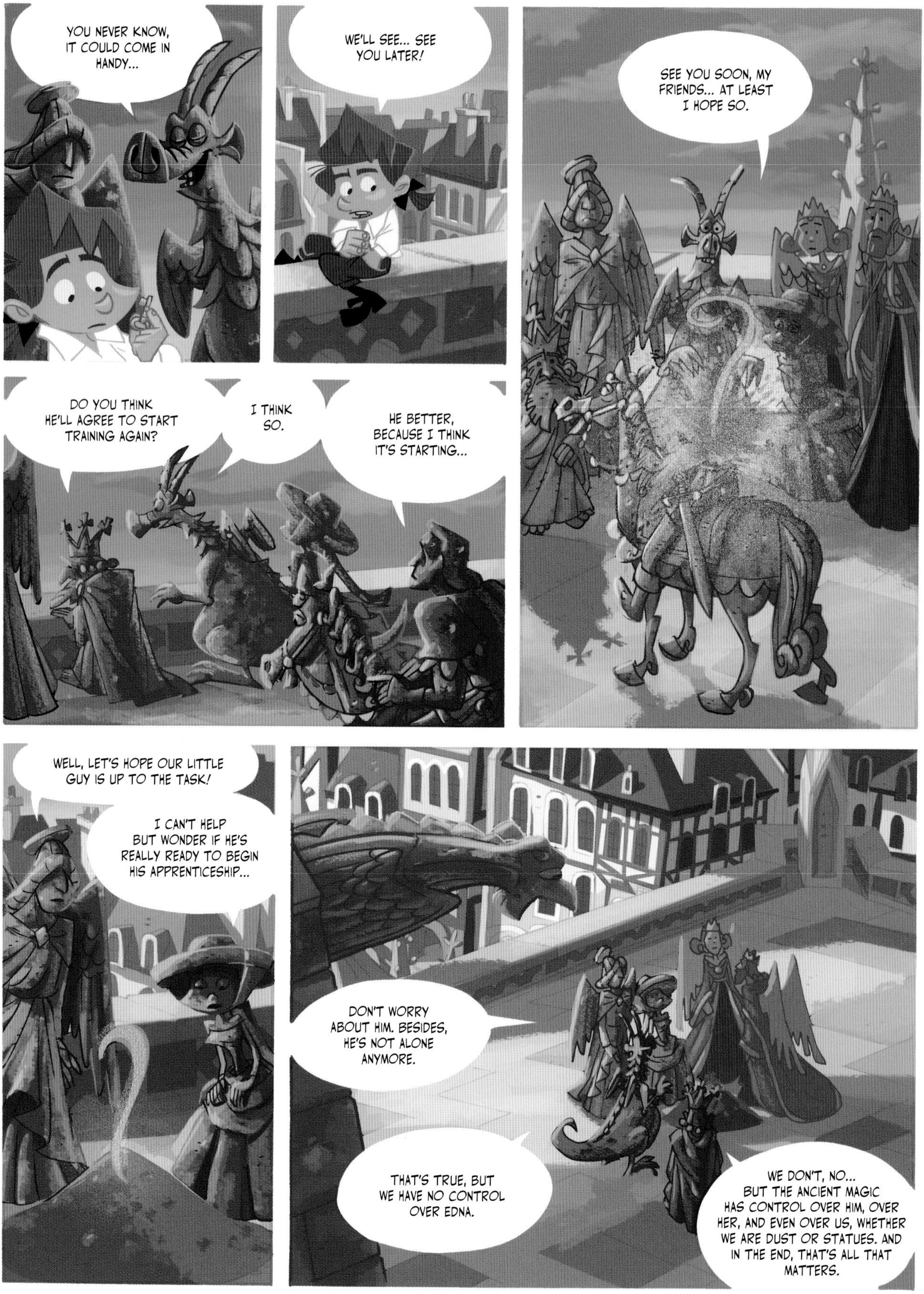
YOU NEVER KNOW, IT COULD COME IN HANDY...
WE'LL SEE... SEE YOU LATER!
SEE YOU SOON, MY FRIENDS... AT LEAST I HOPE SO.
DO YOU THINK HE'LL AGREE TO START TRAINING AGAIN?
I THINK SO.
HE BETTER, BECAUSE I THINK IT'S STARTING...
WELL, LET'S HOPE OUR LITTLE GUY IS UP TO THE TASK!
I CAN'T HELP BUT WONDER IF HE'S REALLY READY TO BEGIN HIS APPRENTICESHIP...
DON'T WORRY ABOUT HIM. BESIDES, HE'S NOT ALONE ANYMORE.
THAT'S TRUE, BUT WE HAVE NO CONTROL OVER EDNA.
WE DON'T, NO... BUT THE ANCIENT MAGIC HAS CONTROL OVER HIM, OVER HER, AND EVEN OVER US, WHETHER WE ARE DUST OR STATUES. AND IN THE END, THAT'S ALL THAT MATTERS.

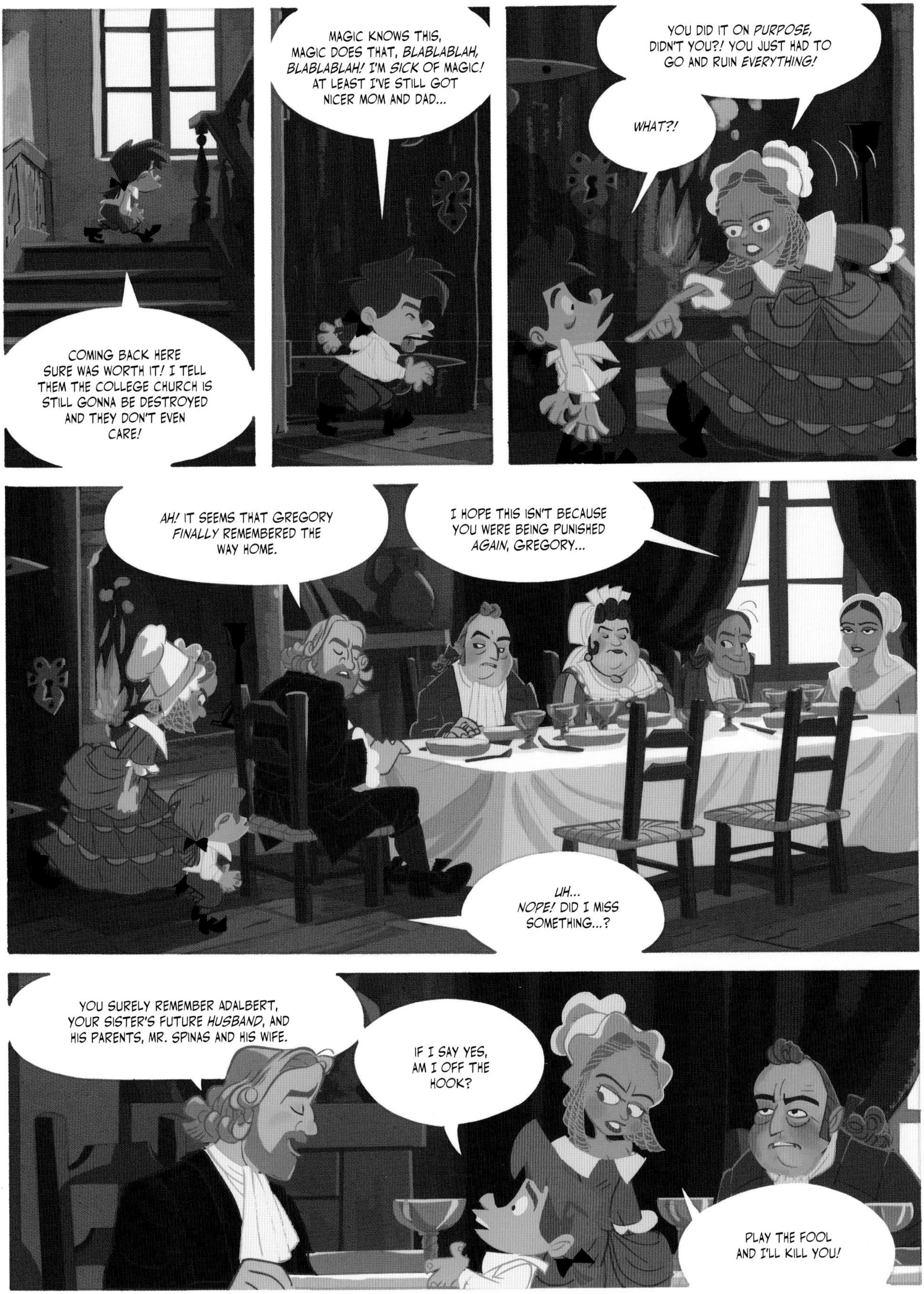
COMING BACK HERE SURE WAS WORTH IT! I TELL THEM THE COLLEGE CHURCH IS STILL GONNA BE DESTROYED AND THEY DON'T EVEN CARE!
MAGIC KNOWS THIS, MAGIC DOES THAT, BLABLABLAH, BLABLABLAH! I'M SICK OF MAGIC! AT LEAST I'VE STILL GOT NICER MOM AND DAD...
YOU DID IT ON PURPOSE, DIDN'T YOU?! YOU JUST HAD TO GO AND RUIN EVERYTHING!
WHAT?!
AH! IT SEEMS THAT GREGORY FINALLY REMEMBERED THE WAY HOME.
I HOPE THIS ISN'T BECAUSE YOU WERE BEING PUNISHED AGAIN, GREGORY...
UH... NOPE! DID I MISS SOMETHING...?
YOU SURELY REMEMBER ADALBERT, YOUR SISTER'S FUTURE HUSBAND, AND HIS PARENTS, MR. SPINAS AND HIS WIFE.
IF I SAY YES, AM I OFF THE HOOK?
PLAY THE FOOL AND I'LL KILL YOU!

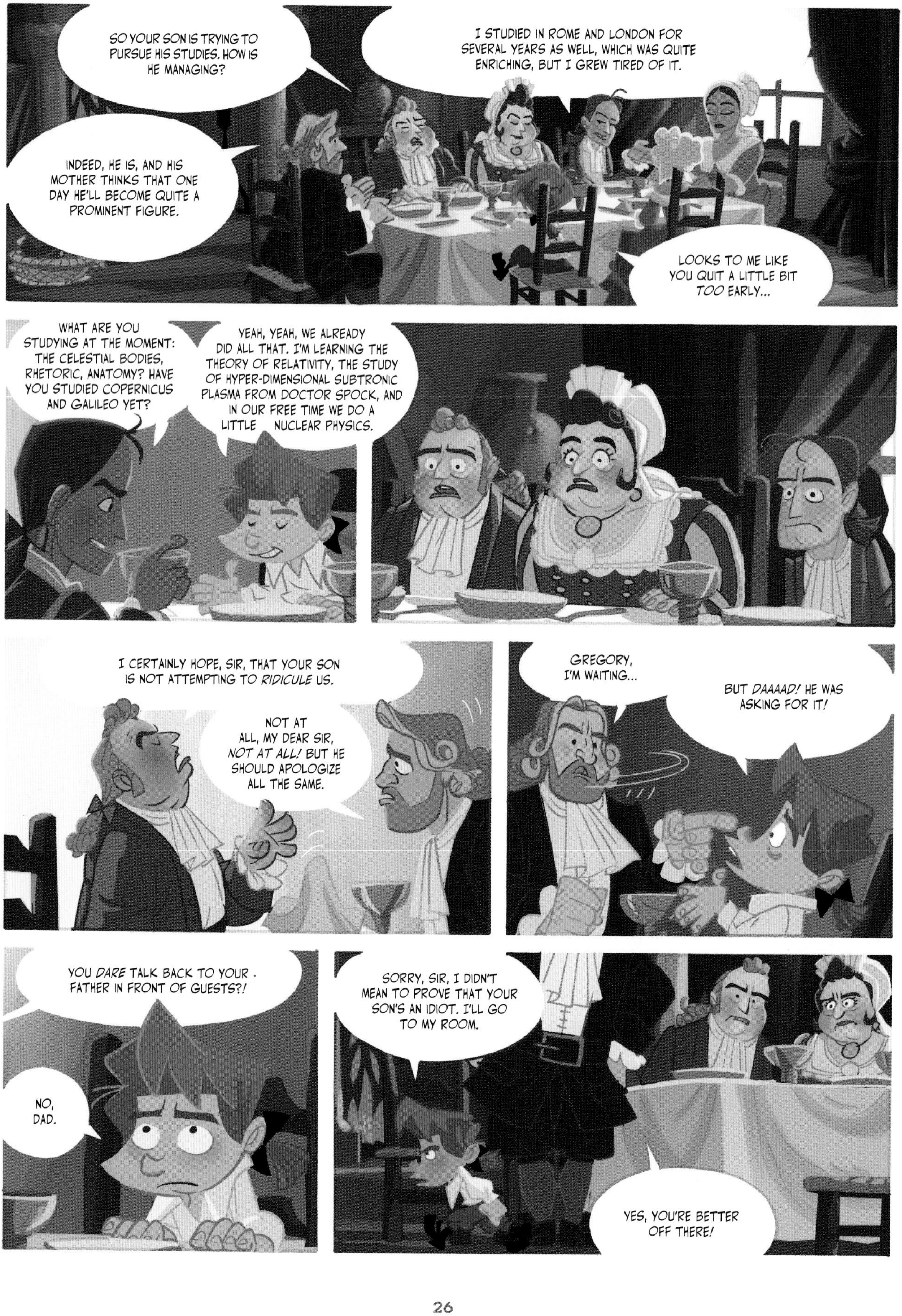
SO YOUR SON IS TRYING TO PURSUE HIS STUDIES. HOW IS HE MANAGING?
INDEED, HE IS, AND HIS MOTHER THINKS THAT ONE DAY HE'LL BECOME QUITE A PROMINENT FIGURE.
I STUDIED IN ROME AND LONDON FOR SEVERAL YEARS AS WELL, WHICH WAS QUITE ENRICHING, BUT I GREW TIRED OF IT.
LOOKS TO ME LIKE YOU QUIT A LITTLE BIT *TOO* EARLY...
WHAT ARE YOU STUDYING AT THE MOMENT: THE CELESTIAL BODIES, RHETORIC, ANATOMY? HAVE YOU STUDIED COPERNICUS AND GALILEO YET?
YEAH, YEAH, WE ALREADY DID ALL THAT. I'M LEARNING THE THEORY OF RELATIVITY, THE STUDY OF HYPER-DIMENSIONAL SUBTRONIC PLASMA FROM DOCTOR SPOCK, AND IN OUR FREE TIME WE DO A LITTLE NUCLEAR PHYSICS.
I CERTAINLY HOPE, SIR, THAT YOUR SON IS NOT ATTEMPTING TO *RIDICULE* US.
NOT AT ALL, MY DEAR SIR, *NOT AT ALL!* BUT HE SHOULD APOLOGIZE ALL THE SAME.
GREGORY, I'M WAITING...
BUT *DAAAAD!* HE WAS ASKING FOR IT!
YOU *DARE* TALK BACK TO YOUR FATHER IN FRONT OF GUESTS?!
NO, DAD.
SORRY, SIR, I DIDN'T MEAN TO PROVE THAT YOUR SON'S AN IDIOT. I'LL GO TO MY ROOM.
YES, YOU'RE BETTER OFF THERE!

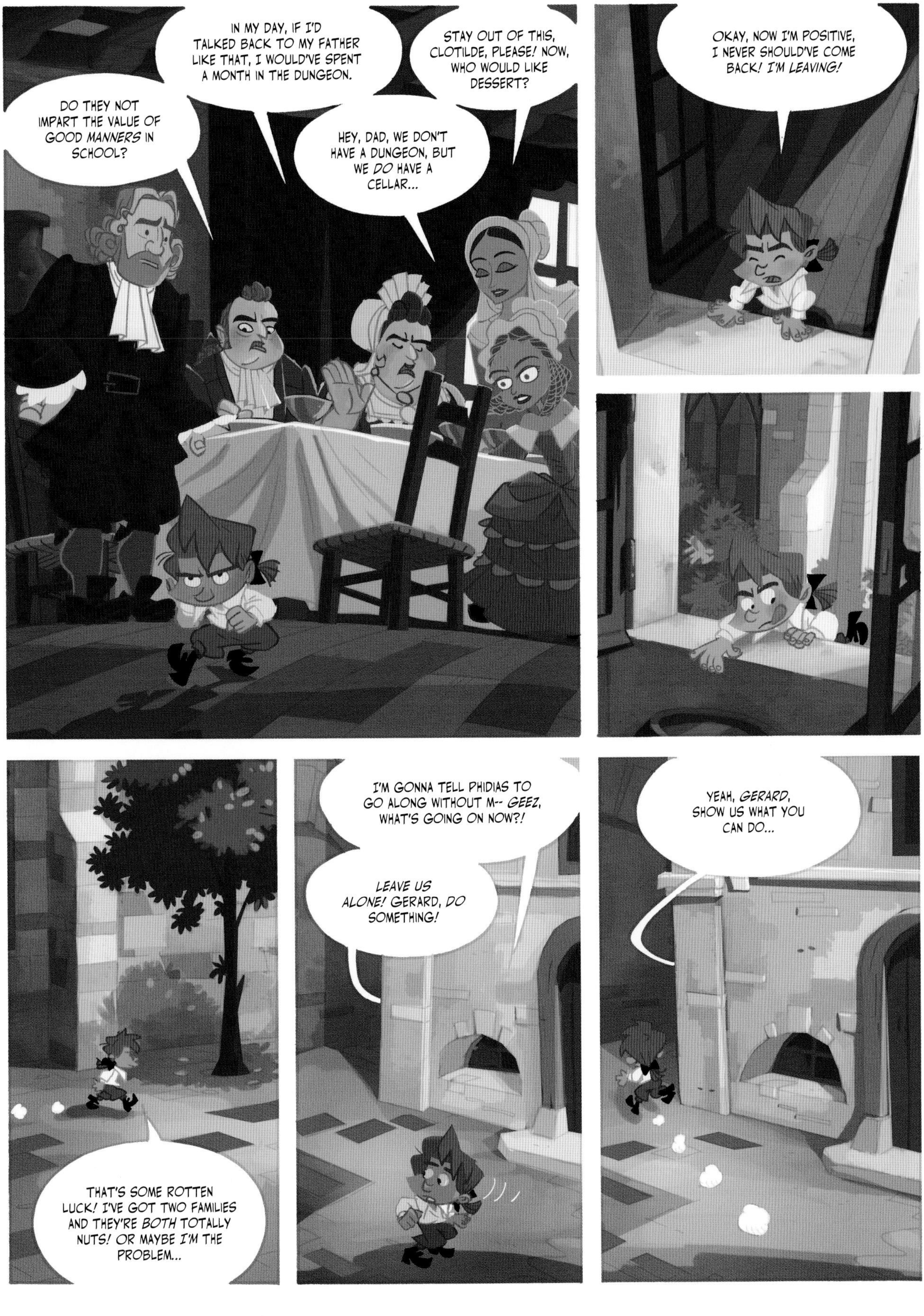
DO THEY NOT IMPART THE VALUE OF GOOD *MANNERS* IN SCHOOL?
IN MY DAY, IF I'D TALKED BACK TO MY FATHER LIKE THAT, I WOULD'VE SPENT A MONTH IN THE DUNGEON.
HEY, DAD, WE DON'T HAVE A DUNGEON, BUT WE *DO* HAVE A CELLAR...
STAY OUT OF THIS, CLOTILDE, PLEASE! NOW, WHO WOULD LIKE DESSERT?
OKAY, NOW I'M POSITIVE, I NEVER SHOULD'VE COME BACK! *I'M LEAVING!*
THAT'S SOME ROTTEN LUCK! I'VE GOT TWO FAMILIES AND THEY'RE *BOTH* TOTALLY NUTS! OR MAYBE *I'M* THE PROBLEM...
I'M GONNA TELL PHIDIAS TO GO ALONG WITHOUT M-- *GEEZ*, WHAT'S GOING ON NOW?!
LEAVE US ALONE! GERARD, DO SOMETHING!
YEAH, *GERARD*, SHOW US WHAT YOU CAN DO...

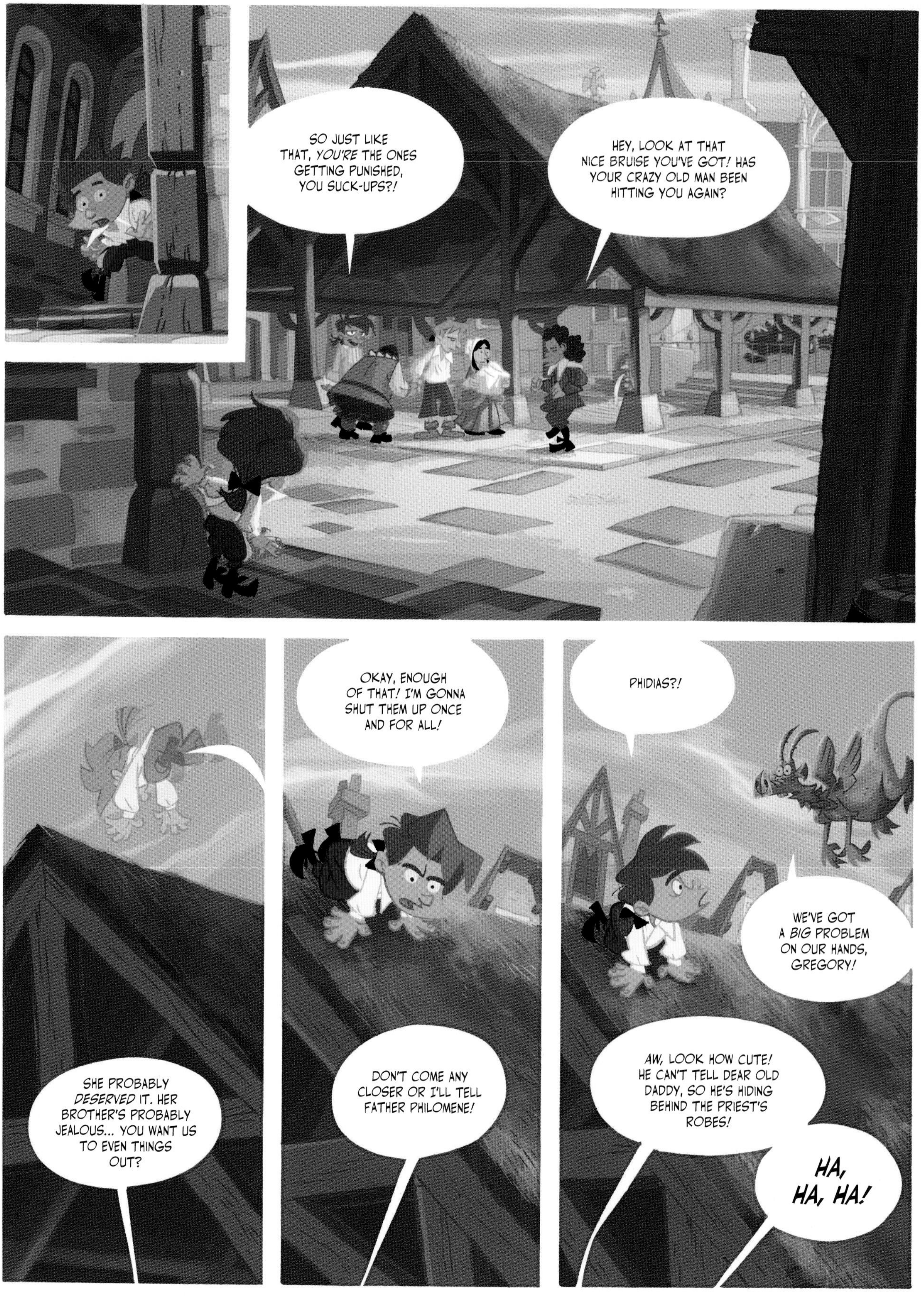
SO JUST LIKE THAT, *YOU'RE* THE ONES GETTING PUNISHED, YOU SUCK-UPS?!
HEY, LOOK AT THAT NICE BRUISE YOU'VE GOT! HAS YOUR CRAZY OLD MAN BEEN HITTING YOU AGAIN?
SHE PROBABLY *DESERVED* IT. HER BROTHER'S PROBABLY JEALOUS... YOU WANT US TO EVEN THINGS OUT?
OKAY, ENOUGH OF THAT! I'M GONNA SHUT THEM UP ONCE AND FOR ALL!
DON'T COME ANY CLOSER OR I'LL TELL FATHER PHILOMENE!
PHIDIAS?!
WE'VE GOT A *BIG* PROBLEM ON OUR HANDS, GREGORY!
AW, LOOK HOW CUTE! HE CAN'T TELL DEAR OLD DADDY, SO HE'S HIDING BEHIND THE PRIEST'S ROBES!
HA, HA, HA!

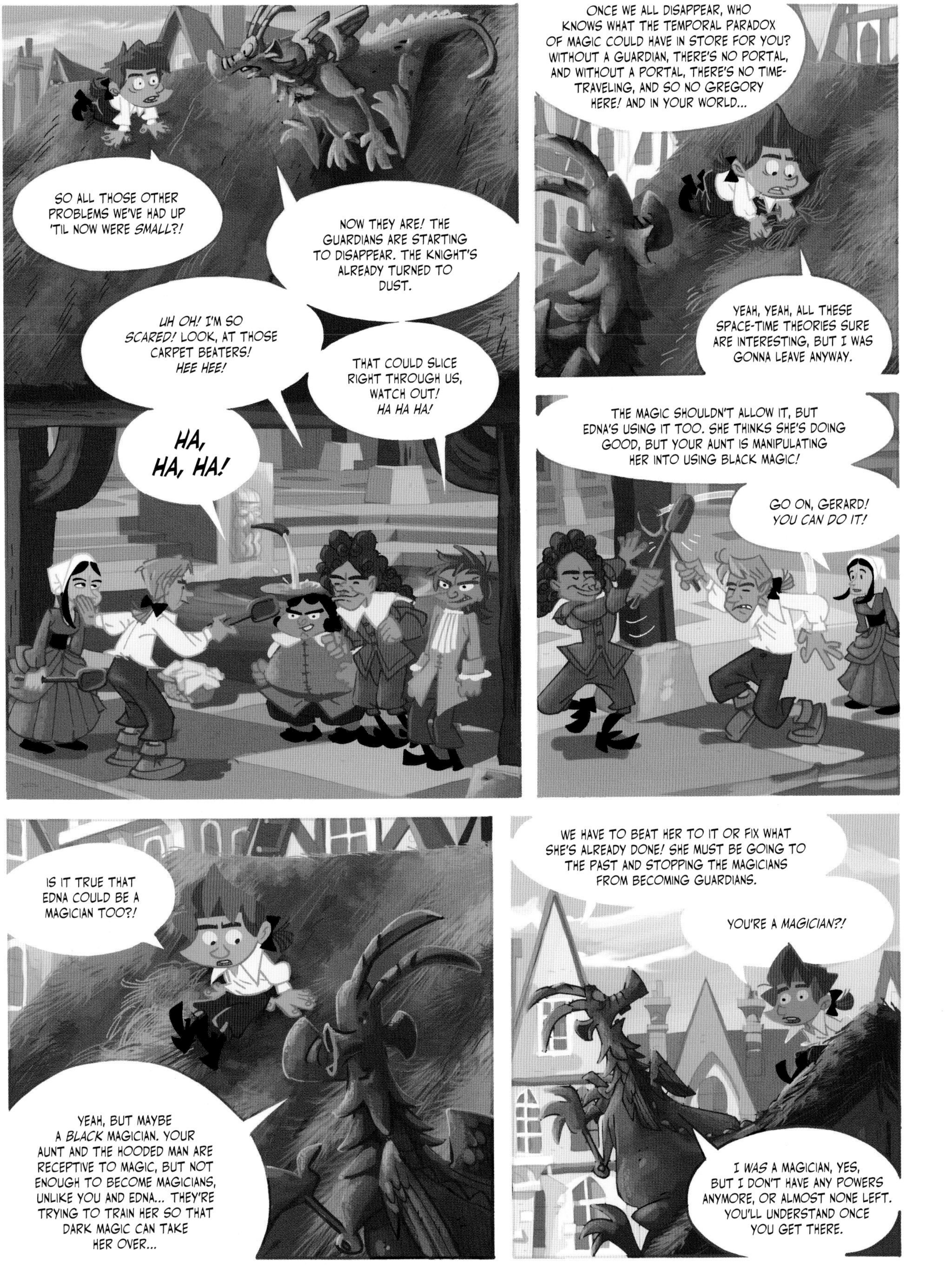
SO ALL THOSE OTHER PROBLEMS WE'VE HAD UP 'TIL NOW WERE *SMALL*?!
NOW THEY ARE! THE GUARDIANS ARE STARTING TO DISAPPEAR. THE KNIGHT'S ALREADY TURNED TO DUST.
UH OH! I'M SO *SCARED!* LOOK, AT THOSE CARPET BEATERS! *HEE HEE!*
THAT COULD SLICE RIGHT THROUGH US, WATCH OUT! *HA HA HA!*
HA, HA, HA!
ONCE WE ALL DISAPPEAR, WHO KNOWS WHAT THE TEMPORAL PARADOX OF MAGIC COULD HAVE IN STORE FOR YOU? WITHOUT A GUARDIAN, THERE'S NO PORTAL, AND WITHOUT A PORTAL, THERE'S NO TIME-TRAVELING, AND SO NO GREGORY HERE! AND IN YOUR WORLD...
YEAH, YEAH, ALL THESE SPACE-TIME THEORIES SURE ARE INTERESTING, BUT I WAS GONNA LEAVE ANYWAY.
THE MAGIC SHOULDN'T ALLOW IT, BUT EDNA'S USING IT TOO. SHE THINKS SHE'S DOING GOOD, BUT YOUR AUNT IS MANIPULATING HER INTO USING BLACK MAGIC!
GO ON, GERARD! YOU CAN DO IT!
IS IT TRUE THAT EDNA COULD BE A MAGICIAN TOO?!
YEAH, BUT MAYBE A *BLACK* MAGICIAN. YOUR AUNT AND THE HOODED MAN ARE RECEPTIVE TO MAGIC, BUT NOT ENOUGH TO BECOME MAGICIANS, UNLIKE YOU AND EDNA... THEY'RE TRYING TO TRAIN HER SO THAT DARK MAGIC CAN TAKE HER OVER...
WE HAVE TO BEAT HER TO IT OR FIX WHAT SHE'S ALREADY DONE! SHE MUST BE GOING TO THE PAST AND STOPPING THE MAGICIANS FROM BECOMING GUARDIANS.
YOU'RE A *MAGICIAN*?!
I *WAS* A MAGICIAN, YES, BUT I DON'T HAVE ANY POWERS ANYMORE, OR ALMOST NONE LEFT. YOU'LL UNDERSTAND ONCE YOU GET THERE.

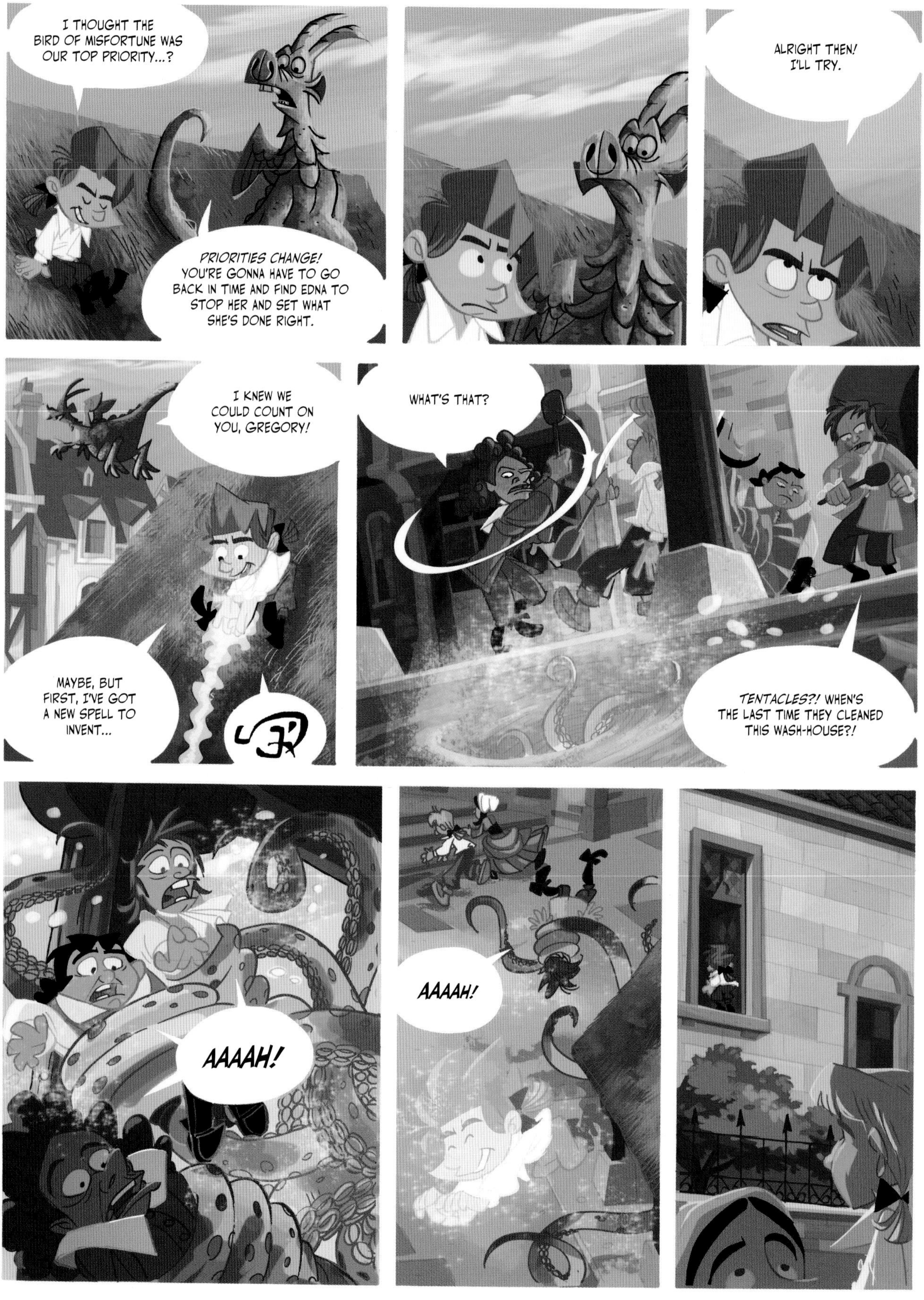
I THOUGHT THE BIRD OF MISFORTUNE WAS OUR TOP PRIORITY...?
PRIORITIES CHANGE! YOU'RE GONNA HAVE TO GO BACK IN TIME AND FIND EDNA TO STOP HER AND SET WHAT SHE'S DONE RIGHT.
ALRIGHT THEN! I'LL TRY.
I KNEW WE COULD COUNT ON YOU, GREGORY!
MAYBE, BUT FIRST, I'VE GOT A NEW SPELL TO INVENT...
WHAT'S THAT?
TENTACLES?! WHEN'S THE LAST TIME THEY CLEANED THIS WASH-HOUSE?!
AAAAH!
AAAAH!

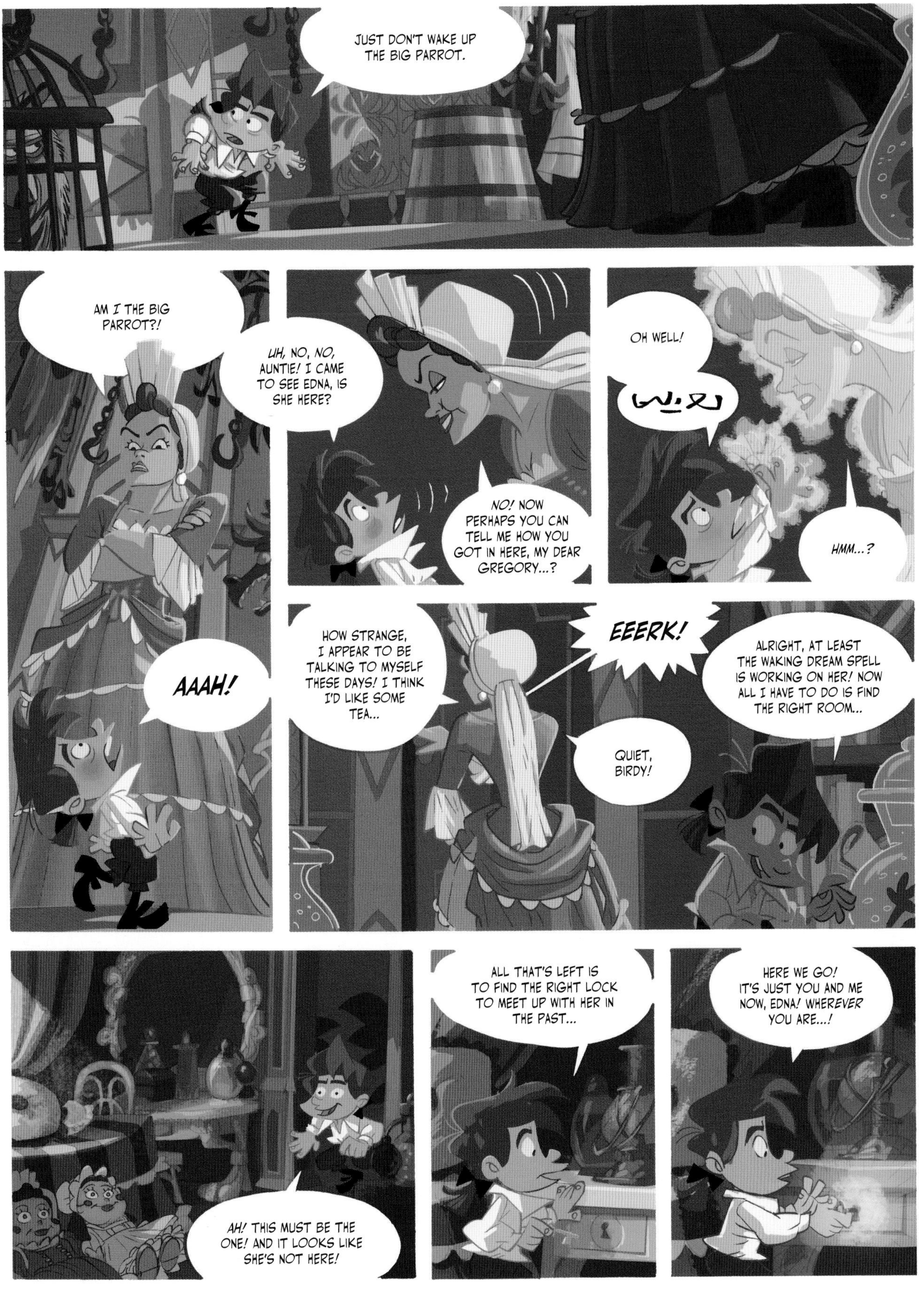
JUST DON'T WAKE UP THE BIG PARROT.
AM I THE BIG PARROT?!
AAAH!
UH, NO, NO, AUNTIE! I CAME TO SEE EDNA, IS SHE HERE?
NO! NOW PERHAPS YOU CAN TELL ME HOW YOU GOT IN HERE, MY DEAR GREGORY...?
OH WELL!
HMM...?
HOW STRANGE, I APPEAR TO BE TALKING TO MYSELF THESE DAYS! I THINK I'D LIKE SOME TEA...
EEERK!
QUIET, BIRDY!
ALRIGHT, AT LEAST THE WAKING DREAM SPELL IS WORKING ON HER! NOW ALL I HAVE TO DO IS FIND THE RIGHT ROOM...
AH! THIS MUST BE THE ONE! AND IT LOOKS LIKE SHE'S NOT HERE!
ALL THAT'S LEFT IS TO FIND THE RIGHT LOCK TO MEET UP WITH HER IN THE PAST...
HERE WE GO! IT'S JUST YOU AND ME NOW, EDNA! WHEREVER YOU ARE...!

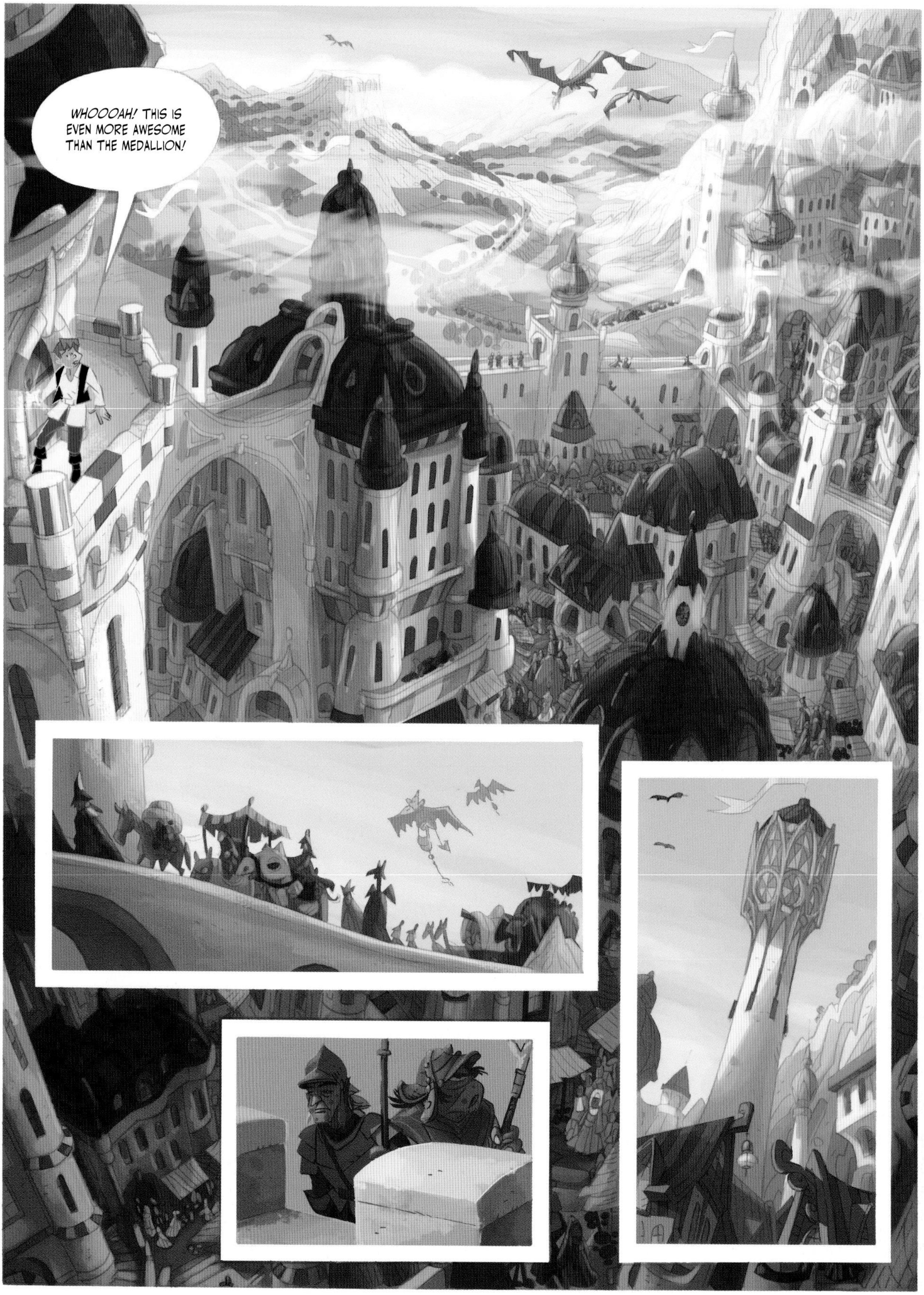
WHOOOAH! THIS IS EVEN MORE AWESOME THAN THE MEDALLION!

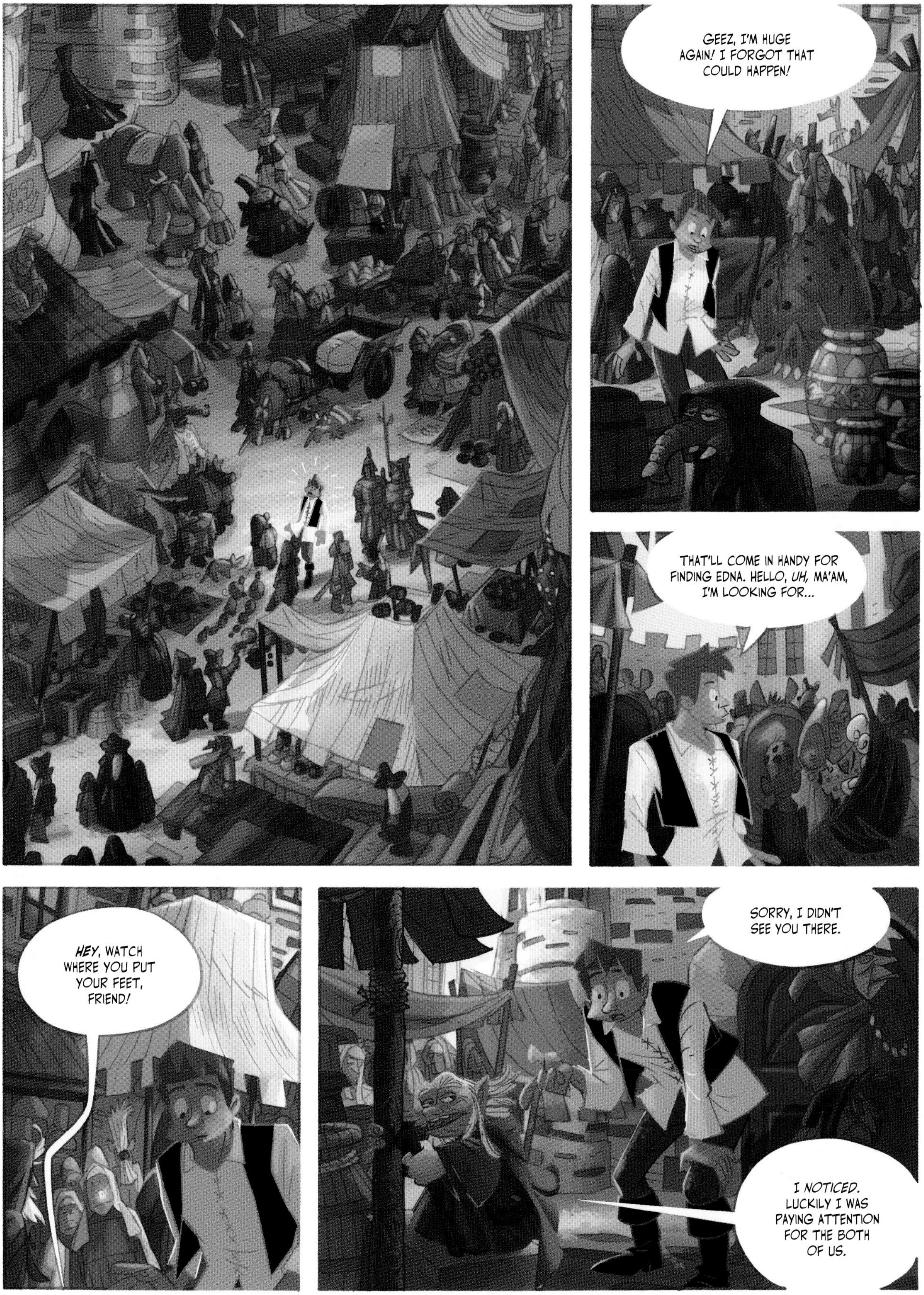
GEEZ, I'M HUGE AGAIN! I FORGOT THAT COULD HAPPEN!
THAT'LL COME IN HANDY FOR FINDING EDNA. HELLO, *UH,* MA'AM, I'M LOOKING FOR...
HEY, WATCH WHERE YOU PUT YOUR FEET, FRIEND!
SORRY, I DIDN'T SEE YOU THERE.
I *NOTICED.* LUCKILY I WAS PAYING ATTENTION FOR THE BOTH OF US.

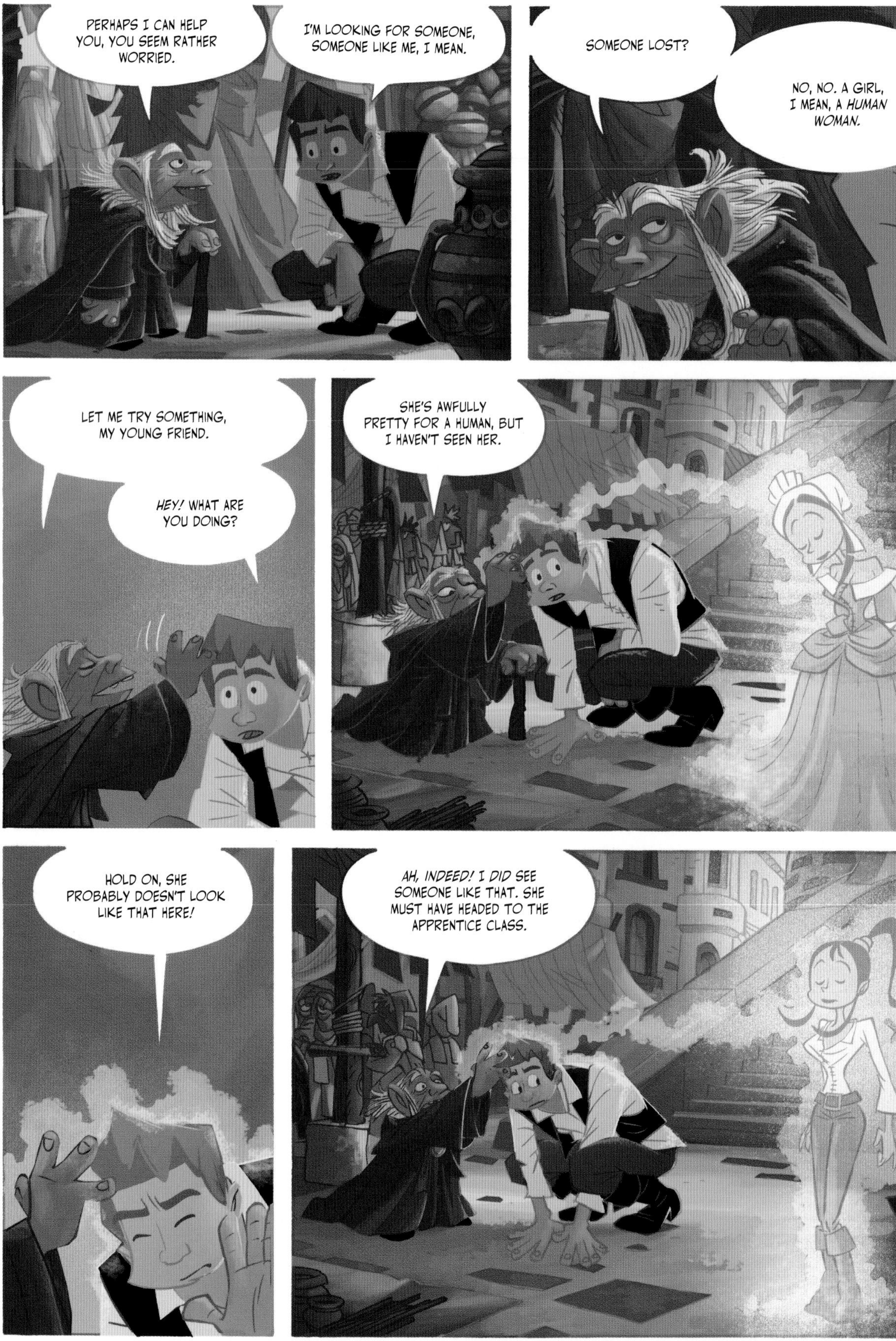
PERHAPS I CAN HELP YOU, YOU SEEM RATHER WORRIED.
I'M LOOKING FOR SOMEONE, SOMEONE LIKE ME, I MEAN.
SOMEONE LOST?
NO, NO. A GIRL, I MEAN, A *HUMAN WOMAN.*
LET ME TRY SOMETHING, MY YOUNG FRIEND.
HEY! WHAT ARE YOU DOING?
SHE'S AWFULLY PRETTY FOR A HUMAN, BUT I HAVEN'T SEEN HER.
HOLD ON, SHE PROBABLY DOESN'T LOOK LIKE THAT HERE!
AH, INDEED! I DID SEE SOMEONE LIKE THAT. SHE MUST HAVE HEADED TO THE APPRENTICE CLASS.

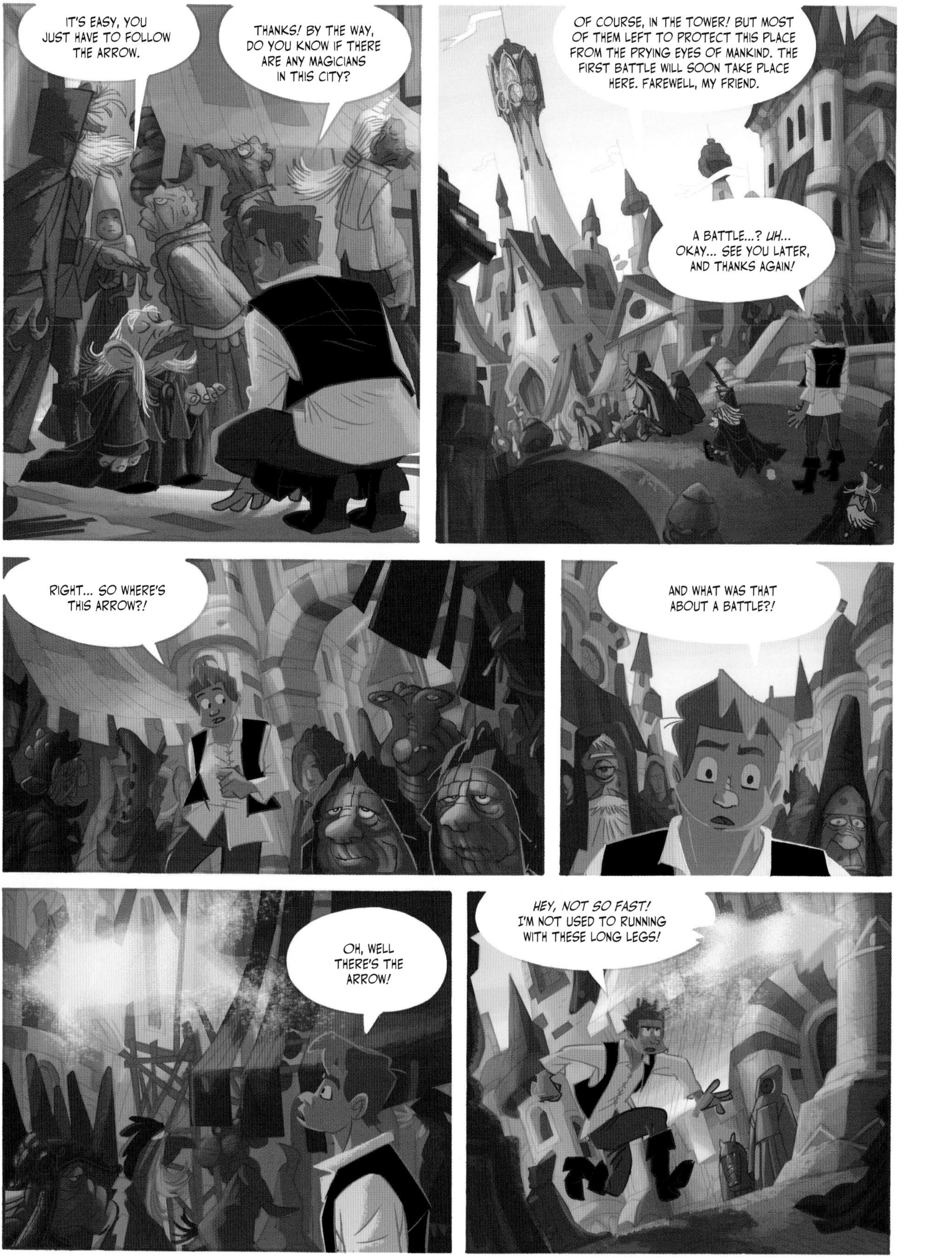
IT'S EASY, YOU JUST HAVE TO FOLLOW THE ARROW.
THANKS! BY THE WAY, DO YOU KNOW IF THERE ARE ANY MAGICIANS IN THIS CITY?
OF COURSE, IN THE TOWER! BUT MOST OF THEM LEFT TO PROTECT THIS PLACE FROM THE PRYING EYES OF MANKIND. THE FIRST BATTLE WILL SOON TAKE PLACE HERE. FAREWELL, MY FRIEND.
A BATTLE...? *UH...* OKAY... SEE YOU LATER, AND THANKS AGAIN!
RIGHT... SO WHERE'S THIS ARROW?!
AND WHAT WAS THAT ABOUT A BATTLE?!
OH, WELL THERE'S THE ARROW!
HEY, NOT SO FAST! I'M NOT USED TO RUNNING WITH THESE LONG LEGS!

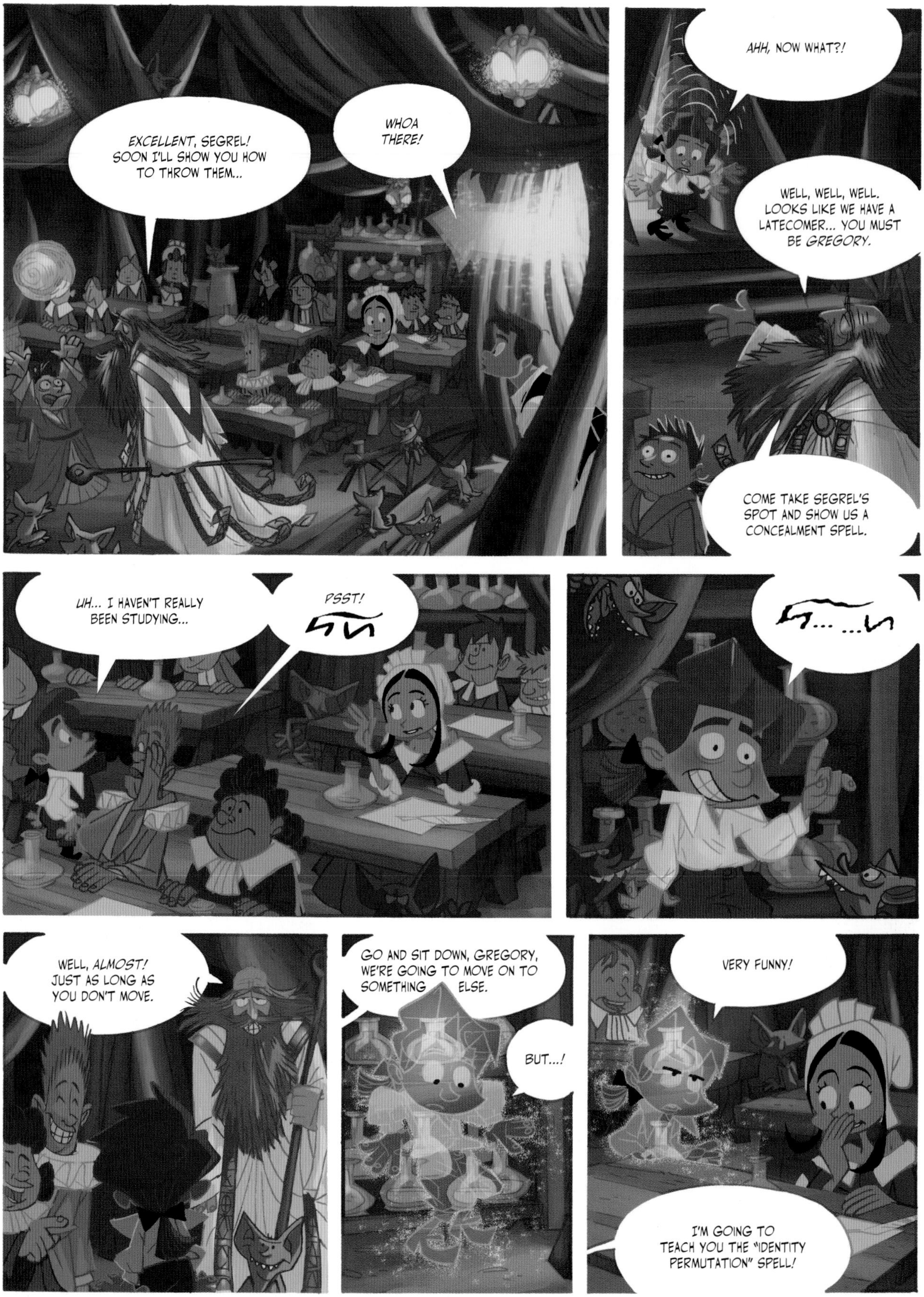

EXCELLENT, SEGREL! SOON I'LL SHOW YOU HOW TO THROW THEM...
WHOA THERE!
AHH, NOW WHAT?!
WELL, WELL, WELL. LOOKS LIKE WE HAVE A LATECOMER... YOU MUST BE GREGORY.
COME TAKE SEGREL'S SPOT AND SHOW US A CONCEALMENT SPELL.
UH... I HAVEN'T REALLY BEEN STUDYING...
PSST!
WELL, ALMOST! JUST AS LONG AS YOU DON'T MOVE.
GO AND SIT DOWN, GREGORY, WE'RE GOING TO MOVE ON TO SOMETHING ELSE.
BUT...!
VERY FUNNY!
I'M GOING TO TEACH YOU THE "IDENTITY PERMUTATION" SPELL!

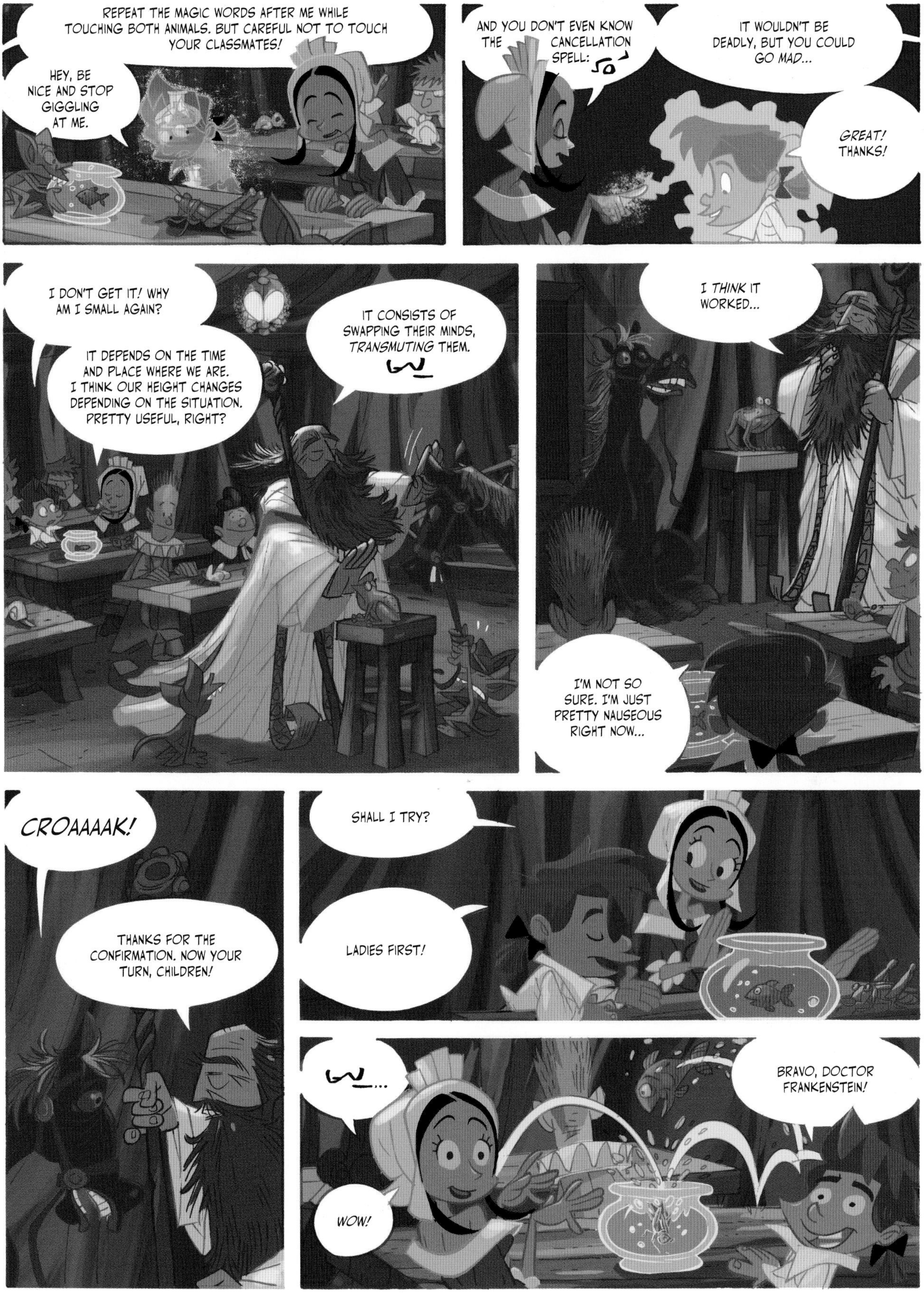
REPEAT THE MAGIC WORDS AFTER ME WHILE TOUCHING BOTH ANIMALS. BUT CAREFUL NOT TO TOUCH YOUR CLASSMATES!
HEY, BE NICE AND STOP GIGGLING AT ME.
AND YOU DON'T EVEN KNOW THE CANCELLATION SPELL:
IT WOULDN'T BE DEADLY, BUT YOU COULD GO MAD...
GREAT! THANKS!
I DON'T GET IT! WHY AM I SMALL AGAIN?
IT DEPENDS ON THE TIME AND PLACE WHERE WE ARE. I THINK OUR HEIGHT CHANGES DEPENDING ON THE SITUATION. PRETTY USEFUL, RIGHT?
IT CONSISTS OF SWAPPING THEIR MINDS, TRANSMUTING THEM.
I THINK IT WORKED...
I'M NOT SO SURE. I'M JUST PRETTY NAUSEOUS RIGHT NOW...
CROAAAAK!
THANKS FOR THE CONFIRMATION. NOW YOUR TURN, CHILDREN!
SHALL I TRY?
LADIES FIRST!
BRAVO, DOCTOR FRANKENSTEIN!
WOW!

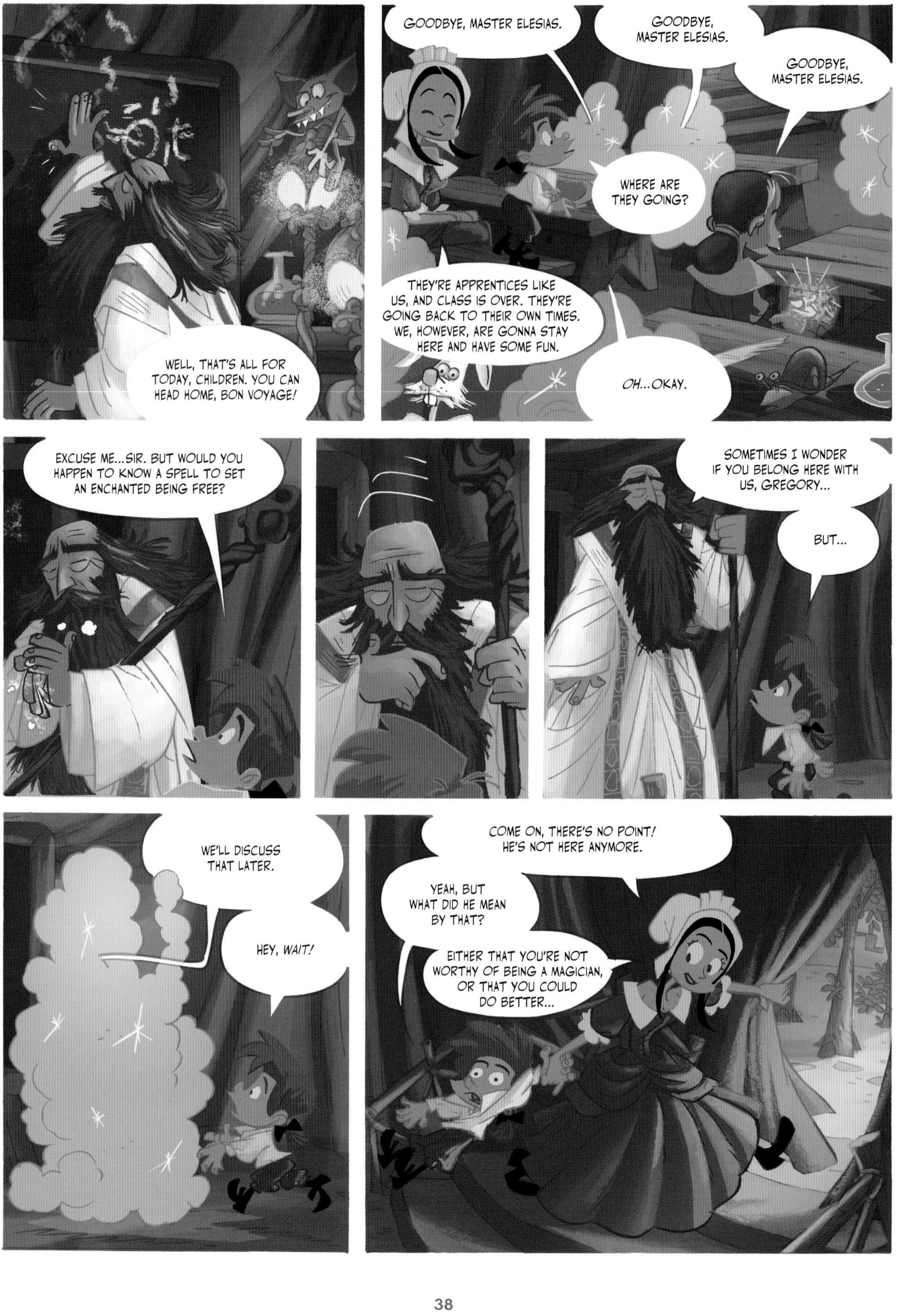
WELL, THAT'S ALL FOR TODAY, CHILDREN. YOU CAN HEAD HOME, BON VOYAGE!
GOODBYE, MASTER ELESIAS.
GOODBYE, MASTER ELESIAS.
GOODBYE, MASTER ELESIAS.
WHERE ARE THEY GOING?
THEY'RE APPRENTICES LIKE US, AND CLASS IS OVER. THEY'RE GOING BACK TO THEIR OWN TIMES. WE, HOWEVER, ARE GONNA STAY HERE AND HAVE SOME FUN.
OH...OKAY.
EXCUSE ME...SIR. BUT WOULD YOU HAPPEN TO KNOW A SPELL TO SET AN ENCHANTED BEING FREE?
SOMETIMES I WONDER IF YOU BELONG HERE WITH US, GREGORY...
BUT...
WE'LL DISCUSS THAT LATER.
HEY, WAIT!
COME ON, THERE'S NO POINT! HE'S NOT HERE ANYMORE.
YEAH, BUT WHAT DID HE MEAN BY THAT?
EITHER THAT YOU'RE NOT WORTHY OF BEING A MAGICIAN, OR THAT YOU COULD DO BETTER...

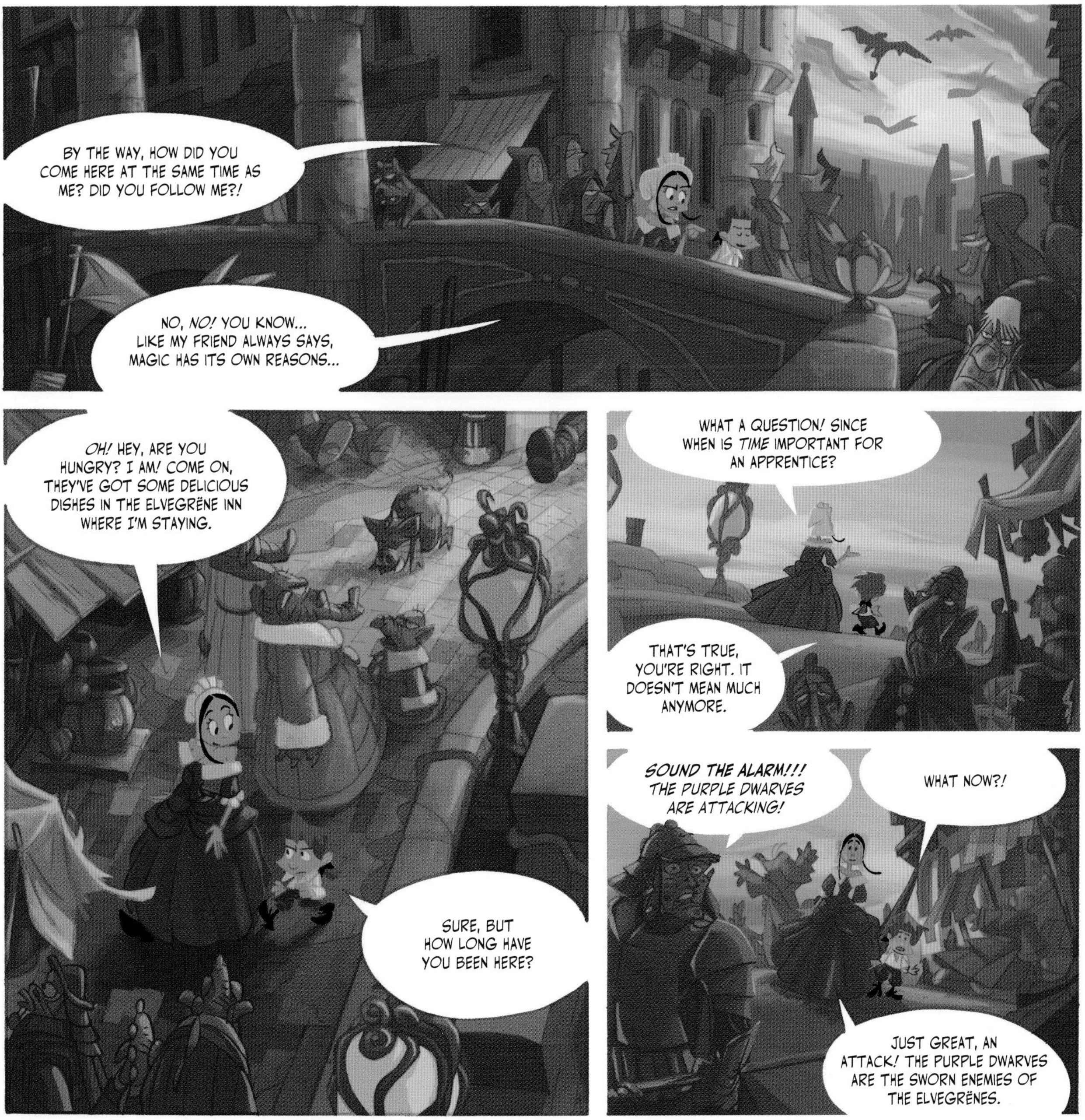
BY THE WAY, HOW DID YOU COME HERE AT THE SAME TIME AS ME? DID YOU FOLLOW ME?!
NO, *NO!* YOU KNOW... LIKE MY FRIEND ALWAYS SAYS, MAGIC HAS ITS OWN REASONS...
OH! HEY, ARE YOU HUNGRY? I AM! COME ON, THEY'VE GOT SOME DELICIOUS DISHES IN THE ELVEGRÈNE INN WHERE I'M STAYING.
SURE, BUT HOW LONG HAVE YOU BEEN HERE?
WHAT A QUESTION! SINCE WHEN IS *TIME* IMPORTANT FOR AN APPRENTICE?
THAT'S TRUE, YOU'RE RIGHT. IT DOESN'T MEAN MUCH ANYMORE.
SOUND THE ALARM!!! *THE PURPLE DWARVES ARE ATTACKING!*
WHAT NOW?!
JUST GREAT, AN ATTACK! THE PURPLE DWARVES ARE THE SWORN ENEMIES OF THE ELVEGRÈNES.
FINALLY, SOME ENTERTAINMENT! *COME QUICK!*

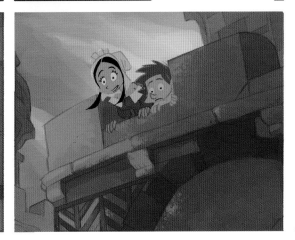

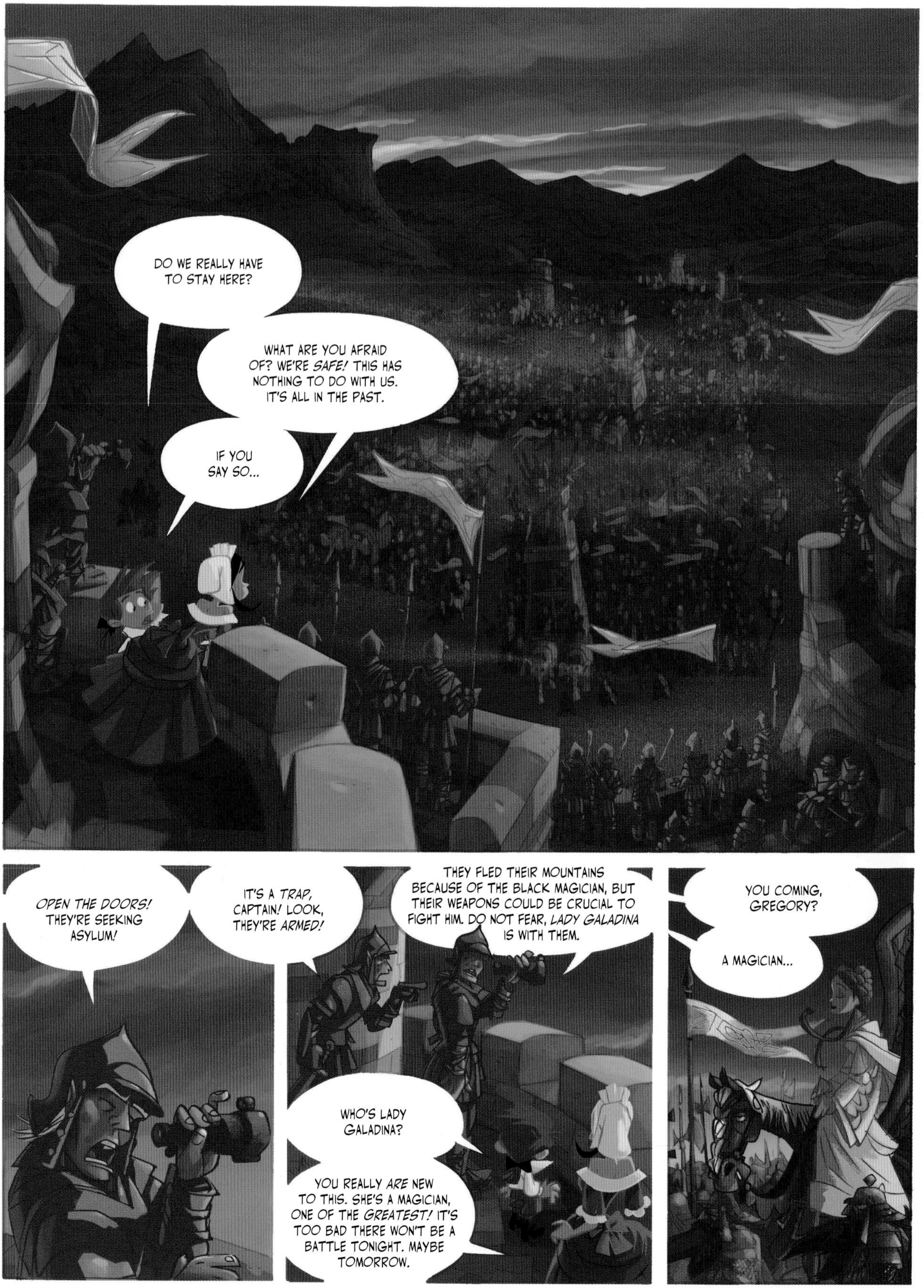
DO WE REALLY HAVE TO STAY HERE?
WHAT ARE YOU AFRAID OF? WE'RE *SAFE!* THIS HAS NOTHING TO DO WITH US. IT'S ALL IN THE PAST.
IF YOU SAY SO...
OPEN THE DOORS! THEY'RE SEEKING ASYLUM!
IT'S A *TRAP,* CAPTAIN! LOOK, THEY'RE *ARMED!*
THEY FLED THEIR MOUNTAINS BECAUSE OF THE BLACK MAGICIAN, BUT THEIR WEAPONS COULD BE CRUCIAL TO FIGHT HIM. DO NOT FEAR, *LADY GALADINA* IS WITH THEM.
WHO'S LADY GALADINA?
YOU REALLY *ARE* NEW TO THIS. SHE'S A MAGICIAN, ONE OF THE *GREATEST!* IT'S TOO BAD THERE WON'T BE A BATTLE TONIGHT. MAYBE TOMORROW.
YOU COMING, GREGORY?
A MAGICIAN...

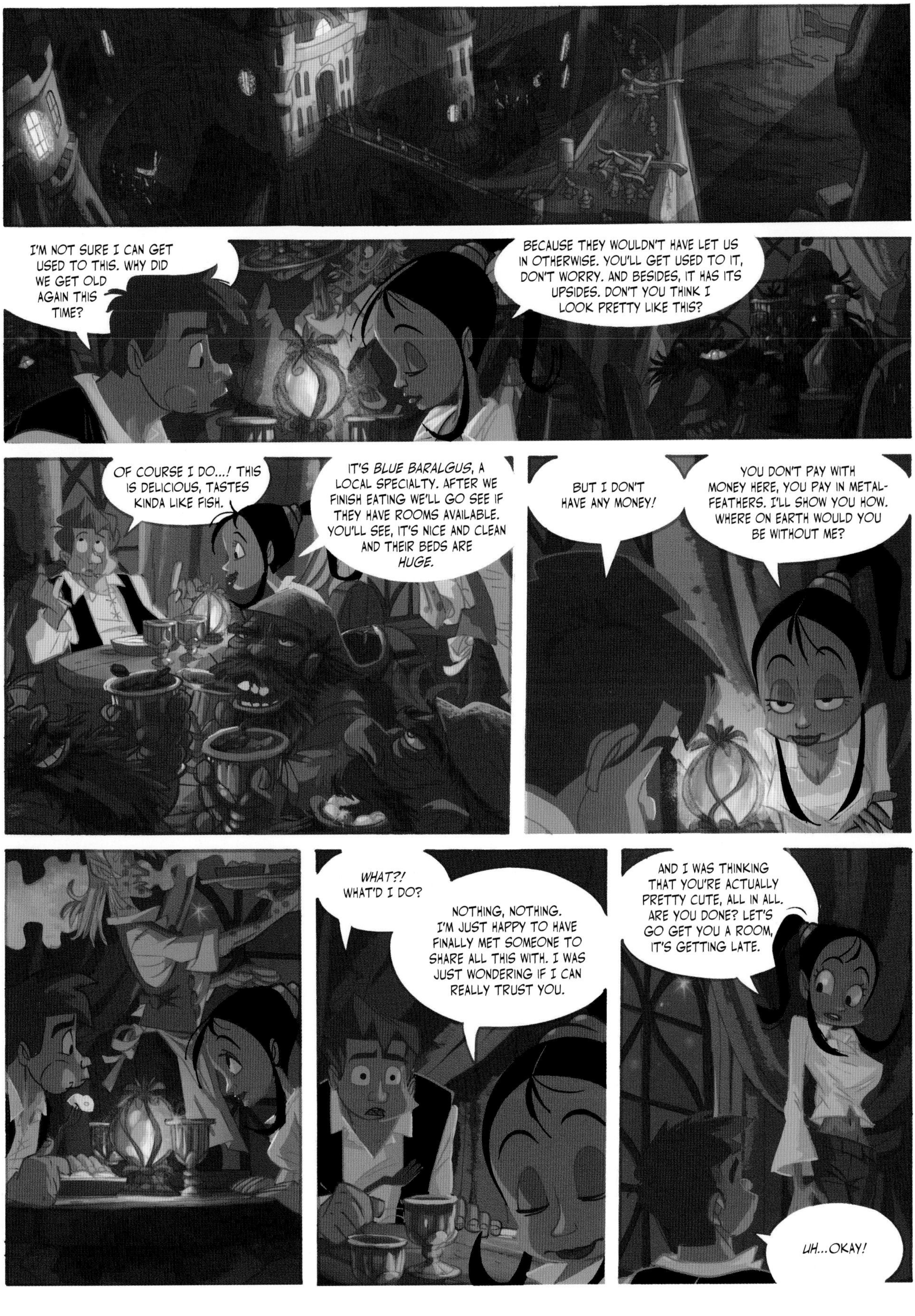
I'M NOT SURE I CAN GET USED TO THIS. WHY DID WE GET OLD AGAIN THIS TIME?
BECAUSE THEY WOULDN'T HAVE LET US IN OTHERWISE. YOU'LL GET USED TO IT, DON'T WORRY. AND BESIDES, IT HAS ITS UPSIDES. DON'T YOU THINK I LOOK PRETTY LIKE THIS?
OF COURSE I DO...! THIS IS DELICIOUS, TASTES KINDA LIKE FISH.
IT'S *BLUE BARALGUS*, A LOCAL SPECIALTY. AFTER WE FINISH EATING WE'LL GO SEE IF THEY HAVE ROOMS AVAILABLE. YOU'LL SEE, IT'S NICE AND CLEAN AND THEIR BEDS ARE *HUGE*.
BUT I DON'T HAVE ANY MONEY!
YOU DON'T PAY WITH MONEY HERE, YOU PAY IN METAL-FEATHERS. I'LL SHOW YOU HOW. WHERE ON EARTH WOULD YOU BE WITHOUT ME?
WHAT?! WHAT'D I DO?
NOTHING, NOTHING. I'M JUST HAPPY TO HAVE FINALLY MET SOMEONE TO SHARE ALL THIS WITH. I WAS JUST WONDERING IF I CAN REALLY TRUST YOU.
AND I WAS THINKING THAT YOU'RE ACTUALLY PRETTY CUTE, ALL IN ALL. ARE YOU DONE? LET'S GO GET YOU A ROOM, IT'S GETTING LATE.
UH...OKAY!

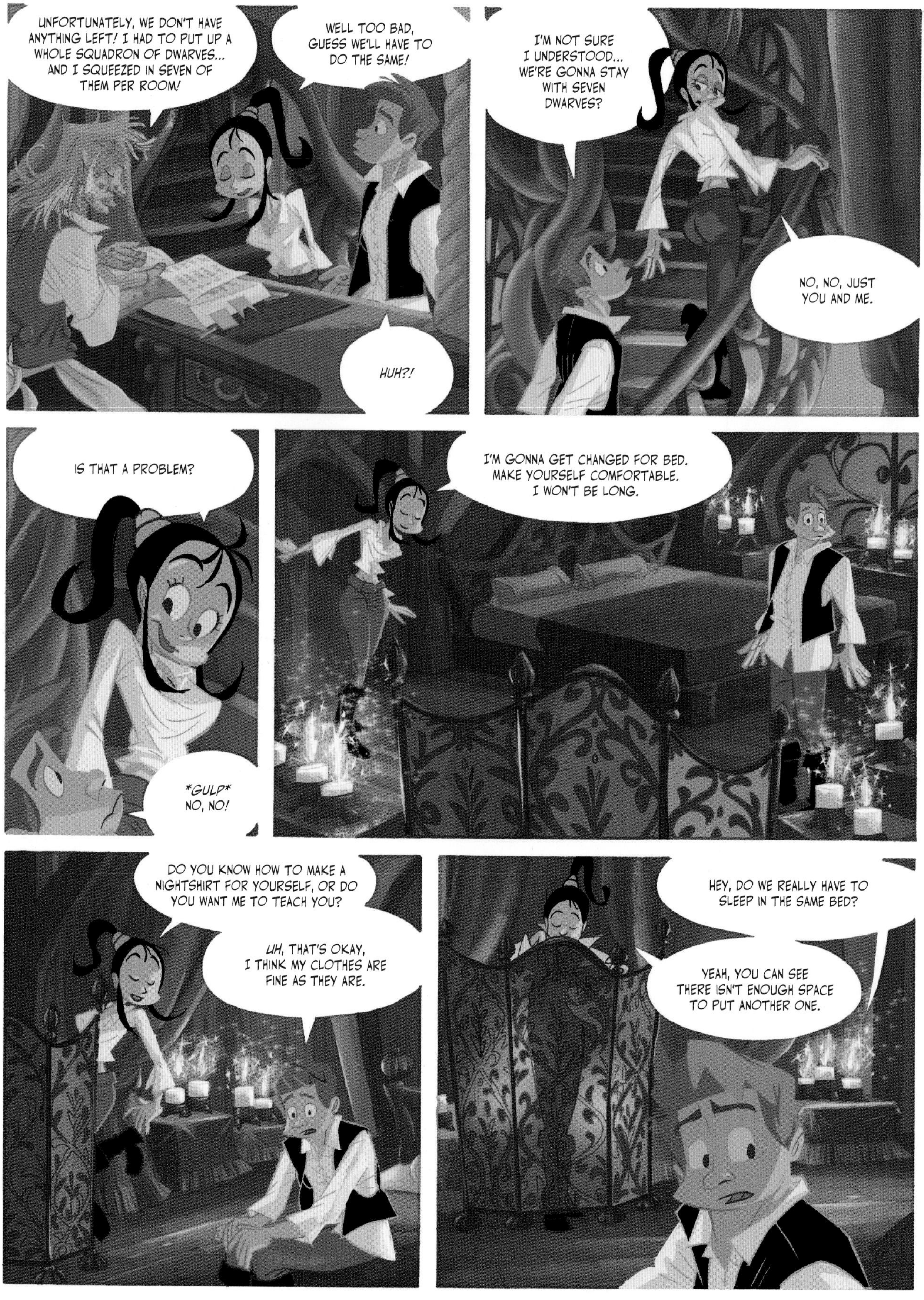

UNFORTUNATELY, WE DON'T HAVE ANYTHING LEFT! I HAD TO PUT UP A WHOLE SQUADRON OF DWARVES... AND I SQUEEZED IN SEVEN OF THEM PER ROOM!
WELL TOO BAD, GUESS WE'LL HAVE TO DO THE SAME!
HUH?!
I'M NOT SURE I UNDERSTOOD... WE'RE GONNA STAY WITH SEVEN DWARVES?
NO, NO, JUST YOU AND ME.
IS THAT A PROBLEM?
GULP NO, NO!
I'M GONNA GET CHANGED FOR BED. MAKE YOURSELF COMFORTABLE. I WON'T BE LONG.
DO YOU KNOW HOW TO MAKE A NIGHTSHIRT FOR YOURSELF, OR DO YOU WANT ME TO TEACH YOU?
UH, THAT'S OKAY, I THINK MY CLOTHES ARE FINE AS THEY ARE.
HEY, DO WE REALLY HAVE TO SLEEP IN THE SAME BED?
YEAH, YOU CAN SEE THERE ISN'T ENOUGH SPACE TO PUT ANOTHER ONE.

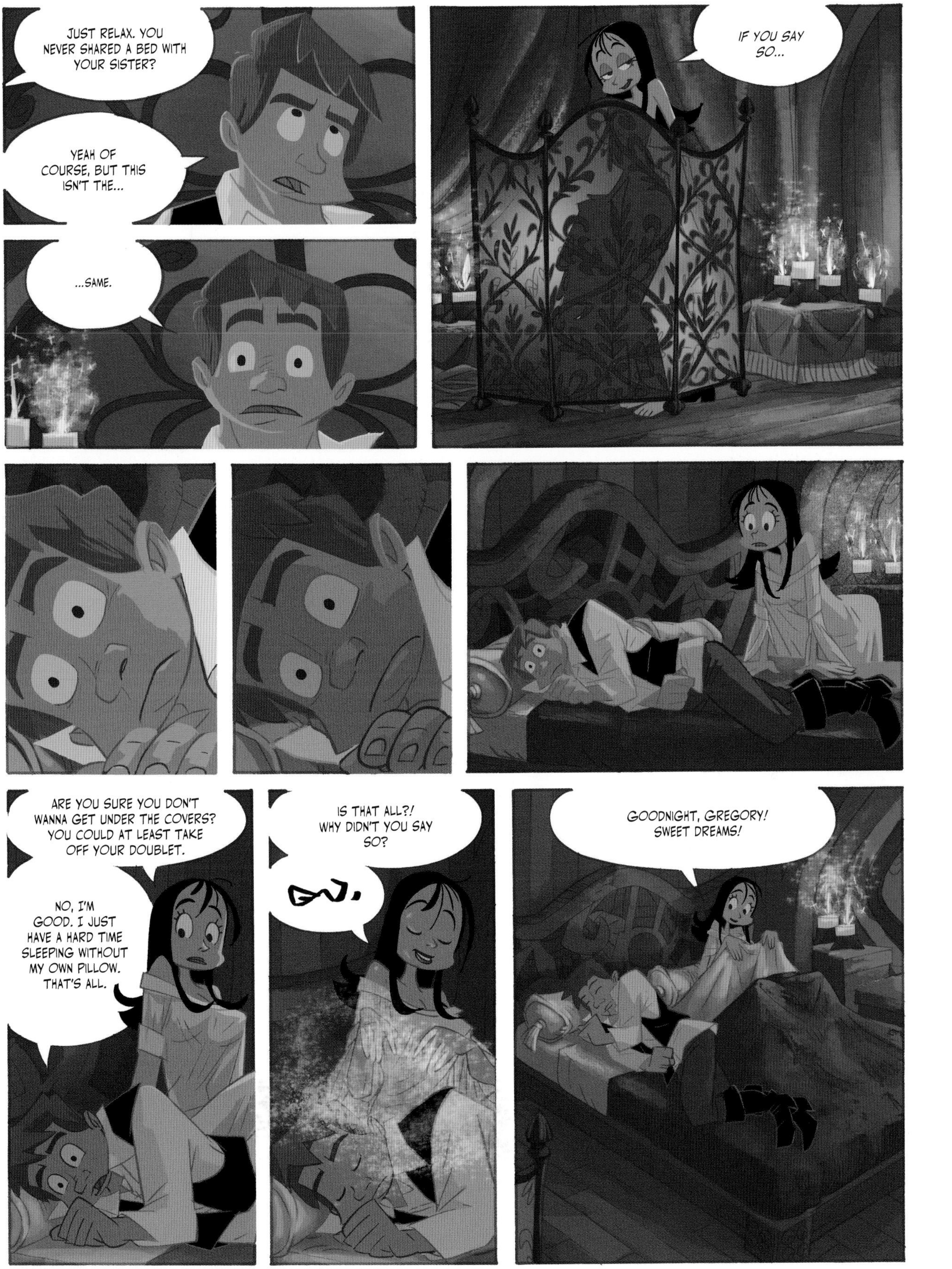

JUST RELAX. YOU NEVER SHARED A BED WITH YOUR SISTER?
YEAH OF COURSE, BUT THIS ISN'T THE...
...SAME.
IF YOU SAY SO...
ARE YOU SURE YOU DON'T WANNA GET UNDER THE COVERS? YOU COULD AT LEAST TAKE OFF YOUR DOUBLET.
NO, I'M GOOD. I JUST HAVE A HARD TIME SLEEPING WITHOUT MY OWN PILLOW. THAT'S ALL.
IS THAT ALL?! WHY DIDN'T YOU SAY SO?
GOODNIGHT, GREGORY! SWEET DREAMS!

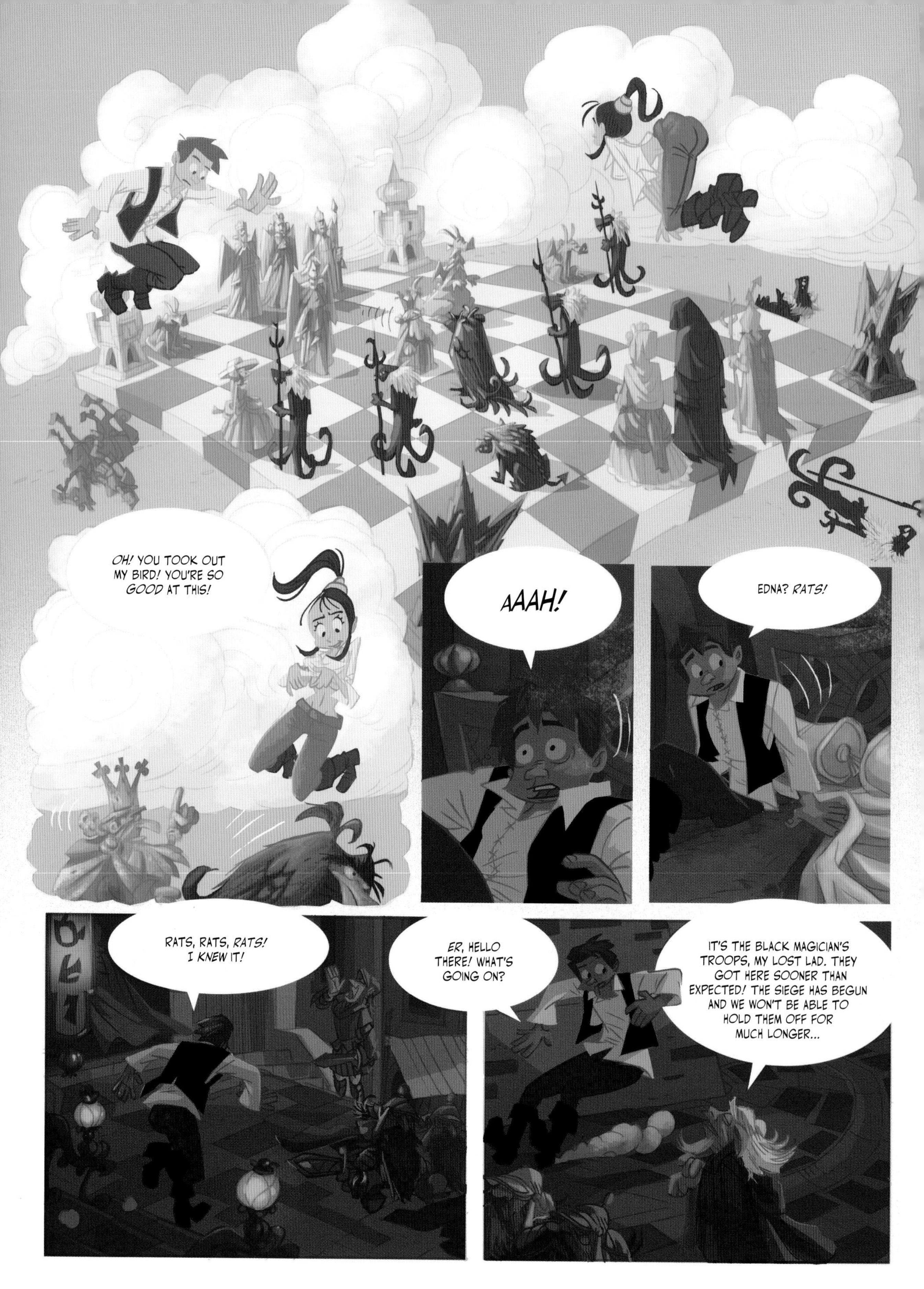
OH! YOU TOOK OUT MY BIRD! YOU'RE SO GOOD AT THIS!
AAAH!
EDNA? RATS!
RATS, RATS, RATS! I KNEW IT!
ER, HELLO THERE! WHAT'S GOING ON?
IT'S THE BLACK MAGICIAN'S TROOPS, MY LOST LAD. THEY GOT HERE SOONER THAN EXPECTED! THE SIEGE HAS BEGUN AND WE WON'T BE ABLE TO HOLD THEM OFF FOR MUCH LONGER...

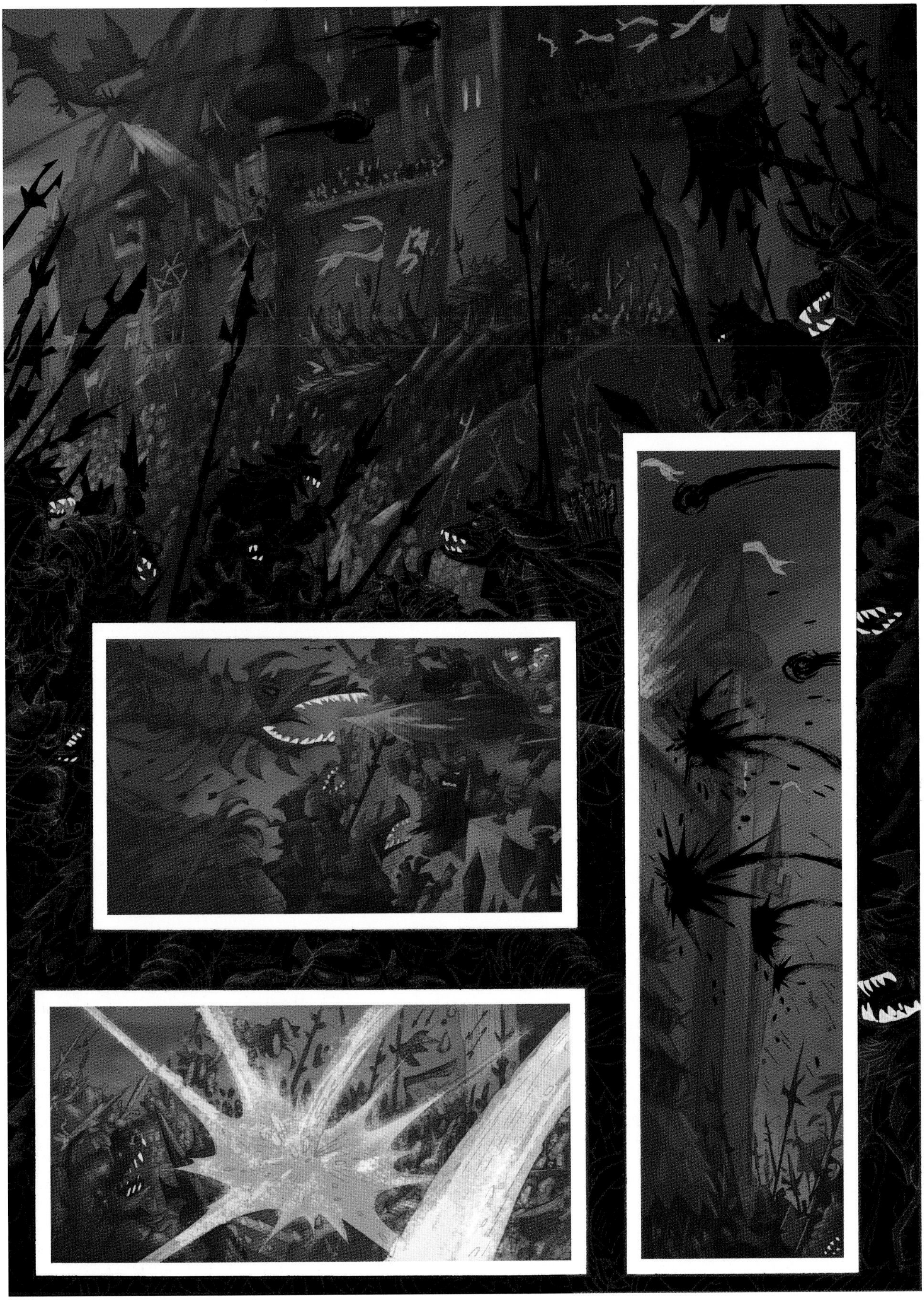

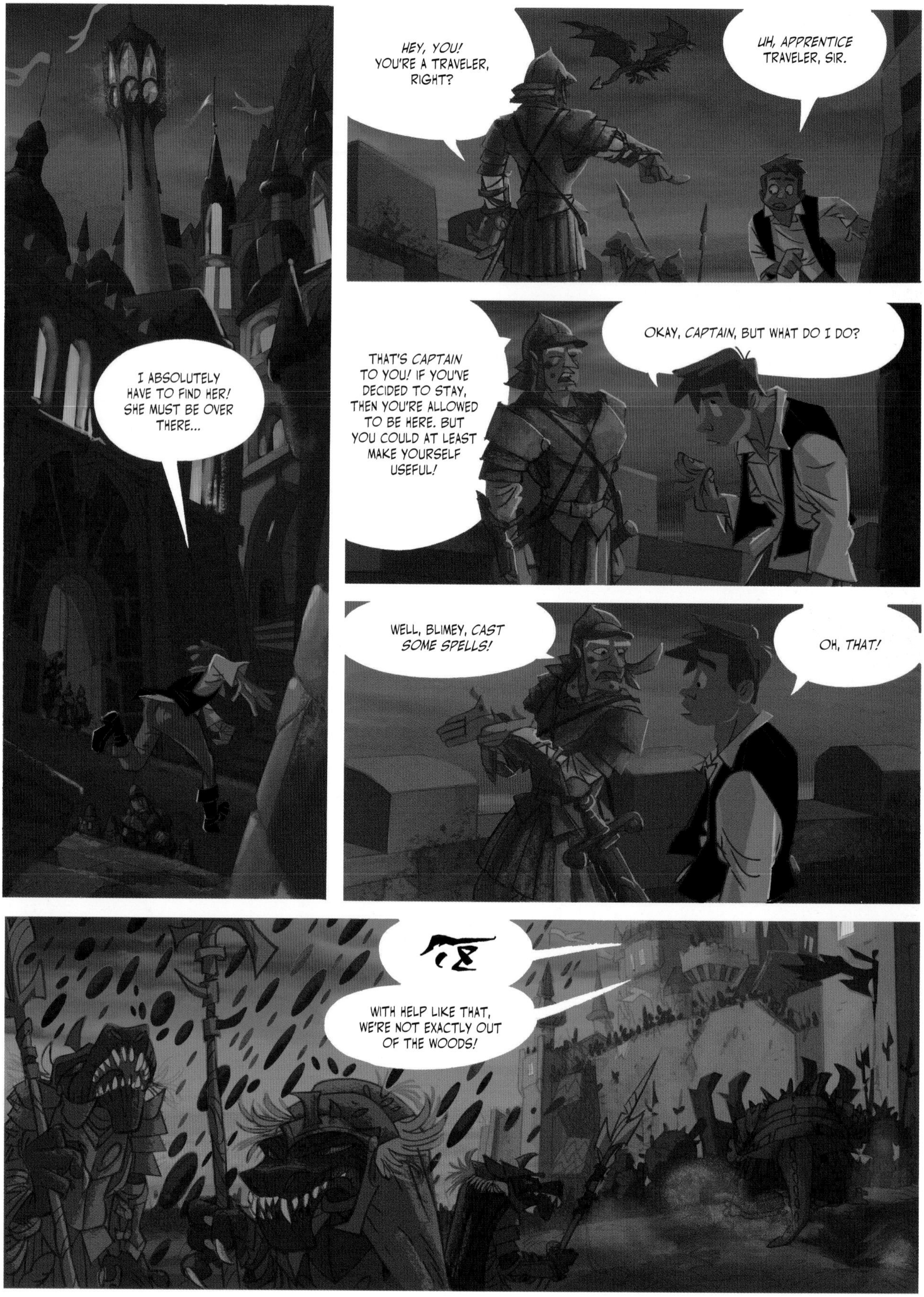
I ABSOLUTELY HAVE TO FIND HER! SHE MUST BE OVER THERE...
HEY, YOU! YOU'RE A TRAVELER, RIGHT?
UH, APPRENTICE TRAVELER, SIR.
THAT'S *CAPTAIN* TO YOU! IF YOU'VE DECIDED TO STAY, THEN YOU'RE ALLOWED TO BE HERE. BUT YOU COULD AT LEAST MAKE YOURSELF USEFUL!
OKAY, *CAPTAIN*, BUT WHAT DO I DO?
WELL, BLIMEY, *CAST SOME SPELLS!*
OH, THAT!
WITH HELP LIKE THAT, WE'RE NOT EXACTLY OUT OF THE WOODS!

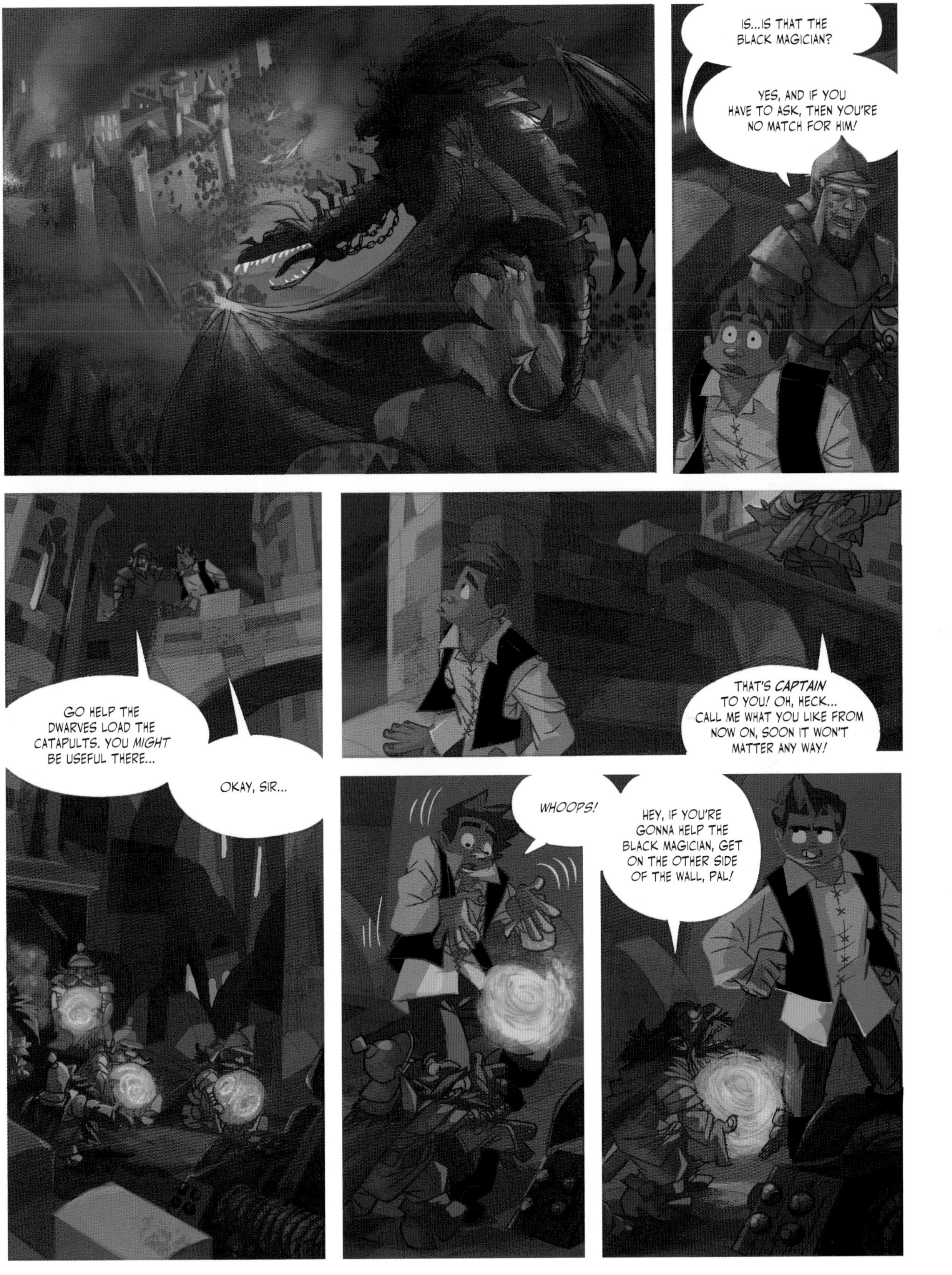

IS...IS THAT THE BLACK MAGICIAN?
YES, AND IF YOU HAVE TO ASK, THEN YOU'RE NO MATCH FOR HIM!
GO HELP THE DWARVES LOAD THE CATAPULTS. YOU *MIGHT* BE USEFUL THERE...
OKAY, SIR...
THAT'S *CAPTAIN* TO YOU! OH, HECK... CALL ME WHAT YOU LIKE FROM NOW ON, SOON IT WON'T MATTER ANY WAY!
WHOOPS!
HEY, IF YOU'RE GONNA HELP THE BLACK MAGICIAN, GET ON THE OTHER SIDE OF THE WALL, PAL!

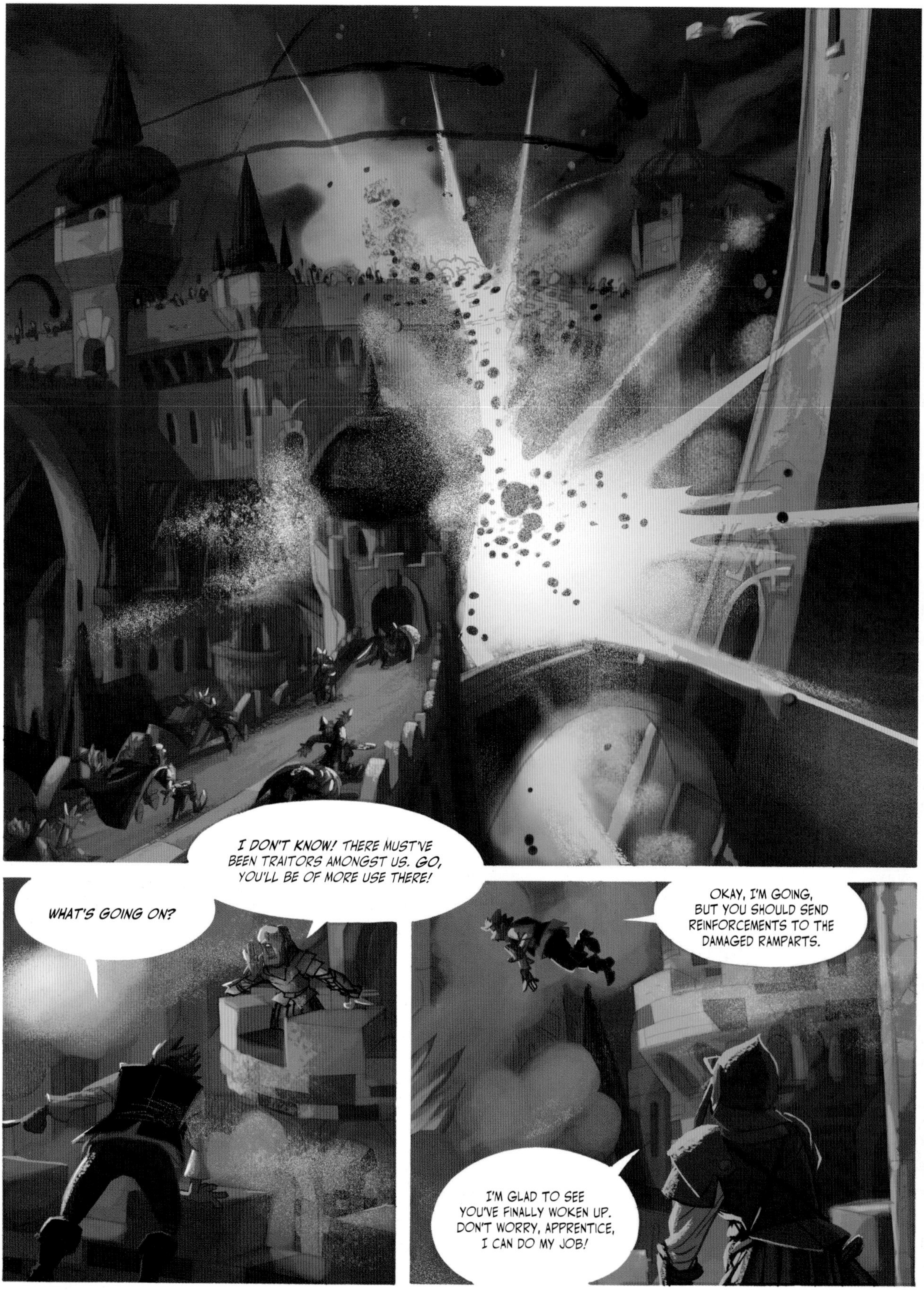
WHAT'S GOING ON?
I DON'T KNOW! THERE MUST'VE BEEN TRAITORS AMONGST US. GO, YOU'LL BE OF MORE USE THERE!
OKAY, I'M GOING, BUT YOU SHOULD SEND REINFORCEMENTS TO THE DAMAGED RAMPARTS.
I'M GLAD TO SEE YOU'VE FINALLY WOKEN UP. DON'T WORRY, APPRENTICE, I CAN DO MY JOB!

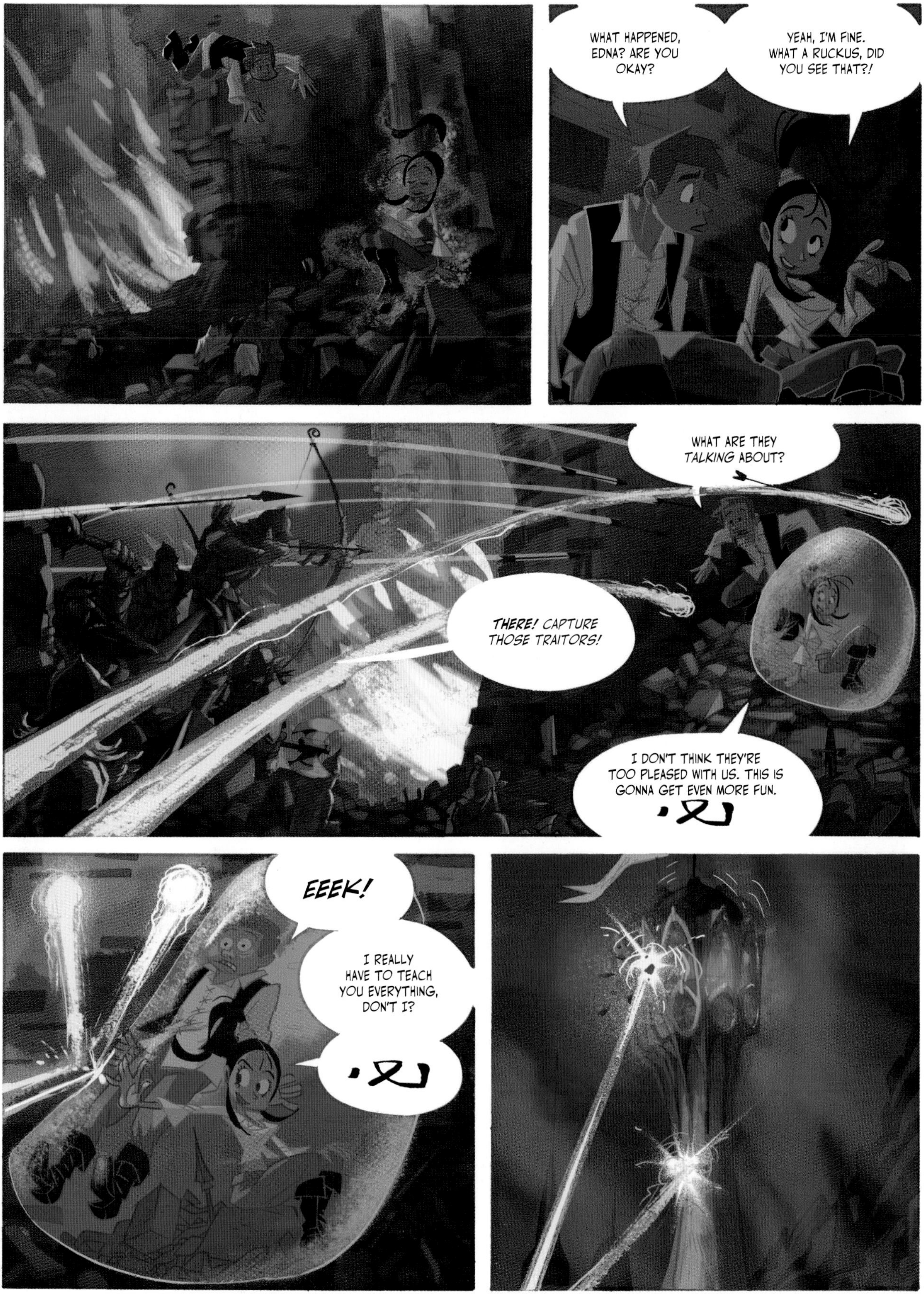
WHAT HAPPENED, EDNA? ARE YOU OKAY?
YEAH, I'M FINE. WHAT A RUCKUS, DID YOU SEE THAT?!
WHAT ARE THEY *TALKING* ABOUT?
THERE! CAPTURE THOSE TRAITORS!
I DON'T THINK THEY'RE TOO PLEASED WITH US. THIS IS GONNA GET EVEN MORE FUN.
EEEK!
I REALLY HAVE TO TEACH YOU EVERYTHING, DON'T I?

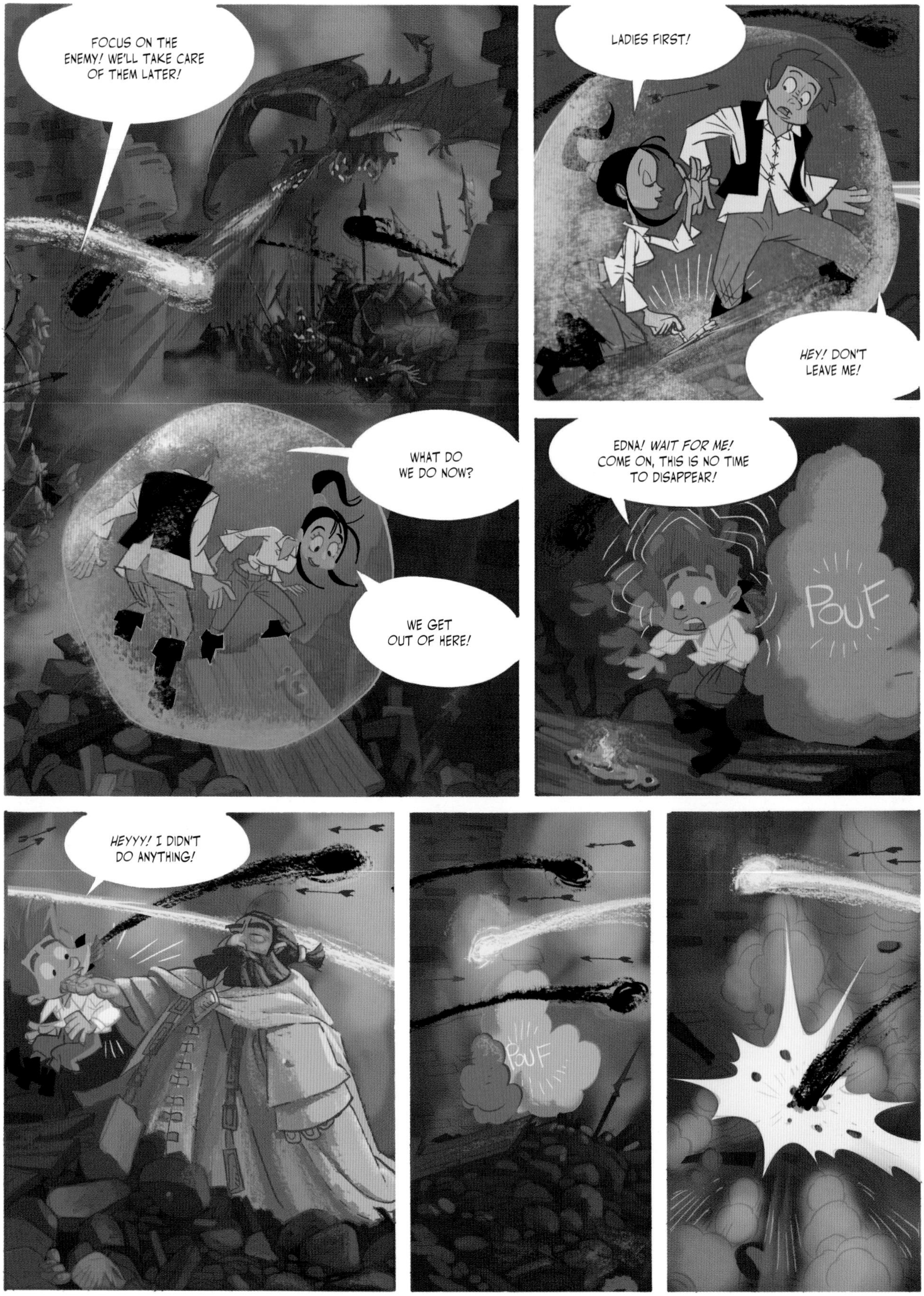
FOCUS ON THE ENEMY! WE'LL TAKE CARE OF THEM LATER!
LADIES FIRST!
HEY! DON'T LEAVE ME!
WHAT DO WE DO NOW?
WE GET OUT OF HERE!
EDNA! WAIT FOR ME! COME ON, THIS IS NO TIME TO DISAPPEAR!
POUF
HEYYY! I DIDN'T DO ANYTHING!
POUF

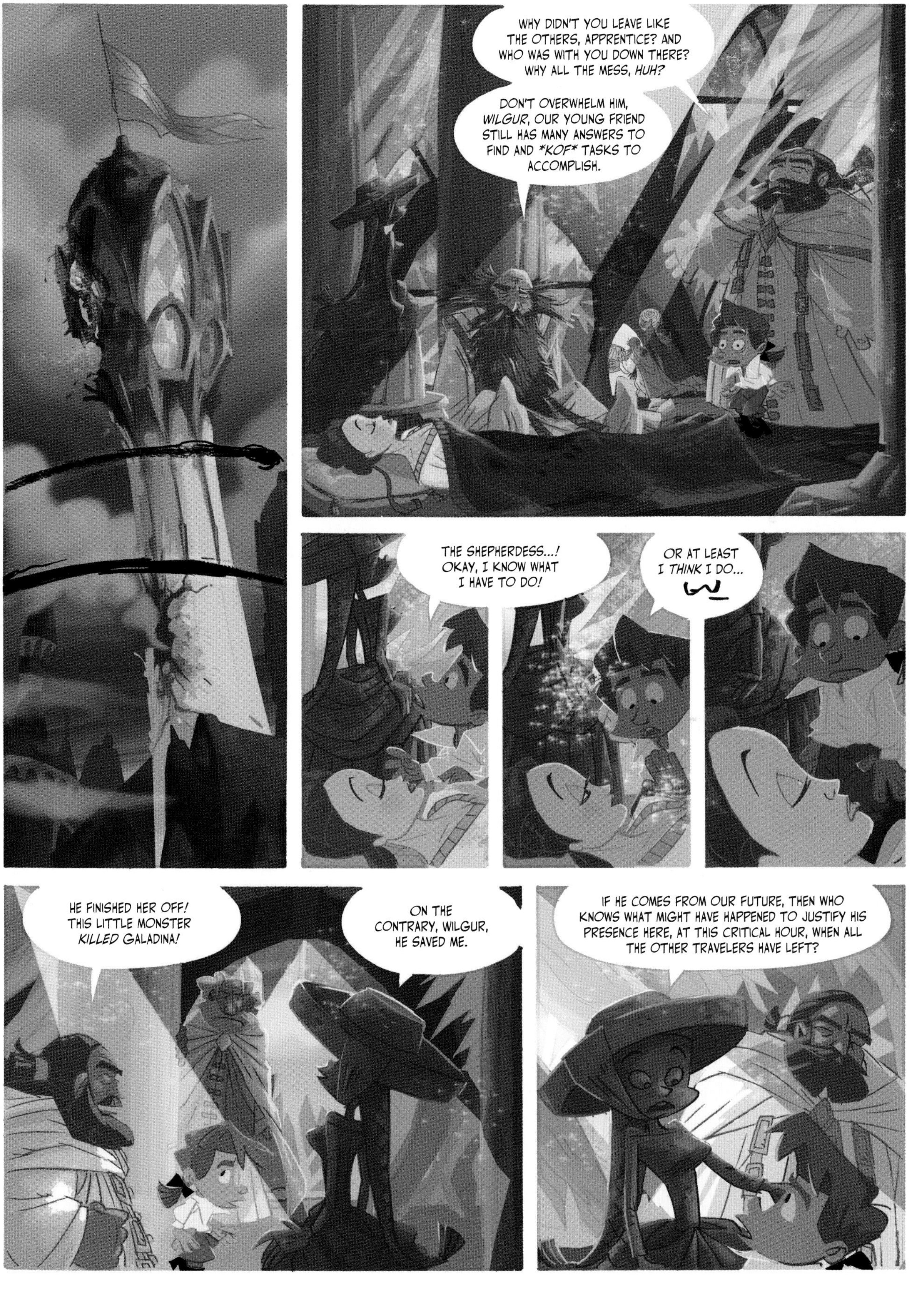

WHY DIDN'T YOU LEAVE LIKE THE OTHERS, APPRENTICE? AND WHO WAS WITH YOU DOWN THERE? WHY ALL THE MESS, *HUH?*
DON'T OVERWHELM HIM, *WILGUR*, OUR YOUNG FRIEND STILL HAS MANY ANSWERS TO FIND AND **KOF** TASKS TO ACCOMPLISH.
THE SHEPHERDESS...! OKAY, I KNOW WHAT I HAVE TO DO!
OR AT LEAST I *THINK* I DO...
HE FINISHED HER OFF! THIS LITTLE MONSTER *KILLED* GALADINA!
ON THE CONTRARY, WILGUR, HE SAVED ME.
IF HE COMES FROM OUR FUTURE, THEN WHO KNOWS WHAT MIGHT HAVE HAPPENED TO JUSTIFY HIS PRESENCE HERE, AT THIS CRITICAL HOUR, WHEN ALL THE OTHER TRAVELERS HAVE LEFT?

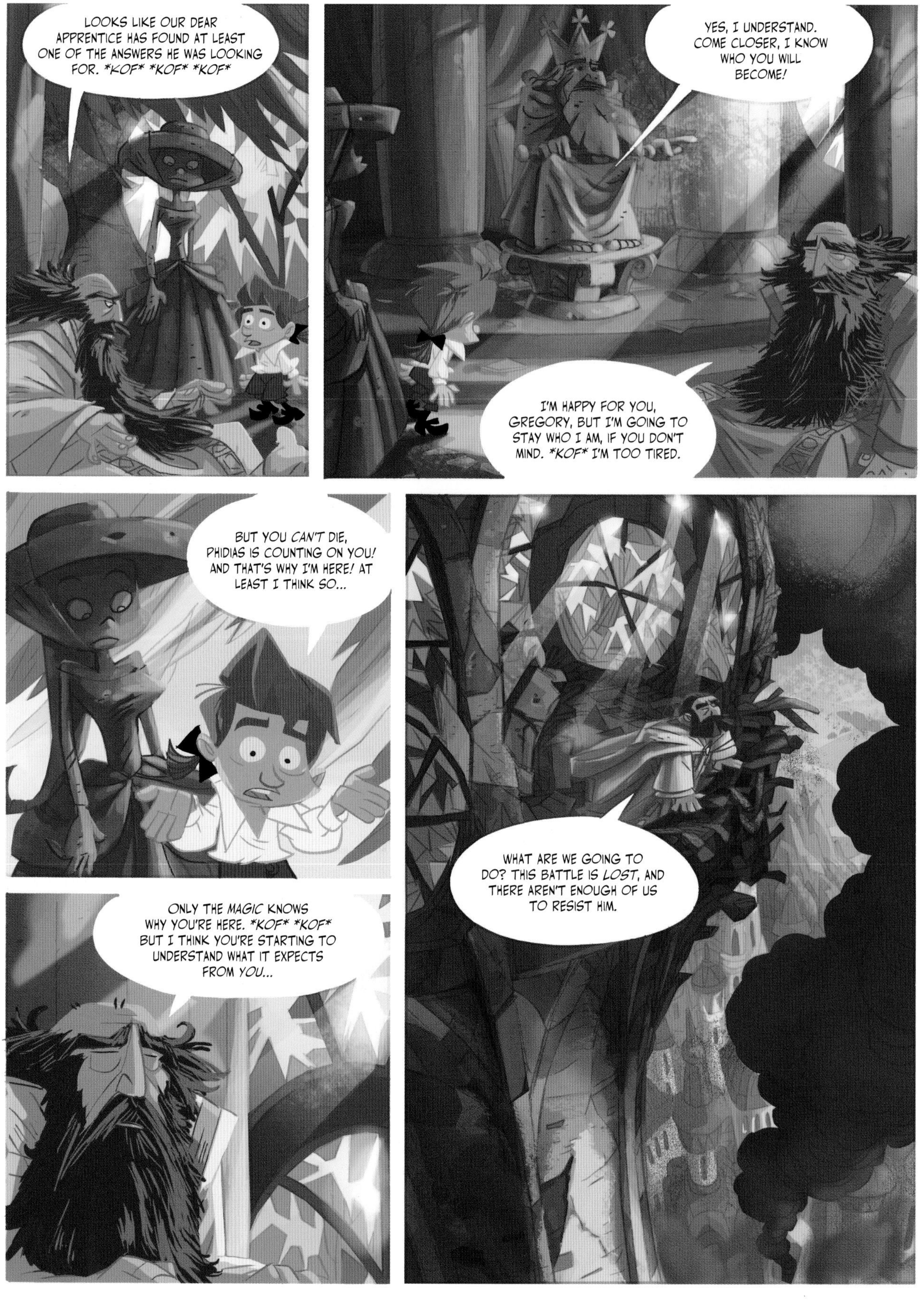
LOOKS LIKE OUR DEAR APPRENTICE HAS FOUND AT LEAST ONE OF THE ANSWERS HE WAS LOOKING FOR. *KOF* *KOF* *KOF*
YES, I UNDERSTAND. COME CLOSER, I KNOW WHO YOU WILL BECOME!
I'M HAPPY FOR YOU, GREGORY, BUT I'M GOING TO STAY WHO I AM, IF YOU DON'T MIND. *KOF* I'M TOO TIRED.
BUT YOU CAN'T DIE, PHIDIAS IS COUNTING ON YOU! AND THAT'S WHY I'M HERE! AT LEAST I THINK SO...
ONLY THE MAGIC KNOWS WHY YOU'RE HERE. *KOF* *KOF* BUT I THINK YOU'RE STARTING TO UNDERSTAND WHAT IT EXPECTS FROM YOU...
WHAT ARE WE GOING TO DO? THIS BATTLE IS LOST, AND THERE AREN'T ENOUGH OF US TO RESIST HIM.

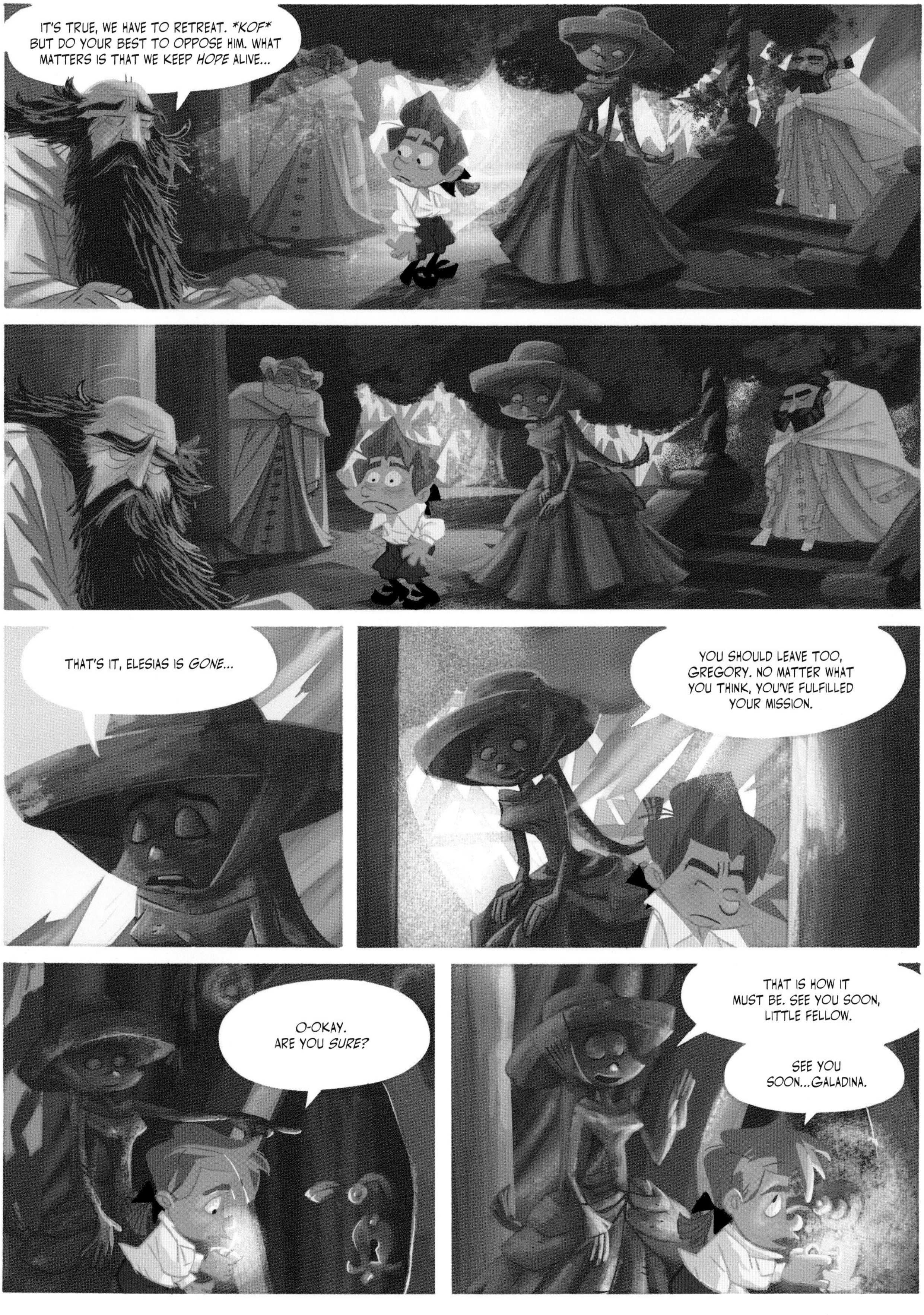
IT'S TRUE, WE HAVE TO RETREAT. *KOF* BUT DO YOUR BEST TO OPPOSE HIM. WHAT MATTERS IS THAT WE KEEP HOPE ALIVE...
THAT'S IT, ELESIAS IS GONE...
YOU SHOULD LEAVE TOO, GREGORY. NO MATTER WHAT YOU THINK, YOU'VE FULFILLED YOUR MISSION.
O-OKAY. ARE YOU SURE?
THAT IS HOW IT MUST BE. SEE YOU SOON, LITTLE FELLOW.
SEE YOU SOON...GALADINA.

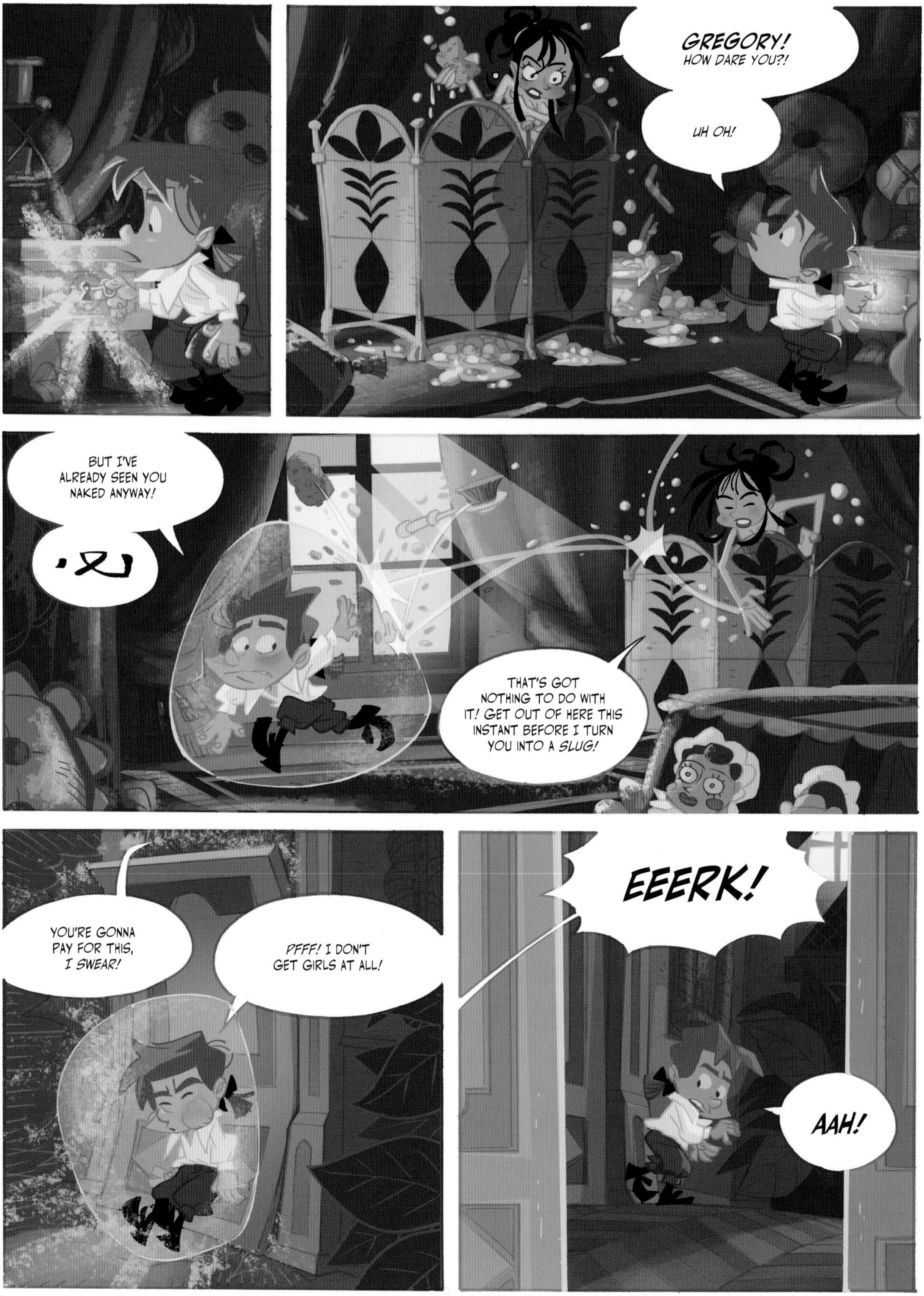
GREGORY! HOW DARE YOU?!
UH OH!
BUT I'VE ALREADY SEEN YOU NAKED ANYWAY!
THAT'S GOT NOTHING TO DO WITH IT! GET OUT OF HERE THIS INSTANT BEFORE I TURN YOU INTO A SLUG!
YOU'RE GONNA PAY FOR THIS, I SWEAR!
PFFF! I DON'T GET GIRLS AT ALL!
EEERK!
AAH!

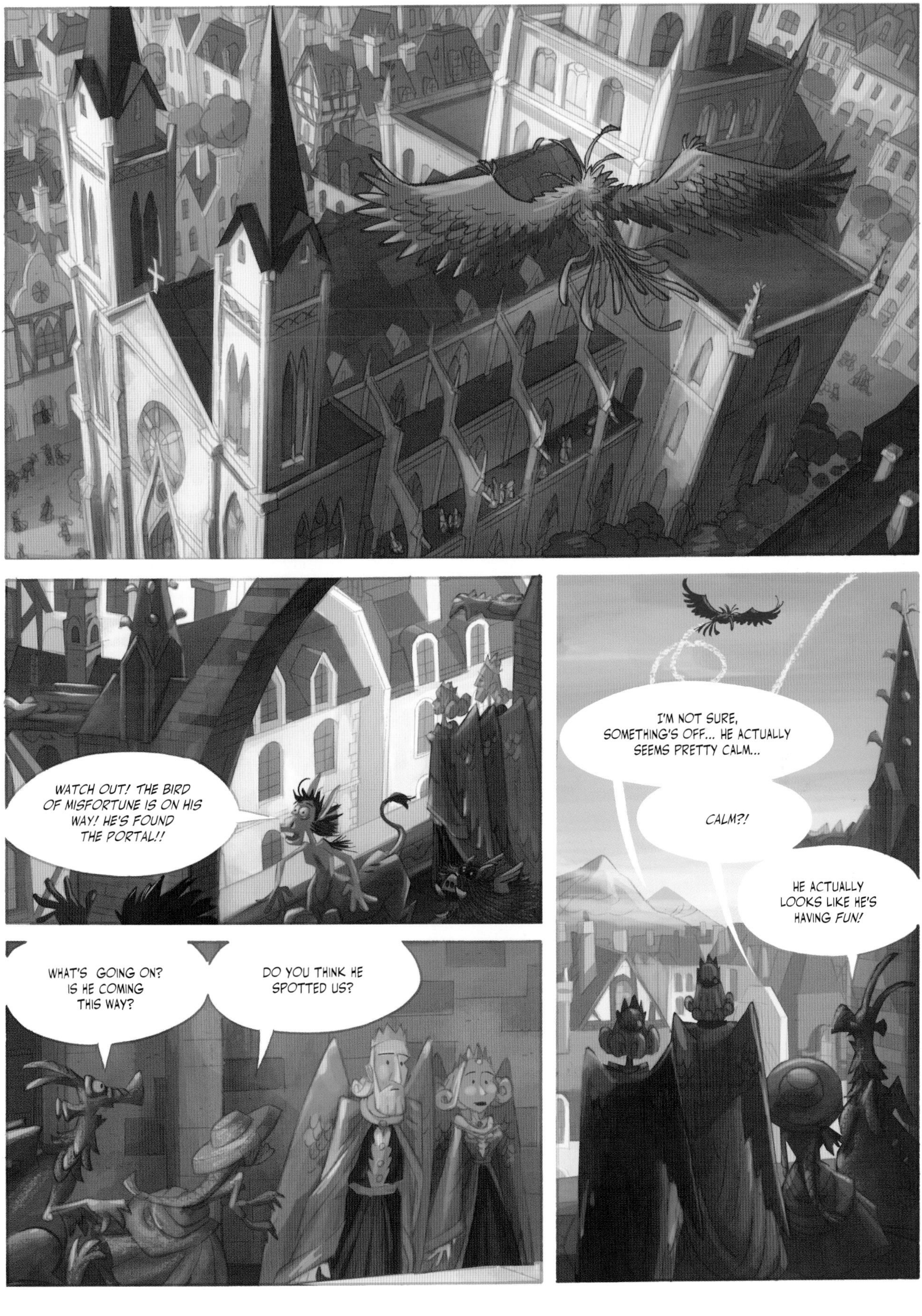

WATCH OUT! THE BIRD OF MISFORTUNE IS ON HIS WAY! HE'S FOUND THE PORTAL!!
WHAT'S GOING ON? IS HE COMING THIS WAY?
DO YOU THINK HE SPOTTED US?
I'M NOT SURE, SOMETHING'S OFF... HE ACTUALLY SEEMS PRETTY CALM...
CALM?!
HE ACTUALLY LOOKS LIKE HE'S HAVING FUN!

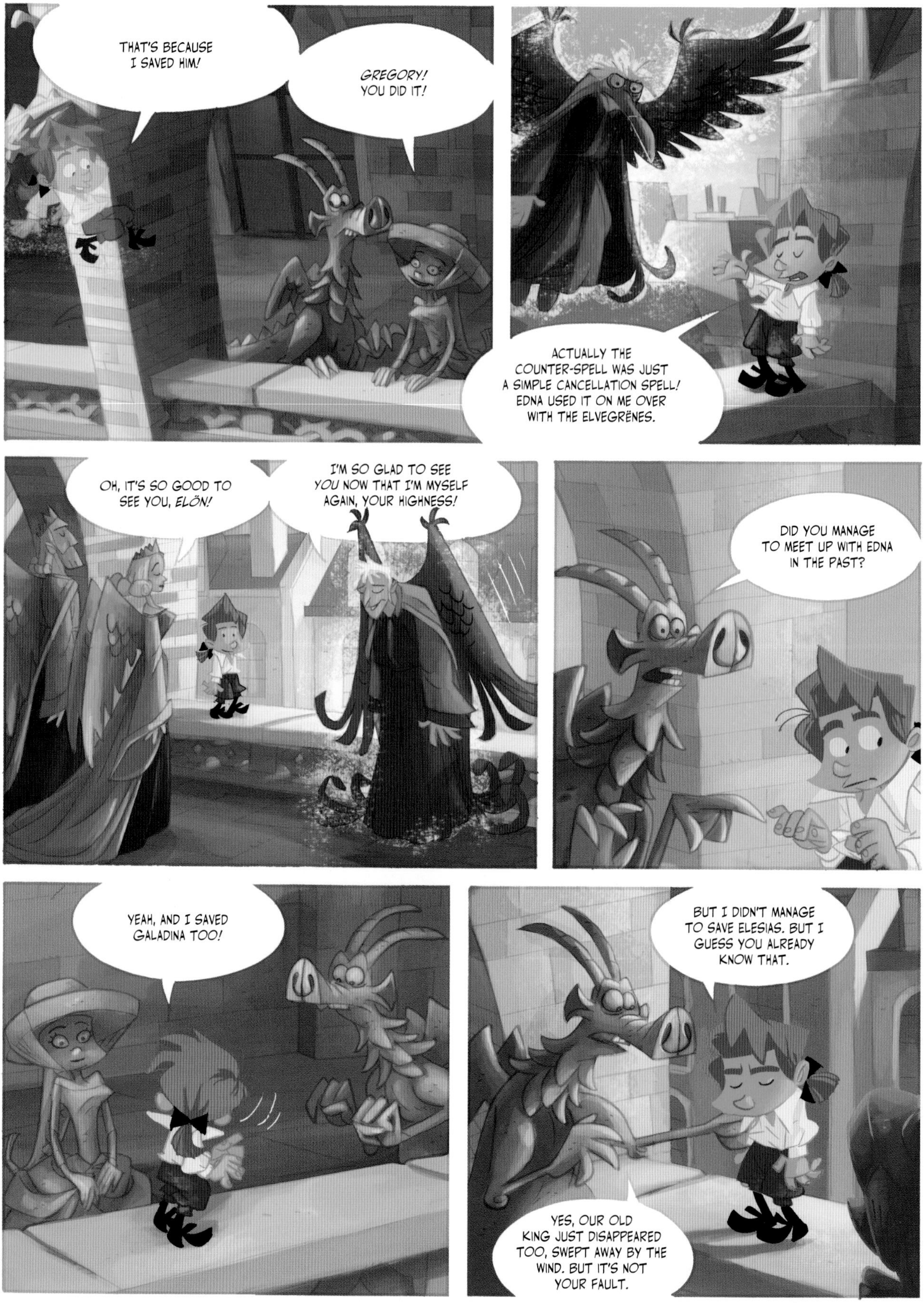

THAT'S BECAUSE I SAVED HIM!
GREGORY! YOU DID IT!
ACTUALLY THE COUNTER-SPELL WAS JUST A SIMPLE CANCELLATION SPELL! EDNA USED IT ON ME OVER WITH THE ELVEGRËNES.
OH, IT'S SO GOOD TO SEE YOU, ELÖN!
I'M SO GLAD TO SEE YOU NOW THAT I'M MYSELF AGAIN, YOUR HIGHNESS!
DID YOU MANAGE TO MEET UP WITH EDNA IN THE PAST?
YEAH, AND I SAVED GALADINA TOO!
BUT I DIDN'T MANAGE TO SAVE ELESIAS. BUT I GUESS YOU ALREADY KNOW THAT.
YES, OUR OLD KING JUST DISAPPEARED TOO, SWEPT AWAY BY THE WIND. BUT IT'S NOT YOUR FAULT.

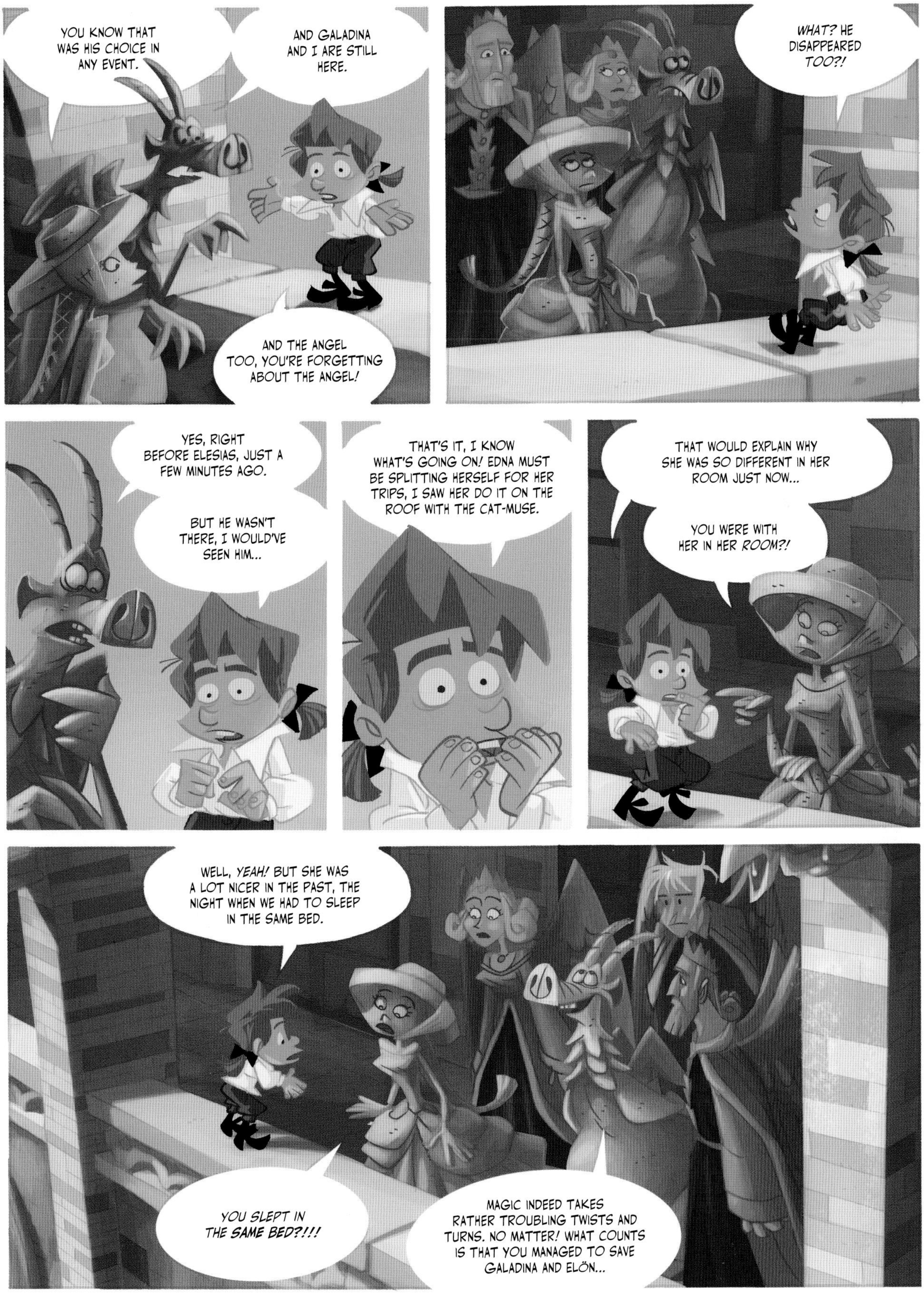

YOU KNOW THAT WAS HIS CHOICE IN ANY EVENT.
AND GALADINA AND I ARE STILL HERE.
AND THE ANGEL TOO, YOU'RE FORGETTING ABOUT THE ANGEL!
WHAT? HE DISAPPEARED *TOO?!*
YES, RIGHT BEFORE ELESIAS, JUST A FEW MINUTES AGO.
BUT HE WASN'T THERE, I WOULD'VE SEEN HIM...
THAT'S IT, I KNOW WHAT'S GOING ON! EDNA MUST BE SPLITTING HERSELF FOR HER TRIPS, I SAW HER DO IT ON THE ROOF WITH THE CAT-MUSE.
THAT WOULD EXPLAIN WHY SHE WAS SO DIFFERENT IN HER ROOM JUST NOW...
YOU WERE WITH HER IN HER *ROOM?!*
WELL, *YEAH!* BUT SHE WAS A LOT NICER IN THE PAST, THE NIGHT WHEN WE HAD TO SLEEP IN THE SAME BED.
*YOU SLEPT IN THE **SAME BED?!!!***
MAGIC INDEED TAKES RATHER TROUBLING TWISTS AND TURNS. NO MATTER! WHAT COUNTS IS THAT YOU MANAGED TO SAVE GALADINA AND ELÖN...

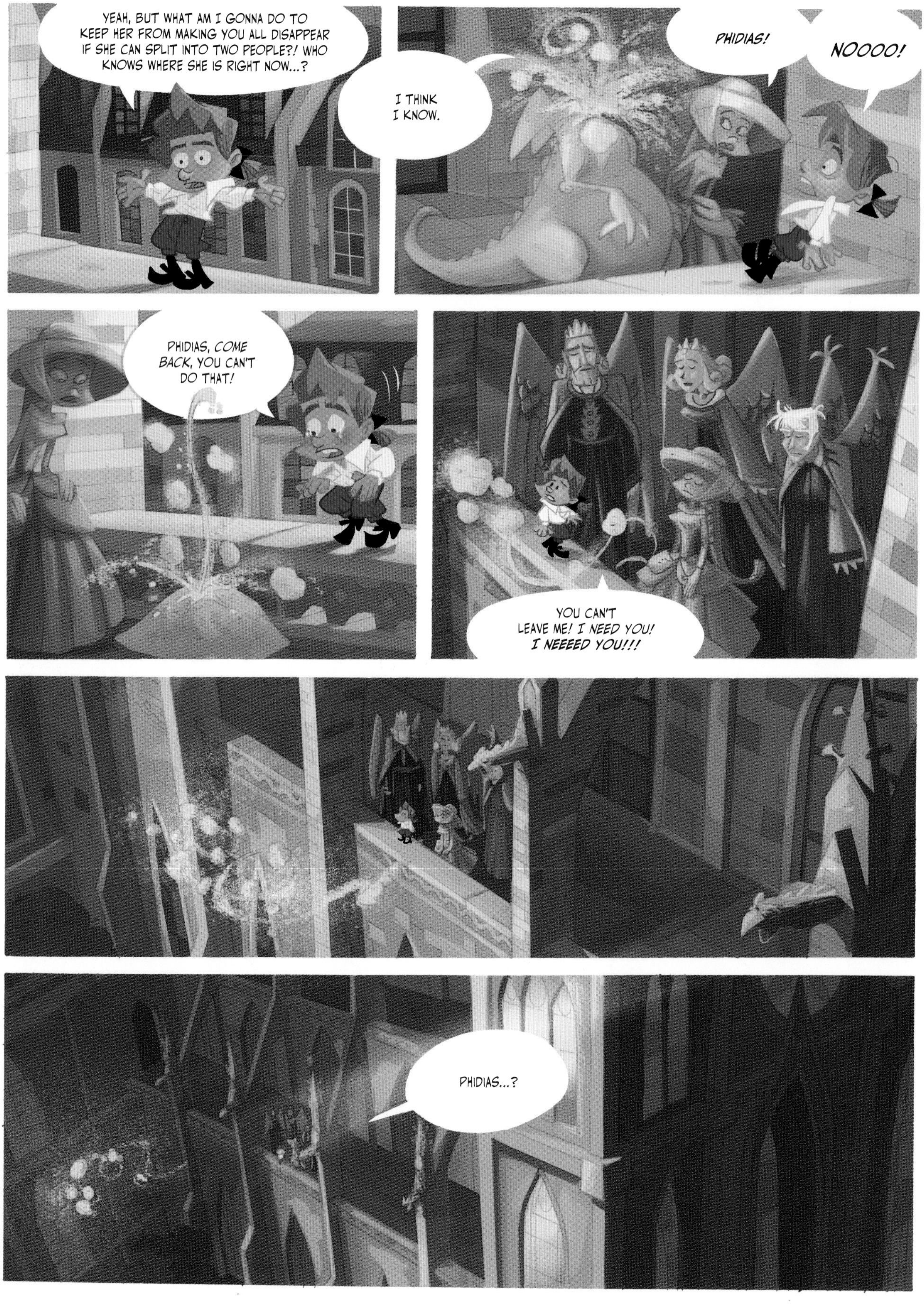
YEAH, BUT WHAT AM I GONNA DO TO KEEP HER FROM MAKING YOU ALL DISAPPEAR IF SHE CAN SPLIT INTO TWO PEOPLE?! WHO KNOWS WHERE SHE IS RIGHT NOW...?
I THINK I KNOW.
PHIDIAS!
NOOOO!
PHIDIAS, COME BACK, YOU CAN'T DO THAT!
YOU CAN'T LEAVE ME! I NEED YOU! I NEEEED YOU!!!
PHIDIAS...?

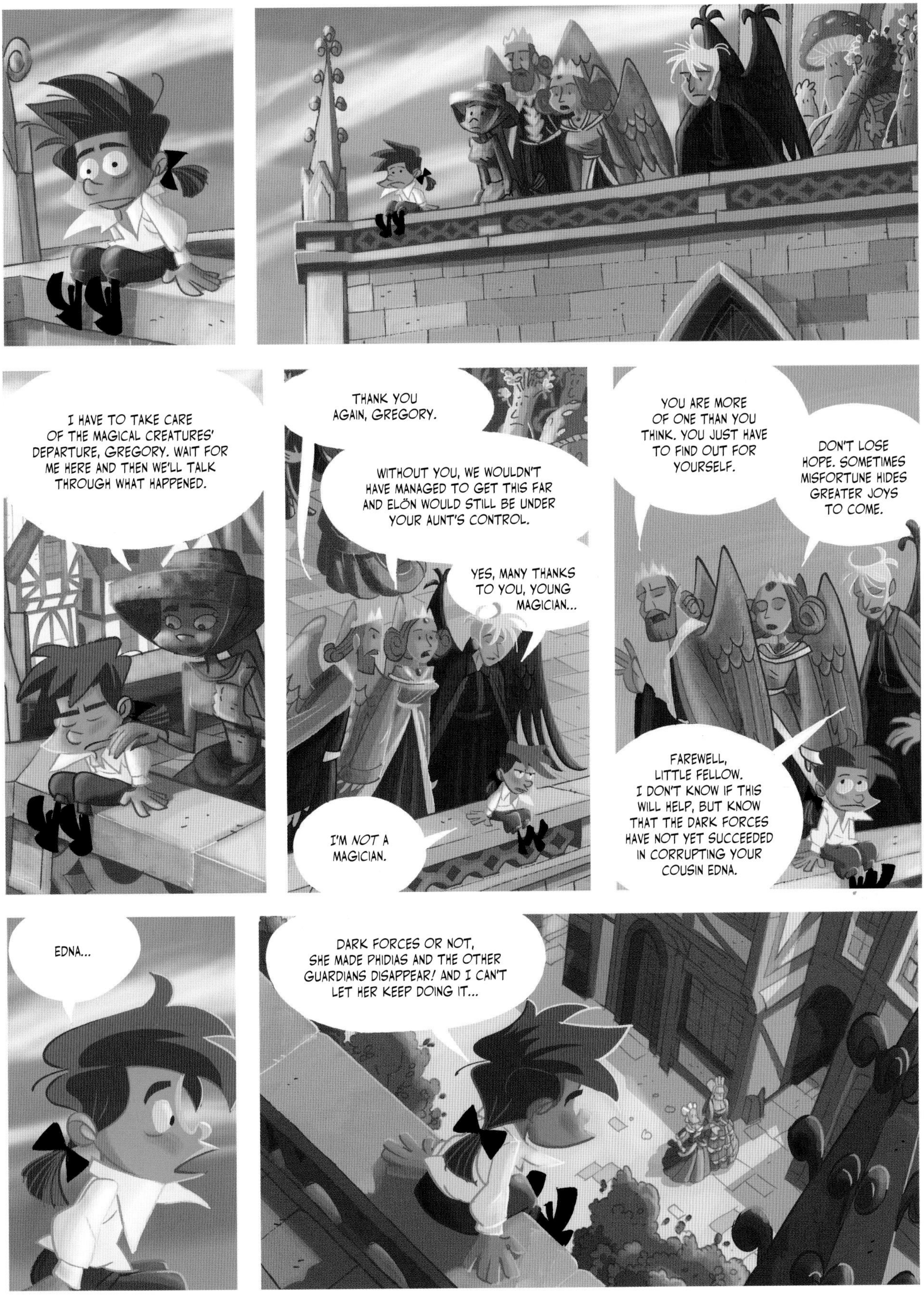
I HAVE TO TAKE CARE OF THE MAGICAL CREATURES' DEPARTURE, GREGORY. WAIT FOR ME HERE AND THEN WE'LL TALK THROUGH WHAT HAPPENED.
THANK YOU AGAIN, GREGORY.
WITHOUT YOU, WE WOULDN'T HAVE MANAGED TO GET THIS FAR AND ELÖN WOULD STILL BE UNDER YOUR AUNT'S CONTROL.
YES, MANY THANKS TO YOU, YOUNG MAGICIAN...
I'M NOT A MAGICIAN.
YOU ARE MORE OF ONE THAN YOU THINK. YOU JUST HAVE TO FIND OUT FOR YOURSELF.
DON'T LOSE HOPE. SOMETIMES MISFORTUNE HIDES GREATER JOYS TO COME.
FAREWELL, LITTLE FELLOW. I DON'T KNOW IF THIS WILL HELP, BUT KNOW THAT THE DARK FORCES HAVE NOT YET SUCCEEDED IN CORRUPTING YOUR COUSIN EDNA.
EDNA...
DARK FORCES OR NOT, SHE MADE PHIDIAS AND THE OTHER GUARDIANS DISAPPEAR! AND I CAN'T LET HER KEEP DOING IT...

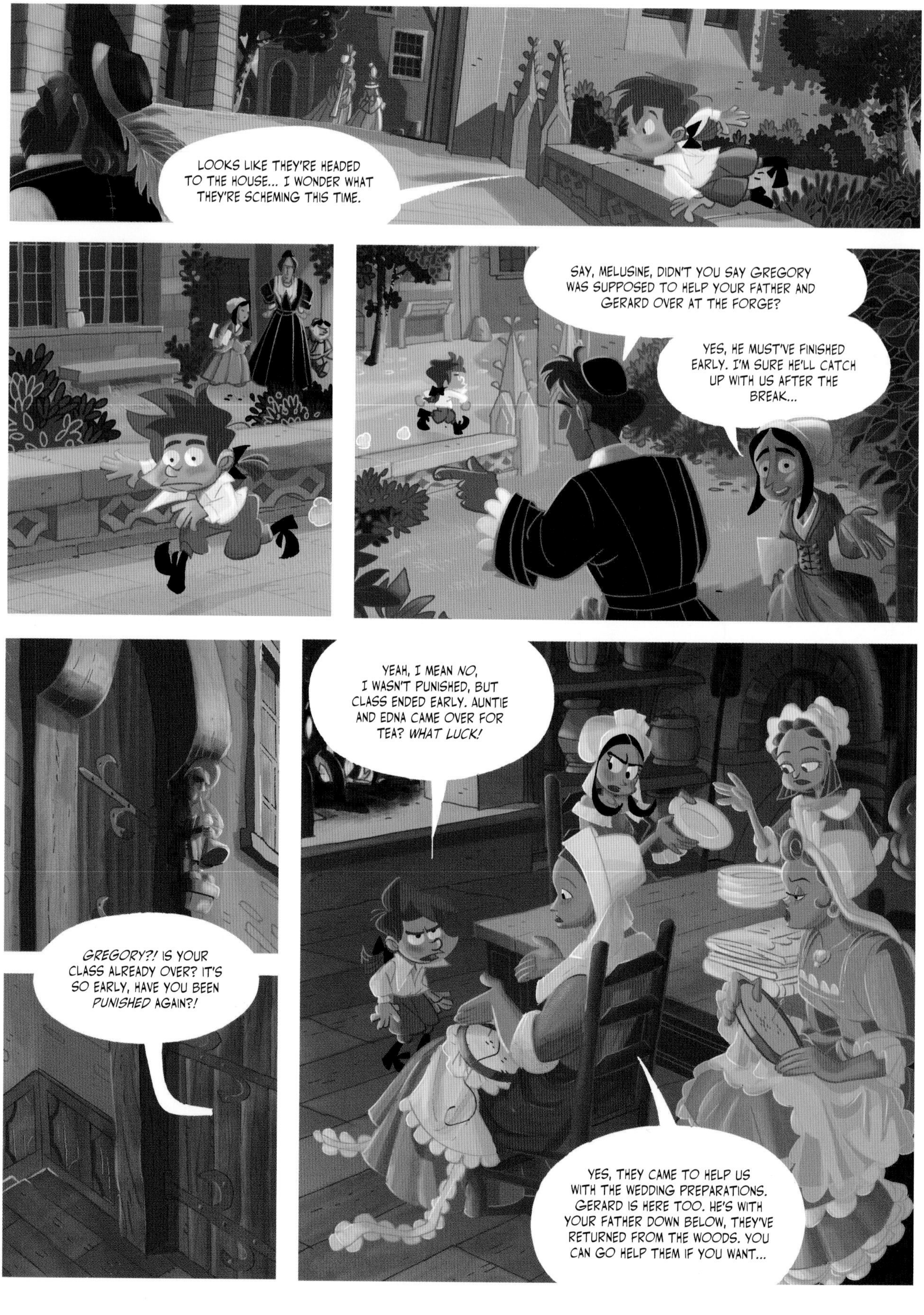

LOOKS LIKE THEY'RE HEADED TO THE HOUSE... I WONDER WHAT THEY'RE SCHEMING THIS TIME.
SAY, MELUSINE, DIDN'T YOU SAY GREGORY WAS SUPPOSED TO HELP YOUR FATHER AND GERARD OVER AT THE FORGE?
YES, HE MUST'VE FINISHED EARLY. I'M SURE HE'LL CATCH UP WITH US AFTER THE BREAK...
GREGORY?! IS YOUR CLASS ALREADY OVER? IT'S SO EARLY, HAVE YOU BEEN PUNISHED AGAIN?!
YEAH, I MEAN NO, I WASN'T PUNISHED, BUT CLASS ENDED EARLY. AUNTIE AND EDNA CAME OVER FOR TEA? WHAT LUCK!
YES, THEY CAME TO HELP US WITH THE WEDDING PREPARATIONS. GERARD IS HERE TOO. HE'S WITH YOUR FATHER DOWN BELOW, THEY'VE RETURNED FROM THE WOODS. YOU CAN GO HELP THEM IF YOU WANT...

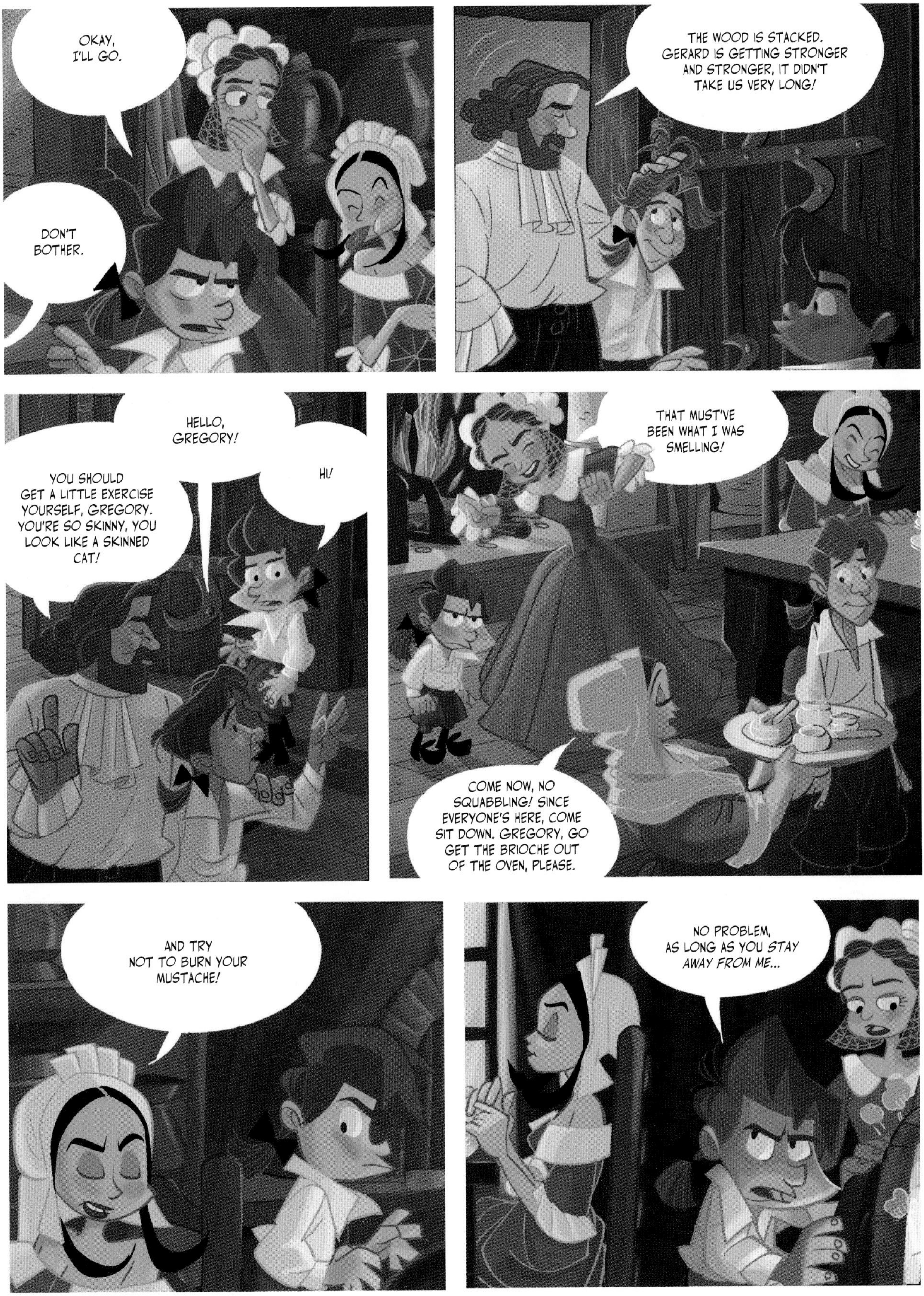
OKAY, I'LL GO.
DON'T BOTHER.
THE WOOD IS STACKED. GERARD IS GETTING STRONGER AND STRONGER, IT DIDN'T TAKE US VERY LONG!
HELLO, GREGORY!
YOU SHOULD GET A LITTLE EXERCISE YOURSELF, GREGORY. YOU'RE SO SKINNY, YOU LOOK LIKE A SKINNED CAT!
HI!
THAT MUST'VE BEEN WHAT I WAS SMELLING!
COME NOW, NO SQUABBLING! SINCE EVERYONE'S HERE, COME SIT DOWN. GREGORY, GO GET THE BRIOCHE OUT OF THE OVEN, PLEASE.
AND TRY NOT TO BURN YOUR MUSTACHE!
NO PROBLEM, AS LONG AS YOU *STAY AWAY FROM ME*...

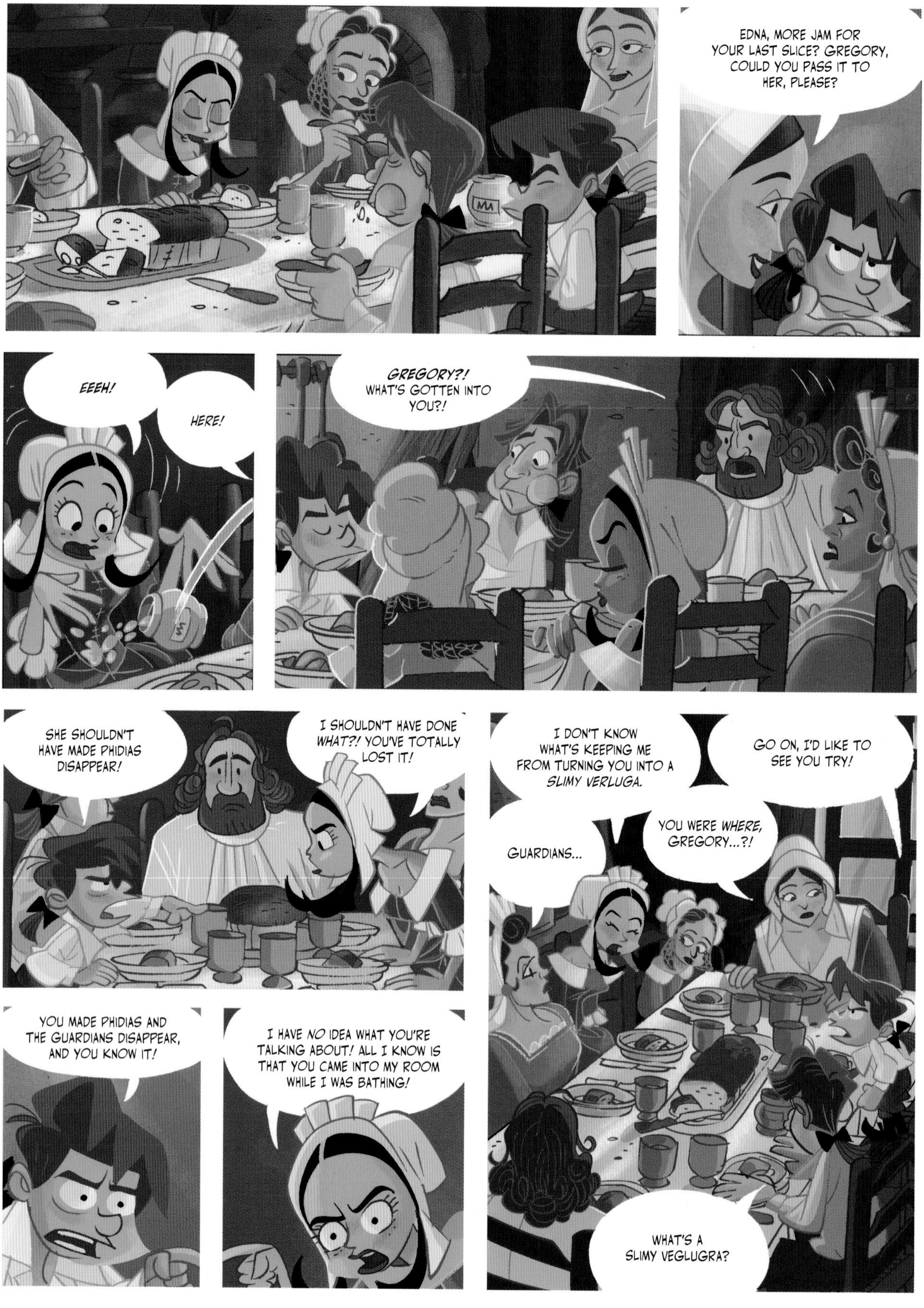
EDNA, MORE JAM FOR YOUR LAST SLICE? GREGORY, COULD YOU PASS IT TO HER, PLEASE?
EEEH!
HERE!
GREGORY?! WHAT'S GOTTEN INTO YOU?!
SHE SHOULDN'T HAVE MADE PHIDIAS DISAPPEAR!
I SHOULDN'T HAVE DONE WHAT?! YOU'VE TOTALLY LOST IT!
YOU MADE PHIDIAS AND THE GUARDIANS DISAPPEAR, AND YOU KNOW IT!
I HAVE NO IDEA WHAT YOU'RE TALKING ABOUT! ALL I KNOW IS THAT YOU CAME INTO MY ROOM WHILE I WAS BATHING!
I DON'T KNOW WHAT'S KEEPING ME FROM TURNING YOU INTO A SLIMY VERLUGA.
GO ON, I'D LIKE TO SEE YOU TRY!
GUARDIANS...
YOU WERE WHERE, GREGORY...?!
WHAT'S A SLIMY VEGLUGRA?

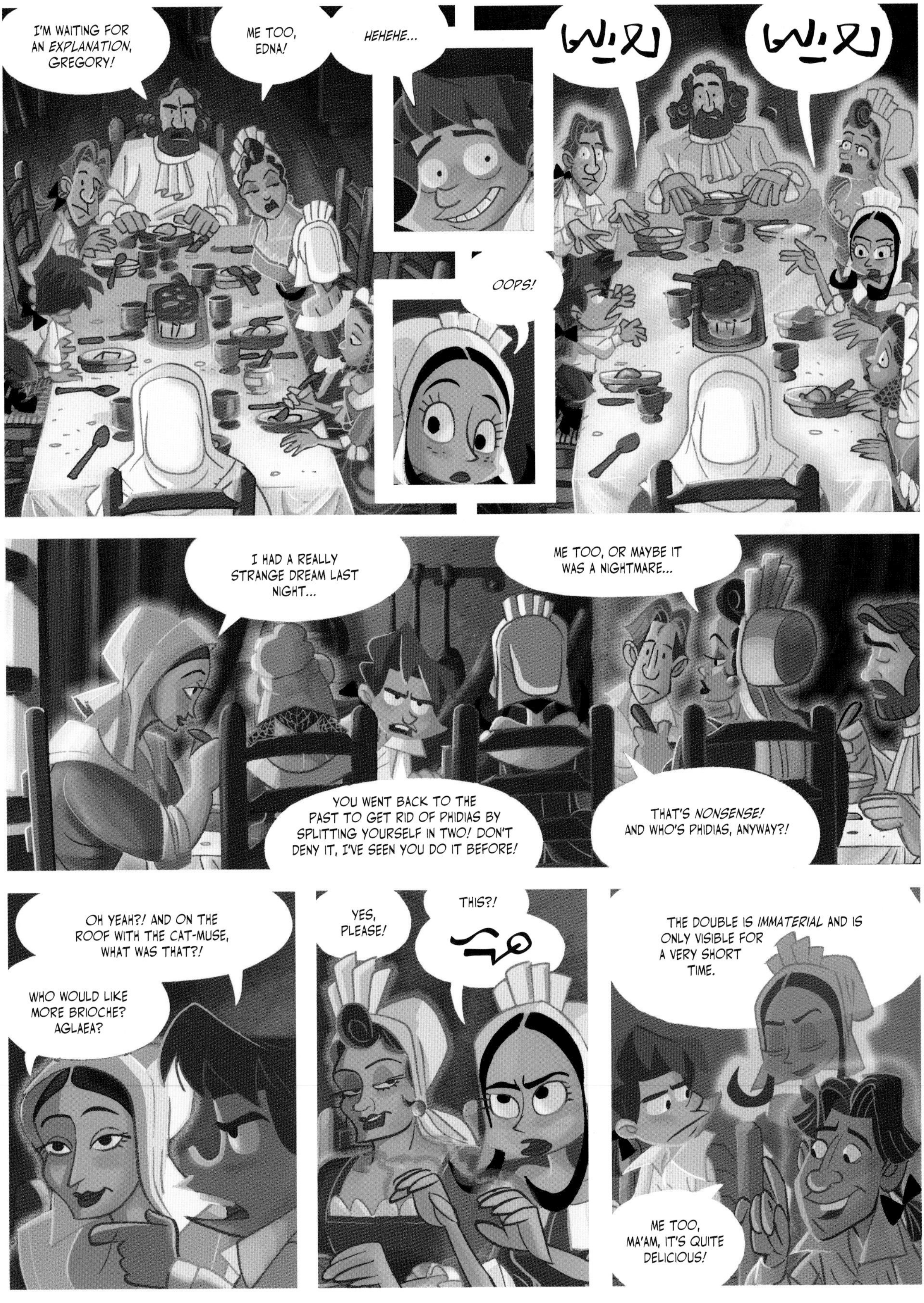
I'M WAITING FOR AN *EXPLANATION*, GREGORY!
ME TOO, EDNA!
HEHEHE...
OOPS!
I HAD A REALLY STRANGE DREAM LAST NIGHT...
ME TOO, OR MAYBE IT WAS A NIGHTMARE...
YOU WENT BACK TO THE PAST TO GET RID OF PHIDIAS BY SPLITTING YOURSELF IN TWO! DON'T DENY IT, I'VE SEEN YOU DO IT BEFORE!
THAT'S *NONSENSE!* AND WHO'S PHIDIAS, ANYWAY?!
OH YEAH?! AND ON THE ROOF WITH THE CAT-MUSE, WHAT WAS THAT?!
WHO WOULD LIKE MORE BRIOCHE? AGLAEA?
YES, PLEASE!
THIS?!
THE DOUBLE IS *IMMATERIAL* AND IS ONLY VISIBLE FOR A VERY SHORT TIME.
ME TOO, MA'AM, IT'S QUITE DELICIOUS!

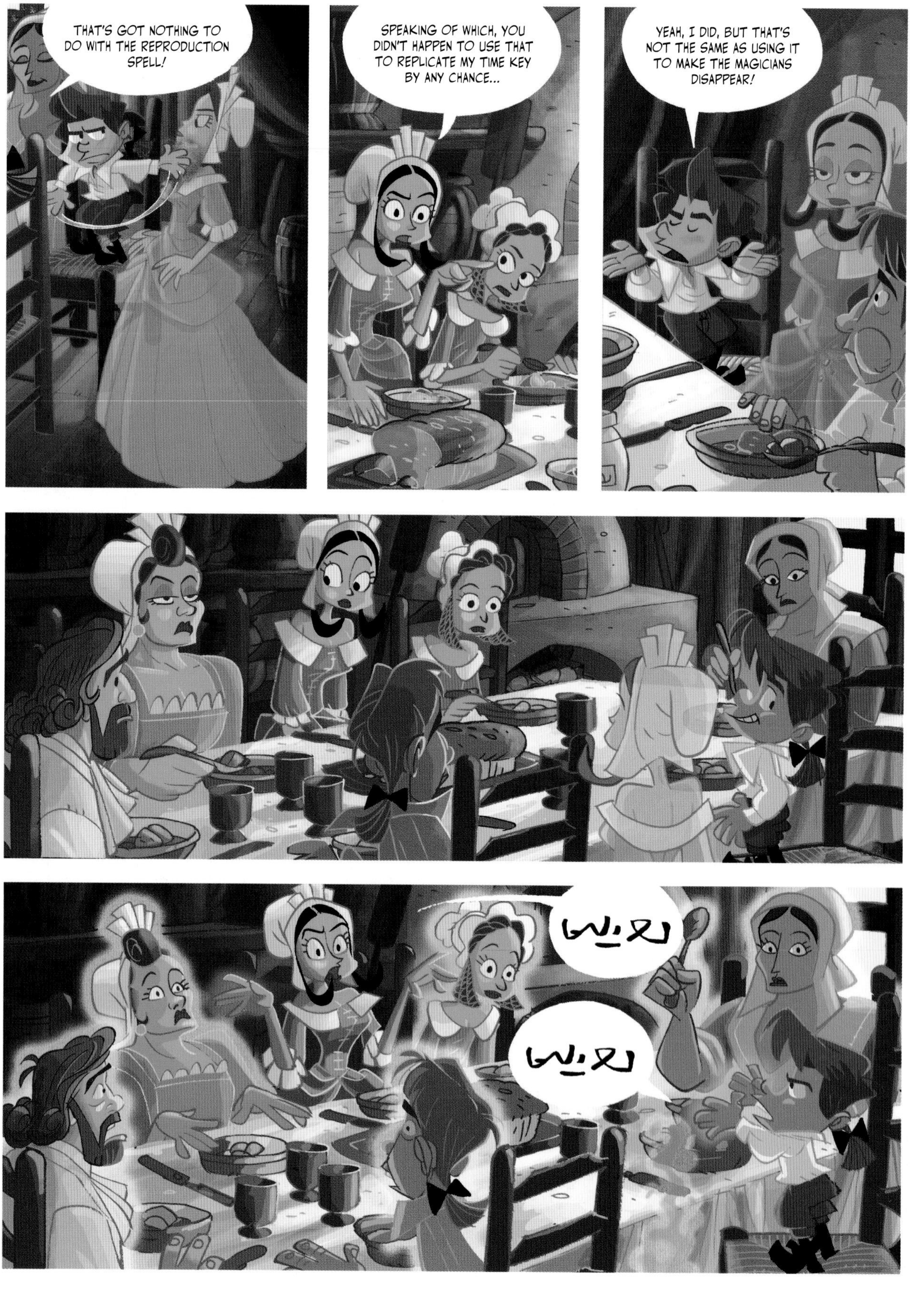
THAT'S GOT NOTHING TO DO WITH THE REPRODUCTION SPELL!
SPEAKING OF WHICH, YOU DIDN'T HAPPEN TO USE THAT TO REPLICATE MY TIME KEY BY ANY CHANCE...
YEAH, I DID, BUT THAT'S NOT THE SAME AS USING IT TO MAKE THE MAGICIANS DISAPPEAR!

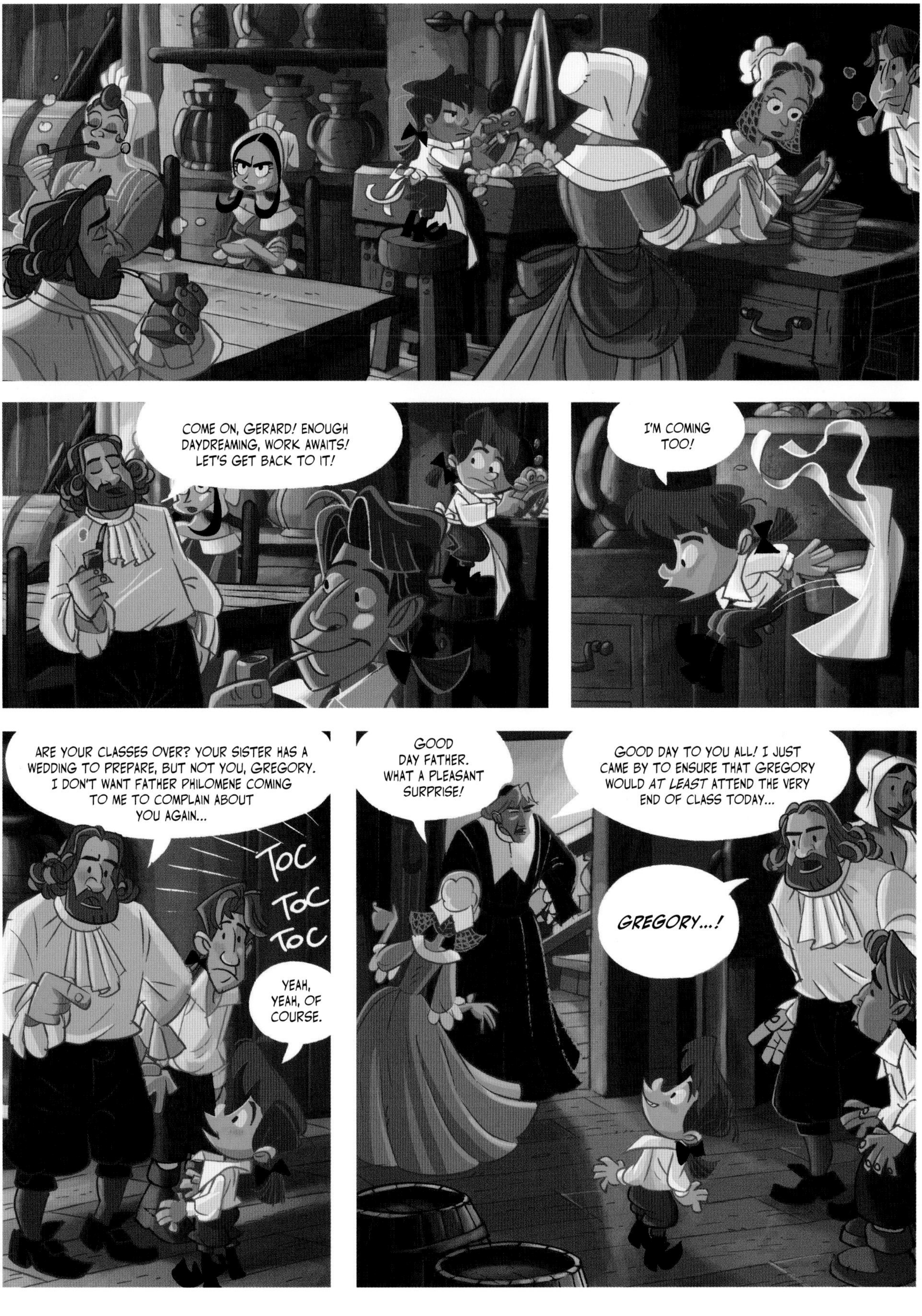
COME ON, GERARD! ENOUGH DAYDREAMING, WORK AWAITS! LET'S GET BACK TO IT!
I'M COMING TOO!
ARE YOUR CLASSES OVER? YOUR SISTER HAS A WEDDING TO PREPARE, BUT NOT YOU, GREGORY. I DON'T WANT FATHER PHILOMENE COMING TO ME TO COMPLAIN ABOUT YOU AGAIN...
TOC TOC TOC
YEAH, YEAH, OF COURSE.
GOOD DAY FATHER. WHAT A PLEASANT SURPRISE!
GOOD DAY TO YOU ALL! I JUST CAME BY TO ENSURE THAT GREGORY WOULD *AT LEAST* ATTEND THE VERY END OF CLASS TODAY...
GREGORY...!

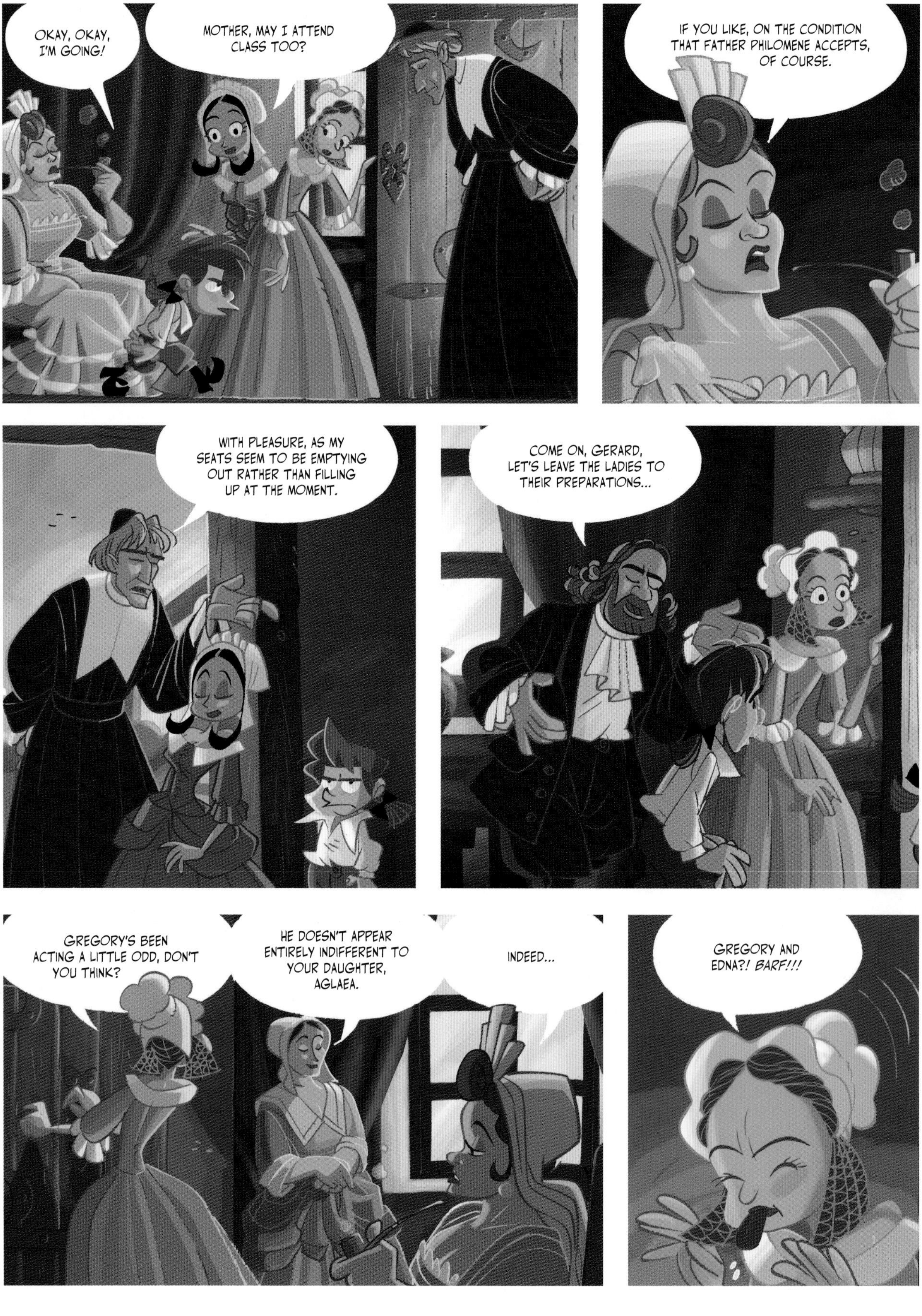
OKAY, OKAY, I'M GOING!
MOTHER, MAY I ATTEND CLASS TOO?
IF YOU LIKE, ON THE CONDITION THAT FATHER PHILOMENE ACCEPTS, OF COURSE.
WITH PLEASURE, AS MY SEATS SEEM TO BE EMPTYING OUT RATHER THAN FILLING UP AT THE MOMENT.
COME ON, GERARD, LET'S LEAVE THE LADIES TO THEIR PREPARATIONS...
GREGORY'S BEEN ACTING A LITTLE ODD, DON'T YOU THINK?
HE DOESN'T APPEAR ENTIRELY INDIFFERENT TO YOUR DAUGHTER, AGLAEA.
INDEED...
GREGORY AND EDNA?! *BARF!!!*

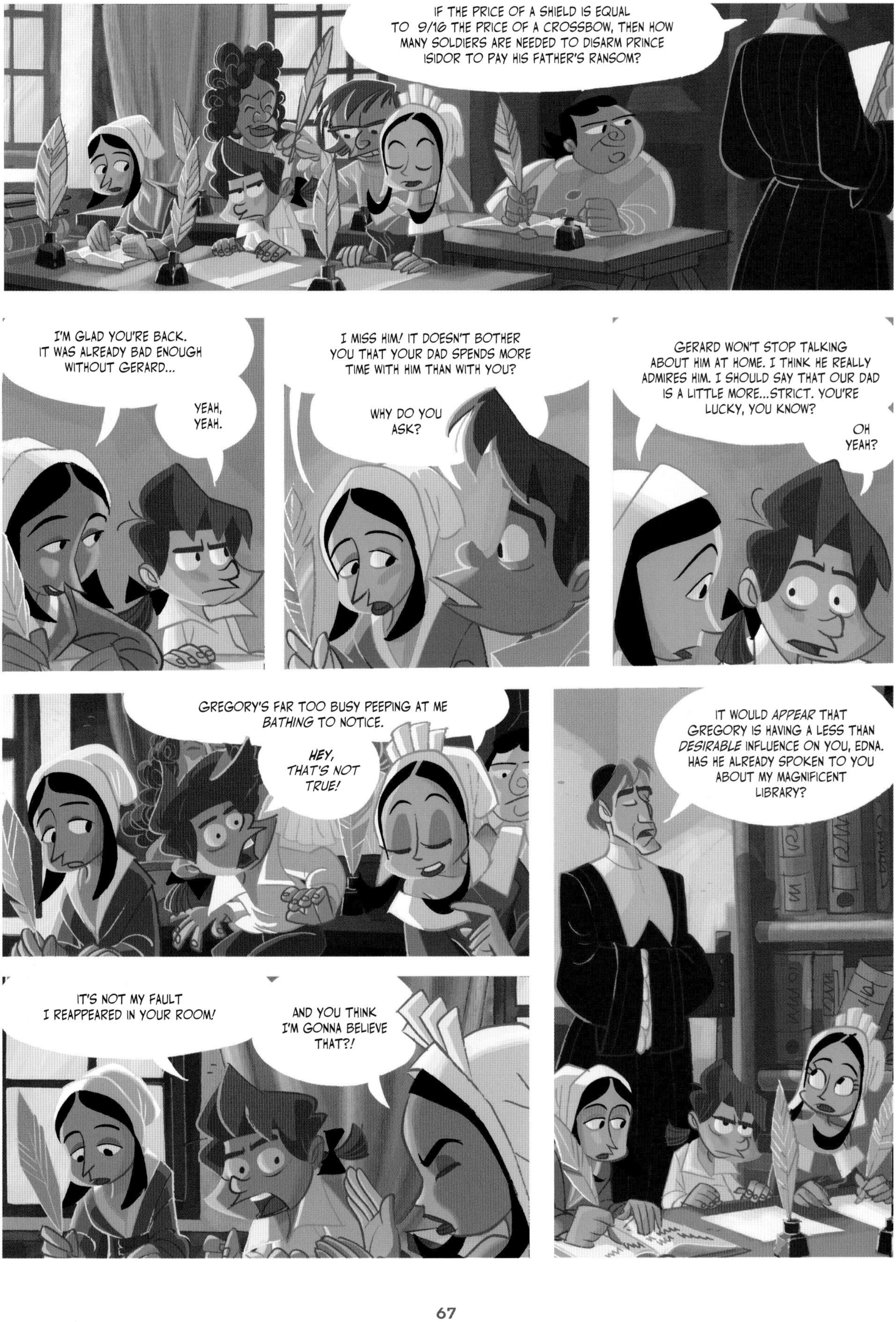

IF THE PRICE OF A SHIELD IS EQUAL TO 9/16 THE PRICE OF A CROSSBOW, THEN HOW MANY SOLDIERS ARE NEEDED TO DISARM PRINCE ISIDOR TO PAY HIS FATHER'S RANSOM?
I'M GLAD YOU'RE BACK. IT WAS ALREADY BAD ENOUGH WITHOUT GERARD...
YEAH, YEAH.
I MISS HIM! IT DOESN'T BOTHER YOU THAT YOUR DAD SPENDS MORE TIME WITH HIM THAN WITH YOU?
WHY DO YOU ASK?
GERARD WON'T STOP TALKING ABOUT HIM AT HOME. I THINK HE REALLY ADMIRES HIM. I SHOULD SAY THAT OUR DAD IS A LITTLE MORE...STRICT. YOU'RE LUCKY, YOU KNOW?
OH YEAH?
GREGORY'S FAR TOO BUSY PEEPING AT ME *BATHING* TO NOTICE.
HEY, THAT'S NOT TRUE!
IT'S NOT MY FAULT I REAPPEARED IN YOUR ROOM!
AND YOU THINK I'M GONNA BELIEVE THAT?!
IT WOULD *APPEAR* THAT GREGORY IS HAVING A LESS THAN *DESIRABLE* INFLUENCE ON YOU, EDNA. HAS HE ALREADY SPOKEN TO YOU ABOUT MY MAGNIFICENT LIBRARY?

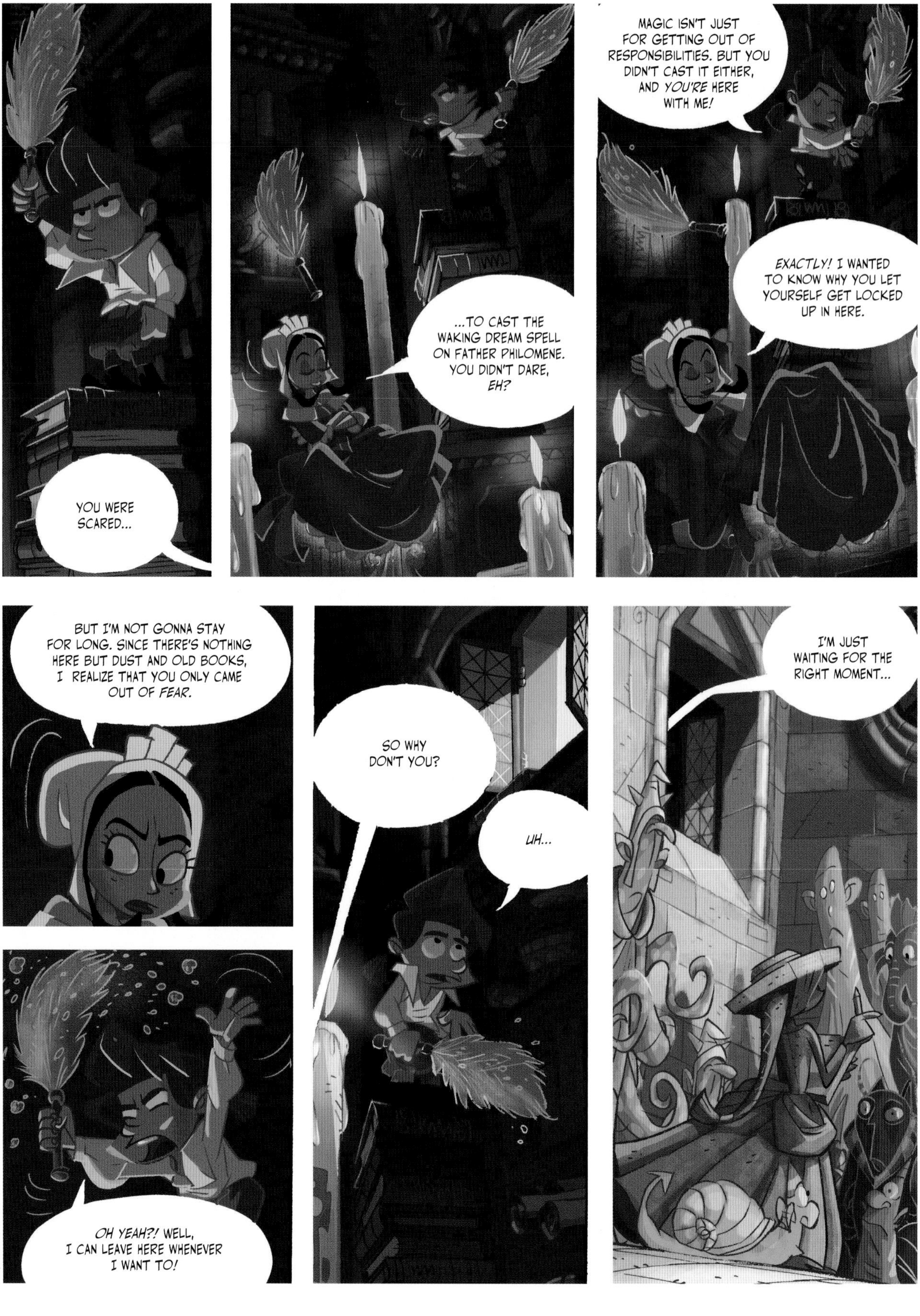
YOU WERE SCARED...
...TO CAST THE WAKING DREAM SPELL ON FATHER PHILOMENE. YOU DIDN'T DARE, EH?
MAGIC ISN'T JUST FOR GETTING OUT OF RESPONSIBILITIES. BUT YOU DIDN'T CAST IT EITHER, AND YOU'RE HERE WITH ME!
EXACTLY! I WANTED TO KNOW WHY YOU LET YOURSELF GET LOCKED UP IN HERE.
BUT I'M NOT GONNA STAY FOR LONG. SINCE THERE'S NOTHING HERE BUT DUST AND OLD BOOKS, I REALIZE THAT YOU ONLY CAME OUT OF FEAR.
OH YEAH?! WELL, I CAN LEAVE HERE WHENEVER I WANT TO!
SO WHY DON'T YOU?
UH...
I'M JUST WAITING FOR THE RIGHT MOMENT...

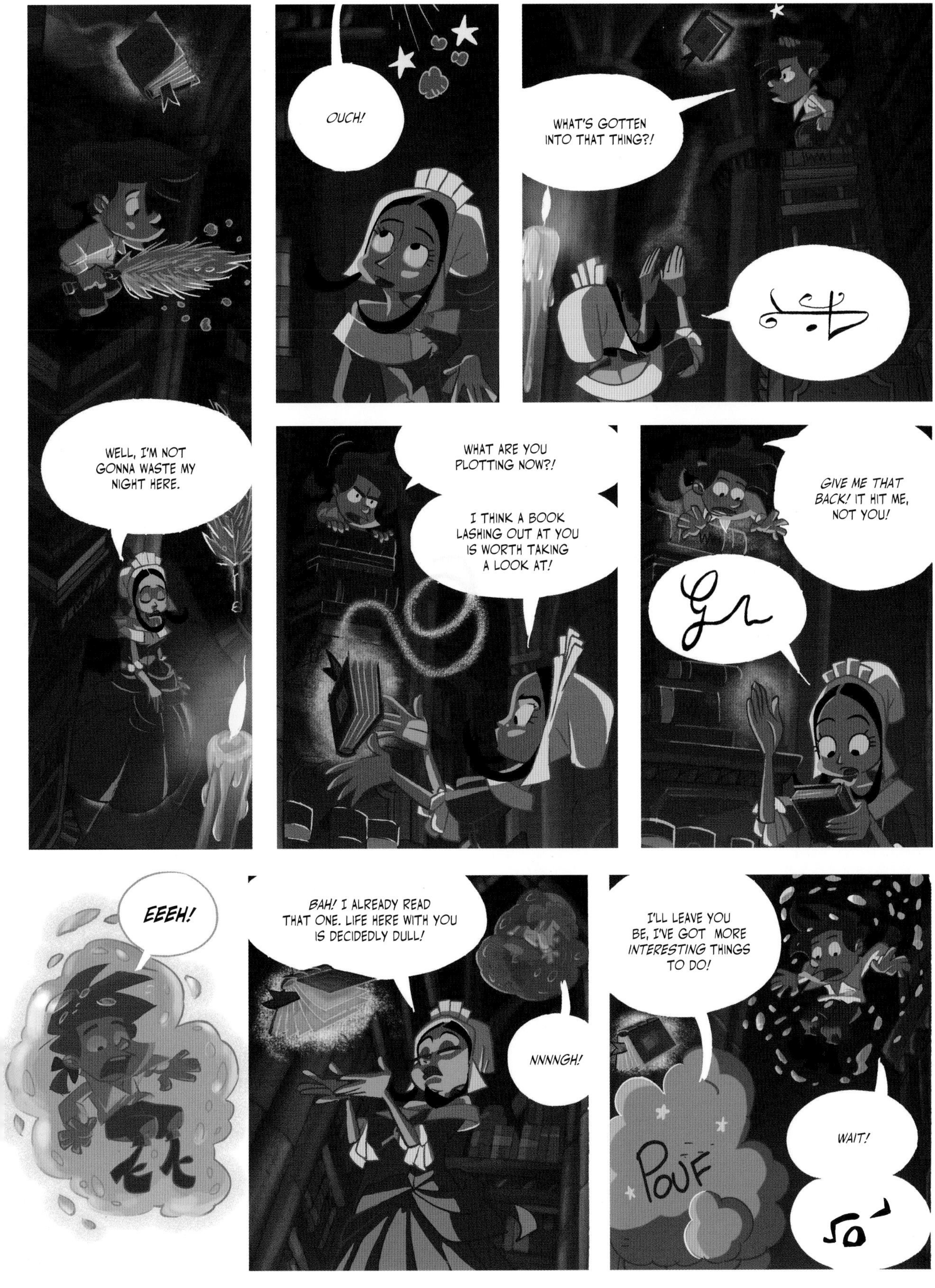
OUCH!
WHAT'S GOTTEN INTO THAT THING?!
WELL, I'M NOT GONNA WASTE MY NIGHT HERE.
WHAT ARE YOU PLOTTING NOW?!
I THINK A BOOK LASHING OUT AT YOU IS WORTH TAKING A LOOK AT!
GIVE ME THAT BACK! IT HIT ME, NOT YOU!
EEEH!
BAH! I ALREADY READ THAT ONE. LIFE HERE WITH YOU IS DECIDEDLY DULL!
NNNNGH!
I'LL LEAVE YOU BE, I'VE GOT MORE INTERESTING THINGS TO DO!
POUF
WAIT!

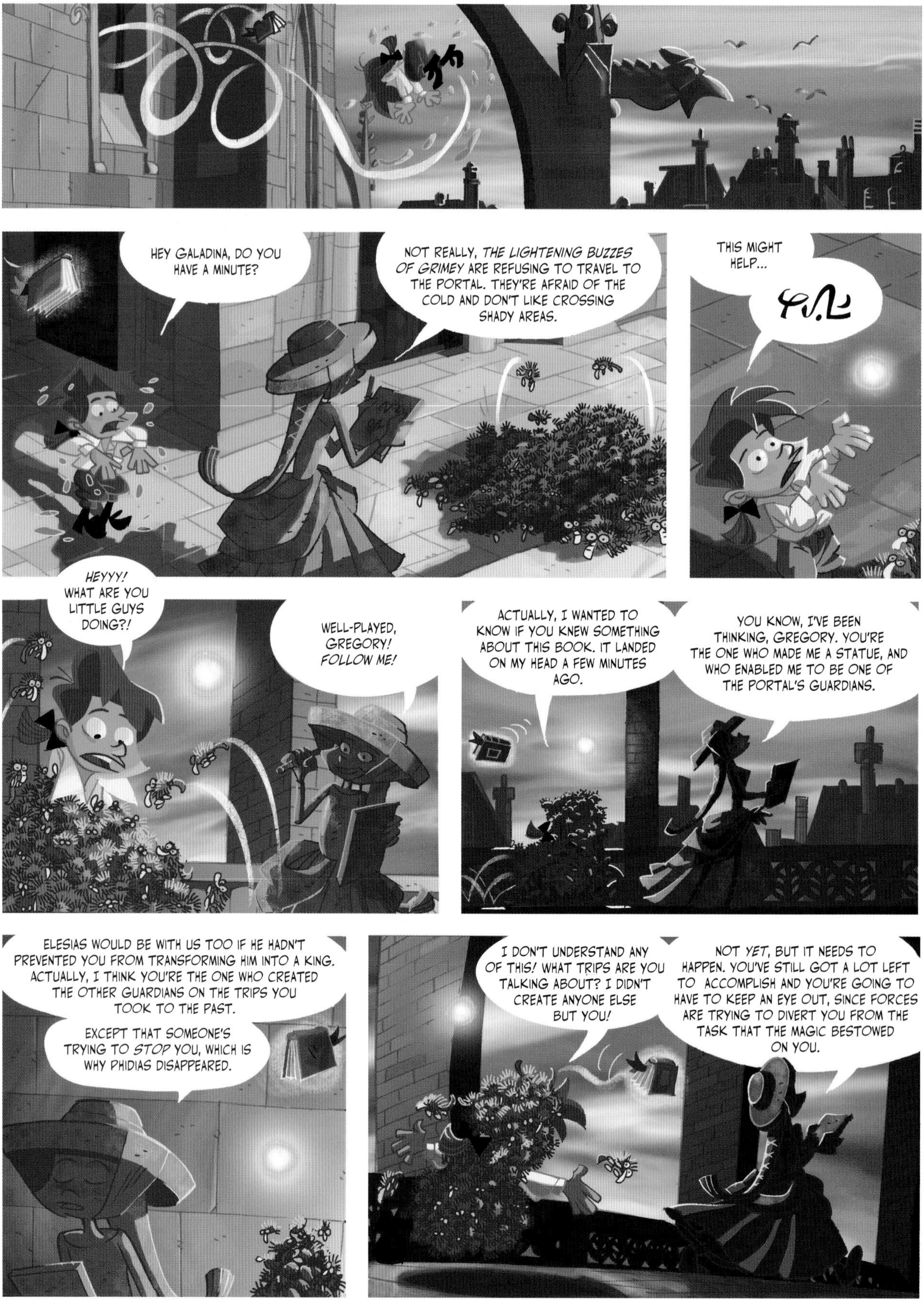

HEY GALADINA, DO YOU HAVE A MINUTE?
NOT REALLY, *THE LIGHTENING BUZZES OF GRIMEY* ARE REFUSING TO TRAVEL TO THE PORTAL. THEY'RE AFRAID OF THE COLD AND DON'T LIKE CROSSING SHADY AREAS.
THIS MIGHT HELP...
HEYYY! WHAT ARE YOU LITTLE GUYS DOING?!
WELL-PLAYED, GREGORY! *FOLLOW ME!*
ACTUALLY, I WANTED TO KNOW IF YOU KNEW SOMETHING ABOUT THIS BOOK. IT LANDED ON MY HEAD A FEW MINUTES AGO.
YOU KNOW, I'VE BEEN THINKING, GREGORY. YOU'RE THE ONE WHO MADE ME A STATUE, AND WHO ENABLED ME TO BE ONE OF THE PORTAL'S GUARDIANS.
ELESIAS WOULD BE WITH US TOO IF HE HADN'T PREVENTED YOU FROM TRANSFORMING HIM INTO A KING. ACTUALLY, I THINK YOU'RE THE ONE WHO CREATED THE OTHER GUARDIANS ON THE TRIPS YOU TOOK TO THE PAST.
EXCEPT THAT SOMEONE'S TRYING TO *STOP* YOU, WHICH IS WHY PHIDIAS DISAPPEARED.
I DON'T UNDERSTAND ANY OF THIS! WHAT TRIPS ARE YOU TALKING ABOUT? I DIDN'T CREATE ANYONE ELSE BUT YOU!
NOT *YET*, BUT IT NEEDS TO HAPPEN. YOU'VE STILL GOT A LOT LEFT TO ACCOMPLISH AND YOU'RE GOING TO HAVE TO KEEP AN EYE OUT, SINCE FORCES ARE TRYING TO DIVERT YOU FROM THE TASK THAT THE MAGIC BESTOWED ON YOU.

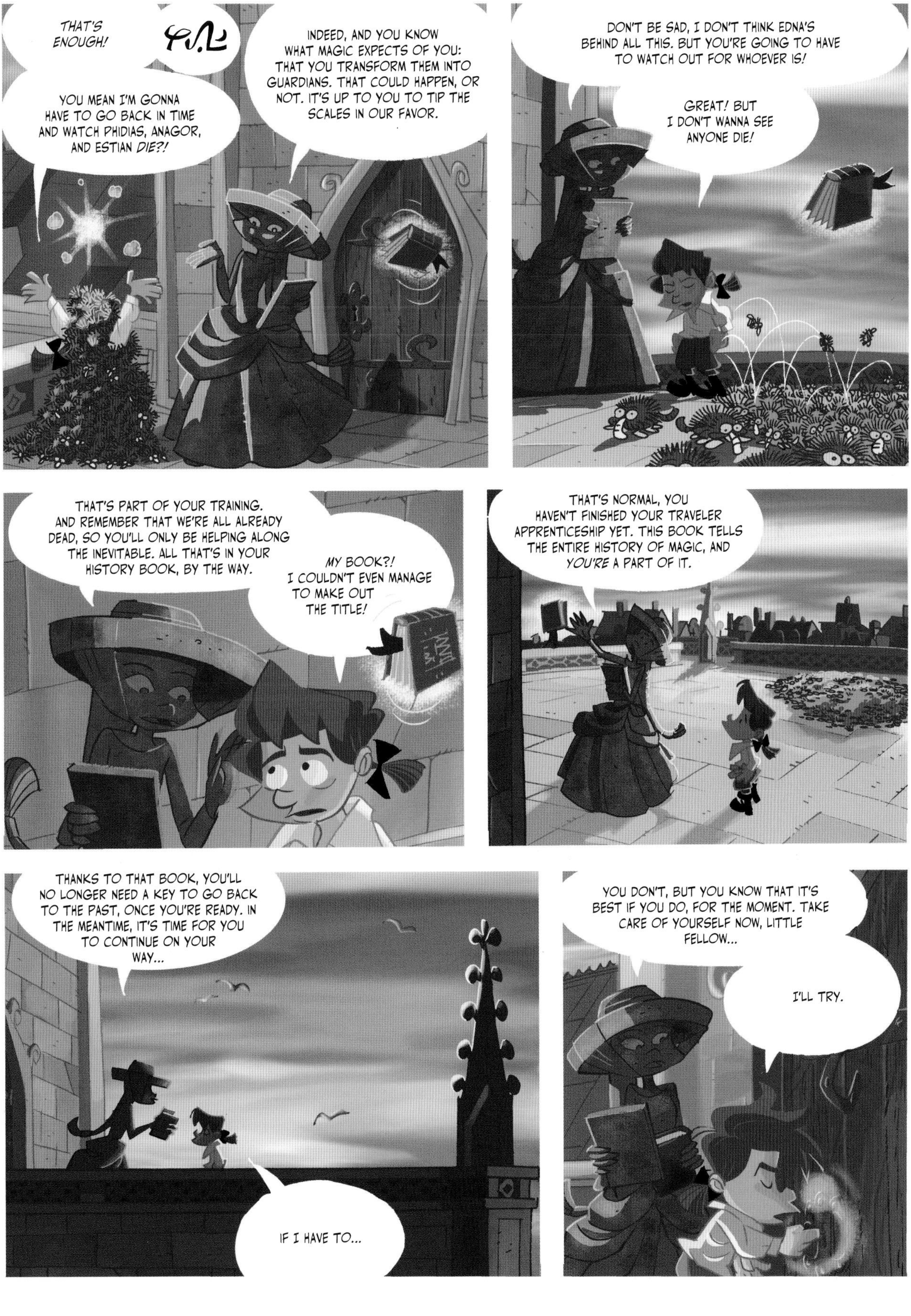
THAT'S ENOUGH!
YOU MEAN I'M GONNA HAVE TO GO BACK IN TIME AND WATCH PHIDIAS, ANAGOR, AND ESTIAN DIE?!
INDEED, AND YOU KNOW WHAT MAGIC EXPECTS OF YOU: THAT YOU TRANSFORM THEM INTO GUARDIANS. THAT COULD HAPPEN, OR NOT. IT'S UP TO YOU TO TIP THE SCALES IN OUR FAVOR.
DON'T BE SAD, I DON'T THINK EDNA'S BEHIND ALL THIS. BUT YOU'RE GOING TO HAVE TO WATCH OUT FOR WHOEVER IS!
GREAT! BUT I DON'T WANNA SEE ANYONE DIE!
THAT'S PART OF YOUR TRAINING. AND REMEMBER THAT WE'RE ALL ALREADY DEAD, SO YOU'LL ONLY BE HELPING ALONG THE INEVITABLE. ALL THAT'S IN YOUR HISTORY BOOK, BY THE WAY.
MY BOOK?! I COULDN'T EVEN MANAGE TO MAKE OUT THE TITLE!
THAT'S NORMAL, YOU HAVEN'T FINISHED YOUR TRAVELER APPRENTICESHIP YET. THIS BOOK TELLS THE ENTIRE HISTORY OF MAGIC, AND YOU'RE A PART OF IT.
THANKS TO THAT BOOK, YOU'LL NO LONGER NEED A KEY TO GO BACK TO THE PAST, ONCE YOU'RE READY. IN THE MEANTIME, IT'S TIME FOR YOU TO CONTINUE ON YOUR WAY...
IF I HAVE TO...
YOU DON'T, BUT YOU KNOW THAT IT'S BEST IF YOU DO, FOR THE MOMENT. TAKE CARE OF YOURSELF NOW, LITTLE FELLOW...
I'LL TRY.

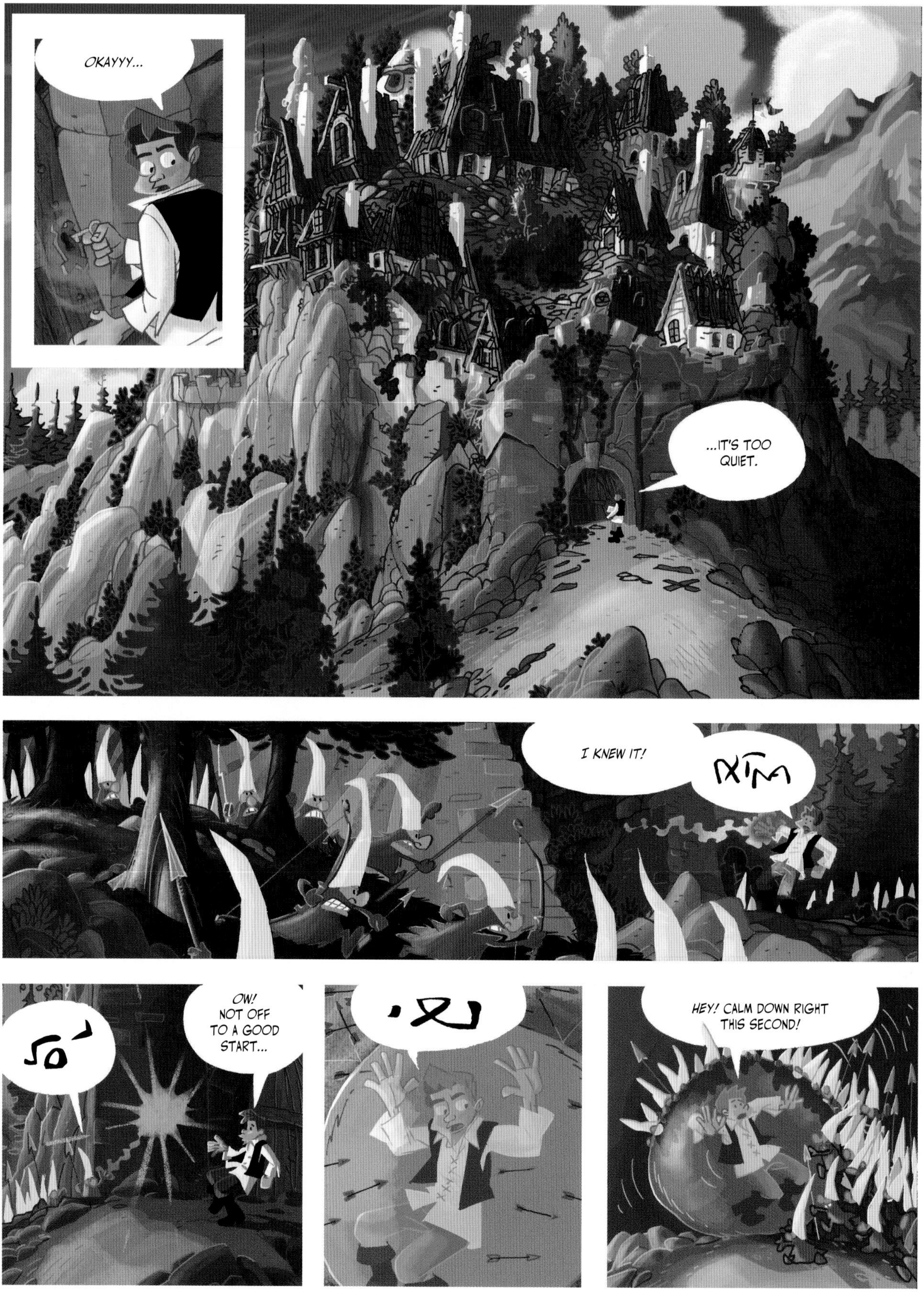
OKAYYY...
...IT'S TOO QUIET.
I KNEW IT!
OW! NOT OFF TO A GOOD START...
HEY! CALM DOWN RIGHT THIS SECOND!

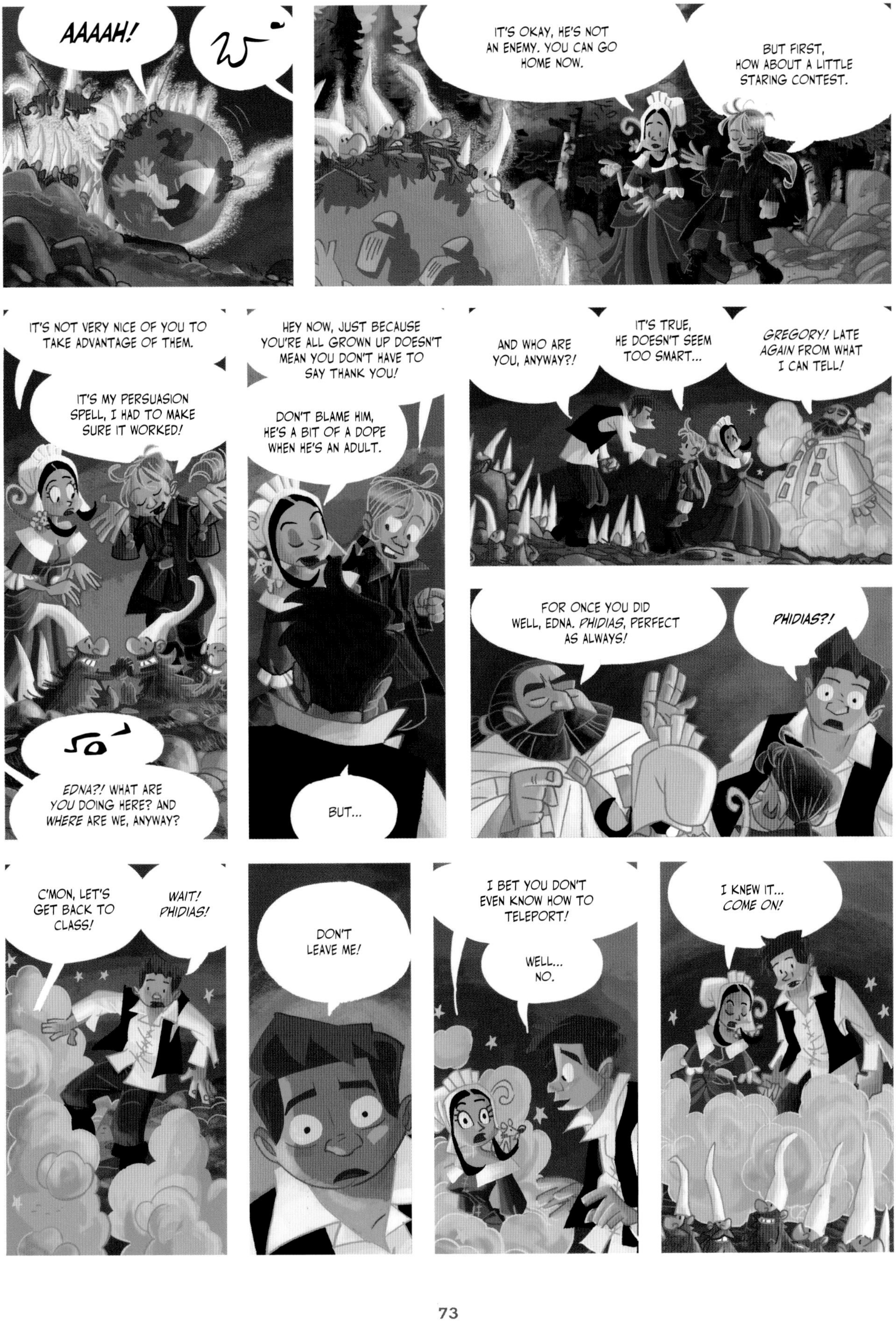
AAAAH!
IT'S OKAY, HE'S NOT AN ENEMY. YOU CAN GO HOME NOW.
BUT FIRST, HOW ABOUT A LITTLE STARING CONTEST.
IT'S NOT VERY NICE OF YOU TO TAKE ADVANTAGE OF THEM.
IT'S MY PERSUASION SPELL, I HAD TO MAKE SURE IT WORKED!
EDNA?! WHAT ARE YOU DOING HERE? AND WHERE ARE WE, ANYWAY?
HEY NOW, JUST BECAUSE YOU'RE ALL GROWN UP DOESN'T MEAN YOU DON'T HAVE TO SAY THANK YOU!
DON'T BLAME HIM, HE'S A BIT OF A DOPE WHEN HE'S AN ADULT.
BUT...
AND WHO ARE YOU, ANYWAY?!
IT'S TRUE, HE DOESN'T SEEM TOO SMART...
GREGORY! LATE AGAIN FROM WHAT I CAN TELL!
FOR ONCE YOU DID WELL, EDNA. PHIDIAS, PERFECT AS ALWAYS!
PHIDIAS?!
C'MON, LET'S GET BACK TO CLASS!
WAIT! PHIDIAS!
DON'T LEAVE ME!
I BET YOU DON'T EVEN KNOW HOW TO TELEPORT!
WELL... NO.
I KNEW IT... COME ON!

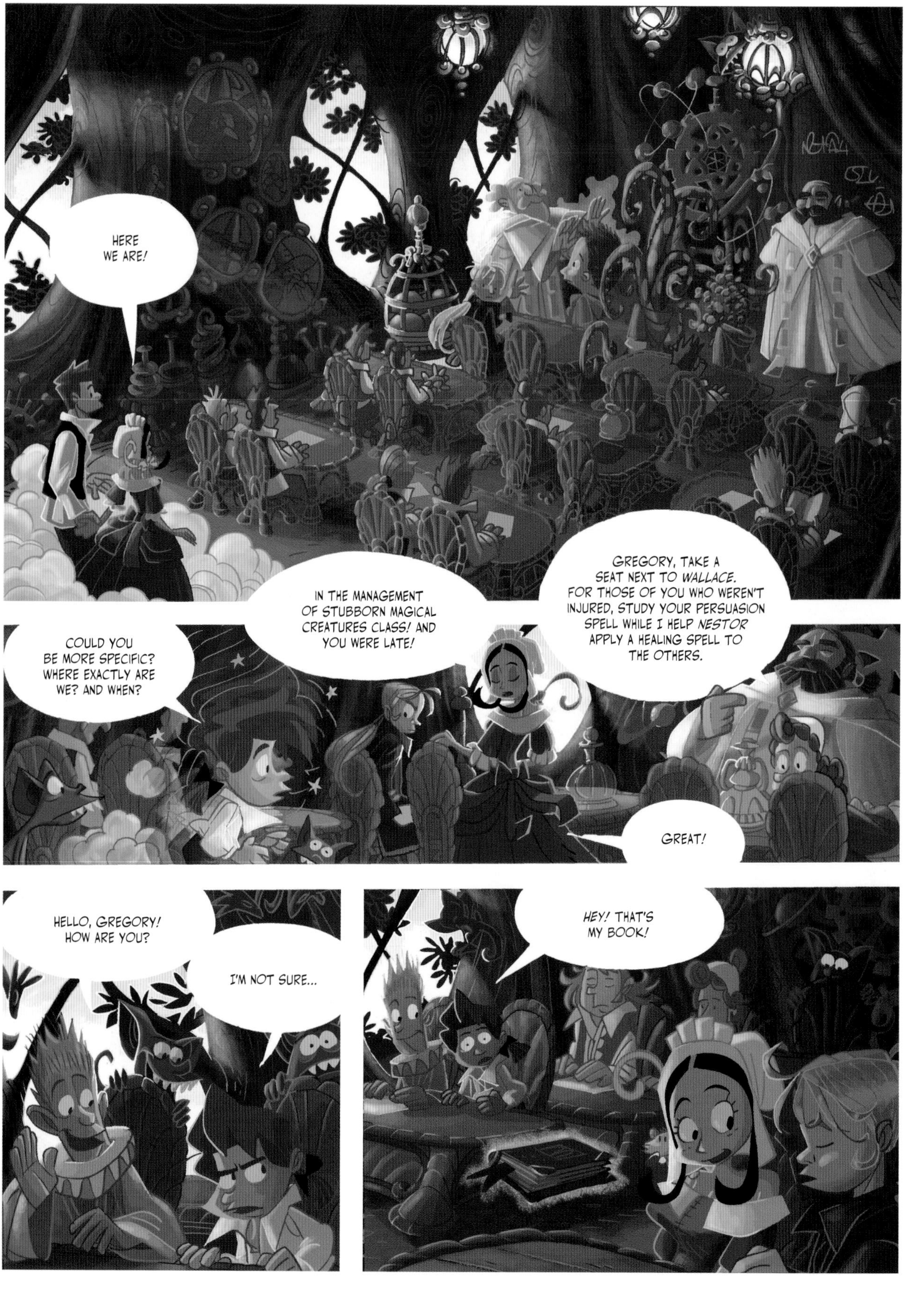
HERE WE ARE!
COULD YOU BE MORE SPECIFIC? WHERE EXACTLY ARE WE? AND WHEN?
IN THE MANAGEMENT OF STUBBORN MAGICAL CREATURES CLASS! AND YOU WERE LATE!
GREGORY, TAKE A SEAT NEXT TO *WALLACE*. FOR THOSE OF YOU WHO WEREN'T INJURED, STUDY YOUR PERSUASION SPELL WHILE I HELP *NESTOR* APPLY A HEALING SPELL TO THE OTHERS.
GREAT!
HELLO, GREGORY! HOW ARE YOU?
I'M NOT SURE...
HEY! THAT'S MY BOOK!

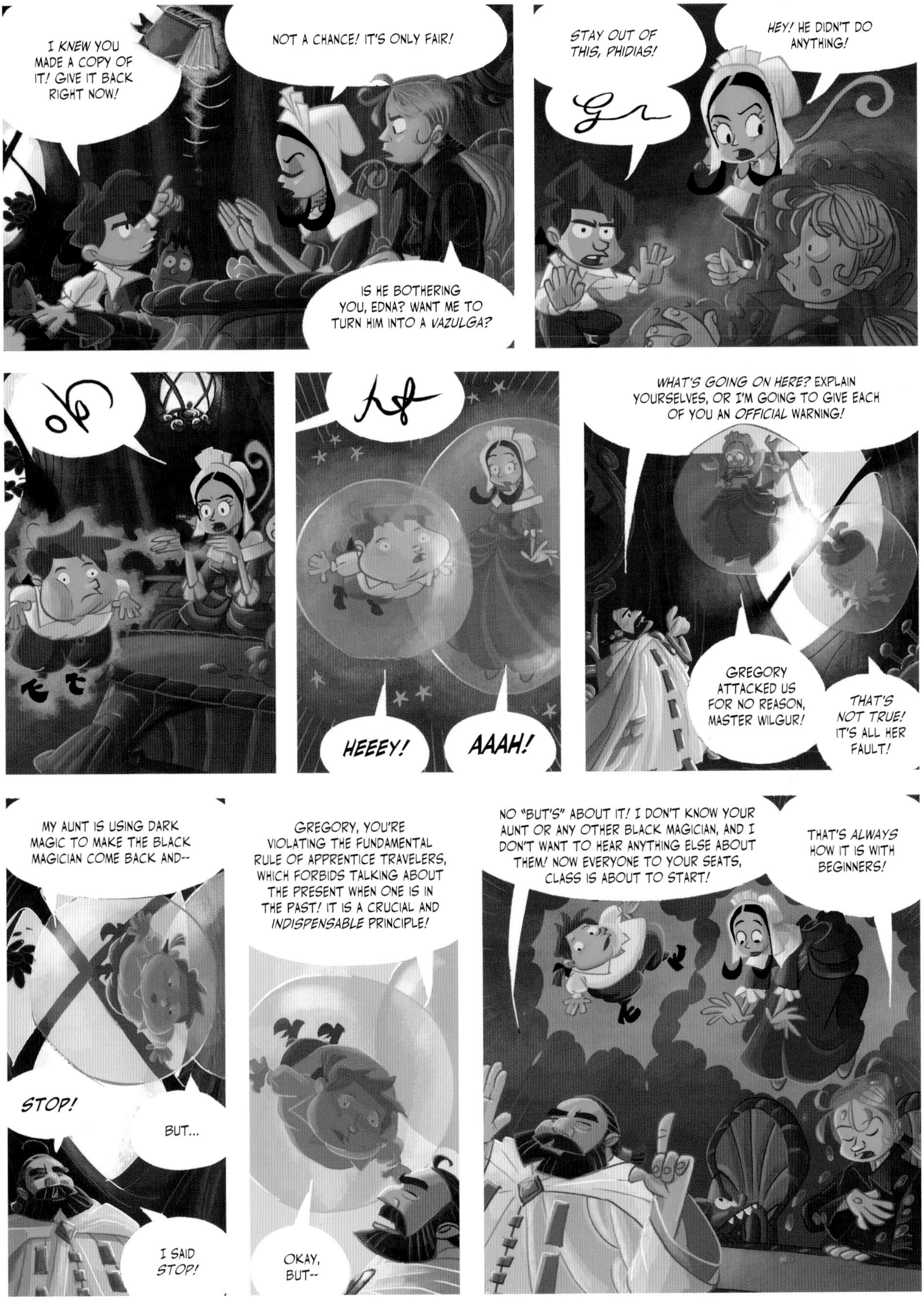
I KNEW YOU MADE A COPY OF IT! GIVE IT BACK RIGHT NOW!
NOT A CHANCE! IT'S ONLY FAIR!
IS HE BOTHERING YOU, EDNA? WANT ME TO TURN HIM INTO A VAZULGA?
STAY OUT OF THIS, PHIDIAS!
HEY! HE DIDN'T DO ANYTHING!
HEEEY!
AAAH!
WHAT'S GOING ON HERE? EXPLAIN YOURSELVES, OR I'M GOING TO GIVE EACH OF YOU AN OFFICIAL WARNING!
GREGORY ATTACKED US FOR NO REASON, MASTER WILGUR!
THAT'S NOT TRUE! IT'S ALL HER FAULT!
MY AUNT IS USING DARK MAGIC TO MAKE THE BLACK MAGICIAN COME BACK AND--
STOP!
BUT...
I SAID STOP!
GREGORY, YOU'RE VIOLATING THE FUNDAMENTAL RULE OF APPRENTICE TRAVELERS, WHICH FORBIDS TALKING ABOUT THE PRESENT WHEN ONE IS IN THE PAST! IT IS A CRUCIAL AND INDISPENSABLE PRINCIPLE!
OKAY, BUT--
NO "BUT'S" ABOUT IT! I DON'T KNOW YOUR AUNT OR ANY OTHER BLACK MAGICIAN, AND I DON'T WANT TO HEAR ANYTHING ELSE ABOUT THEM! NOW EVERYONE TO YOUR SEATS, CLASS IS ABOUT TO START!
THAT'S ALWAYS HOW IT IS WITH BEGINNERS!

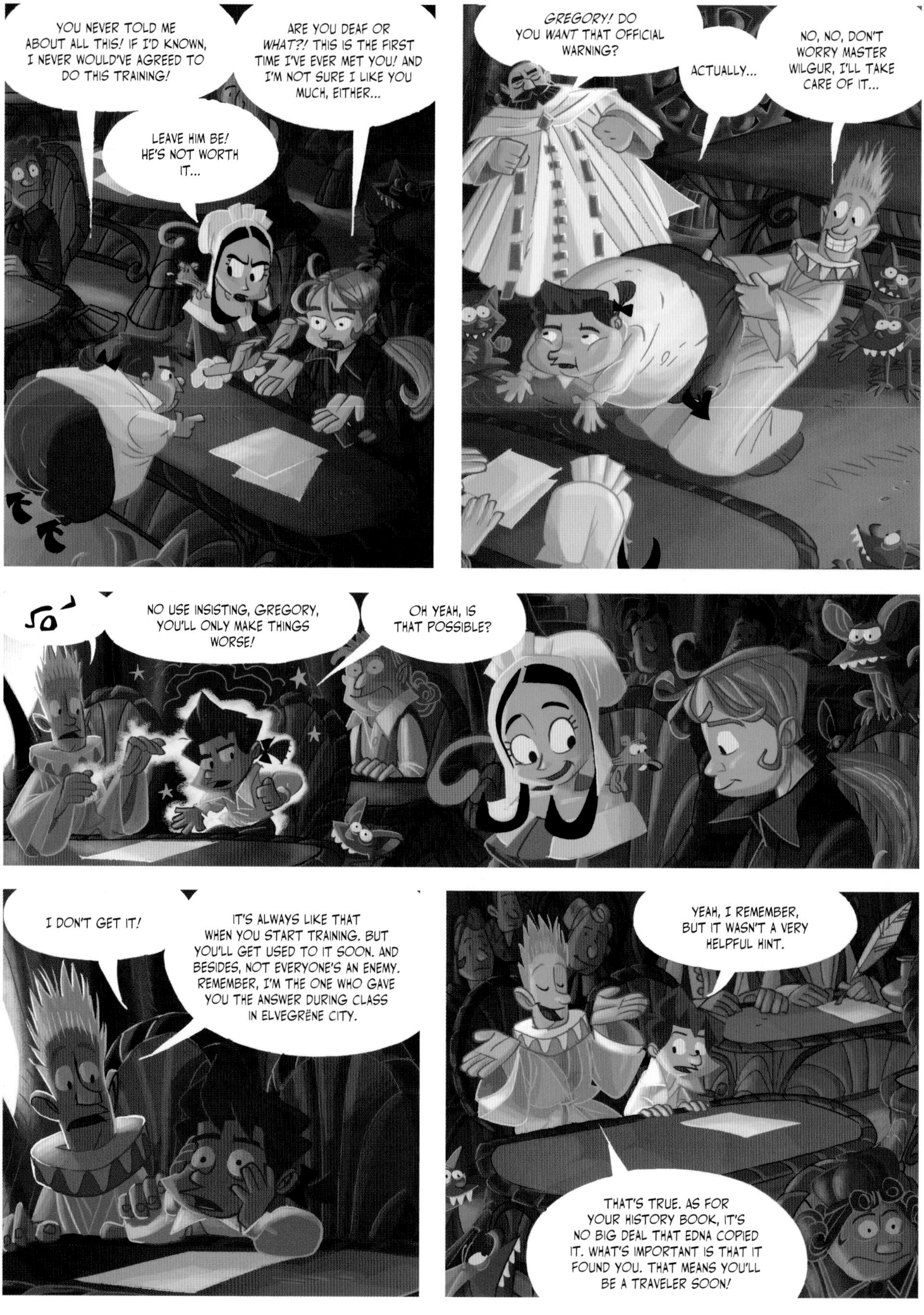

YOU NEVER TOLD ME ABOUT ALL THIS! IF I'D KNOWN, I NEVER WOULD'VE AGREED TO DO THIS TRAINING!
ARE YOU DEAF OR WHAT?! THIS IS THE FIRST TIME I'VE EVER MET YOU! AND I'M NOT SURE I LIKE YOU MUCH, EITHER...
LEAVE HIM BE! HE'S NOT WORTH IT...
GREGORY! DO YOU WANT THAT OFFICIAL WARNING?
ACTUALLY...
NO, NO, DON'T WORRY MASTER WILGUR, I'LL TAKE CARE OF IT...
NO USE INSISTING, GREGORY, YOU'LL ONLY MAKE THINGS WORSE!
OH YEAH, IS THAT POSSIBLE?
I DON'T GET IT!
IT'S ALWAYS LIKE THAT WHEN YOU START TRAINING. BUT YOU'LL GET USED TO IT SOON. AND BESIDES, NOT EVERYONE'S AN ENEMY. REMEMBER, I'M THE ONE WHO GAVE YOU THE ANSWER DURING CLASS IN ELVEGRËNE CITY.
YEAH, I REMEMBER, BUT IT WASN'T A VERY HELPFUL HINT.
THAT'S TRUE. AS FOR YOUR HISTORY BOOK, IT'S NO BIG DEAL THAT EDNA COPIED IT. WHAT'S IMPORTANT IS THAT IT FOUND YOU. THAT MEANS YOU'LL BE A TRAVELER SOON!

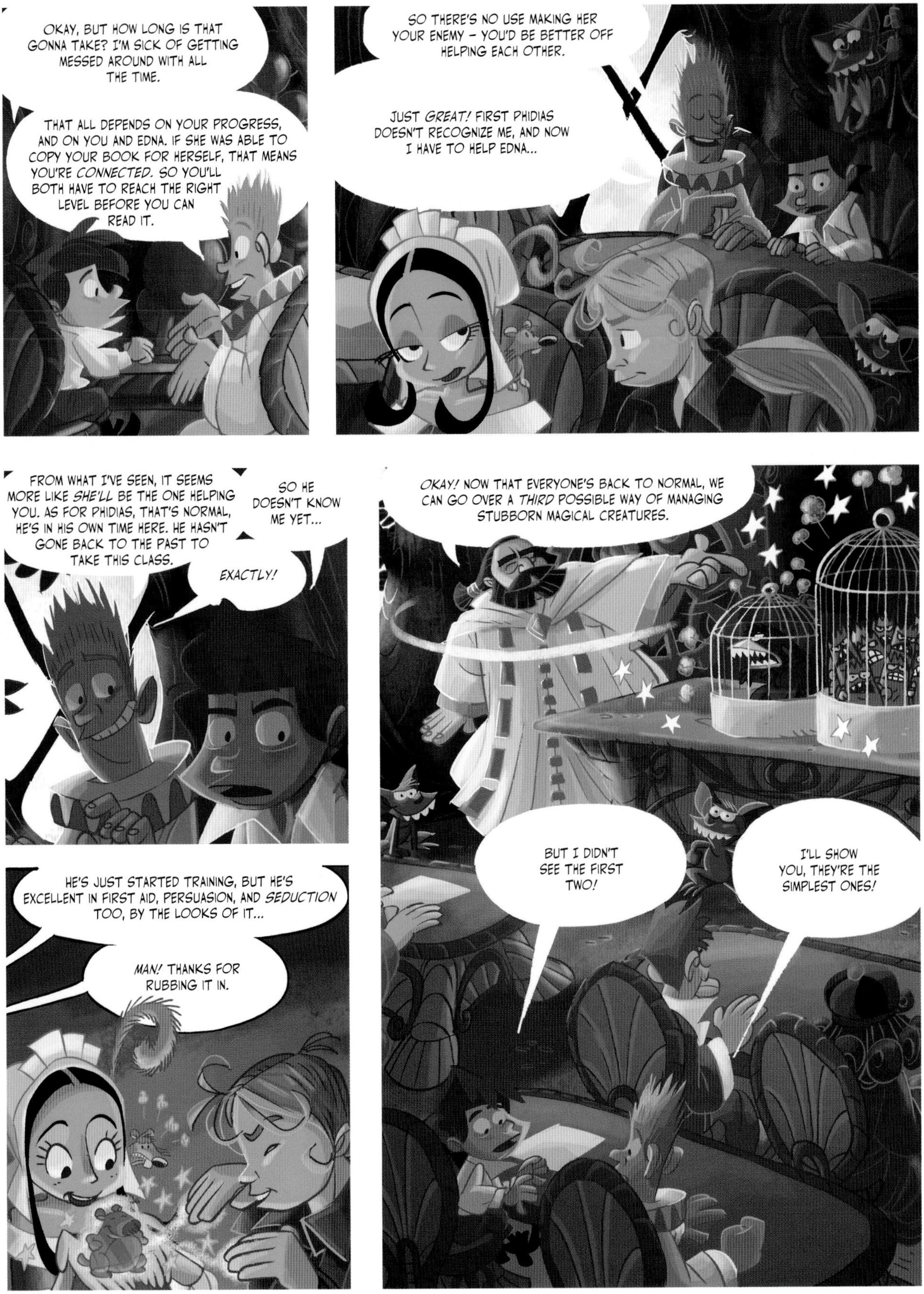
OKAY, BUT HOW LONG IS THAT GONNA TAKE? I'M SICK OF GETTING MESSED AROUND WITH ALL THE TIME.
THAT ALL DEPENDS ON YOUR PROGRESS, AND ON YOU AND EDNA. IF SHE WAS ABLE TO COPY YOUR BOOK FOR HERSELF, THAT MEANS YOU'RE *CONNECTED.* SO YOU'LL BOTH HAVE TO REACH THE RIGHT LEVEL BEFORE YOU CAN READ IT.
SO THERE'S NO USE MAKING HER YOUR ENEMY – YOU'D BE BETTER OFF HELPING EACH OTHER.
JUST *GREAT!* FIRST PHIDIAS DOESN'T RECOGNIZE ME, AND NOW I HAVE TO HELP EDNA...
FROM WHAT I'VE SEEN, IT SEEMS MORE LIKE *SHE'LL* BE THE ONE HELPING YOU. AS FOR PHIDIAS, THAT'S NORMAL, HE'S IN HIS OWN TIME HERE. HE HASN'T GONE BACK TO THE PAST TO TAKE THIS CLASS.
SO HE DOESN'T KNOW ME YET...
EXACTLY!
HE'S JUST STARTED TRAINING, BUT HE'S EXCELLENT IN FIRST AID, PERSUASION, AND *SEDUCTION* TOO, BY THE LOOKS OF IT...
MAN! THANKS FOR RUBBING IT IN.
OKAY! NOW THAT EVERYONE'S BACK TO NORMAL, WE CAN GO OVER A *THIRD* POSSIBLE WAY OF MANAGING STUBBORN MAGICAL CREATURES.
BUT I DIDN'T SEE THE FIRST TWO!
I'LL SHOW YOU, THEY'RE THE SIMPLEST ONES!

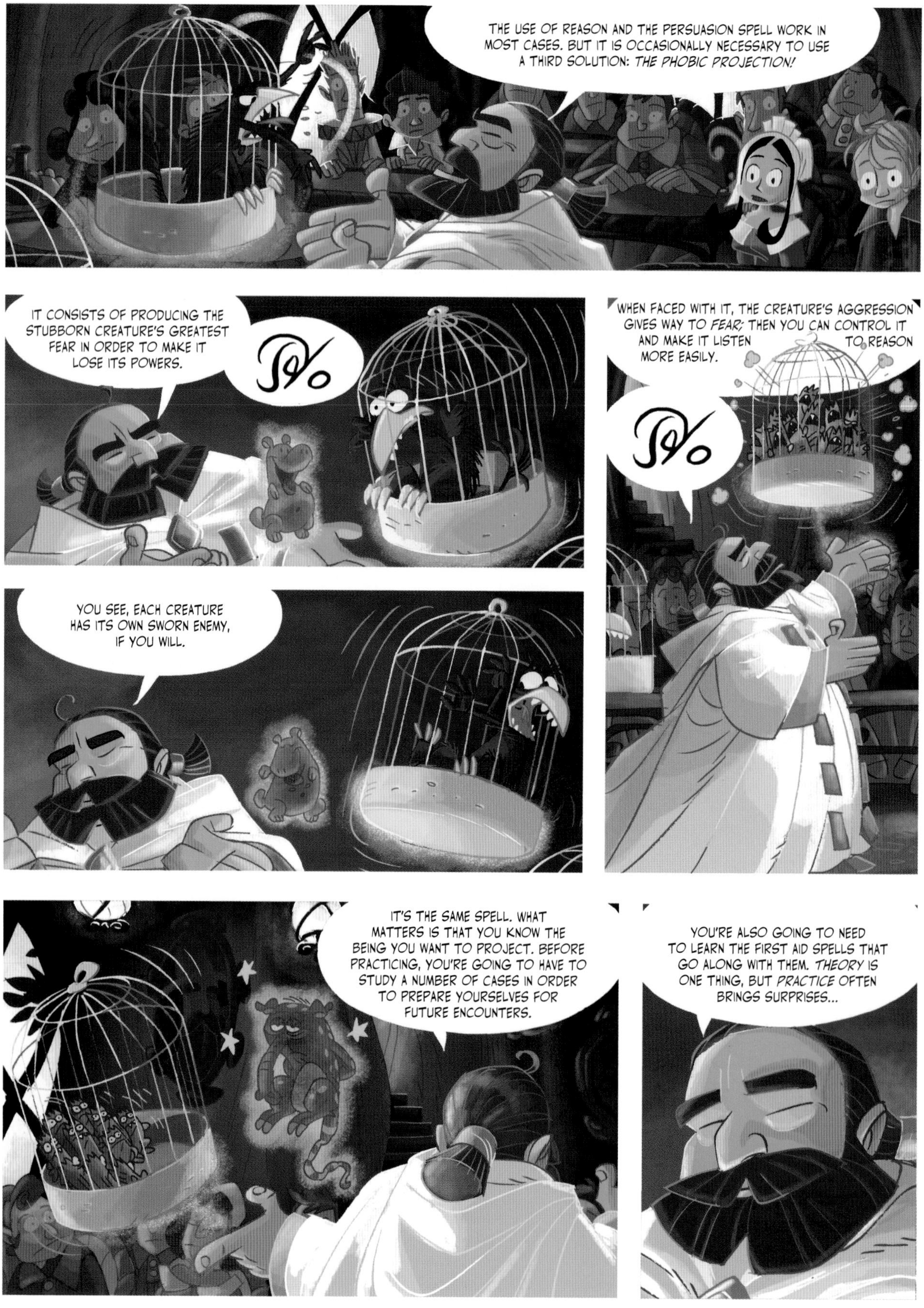
THE USE OF REASON AND THE PERSUASION SPELL WORK IN MOST CASES. BUT IT IS OCCASIONALLY NECESSARY TO USE A THIRD SOLUTION: *THE PHOBIC PROJECTION!*
IT CONSISTS OF PRODUCING THE STUBBORN CREATURE'S GREATEST FEAR IN ORDER TO MAKE IT LOSE ITS POWERS.
WHEN FACED WITH IT, THE CREATURE'S AGGRESSION GIVES WAY TO *FEAR;* THEN YOU CAN CONTROL IT AND MAKE IT LISTEN TO REASON MORE EASILY.
YOU SEE, EACH CREATURE HAS ITS OWN SWORN ENEMY, IF YOU WILL.
IT'S THE SAME SPELL. WHAT MATTERS IS THAT YOU KNOW THE BEING YOU WANT TO PROJECT. BEFORE PRACTICING, YOU'RE GOING TO HAVE TO STUDY A NUMBER OF CASES IN ORDER TO PREPARE YOURSELVES FOR FUTURE ENCOUNTERS.
YOU'RE ALSO GOING TO NEED TO LEARN THE FIRST AID SPELLS THAT GO ALONG WITH THEM. *THEORY* IS ONE THING, BUT *PRACTICE* OFTEN BRINGS SURPRISES...

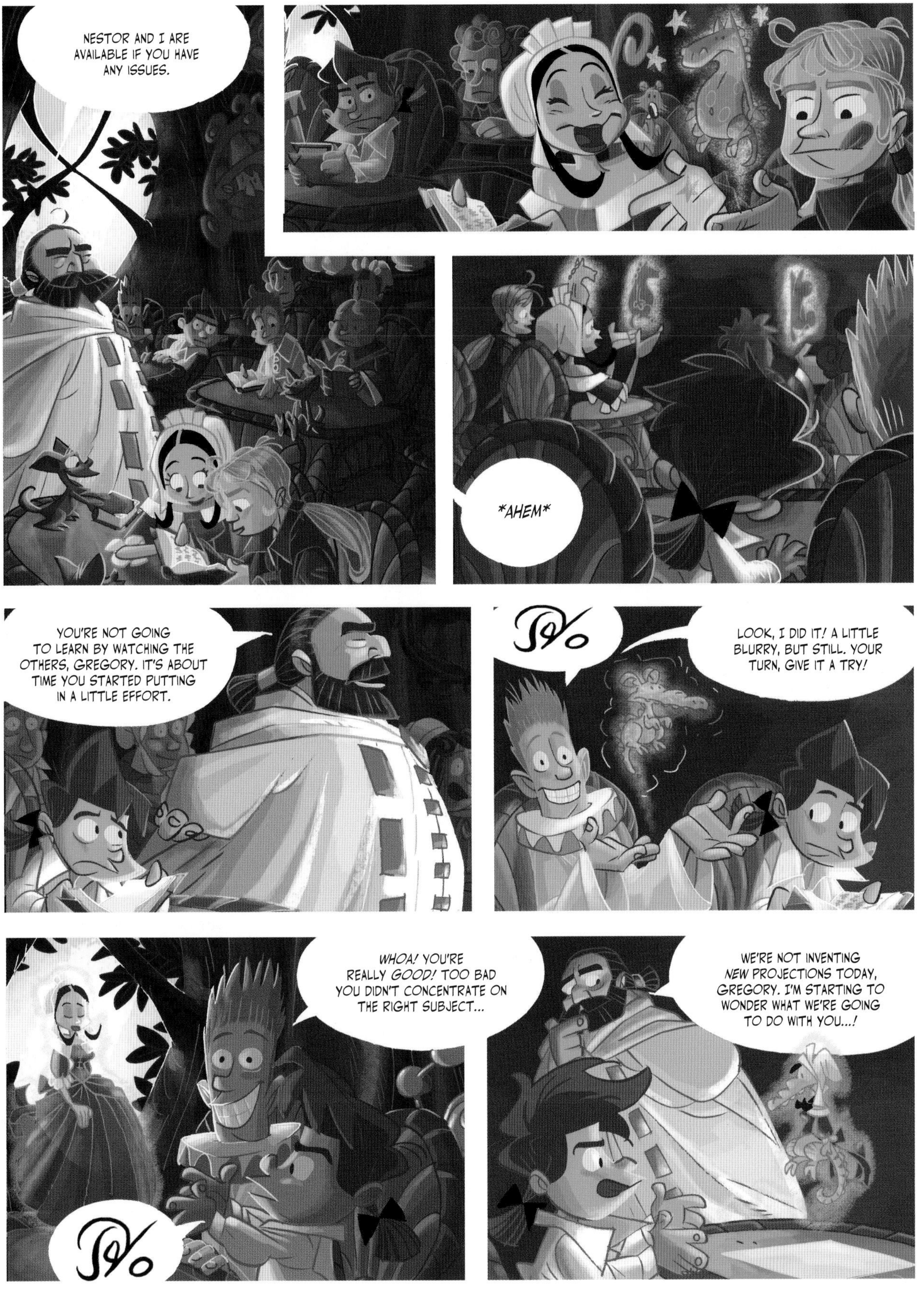
NESTOR AND I ARE AVAILABLE IF YOU HAVE ANY ISSUES.
AHEM
YOU'RE NOT GOING TO LEARN BY WATCHING THE OTHERS, GREGORY. IT'S ABOUT TIME YOU STARTED PUTTING IN A LITTLE EFFORT.
LOOK, I DID IT! A LITTLE BLURRY, BUT STILL. YOUR TURN, GIVE IT A TRY!
WHOA! YOU'RE REALLY GOOD! TOO BAD YOU DIDN'T CONCENTRATE ON THE RIGHT SUBJECT...
WE'RE NOT INVENTING NEW PROJECTIONS TODAY, GREGORY. I'M STARTING TO WONDER WHAT WE'RE GOING TO DO WITH YOU...!

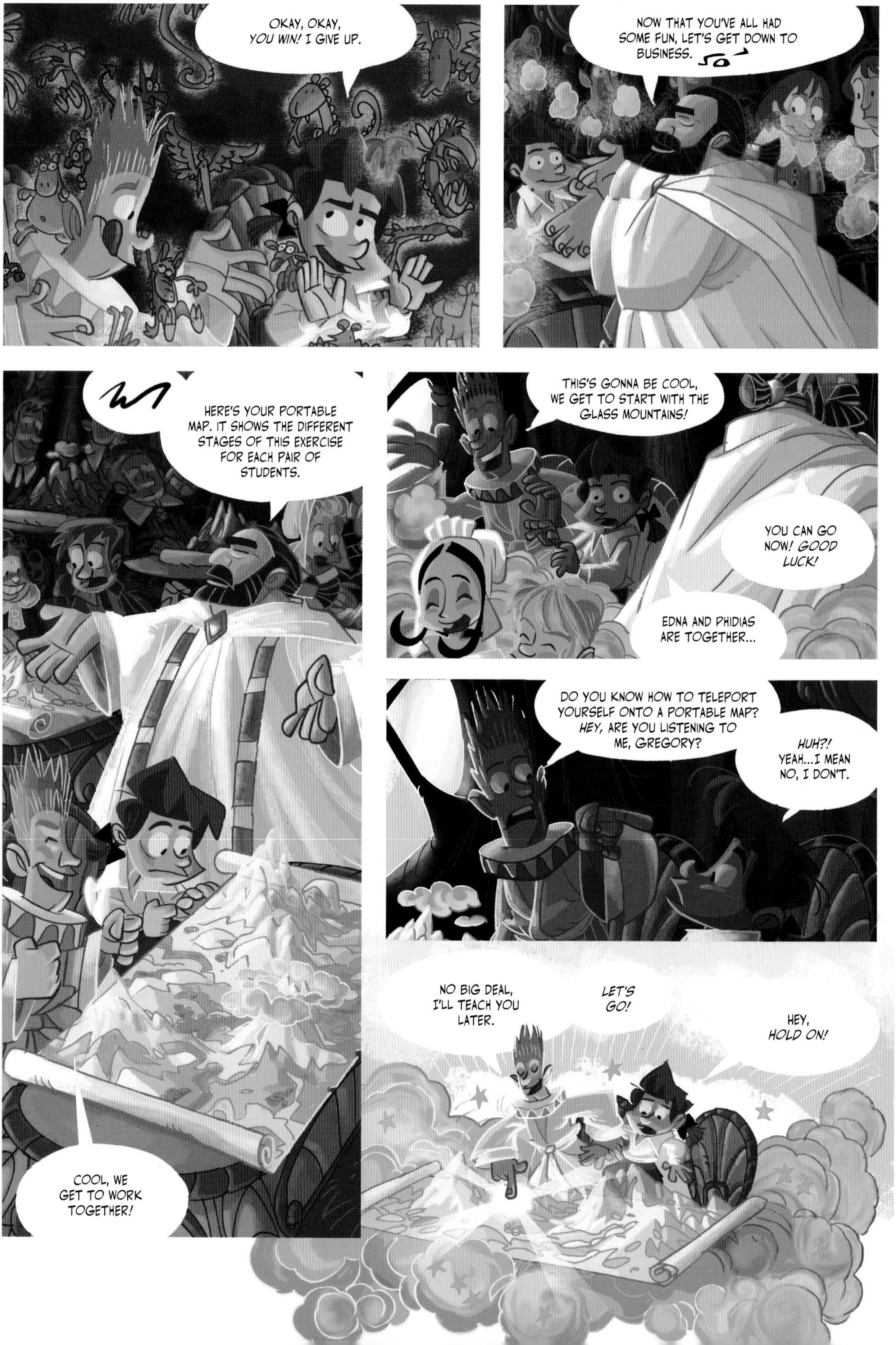

OKAY, OKAY, *YOU WIN!* I GIVE UP.
NOW THAT YOU'VE ALL HAD SOME FUN, LET'S GET DOWN TO BUSINESS.
HERE'S YOUR PORTABLE MAP. IT SHOWS THE DIFFERENT STAGES OF THIS EXERCISE FOR EACH PAIR OF STUDENTS.
COOL, WE GET TO WORK TOGETHER!
EDNA AND PHIDIAS ARE TOGETHER...
YOU CAN GO NOW! *GOOD LUCK!*
THIS'S GONNA BE COOL, WE GET TO START WITH THE GLASS MOUNTAINS!
DO YOU KNOW HOW TO TELEPORT YOURSELF ONTO A PORTABLE MAP? *HEY, ARE YOU LISTENING TO ME, GREGORY?*
HUH?! YEAH...I MEAN NO, I DON'T.
NO BIG DEAL, I'LL TEACH YOU LATER.
LET'S GO!
HEY, *HOLD ON!*

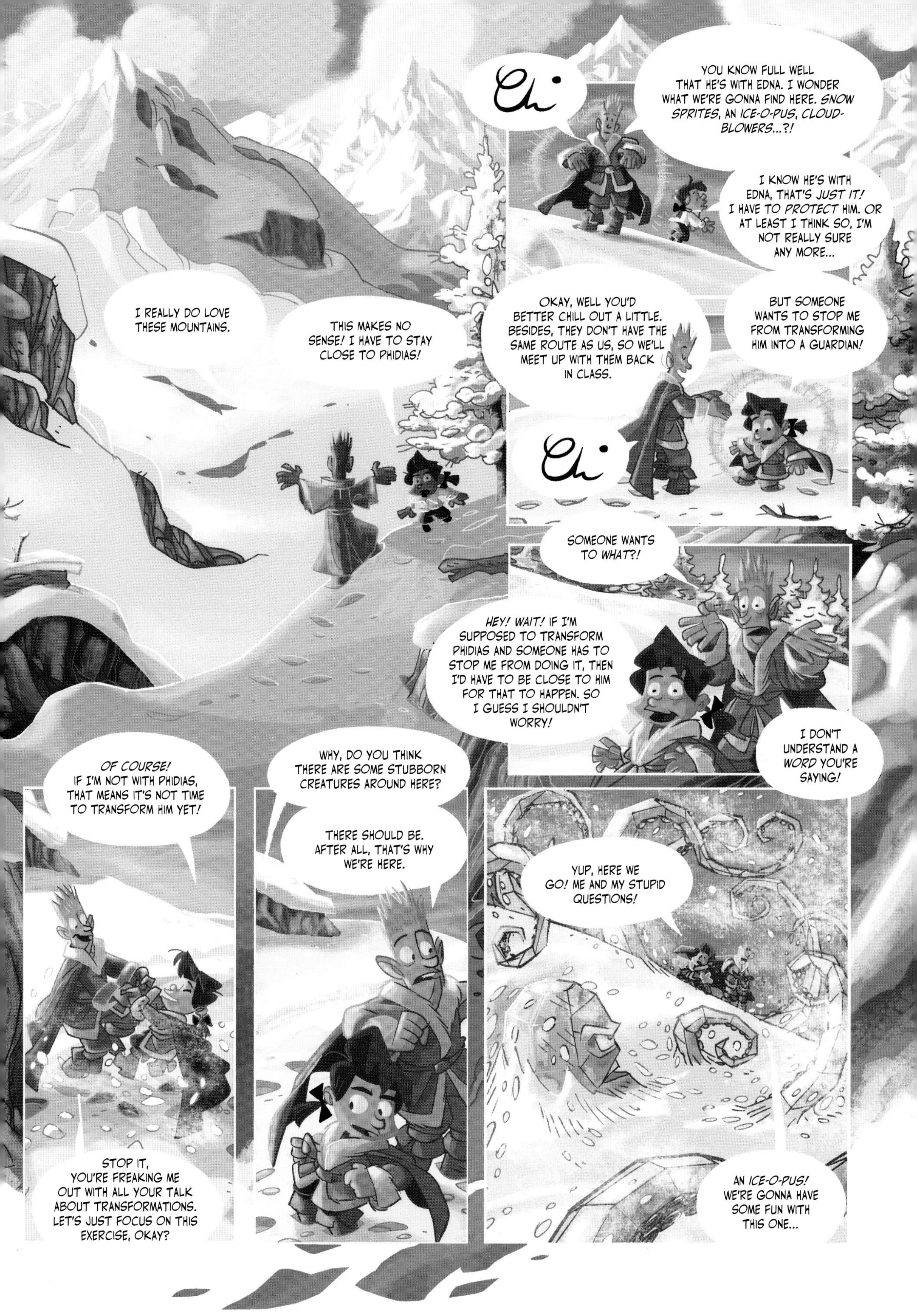
I REALLY DO LOVE THESE MOUNTAINS.
THIS MAKES NO SENSE! I HAVE TO STAY CLOSE TO PHIDIAS!
Chi
YOU KNOW FULL WELL THAT HE'S WITH EDNA. I WONDER WHAT WE'RE GONNA FIND HERE. SNOW SPRITES, AN ICE-O-PUS, CLOUD-BLOWERS...?!
I KNOW HE'S WITH EDNA, THAT'S JUST IT! I HAVE TO PROTECT HIM. OR AT LEAST I THINK SO, I'M NOT REALLY SURE ANY MORE...
OKAY, WELL YOU'D BETTER CHILL OUT A LITTLE. BESIDES, THEY DON'T HAVE THE SAME ROUTE AS US, SO WE'LL MEET UP WITH THEM BACK IN CLASS.
BUT SOMEONE WANTS TO STOP ME FROM TRANSFORMING HIM INTO A GUARDIAN!
Chi
SOMEONE WANTS TO WHAT?!
HEY! WAIT! IF I'M SUPPOSED TO TRANSFORM PHIDIAS AND SOMEONE HAS TO STOP ME FROM DOING IT, THEN I'D HAVE TO BE CLOSE TO HIM FOR THAT TO HAPPEN. SO I GUESS I SHOULDN'T WORRY!
I DON'T UNDERSTAND A WORD YOU'RE SAYING!
OF COURSE! IF I'M NOT WITH PHIDIAS, THAT MEANS IT'S NOT TIME TO TRANSFORM HIM YET!
STOP IT, YOU'RE FREAKING ME OUT WITH ALL YOUR TALK ABOUT TRANSFORMATIONS. LET'S JUST FOCUS ON THIS EXERCISE, OKAY?
WHY, DO YOU THINK THERE ARE SOME STUBBORN CREATURES AROUND HERE?
THERE SHOULD BE. AFTER ALL, THAT'S WHY WE'RE HERE.
YUP, HERE WE GO! ME AND MY STUPID QUESTIONS!
AN ICE-O-PUS! WE'RE GONNA HAVE SOME FUN WITH THIS ONE...

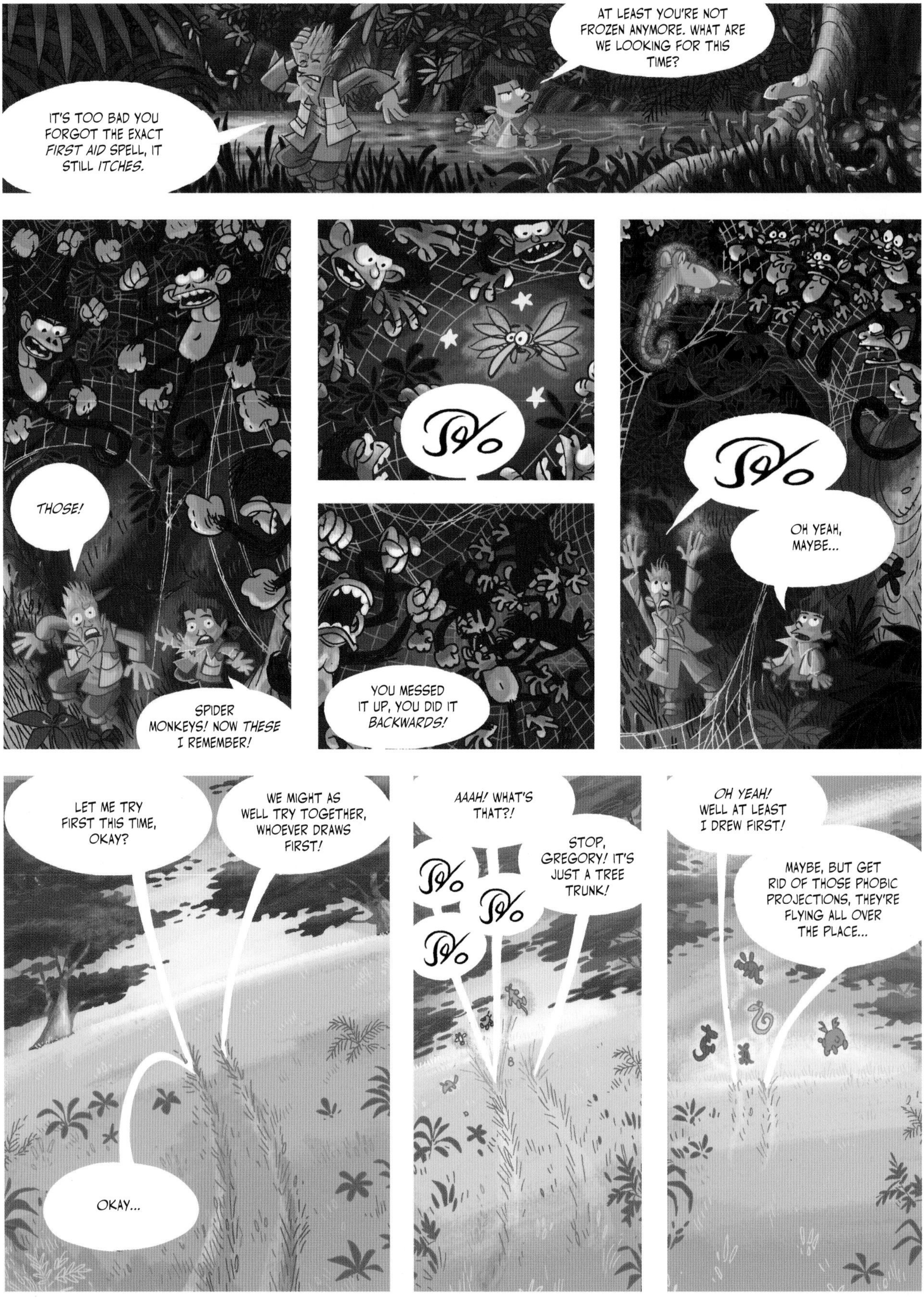
AT LEAST YOU'RE NOT FROZEN ANYMORE. WHAT ARE WE LOOKING FOR THIS TIME?
IT'S TOO BAD YOU FORGOT THE EXACT *FIRST AID* SPELL, IT STILL *ITCHES.*
THOSE!
SPIDER MONKEYS! NOW *THESE* I REMEMBER!
YOU MESSED IT UP, YOU DID IT *BACKWARDS!*
OH YEAH, MAYBE...
LET ME TRY FIRST THIS TIME, OKAY?
WE MIGHT AS WELL TRY TOGETHER, WHOEVER DRAWS FIRST!
OKAY...
AAAH! WHAT'S THAT?!
STOP, GREGORY! IT'S JUST A TREE TRUNK!
OH YEAH! WELL AT LEAST I DREW FIRST!
MAYBE, BUT GET RID OF THOSE PHOBIC PROJECTIONS, THEY'RE FLYING ALL OVER THE PLACE...

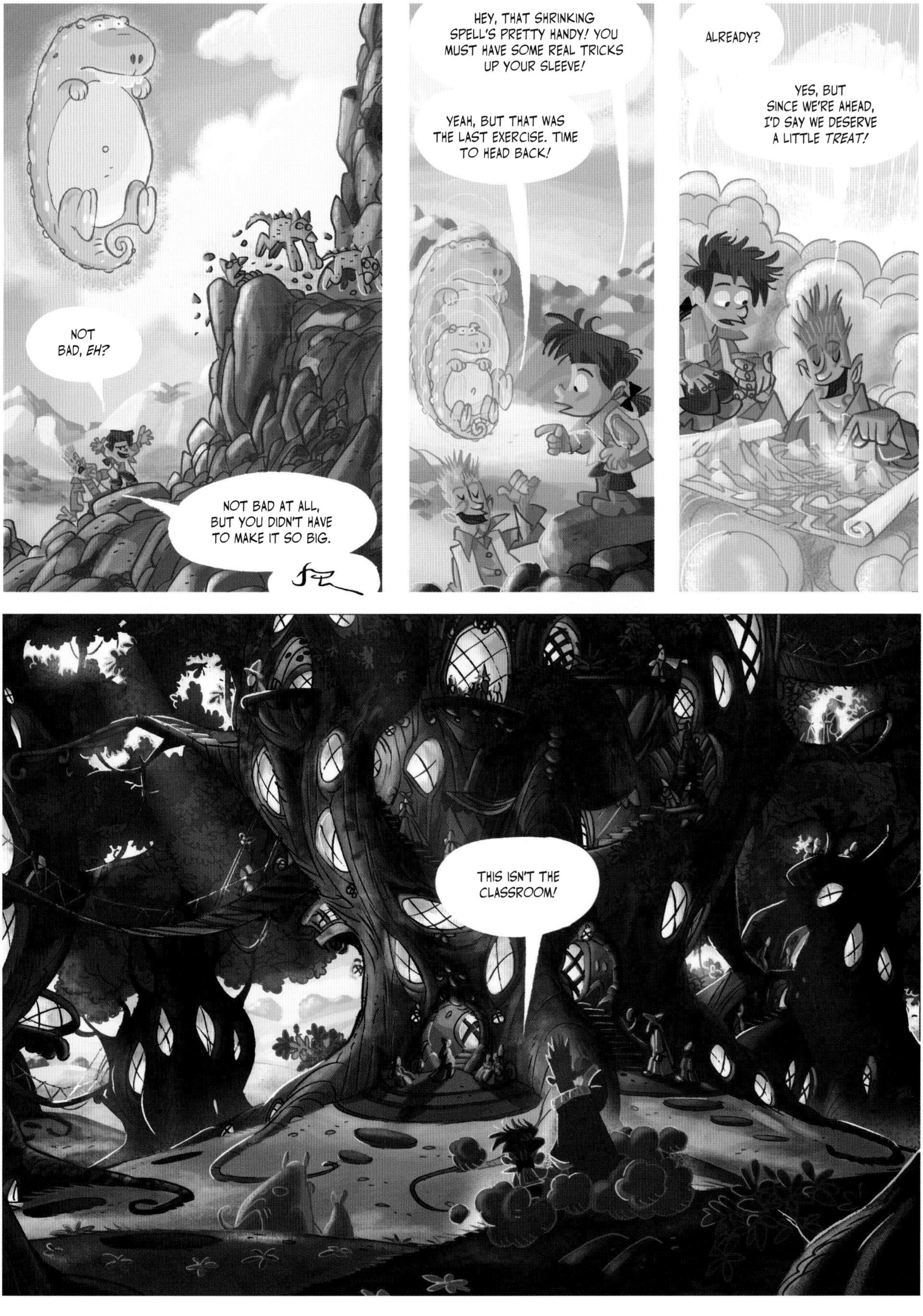
NOT BAD, EH?
NOT BAD AT ALL, BUT YOU DIDN'T HAVE TO MAKE IT SO BIG.
HEY, THAT SHRINKING SPELL'S PRETTY HANDY! YOU MUST HAVE SOME REAL TRICKS UP YOUR SLEEVE!
YEAH, BUT THAT WAS THE LAST EXERCISE. TIME TO HEAD BACK!
ALREADY?
YES, BUT SINCE WE'RE AHEAD, I'D SAY WE DESERVE A LITTLE *TREAT!*
THIS ISN'T THE CLASSROOM!

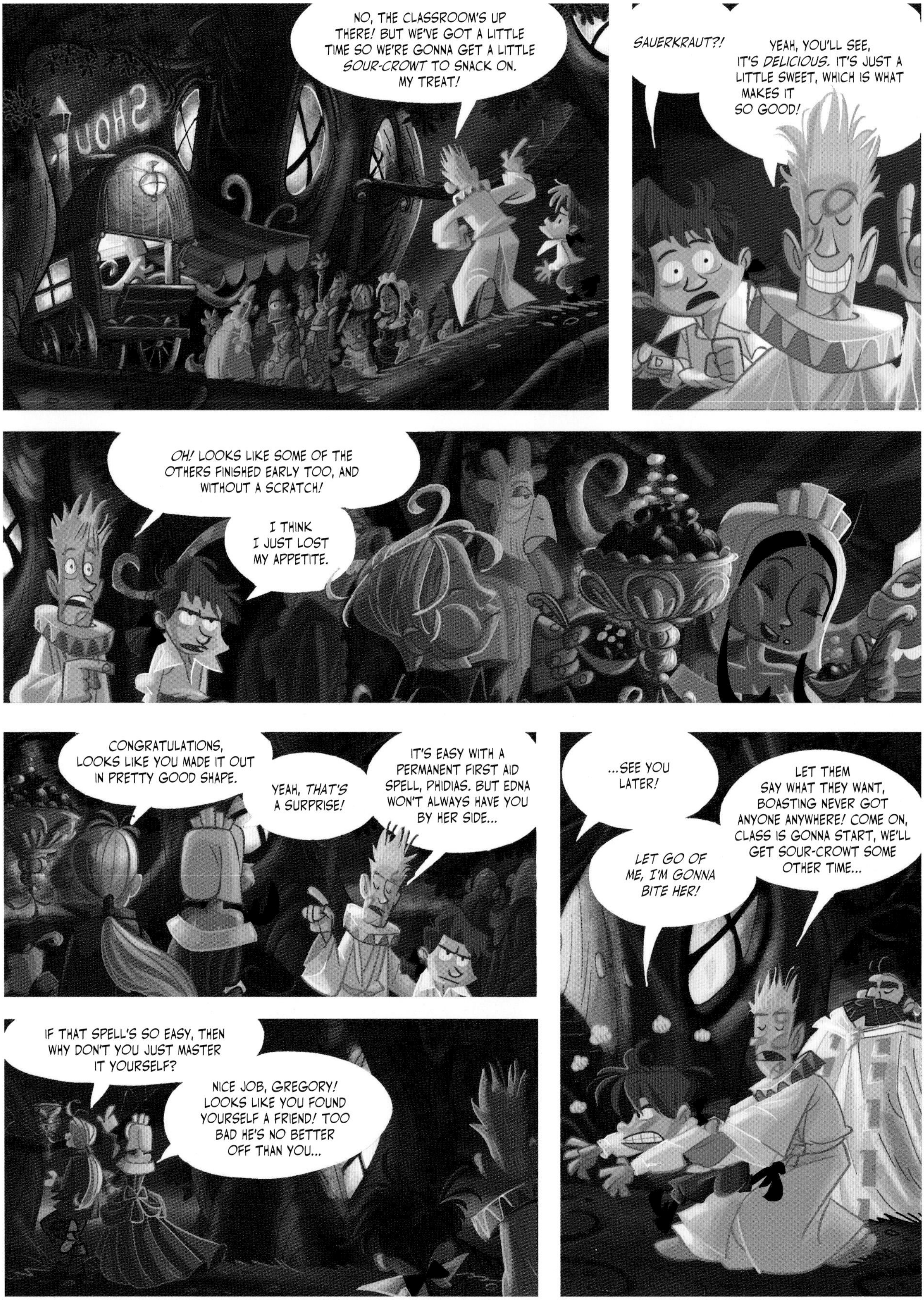
NO, THE CLASSROOM'S UP THERE! BUT WE'VE GOT A LITTLE TIME SO WE'RE GONNA GET A LITTLE SOUR-CROWT TO SNACK ON. MY TREAT!
SAUERKRAUT?!
YEAH, YOU'LL SEE, IT'S DELICIOUS. IT'S JUST A LITTLE SWEET, WHICH IS WHAT MAKES IT SO GOOD!
OH! LOOKS LIKE SOME OF THE OTHERS FINISHED EARLY TOO, AND WITHOUT A SCRATCH!
I THINK I JUST LOST MY APPETITE.
CONGRATULATIONS, LOOKS LIKE YOU MADE IT OUT IN PRETTY GOOD SHAPE.
YEAH, THAT'S A SURPRISE!
IT'S EASY WITH A PERMANENT FIRST AID SPELL, PHIDIAS. BUT EDNA WON'T ALWAYS HAVE YOU BY HER SIDE...
IF THAT SPELL'S SO EASY, THEN WHY DON'T YOU JUST MASTER IT YOURSELF?
NICE JOB, GREGORY! LOOKS LIKE YOU FOUND YOURSELF A FRIEND! TOO BAD HE'S NO BETTER OFF THAN YOU...
...SEE YOU LATER!
LET GO OF ME, I'M GONNA BITE HER!
LET THEM SAY WHAT THEY WANT, BOASTING NEVER GOT ANYONE ANYWHERE! COME ON, CLASS IS GONNA START, WE'LL GET SOUR-CROWT SOME OTHER TIME...

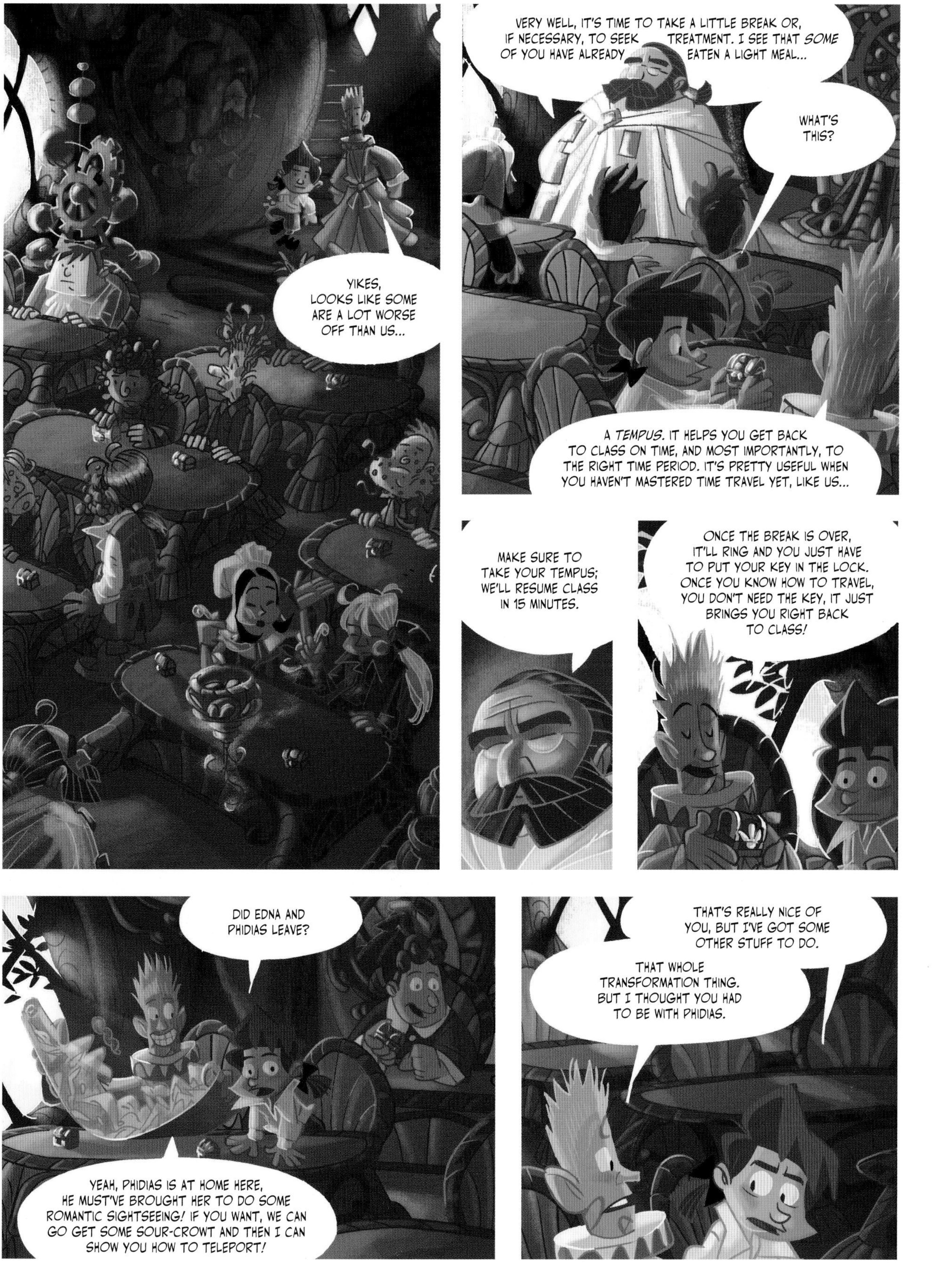
YIKES, LOOKS LIKE SOME ARE A LOT WORSE OFF THAN US...
VERY WELL, IT'S TIME TO TAKE A LITTLE BREAK OR, IF NECESSARY, TO SEEK TREATMENT. I SEE THAT *SOME* OF YOU HAVE ALREADY EATEN A LIGHT MEAL...
WHAT'S THIS?
A *TEMPUS*. IT HELPS YOU GET BACK TO CLASS ON TIME, AND MOST IMPORTANTLY, TO THE RIGHT TIME PERIOD. IT'S PRETTY USEFUL WHEN YOU HAVEN'T MASTERED TIME TRAVEL YET, LIKE US...
MAKE SURE TO TAKE YOUR TEMPUS; WE'LL RESUME CLASS IN 15 MINUTES.
ONCE THE BREAK IS OVER, IT'LL RING AND YOU JUST HAVE TO PUT YOUR KEY IN THE LOCK. ONCE YOU KNOW HOW TO TRAVEL, YOU DON'T NEED THE KEY, IT JUST BRINGS YOU RIGHT BACK TO CLASS!
DID EDNA AND PHIDIAS LEAVE?
YEAH, PHIDIAS IS AT HOME HERE, HE MUST'VE BROUGHT HER TO DO SOME ROMANTIC SIGHTSEEING! IF YOU WANT, WE CAN GO GET SOME SOUR-CROWT AND THEN I CAN SHOW YOU HOW TO TELEPORT!
THAT'S REALLY NICE OF YOU, BUT I'VE GOT SOME OTHER STUFF TO DO.
THAT WHOLE TRANSFORMATION THING. BUT I THOUGHT YOU HAD TO BE WITH PHIDIAS.

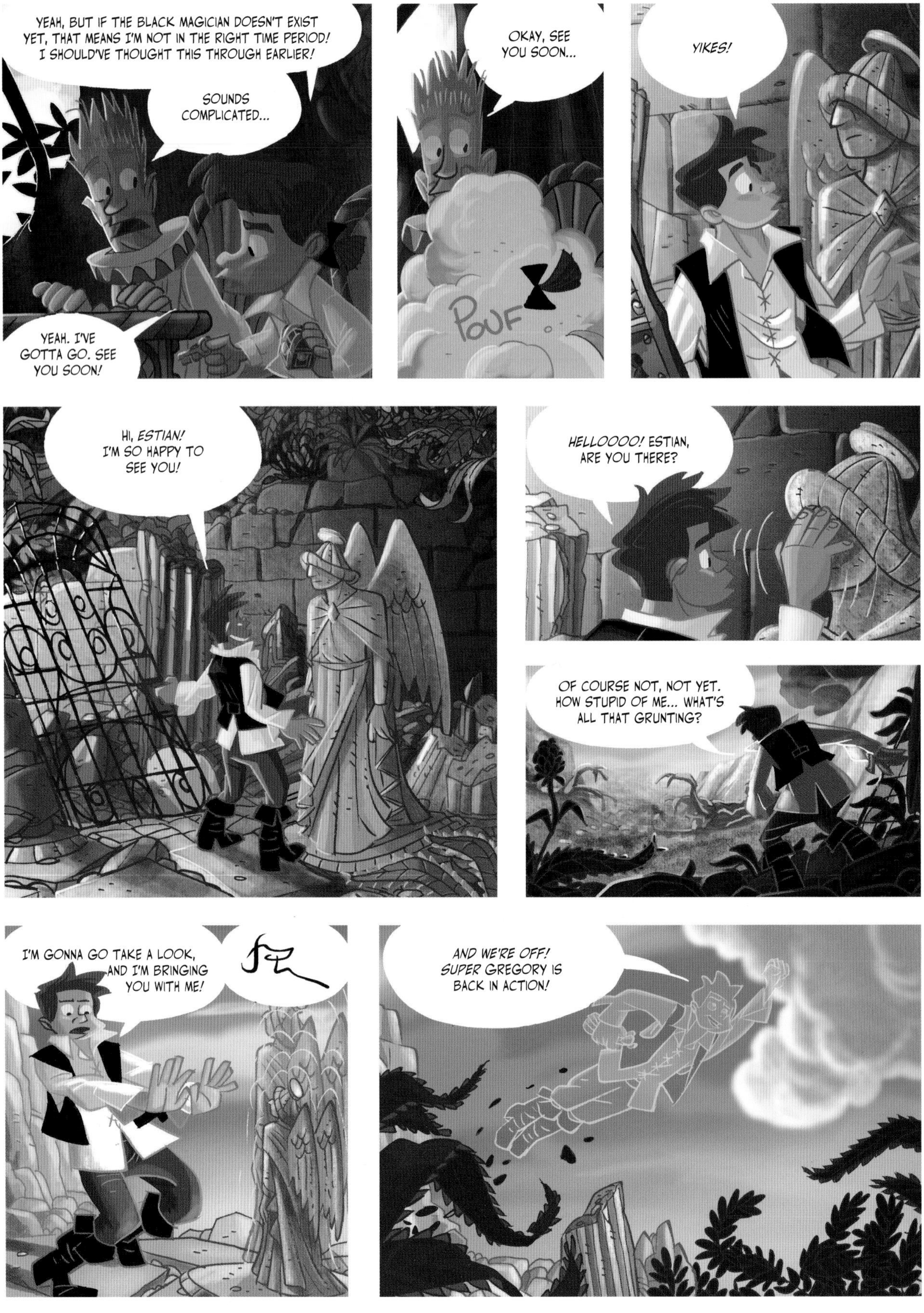
YEAH, BUT IF THE BLACK MAGICIAN DOESN'T EXIST YET, THAT MEANS I'M NOT IN THE RIGHT TIME PERIOD! I SHOULD'VE THOUGHT THIS THROUGH EARLIER!
SOUNDS COMPLICATED...
YEAH. I'VE GOTTA GO. SEE YOU SOON!
OKAY, SEE YOU SOON...
POUF
YIKES!
HI, ESTIAN! I'M SO HAPPY TO SEE YOU!
HELLOOOO! ESTIAN, ARE YOU THERE?
OF COURSE NOT, NOT YET. HOW STUPID OF ME... WHAT'S ALL THAT GRUNTING?
I'M GONNA GO TAKE A LOOK, AND I'M BRINGING YOU WITH ME!
AND WE'RE OFF! SUPER GREGORY IS BACK IN ACTION!

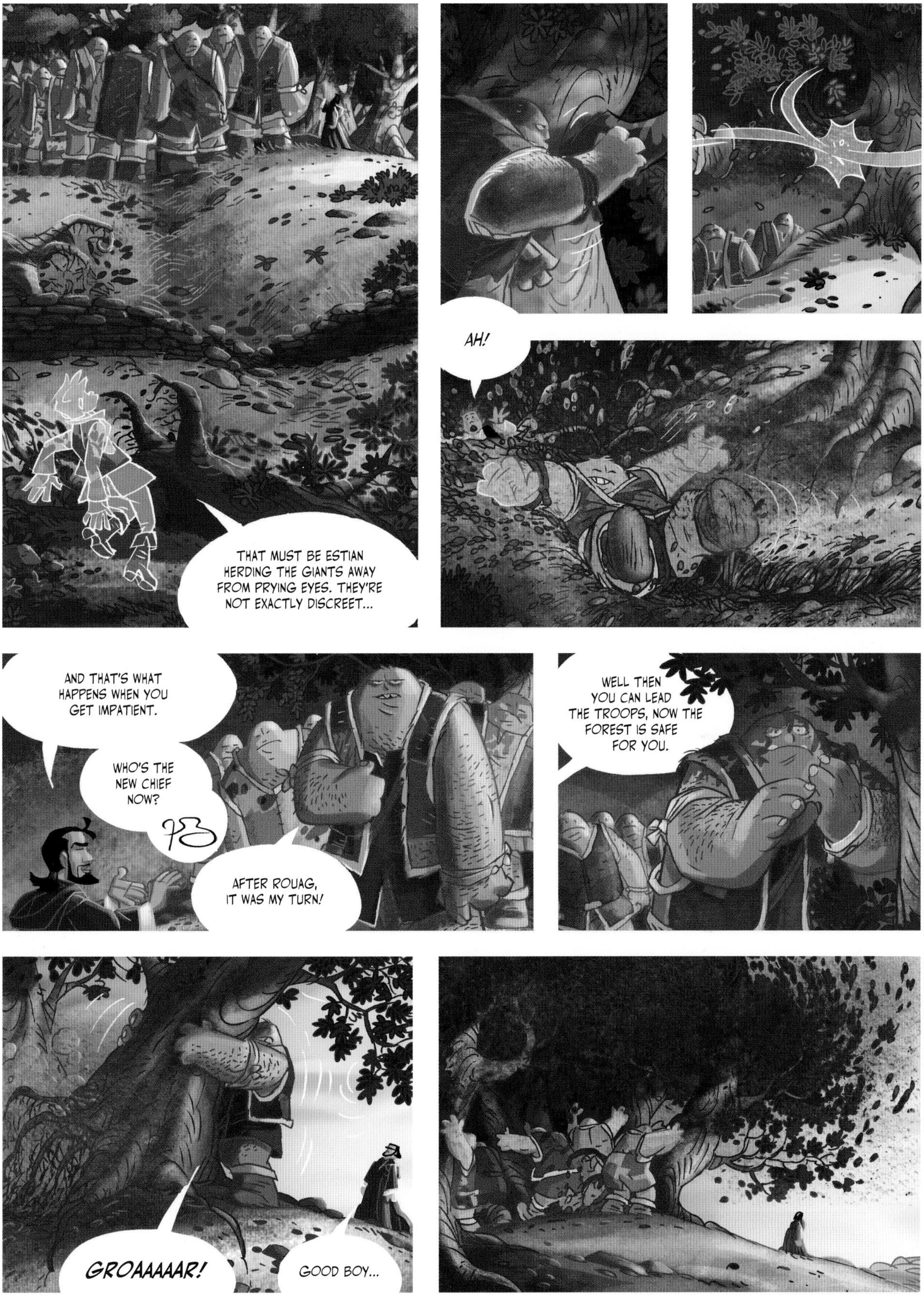
THAT MUST BE ESTIAN HERDING THE GIANTS AWAY FROM PRYING EYES. THEY'RE NOT EXACTLY DISCREET...
AH!
AND THAT'S WHAT HAPPENS WHEN YOU GET IMPATIENT.
WHO'S THE NEW CHIEF NOW?
AFTER ROUAG, IT WAS MY TURN!
WELL THEN YOU CAN LEAD THE TROOPS, NOW THE FOREST IS SAFE FOR YOU.
GROAAAAAR!
GOOD BOY...

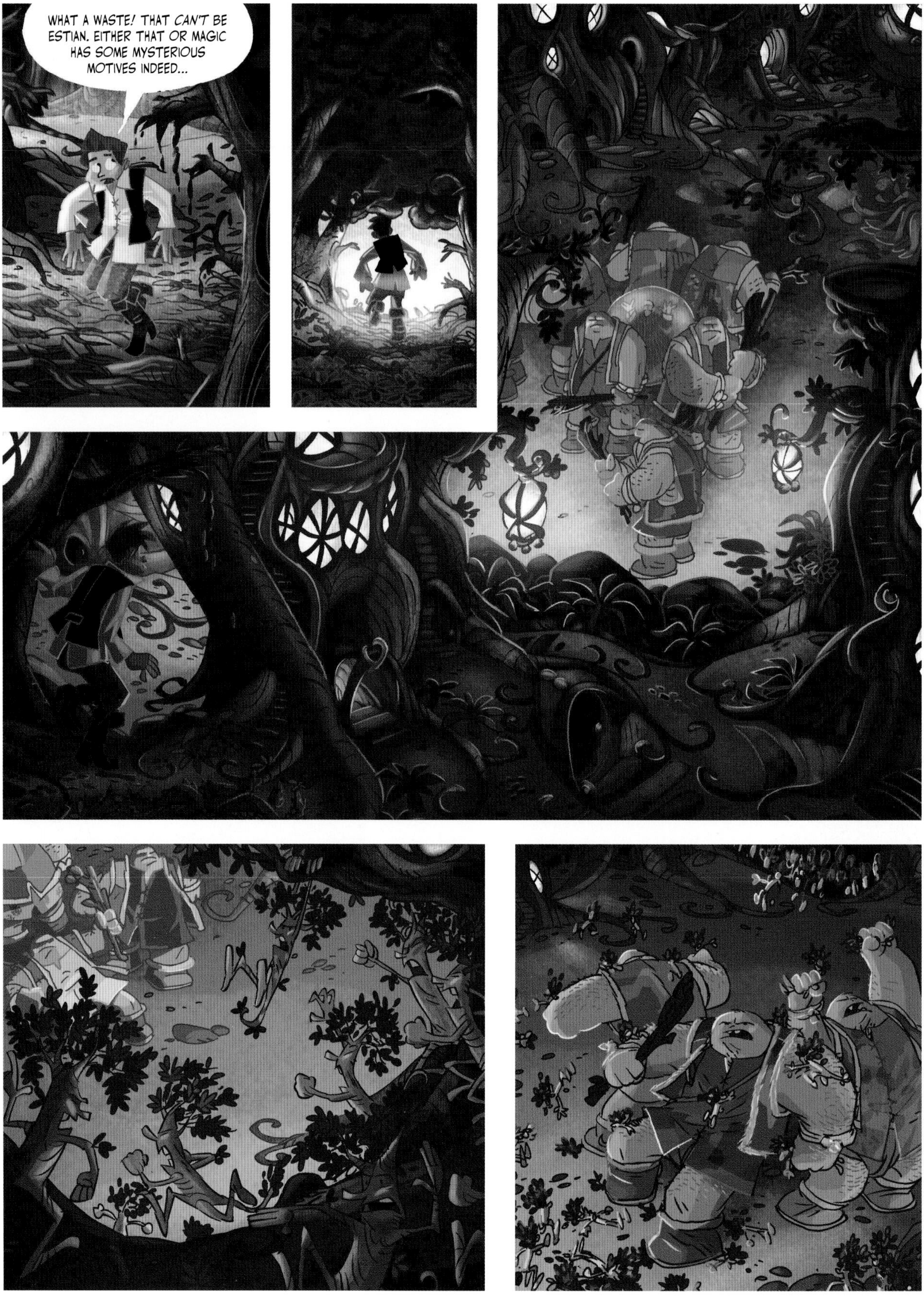
WHAT A WASTE! THAT CAN'T BE ESTIAN. EITHER THAT OR MAGIC HAS SOME MYSTERIOUS MOTIVES INDEED...

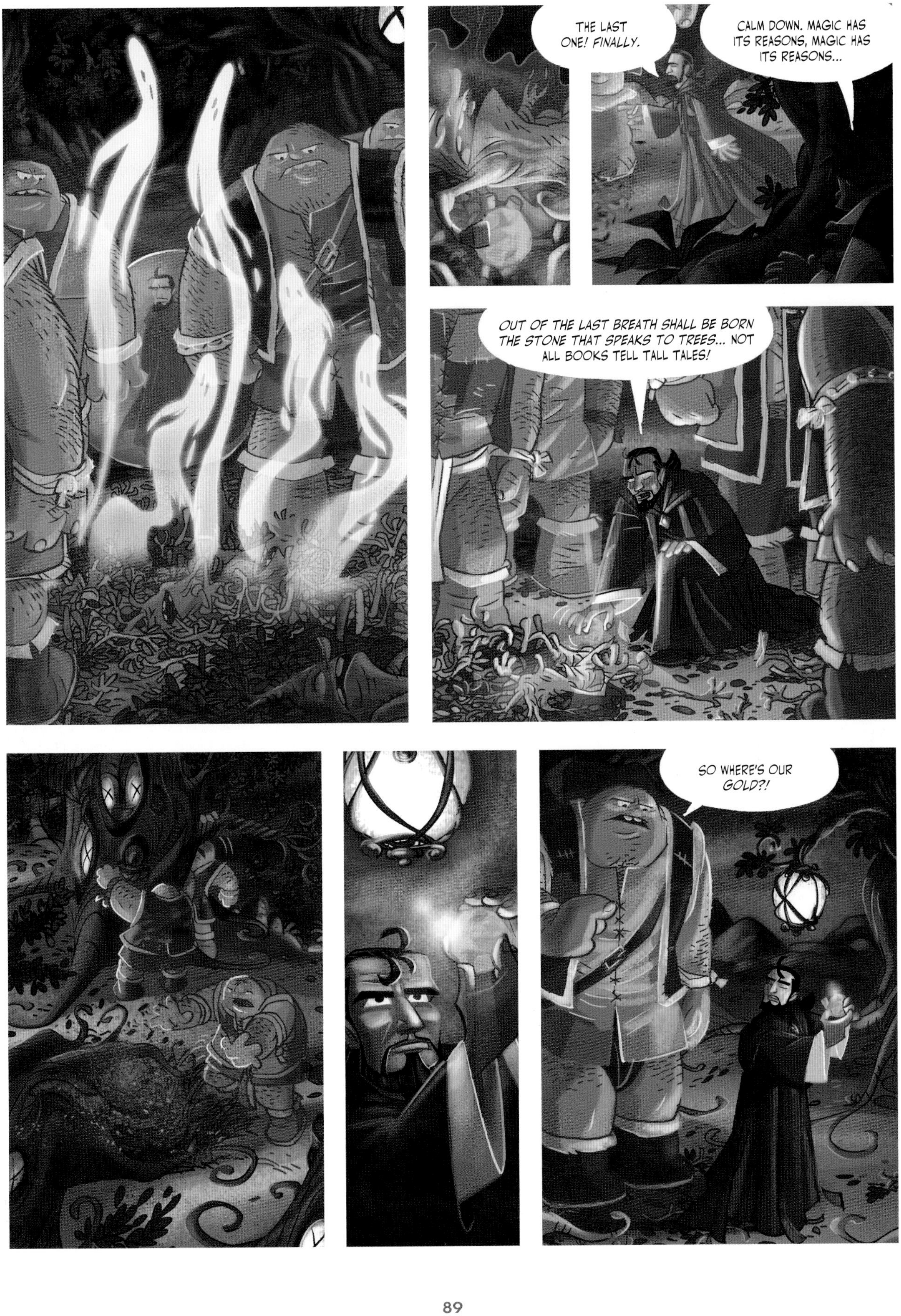
THE LAST ONE! *FINALLY.*
CALM DOWN. MAGIC HAS ITS REASONS, MAGIC HAS ITS REASONS...
OUT OF THE LAST BREATH SHALL BE BORN THE STONE THAT SPEAKS TO TREES... NOT ALL BOOKS TELL TALL TALES!
SO WHERE'S OUR *GOLD?!*

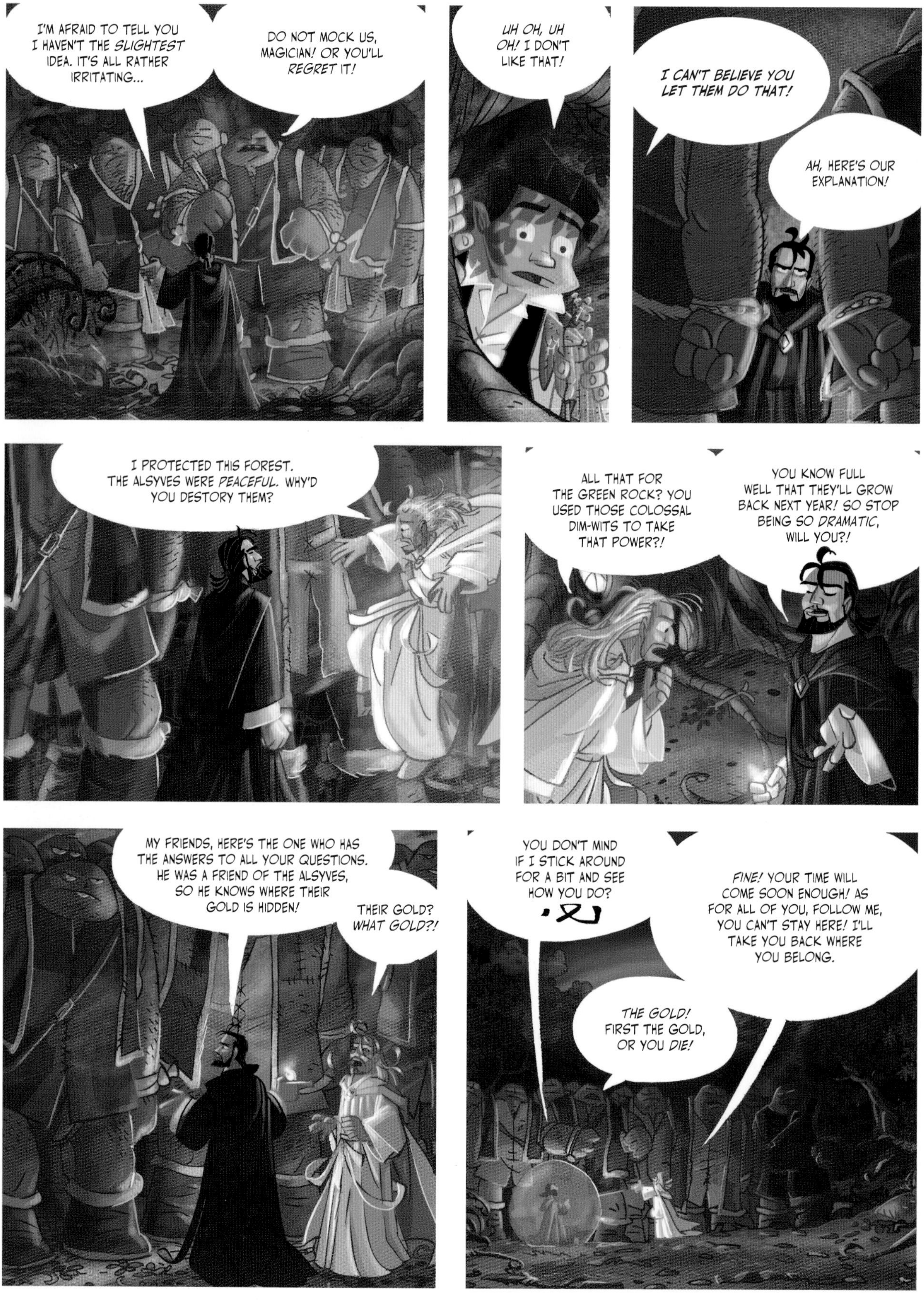
I'M AFRAID TO TELL YOU I HAVEN'T THE *SLIGHTEST* IDEA. IT'S ALL RATHER IRRITATING...
DO NOT MOCK US, MAGICIAN! OR YOU'LL *REGRET* IT!
UH OH, UH OH! I DON'T LIKE THAT!
I CAN'T BELIEVE YOU LET THEM DO THAT!
AH, HERE'S OUR EXPLANATION!
I PROTECTED THIS FOREST. THE ALSYVES WERE *PEACEFUL*. WHY'D YOU DESTORY THEM?
ALL THAT FOR THE GREEN ROCK? YOU USED THOSE COLOSSAL DIM-WITS TO TAKE THAT POWER?!
YOU KNOW FULL WELL THAT THEY'LL GROW BACK NEXT YEAR! SO STOP BEING SO *DRAMATIC*, WILL YOU?!
MY FRIENDS, HERE'S THE ONE WHO HAS THE ANSWERS TO ALL YOUR QUESTIONS. HE WAS A FRIEND OF THE ALSYVES, SO HE KNOWS WHERE THEIR GOLD IS HIDDEN!
THEIR GOLD? *WHAT GOLD?!*
YOU DON'T MIND IF I STICK AROUND FOR A BIT AND SEE HOW YOU DO?
FINE! YOUR TIME WILL COME SOON ENOUGH! AS FOR ALL OF YOU, FOLLOW ME, YOU CAN'T STAY HERE! I'LL TAKE YOU BACK WHERE YOU BELONG.
THE GOLD! FIRST THE GOLD, OR YOU *DIE!*

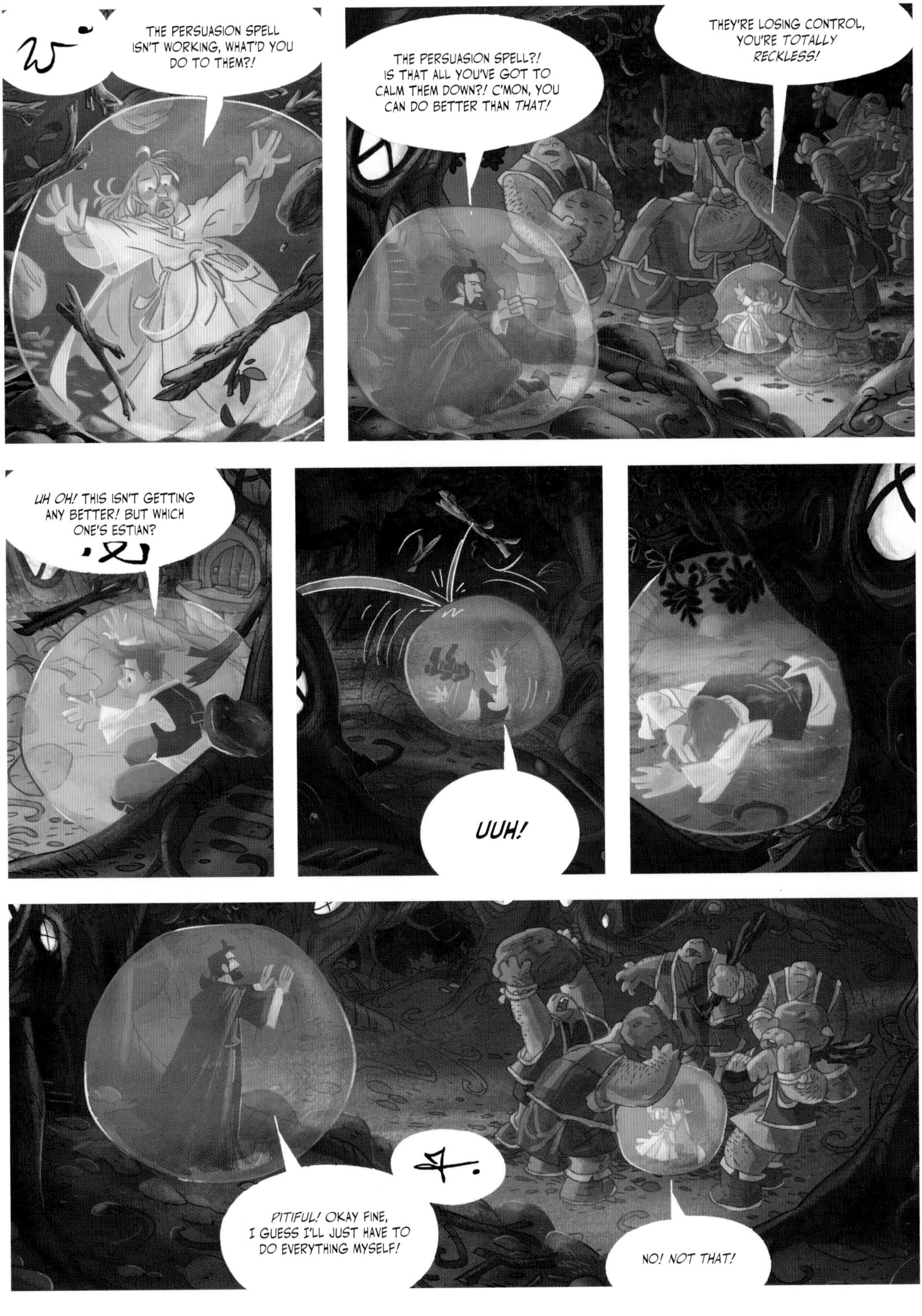
THE PERSUASION SPELL ISN'T WORKING, WHAT'D YOU DO TO THEM?!
THE PERSUASION SPELL?! IS THAT ALL YOU'VE GOT TO CALM THEM DOWN?! C'MON, YOU CAN DO BETTER THAN THAT!
THEY'RE LOSING CONTROL, YOU'RE TOTALLY RECKLESS!
UH OH! THIS ISN'T GETTING ANY BETTER! BUT WHICH ONE'S ESTIAN?
UUH!
PITIFUL! OKAY FINE, I GUESS I'LL JUST HAVE TO DO EVERYTHING MYSELF!
NO! NOT THAT!

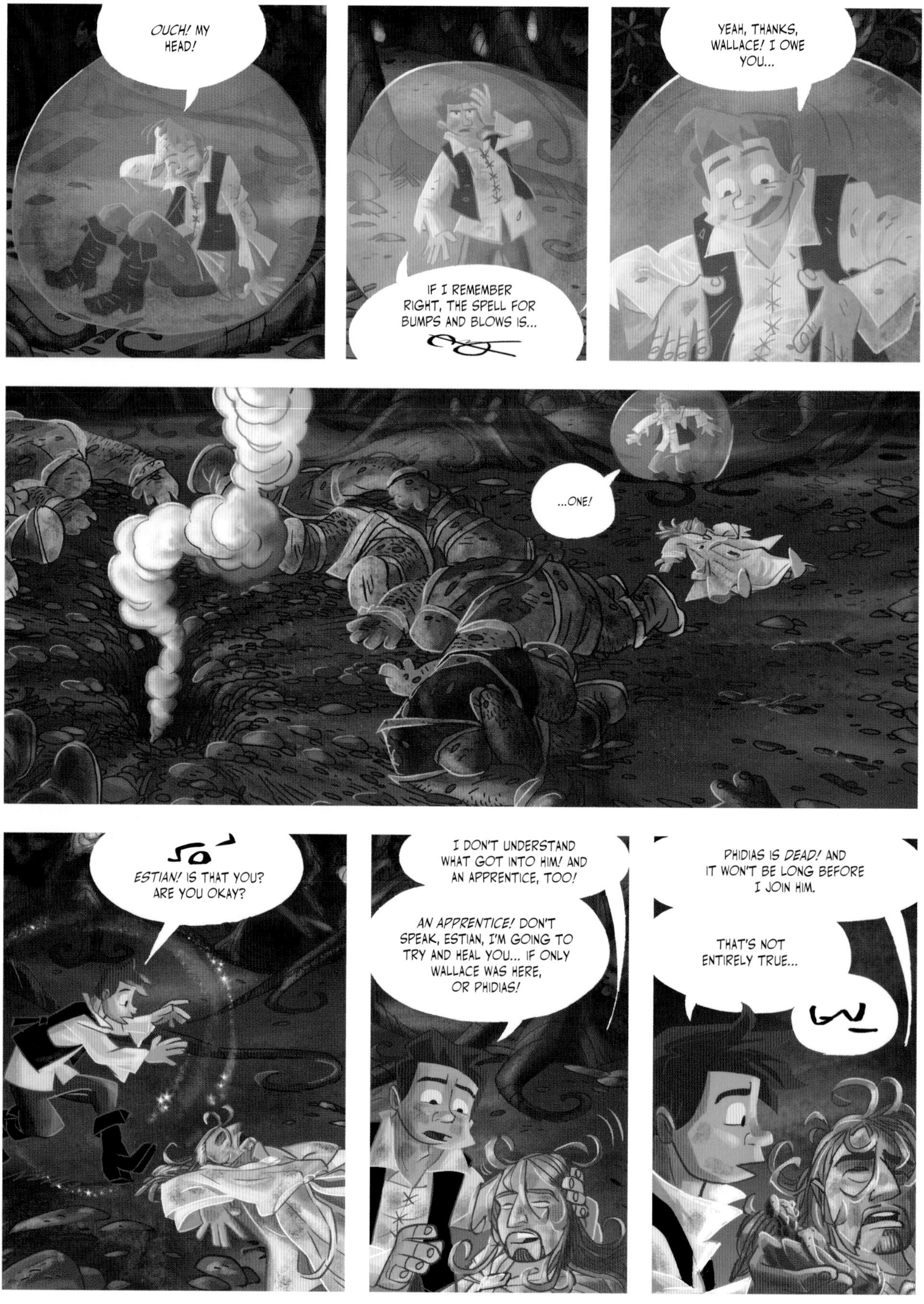
OUCH! MY HEAD!
IF I REMEMBER RIGHT, THE SPELL FOR BUMPS AND BLOWS IS...
YEAH, THANKS, WALLACE! I OWE YOU...
...ONE!
ESTIAN! IS THAT YOU? ARE YOU OKAY?
I DON'T UNDERSTAND WHAT GOT INTO HIM! AND AN APPRENTICE, TOO!
AN APPRENTICE! DON'T SPEAK, ESTIAN, I'M GOING TO TRY AND HEAL YOU... IF ONLY WALLACE WAS HERE, OR PHIDIAS!
PHIDIAS IS DEAD! AND IT WON'T BE LONG BEFORE I JOIN HIM.
THAT'S NOT ENTIRELY TRUE...

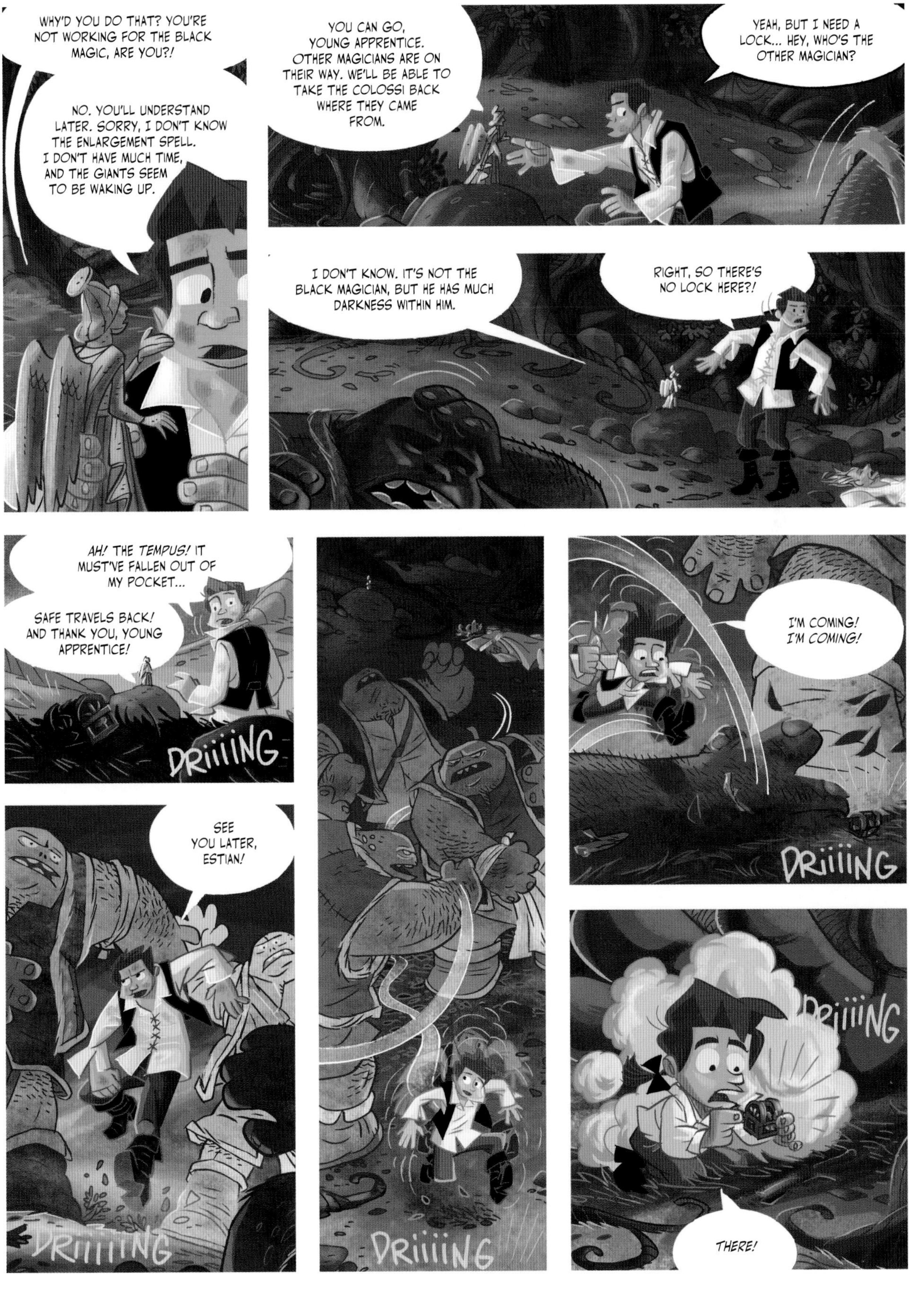
WHY'D YOU DO THAT? YOU'RE NOT WORKING FOR THE BLACK MAGIC, ARE YOU?!
NO. YOU'LL UNDERSTAND LATER. SORRY, I DON'T KNOW THE ENLARGEMENT SPELL. I DON'T HAVE MUCH TIME, AND THE GIANTS SEEM TO BE WAKING UP.
YOU CAN GO, YOUNG APPRENTICE. OTHER MAGICIANS ARE ON THEIR WAY. WE'LL BE ABLE TO TAKE THE COLOSSI BACK WHERE THEY CAME FROM.
YEAH, BUT I NEED A LOCK... HEY, WHO'S THE OTHER MAGICIAN?
I DON'T KNOW. IT'S NOT THE BLACK MAGICIAN, BUT HE HAS MUCH DARKNESS WITHIN HIM.
RIGHT, SO THERE'S NO LOCK HERE?!
AH! THE TEMPUS! IT MUST'VE FALLEN OUT OF MY POCKET...
SAFE TRAVELS BACK! AND THANK YOU, YOUNG APPRENTICE!
DRIIIING
I'M COMING! I'M COMING!
DRIIIING
SEE YOU LATER, ESTIAN!
DRIIIIING
DRIIIING
DRIIIING
THERE!

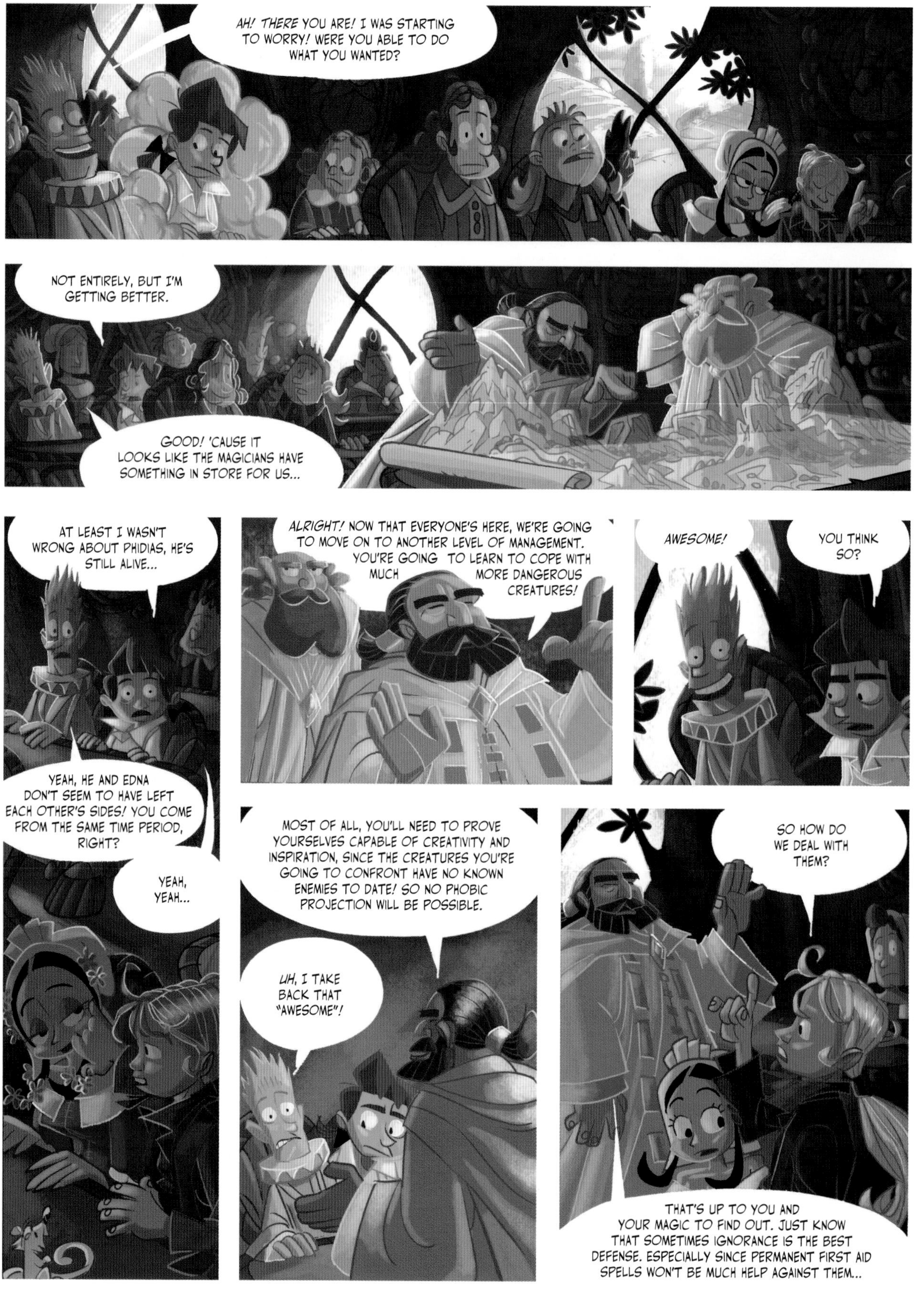
AH! THERE YOU ARE! I WAS STARTING TO WORRY! WERE YOU ABLE TO DO WHAT YOU WANTED?
NOT ENTIRELY, BUT I'M GETTING BETTER.
GOOD! 'CAUSE IT LOOKS LIKE THE MAGICIANS HAVE SOMETHING IN STORE FOR US...
AT LEAST I WASN'T WRONG ABOUT PHIDIAS, HE'S STILL ALIVE...
ALRIGHT! NOW THAT EVERYONE'S HERE, WE'RE GOING TO MOVE ON TO ANOTHER LEVEL OF MANAGEMENT. YOU'RE GOING TO LEARN TO COPE WITH MUCH MORE DANGEROUS CREATURES!
AWESOME!
YOU THINK SO?
YEAH, HE AND EDNA DON'T SEEM TO HAVE LEFT EACH OTHER'S SIDES! YOU COME FROM THE SAME TIME PERIOD, RIGHT?
YEAH, YEAH...
MOST OF ALL, YOU'LL NEED TO PROVE YOURSELVES CAPABLE OF CREATIVITY AND INSPIRATION, SINCE THE CREATURES YOU'RE GOING TO CONFRONT HAVE NO KNOWN ENEMIES TO DATE! SO NO PHOBIC PROJECTION WILL BE POSSIBLE.
UH, I TAKE BACK THAT "AWESOME"!
SO HOW DO WE DEAL WITH THEM?
THAT'S UP TO YOU AND YOUR MAGIC TO FIND OUT. JUST KNOW THAT SOMETIMES IGNORANCE IS THE BEST DEFENSE. ESPECIALLY SINCE PERMANENT FIRST AID SPELLS WON'T BE MUCH HELP AGAINST THEM...

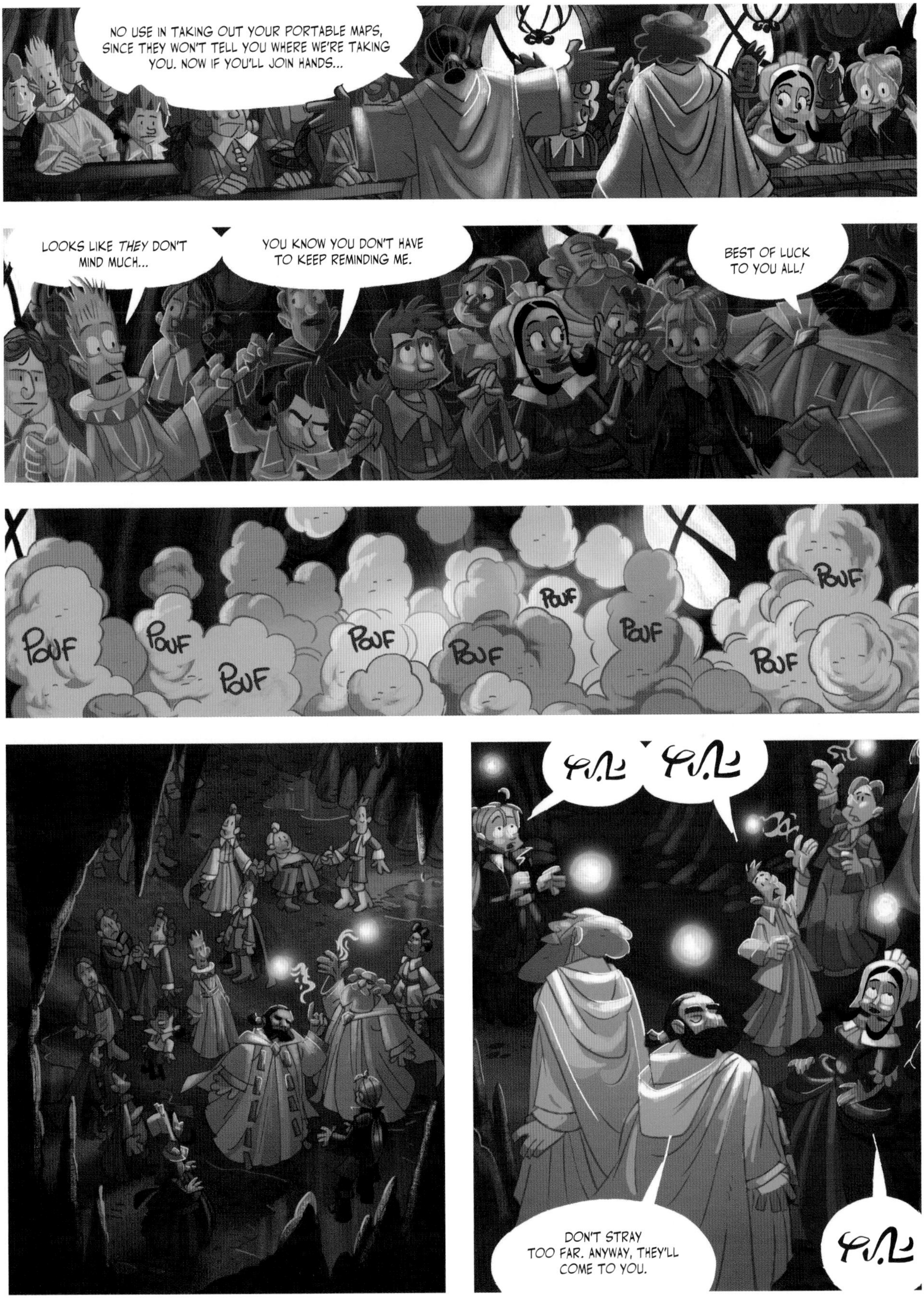
NO USE IN TAKING OUT YOUR PORTABLE MAPS, SINCE THEY WON'T TELL YOU WHERE WE'RE TAKING YOU. NOW IF YOU'LL JOIN HANDS...
LOOKS LIKE *THEY* DON'T MIND MUCH...
YOU KNOW YOU DON'T HAVE TO KEEP REMINDING ME.
BEST OF LUCK TO YOU ALL!
POUF
POUF
POUF
POUF
POUF
POUF
POUF
POUF
POUF
DON'T STRAY TOO FAR. ANYWAY, THEY'LL COME TO YOU.

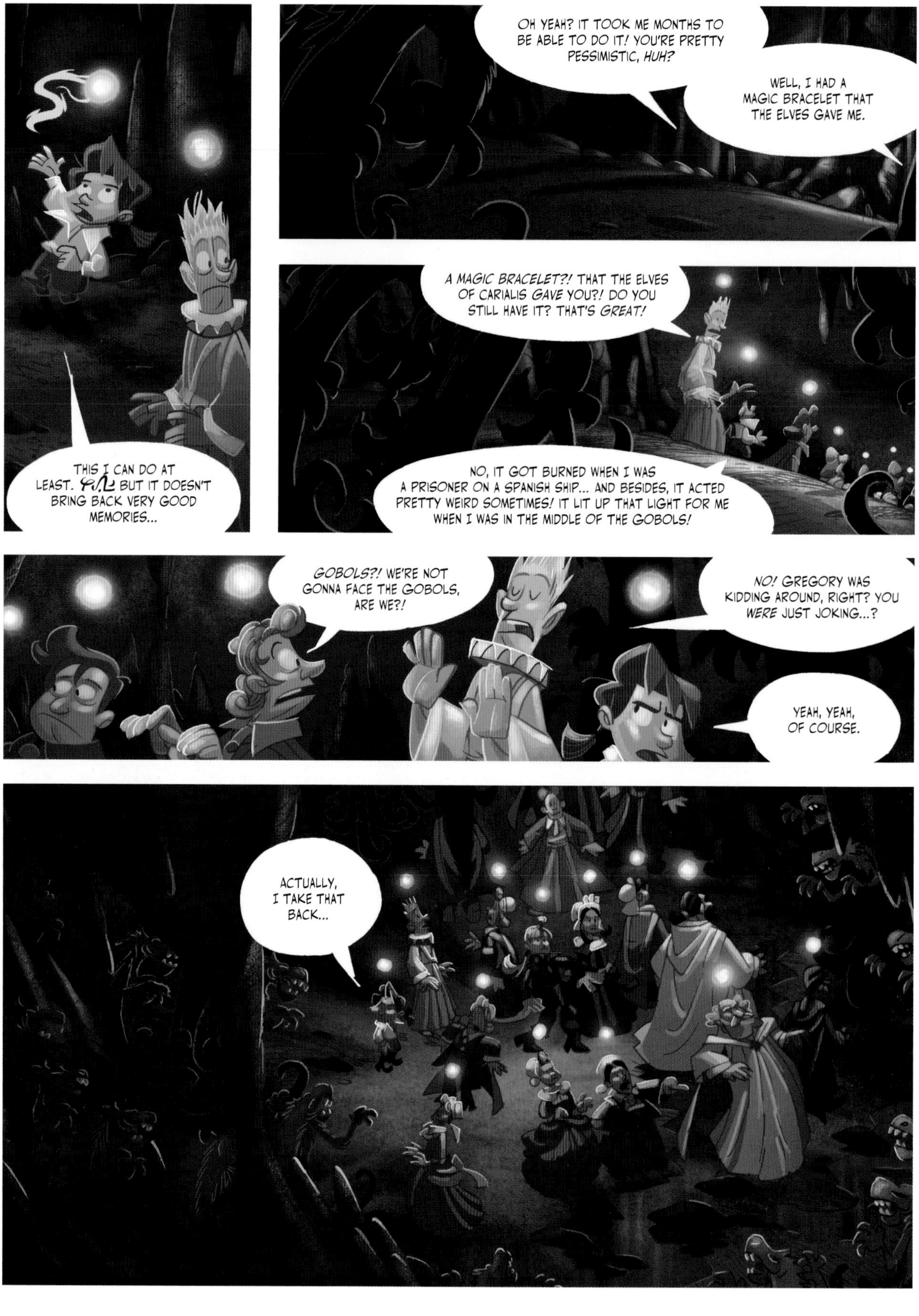
THIS I CAN DO AT LEAST. BUT IT DOESN'T BRING BACK VERY GOOD MEMORIES...
OH YEAH? IT TOOK ME MONTHS TO BE ABLE TO DO IT! YOU'RE PRETTY PESSIMISTIC, *HUH?*
WELL, I HAD A MAGIC BRACELET THAT THE ELVES GAVE ME.
A MAGIC BRACELET?! THAT THE ELVES OF CARIALIS *GAVE* YOU?! DO YOU STILL HAVE IT? THAT'S *GREAT!*
NO, IT GOT BURNED WHEN I WAS A PRISONER ON A SPANISH SHIP... AND BESIDES, IT ACTED PRETTY WEIRD SOMETIMES! IT LIT UP THAT LIGHT FOR ME WHEN I WAS IN THE MIDDLE OF THE GOBOLS!
GOBOLS?! WE'RE NOT GONNA FACE THE GOBOLS, ARE WE?!
NO! GREGORY WAS KIDDING AROUND, RIGHT? YOU *WERE* JUST JOKING...?
YEAH, YEAH, OF COURSE.
ACTUALLY, I TAKE THAT BACK...

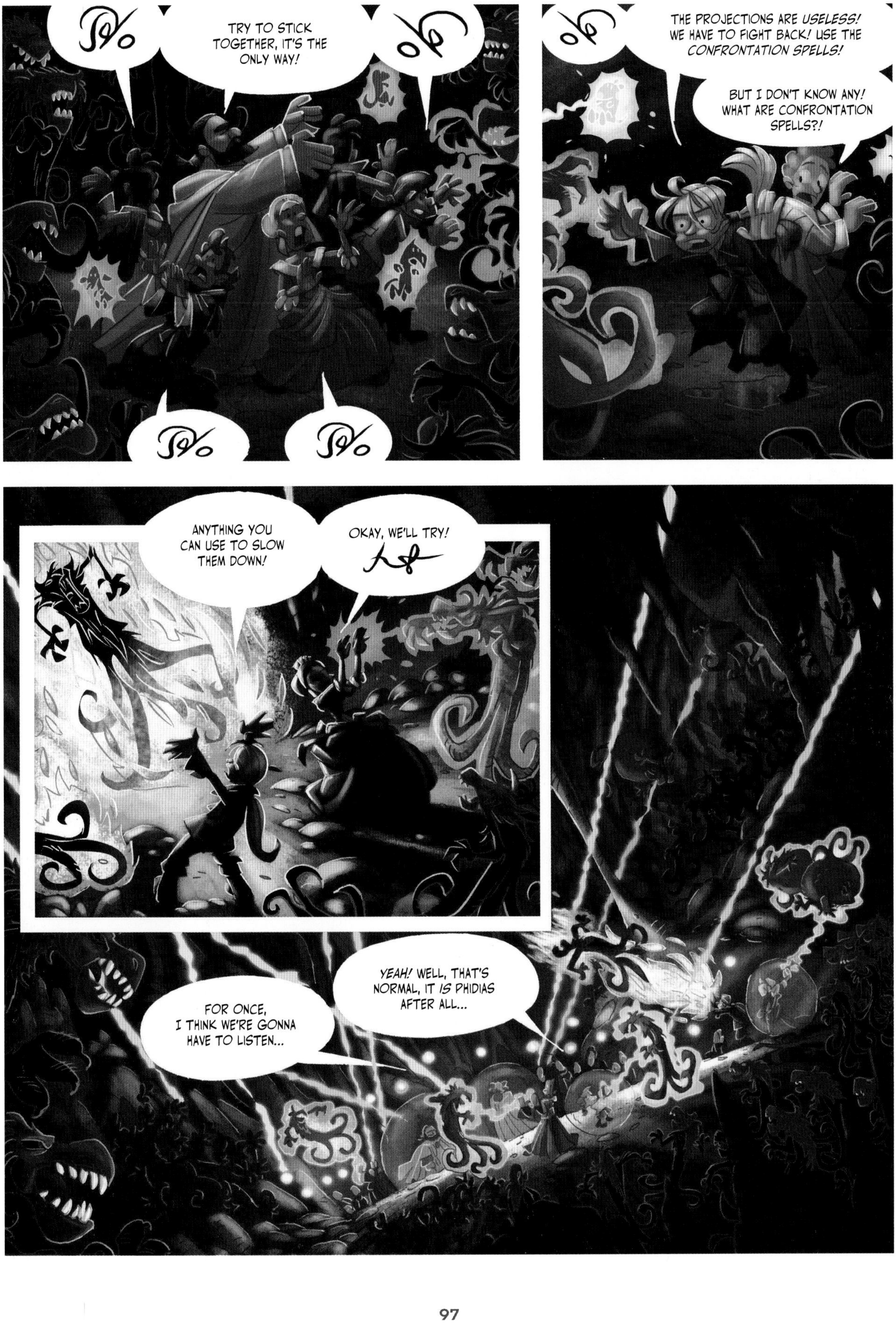
TRY TO STICK TOGETHER, IT'S THE ONLY WAY!
THE PROJECTIONS ARE USELESS! WE HAVE TO FIGHT BACK! USE THE CONFRONTATION SPELLS!
BUT I DON'T KNOW ANY! WHAT ARE CONFRONTATION SPELLS?!
ANYTHING YOU CAN USE TO SLOW THEM DOWN!
OKAY, WE'LL TRY!
YEAH! WELL, THAT'S NORMAL, IT IS PHIDIAS AFTER ALL...
FOR ONCE, I THINK WE'RE GONNA HAVE TO LISTEN...

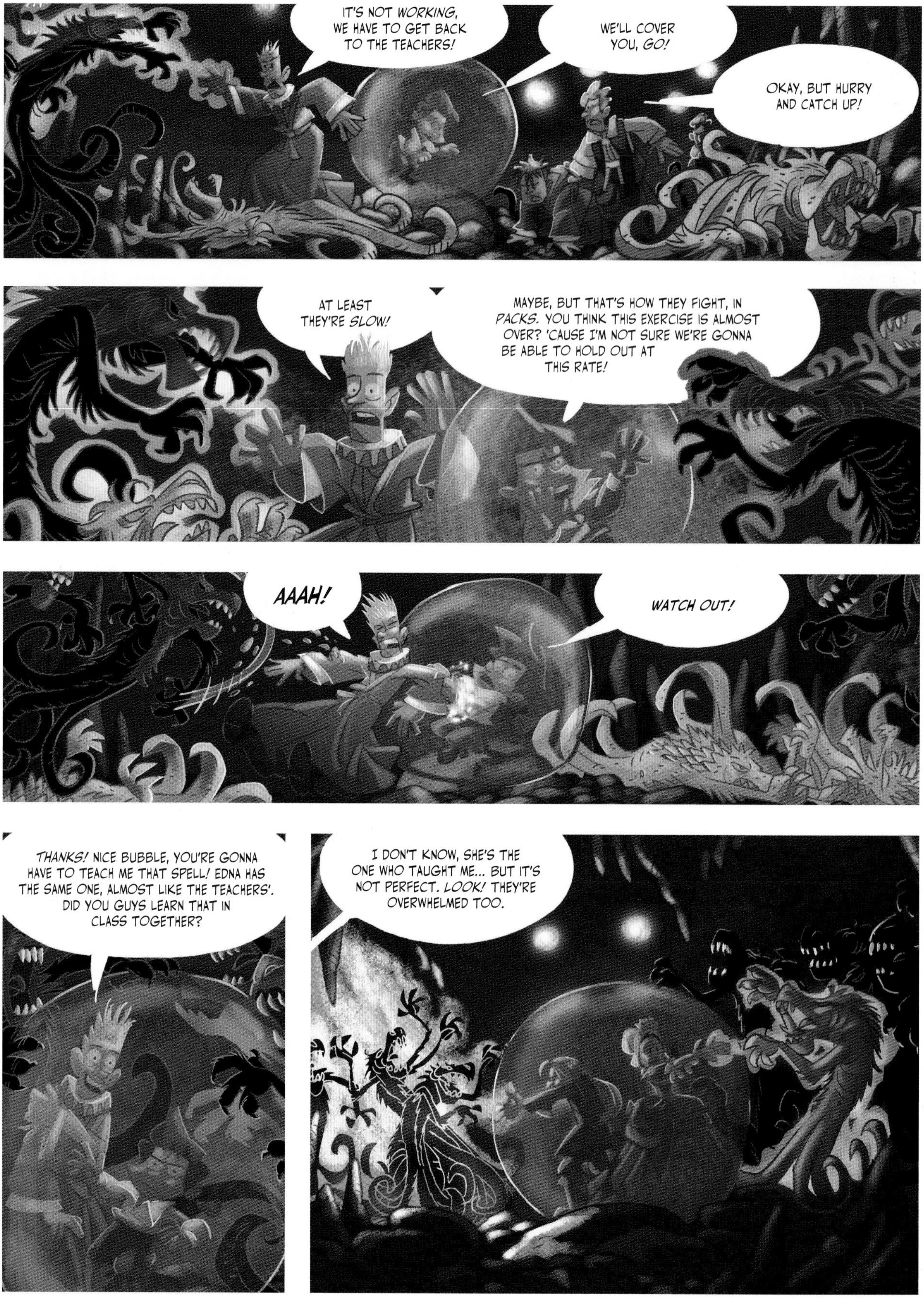
IT'S NOT *WORKING*, WE HAVE TO GET BACK TO THE TEACHERS!
WE'LL COVER YOU, *GO!*
OKAY, BUT HURRY AND CATCH UP!
AT LEAST THEY'RE *SLOW!*
MAYBE, BUT THAT'S HOW THEY FIGHT, IN *PACKS.* YOU THINK THIS EXERCISE IS ALMOST OVER? 'CAUSE I'M NOT SURE WE'RE GONNA BE ABLE TO HOLD OUT AT THIS RATE!
AAAH!
WATCH OUT!
THANKS! NICE BUBBLE, YOU'RE GONNA HAVE TO TEACH ME THAT SPELL! EDNA HAS THE SAME ONE, ALMOST LIKE THE TEACHERS'. DID YOU GUYS LEARN THAT IN CLASS TOGETHER?
I DON'T KNOW, SHE'S THE ONE WHO TAUGHT ME... BUT IT'S NOT PERFECT. *LOOK!* THEY'RE OVERWHELMED TOO.

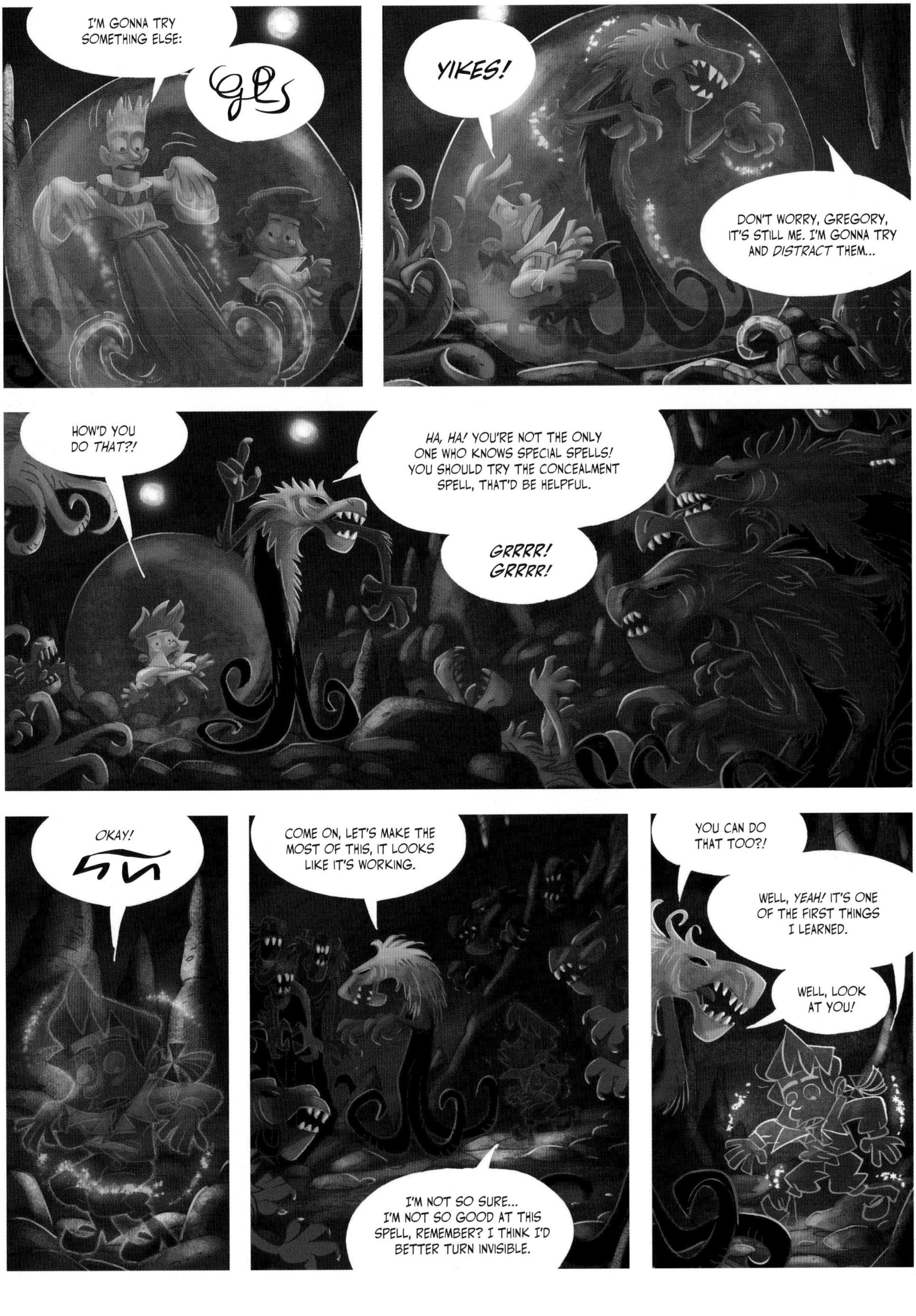
I'M GONNA TRY SOMETHING ELSE:
YIKES!
DON'T WORRY, GREGORY, IT'S STILL ME. I'M GONNA TRY AND DISTRACT THEM...
HOW'D YOU DO THAT?!
HA, HA! YOU'RE NOT THE ONLY ONE WHO KNOWS SPECIAL SPELLS! YOU SHOULD TRY THE CONCEALMENT SPELL, THAT'D BE HELPFUL.
GRRRR! GRRRR!
OKAY!
COME ON, LET'S MAKE THE MOST OF THIS, IT LOOKS LIKE IT'S WORKING.
I'M NOT SO SURE... I'M NOT SO GOOD AT THIS SPELL, REMEMBER? I THINK I'D BETTER TURN INVISIBLE.
YOU CAN DO THAT TOO?!
WELL, YEAH! IT'S ONE OF THE FIRST THINGS I LEARNED.
WELL, LOOK AT YOU!

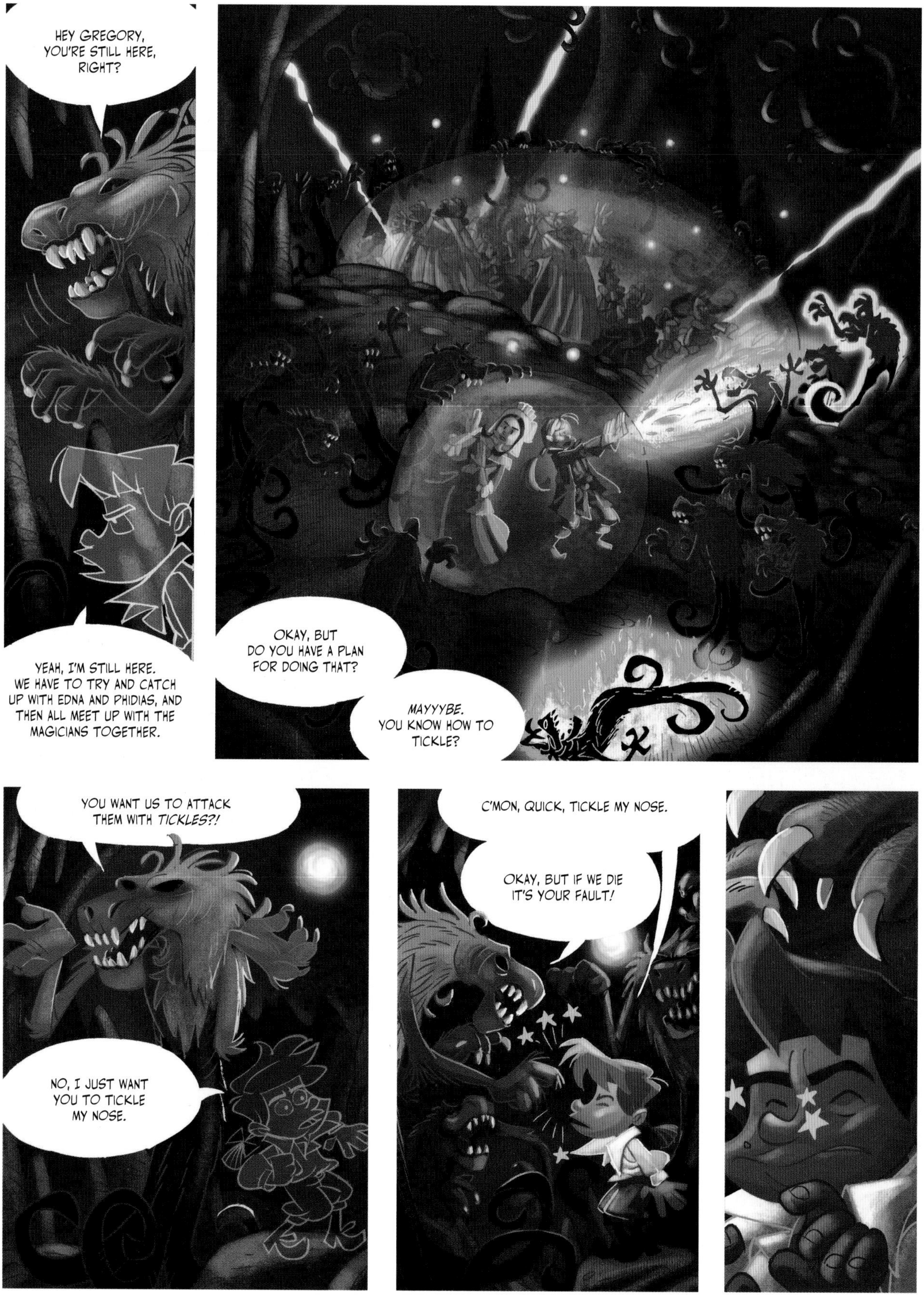
HEY GREGORY, YOU'RE STILL HERE, RIGHT?
YEAH, I'M STILL HERE. WE HAVE TO TRY AND CATCH UP WITH EDNA AND PHIDIAS, AND THEN ALL MEET UP WITH THE MAGICIANS TOGETHER.
OKAY, BUT DO YOU HAVE A PLAN FOR DOING THAT?
MAYYYBE. YOU KNOW HOW TO TICKLE?
YOU WANT US TO ATTACK THEM WITH TICKLES?!
NO, I JUST WANT YOU TO TICKLE MY NOSE.
C'MON, QUICK, TICKLE MY NOSE.
OKAY, BUT IF WE DIE IT'S YOUR FAULT!

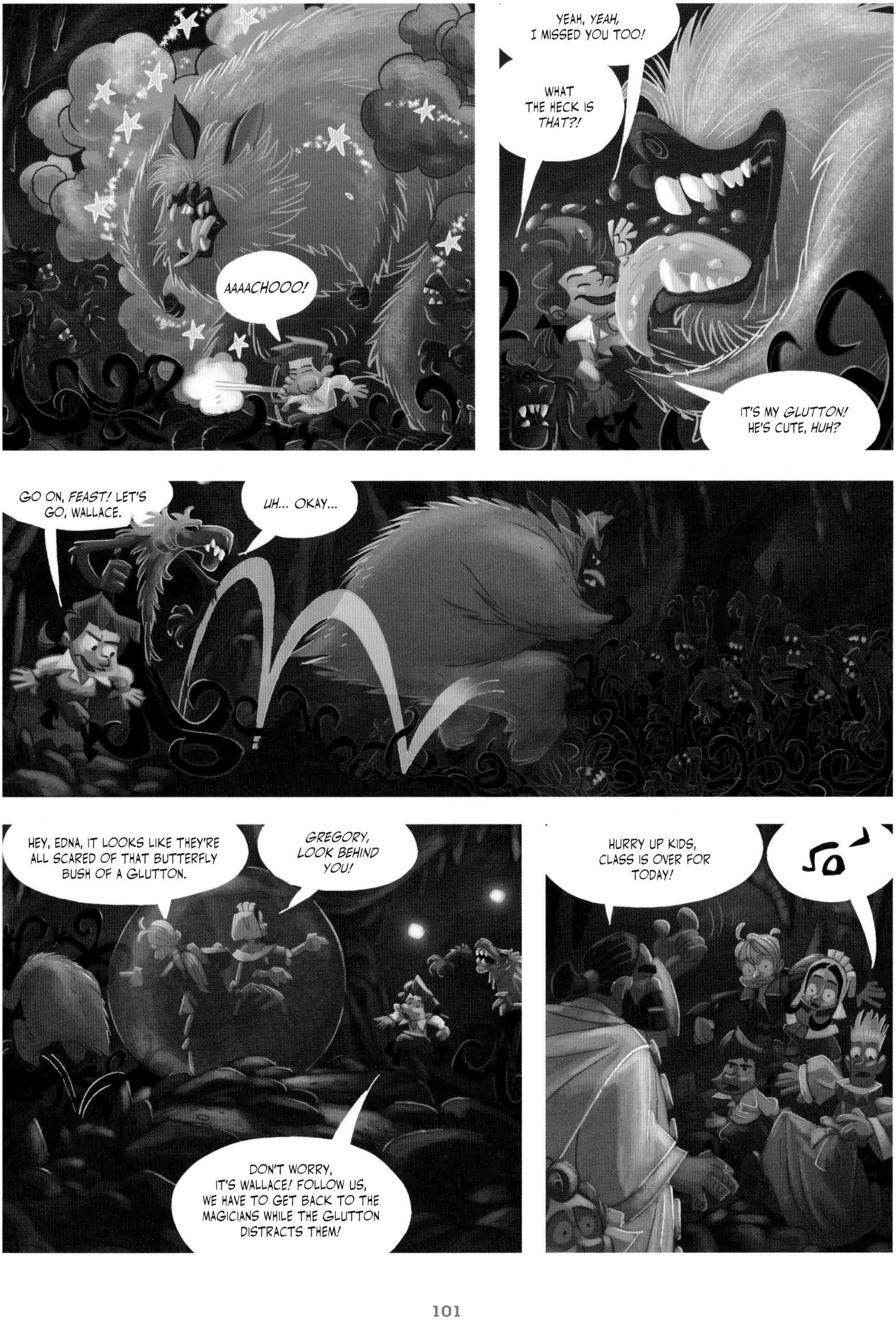
AAAACHOOO!
YEAH, *YEAH,* I MISSED YOU TOO!
WHAT THE HECK IS *THAT?!*
IT'S MY *GLUTTON!* HE'S CUTE, *HUH?*
GO ON, *FEAST!* LET'S GO, WALLACE.
UH... OKAY...
HEY, EDNA, IT LOOKS LIKE THEY'RE ALL SCARED OF THAT BUTTERFLY BUSH OF A GLUTTON.
GREGORY, LOOK BEHIND YOU!
DON'T WORRY, IT'S WALLACE! FOLLOW US, WE HAVE TO GET BACK TO THE MAGICIANS WHILE THE GLUTTON DISTRACTS THEM!
HURRY UP KIDS, CLASS IS OVER FOR TODAY!

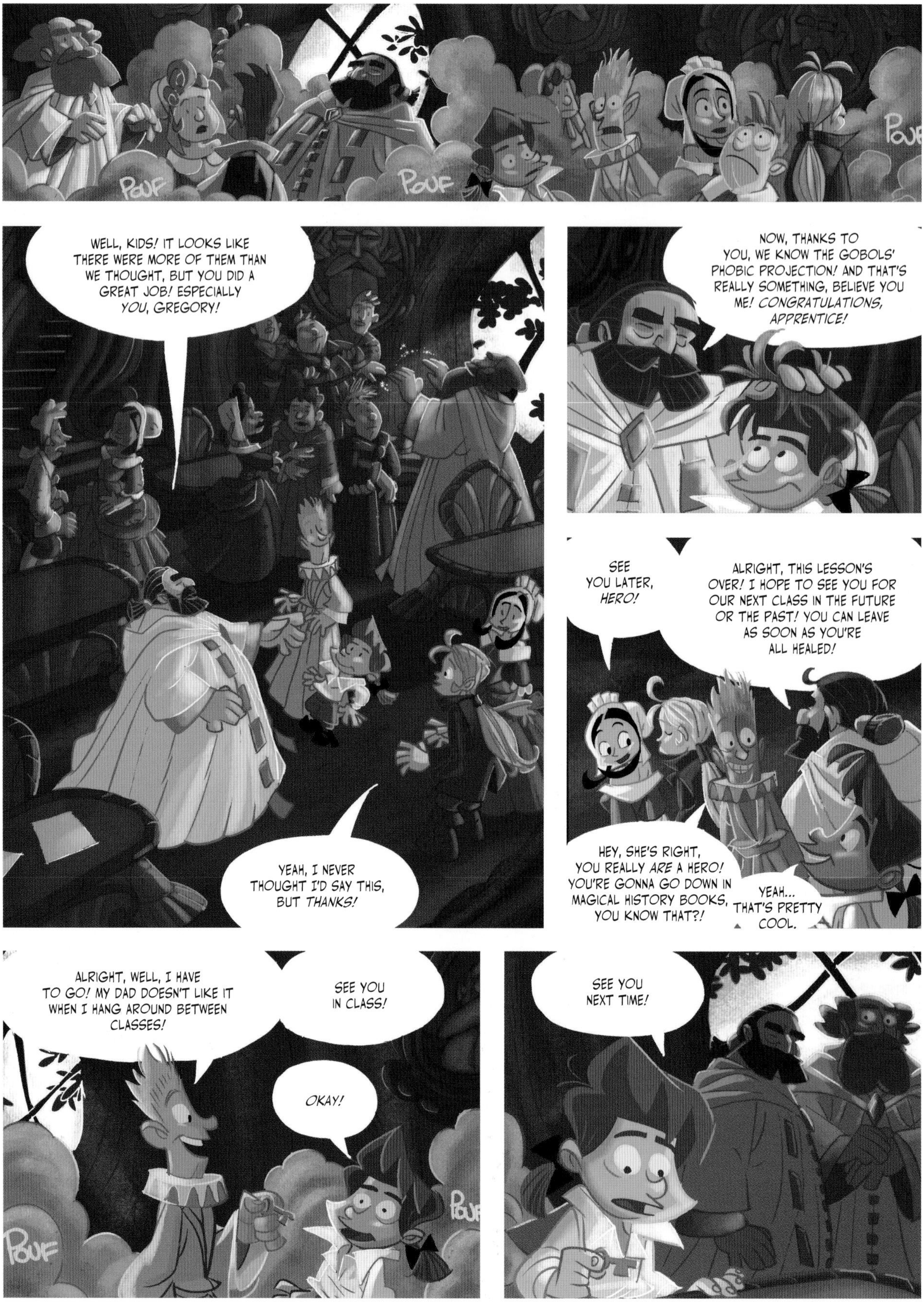
POUF
POUF
POUF
WELL, KIDS! IT LOOKS LIKE THERE WERE MORE OF THEM THAN WE THOUGHT, BUT YOU DID A GREAT JOB! ESPECIALLY YOU, GREGORY!
YEAH, I NEVER THOUGHT I'D SAY THIS, BUT THANKS!
NOW, THANKS TO YOU, WE KNOW THE GOBOLS' PHOBIC PROJECTION! AND THAT'S REALLY SOMETHING, BELIEVE YOU ME! CONGRATULATIONS, APPRENTICE!
SEE YOU LATER, HERO!
ALRIGHT, THIS LESSON'S OVER! I HOPE TO SEE YOU FOR OUR NEXT CLASS IN THE FUTURE OR THE PAST! YOU CAN LEAVE AS SOON AS YOU'RE ALL HEALED!
HEY, SHE'S RIGHT, YOU REALLY ARE A HERO! YOU'RE GONNA GO DOWN IN MAGICAL HISTORY BOOKS, YOU KNOW THAT?!
YEAH... THAT'S PRETTY COOL.
ALRIGHT, WELL, I HAVE TO GO! MY DAD DOESN'T LIKE IT WHEN I HANG AROUND BETWEEN CLASSES!
SEE YOU IN CLASS!
OKAY!
POUF
POUF
SEE YOU NEXT TIME!

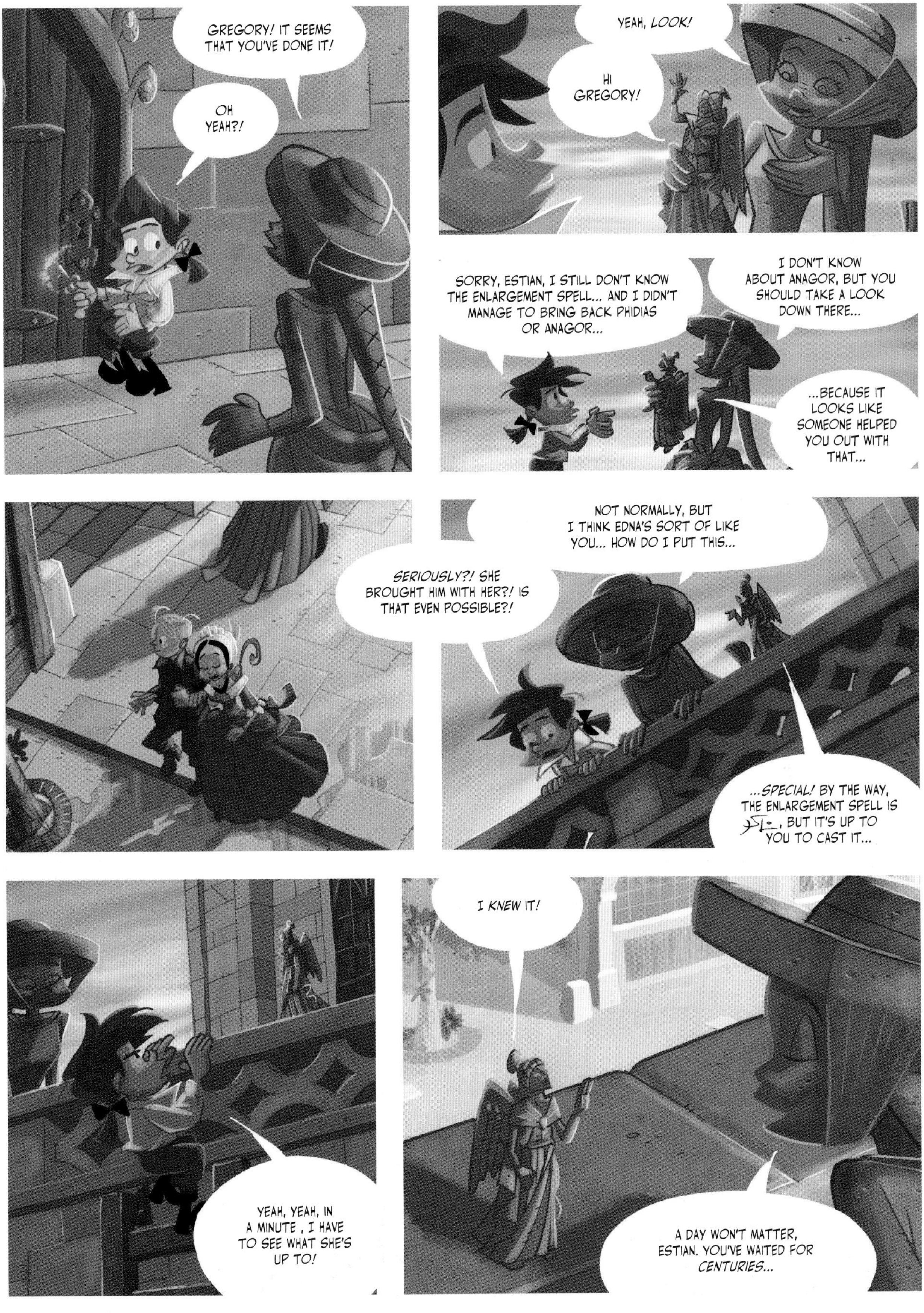
GREGORY! IT SEEMS THAT YOU'VE DONE IT!
OH YEAH?!
YEAH, *LOOK!*
HI GREGORY!
SORRY, ESTIAN, I STILL DON'T KNOW THE ENLARGEMENT SPELL... AND I DIDN'T MANAGE TO BRING BACK PHIDIAS OR ANAGOR...
I DON'T KNOW ABOUT ANAGOR, BUT YOU SHOULD TAKE A LOOK DOWN THERE...
...BECAUSE IT LOOKS LIKE SOMEONE HELPED YOU OUT WITH THAT...
SERIOUSLY?! SHE BROUGHT HIM WITH HER?! IS THAT EVEN POSSIBLE?!
NOT NORMALLY, BUT I THINK EDNA'S SORT OF LIKE YOU... HOW DO I PUT THIS...
...*SPECIAL!* BY THE WAY, THE ENLARGEMENT SPELL IS , BUT IT'S UP TO YOU TO CAST IT...
YEAH, YEAH, IN A MINUTE , I HAVE TO SEE WHAT SHE'S UP TO!
I *KNEW* IT!
A DAY WON'T MATTER, ESTIAN. YOU'VE WAITED FOR *CENTURIES*...

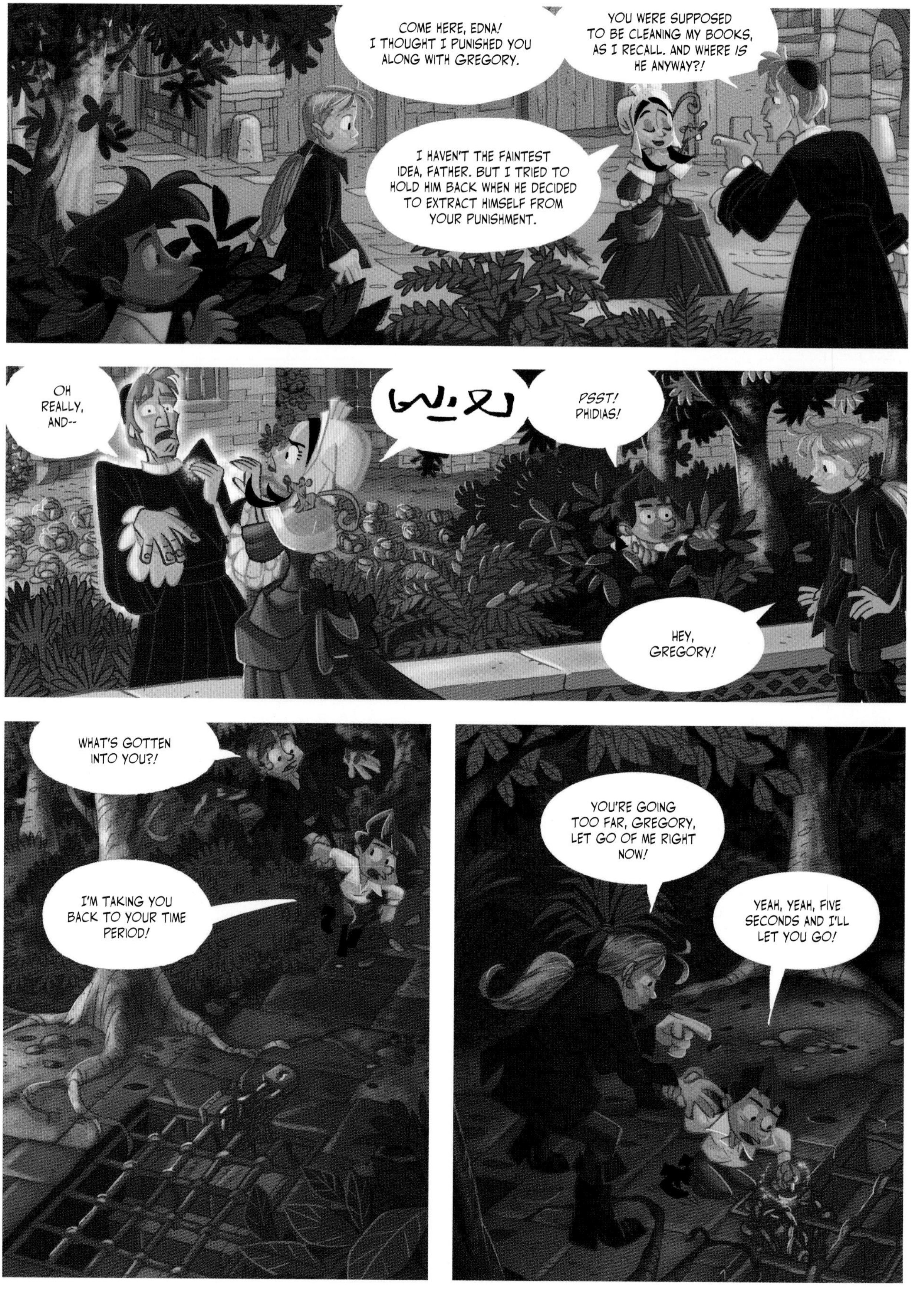
COME HERE, EDNA! I THOUGHT I PUNISHED YOU ALONG WITH GREGORY.
YOU WERE SUPPOSED TO BE CLEANING MY BOOKS, AS I RECALL. AND WHERE *IS* HE ANYWAY?!
I HAVEN'T THE FAINTEST IDEA, FATHER. BUT I TRIED TO HOLD HIM BACK WHEN HE DECIDED TO EXTRACT HIMSELF FROM YOUR PUNISHMENT.
OH REALLY, AND--
PSST! PHIDIAS!
HEY, GREGORY!
WHAT'S GOTTEN INTO YOU?!
I'M TAKING YOU BACK TO YOUR TIME PERIOD!
YOU'RE GOING TOO FAR, GREGORY, LET GO OF ME RIGHT NOW!
YEAH, YEAH, FIVE SECONDS AND I'LL LET YOU GO!

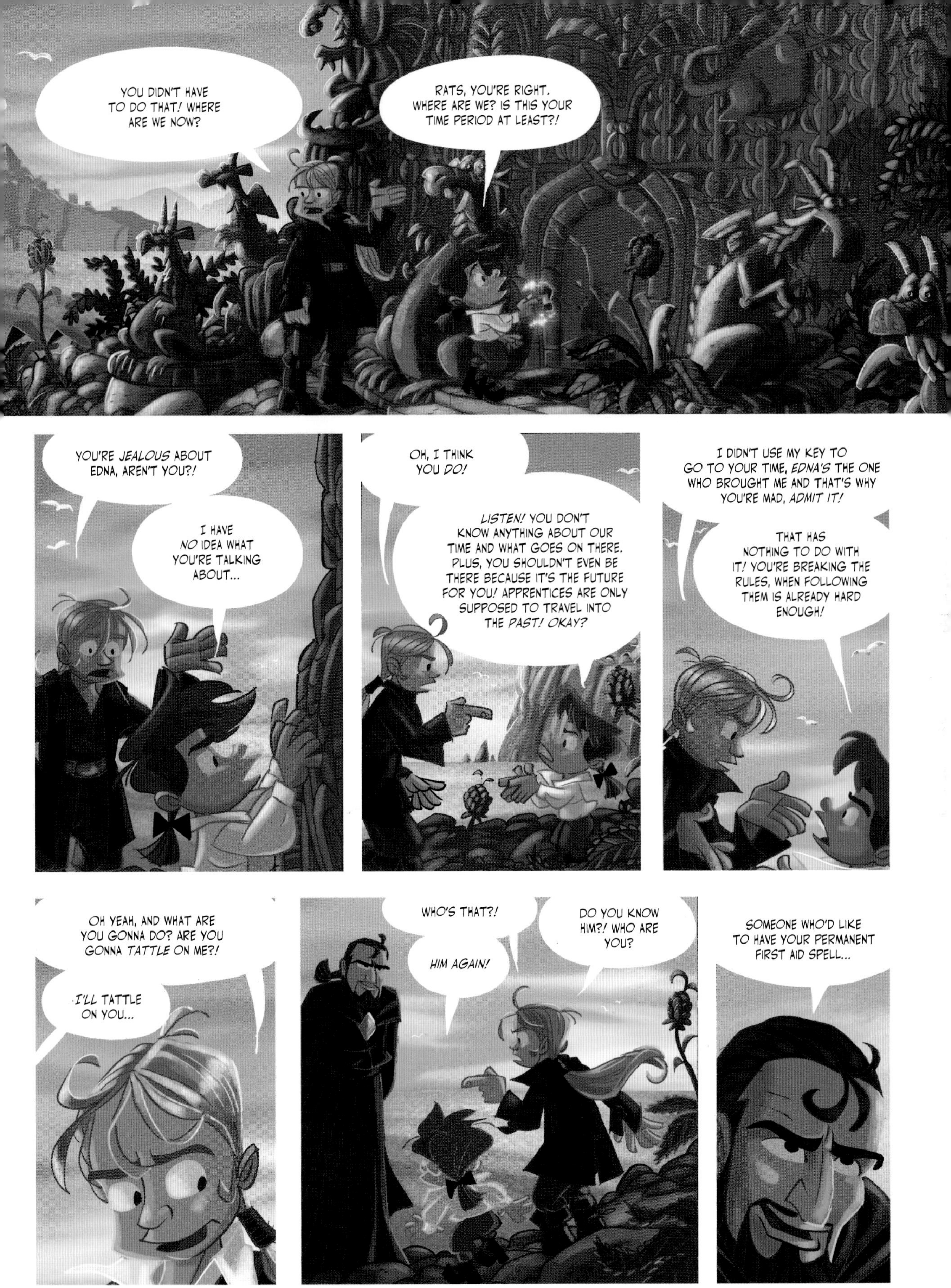
YOU DIDN'T HAVE TO DO THAT! WHERE ARE WE NOW?
RATS, YOU'RE RIGHT. WHERE ARE WE? IS THIS YOUR TIME PERIOD AT LEAST?!
YOU'RE *JEALOUS* ABOUT EDNA, AREN'T YOU?!
I HAVE *NO* IDEA WHAT YOU'RE TALKING ABOUT...
OH, I THINK YOU *DO!*
LISTEN! YOU DON'T KNOW ANYTHING ABOUT OUR TIME AND WHAT GOES ON THERE. PLUS, YOU SHOULDN'T EVEN BE THERE BECAUSE IT'S THE FUTURE FOR YOU! APPRENTICES ARE ONLY SUPPOSED TO TRAVEL INTO THE *PAST! OKAY?*
I DIDN'T USE MY KEY TO GO TO YOUR TIME, *EDNA'S* THE ONE WHO BROUGHT ME AND THAT'S WHY YOU'RE MAD, *ADMIT IT!*
THAT HAS NOTHING TO DO WITH IT! YOU'RE BREAKING THE RULES, WHEN FOLLOWING THEM IS ALREADY HARD ENOUGH!
OH YEAH, AND WHAT ARE YOU GONNA DO? ARE YOU GONNA *TATTLE* ON ME?!
I'LL TATTLE ON YOU...
WHO'S THAT?!
HIM AGAIN!
DO YOU KNOW HIM?! WHO ARE YOU?
SOMEONE WHO'D LIKE TO HAVE YOUR PERMANENT FIRST AID SPELL...

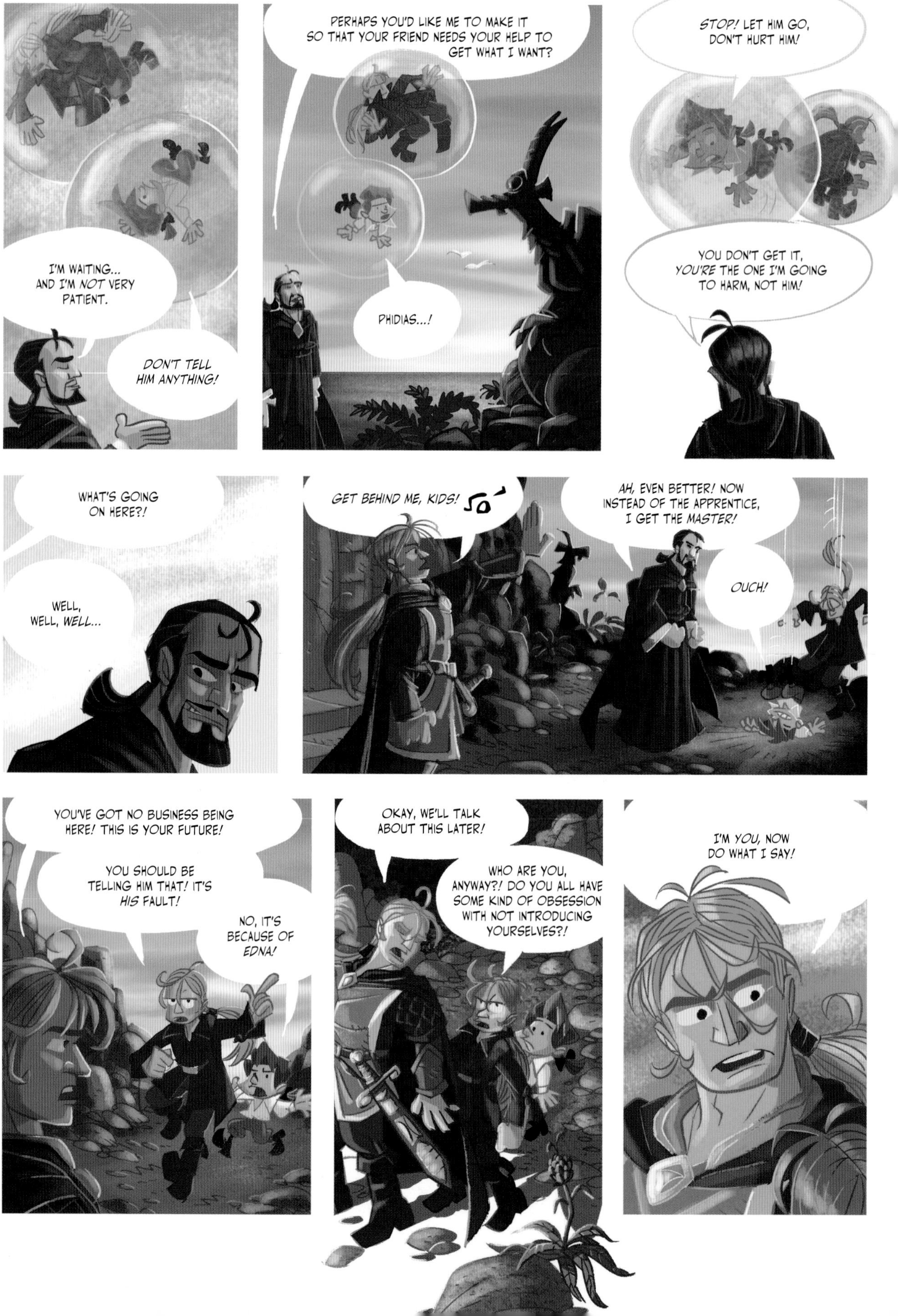
I'M WAITING... AND I'M *NOT* VERY PATIENT.
DON'T TELL HIM ANYTHING!
PERHAPS YOU'D LIKE ME TO MAKE IT SO THAT YOUR FRIEND NEEDS YOUR HELP TO GET WHAT I WANT?
PHIDIAS...!
STOP! LET HIM GO, DON'T HURT HIM!
YOU DON'T GET IT, *YOU'RE* THE ONE I'M GOING TO HARM, NOT HIM!
WHAT'S GOING ON HERE?!
WELL, WELL, *WELL*...
GET BEHIND ME, KIDS!
AH, EVEN BETTER! NOW INSTEAD OF THE APPRENTICE, I GET THE *MASTER!*
OUCH!
YOU'VE GOT NO BUSINESS BEING HERE! THIS IS YOUR FUTURE!
YOU SHOULD BE TELLING HIM THAT! IT'S *HIS* FAULT!
NO, IT'S BECAUSE OF *EDNA!*
OKAY, WE'LL TALK ABOUT THIS LATER!
WHO ARE YOU, ANYWAY?! DO YOU ALL HAVE SOME KIND OF OBSESSION WITH NOT INTRODUCING YOURSELVES?!
I'M *YOU*, NOW DO WHAT I SAY!

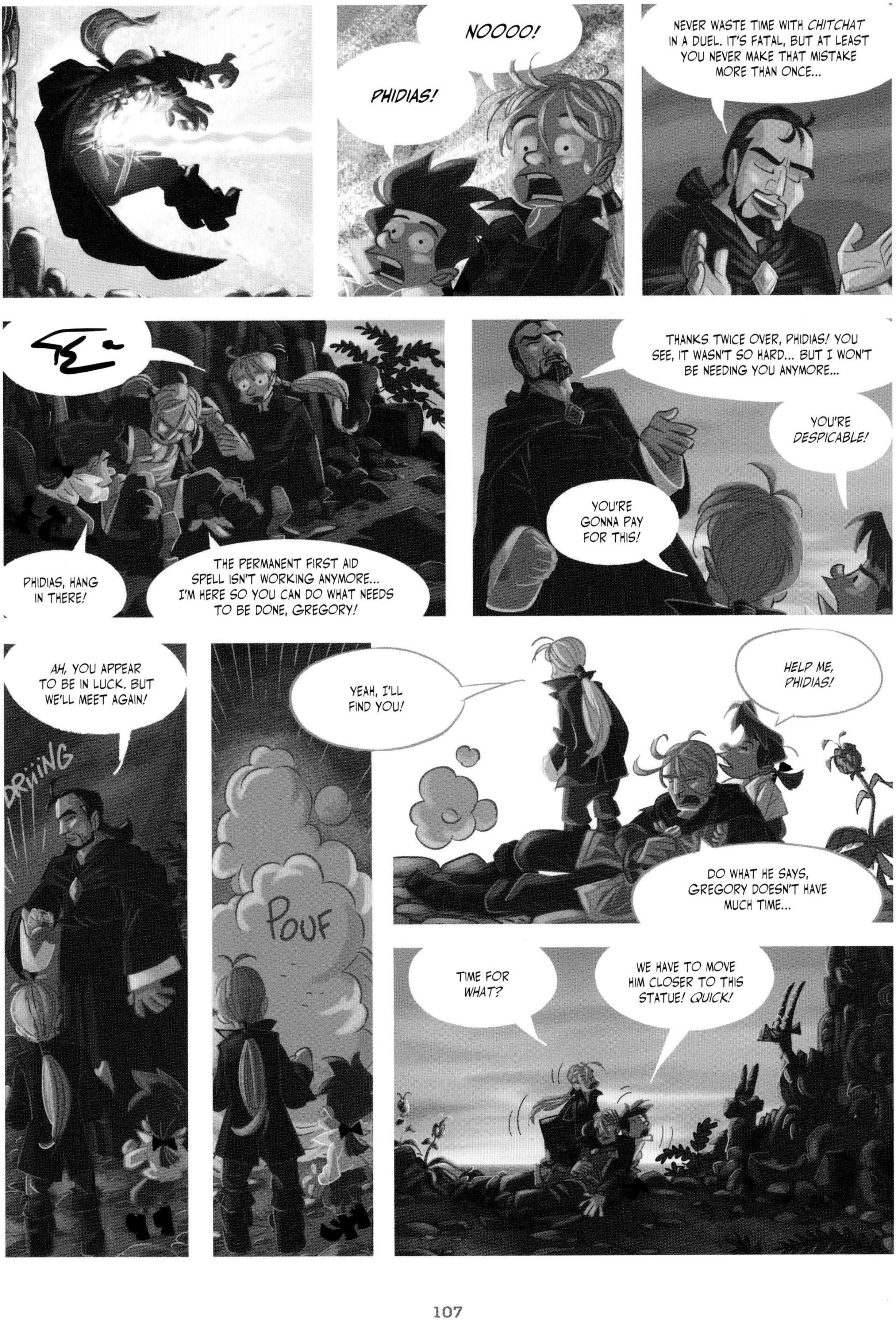
NOOOO!
PHIDIAS!
NEVER WASTE TIME WITH CHITCHAT IN A DUEL. IT'S FATAL, BUT AT LEAST YOU NEVER MAKE THAT MISTAKE MORE THAN ONCE...
PHIDIAS, HANG IN THERE!
THE PERMANENT FIRST AID SPELL ISN'T WORKING ANYMORE... I'M HERE SO YOU CAN DO WHAT NEEDS TO BE DONE, GREGORY!
THANKS TWICE OVER, PHIDIAS! YOU SEE, IT WASN'T SO HARD... BUT I WON'T BE NEEDING YOU ANYMORE...
YOU'RE DESPICABLE!
YOU'RE GONNA PAY FOR THIS!
AH, YOU APPEAR TO BE IN LUCK. BUT WE'LL MEET AGAIN!
DRiiiNG
POUF
YEAH, I'LL FIND YOU!
HELP ME, PHIDIAS!
DO WHAT HE SAYS, GREGORY DOESN'T HAVE MUCH TIME...
TIME FOR WHAT?
WE HAVE TO MOVE HIM CLOSER TO THIS STATUE! QUICK!

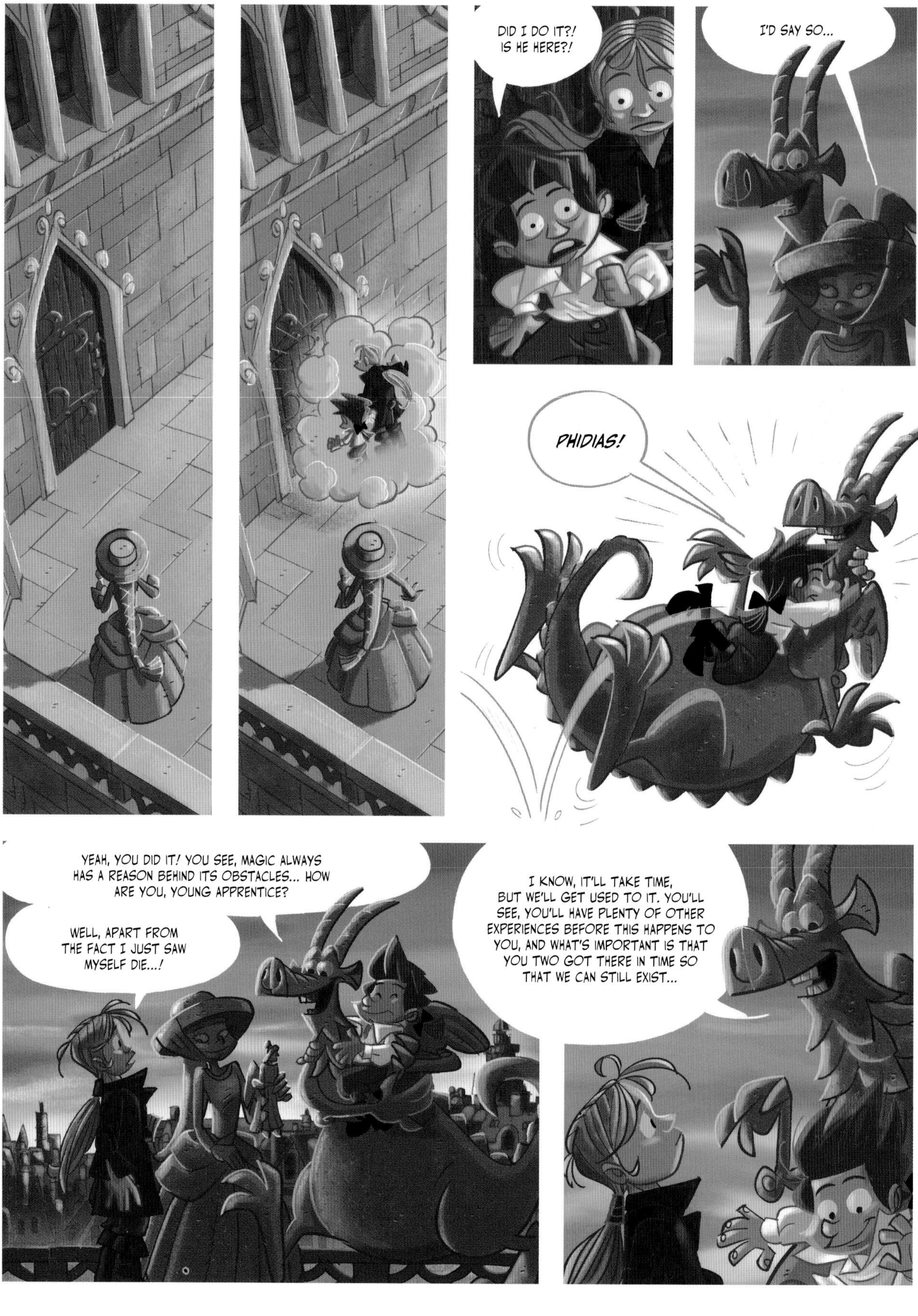
DID I DO IT?! IS HE HERE?!
I'D SAY SO...
PHIDIAS!
YEAH, YOU DID IT! YOU SEE, MAGIC ALWAYS HAS A REASON BEHIND ITS OBSTACLES... HOW ARE YOU, YOUNG APPRENTICE?
WELL, APART FROM THE FACT I JUST SAW MYSELF DIE...!
I KNOW, IT'LL TAKE TIME, BUT WE'LL GET USED TO IT. YOU'LL SEE, YOU'LL HAVE PLENTY OF OTHER EXPERIENCES BEFORE THIS HAPPENS TO YOU, AND WHAT'S IMPORTANT IS THAT YOU TWO GOT THERE IN TIME SO THAT WE CAN STILL EXIST...

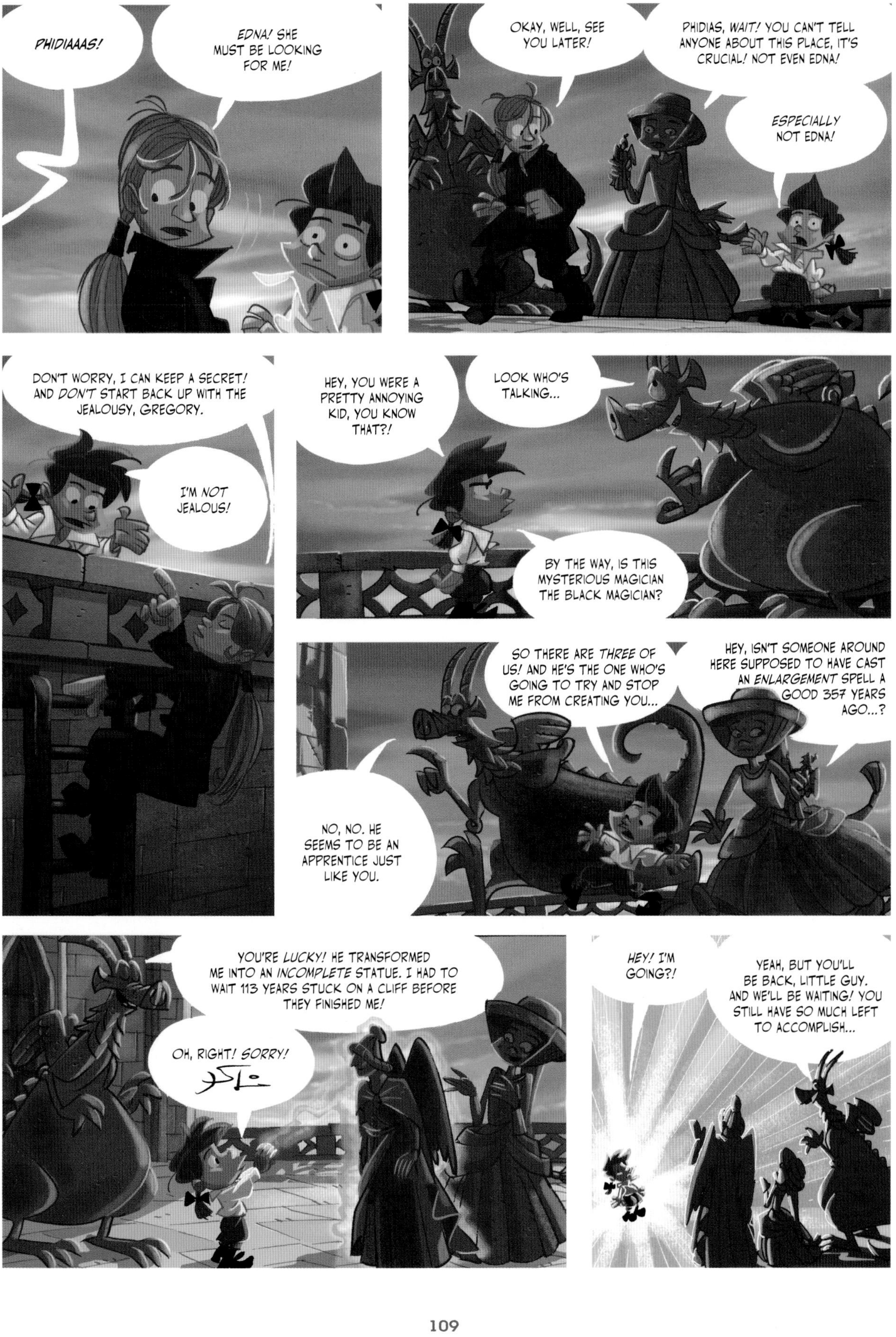
PHIDIAAAS!
EDNA! SHE MUST BE LOOKING FOR ME!
OKAY, WELL, SEE YOU LATER!
PHIDIAS, WAIT! YOU CAN'T TELL ANYONE ABOUT THIS PLACE, IT'S CRUCIAL! NOT EVEN EDNA!
ESPECIALLY NOT EDNA!
DON'T WORRY, I CAN KEEP A SECRET! AND DON'T START BACK UP WITH THE JEALOUSY, GREGORY.
I'M NOT JEALOUS!
HEY, YOU WERE A PRETTY ANNOYING KID, YOU KNOW THAT?!
LOOK WHO'S TALKING...
BY THE WAY, IS THIS MYSTERIOUS MAGICIAN THE BLACK MAGICIAN?
NO, NO. HE SEEMS TO BE AN APPRENTICE JUST LIKE YOU.
SO THERE ARE THREE OF US! AND HE'S THE ONE WHO'S GOING TO TRY AND STOP ME FROM CREATING YOU...
HEY, ISN'T SOMEONE AROUND HERE SUPPOSED TO HAVE CAST AN ENLARGEMENT SPELL A GOOD 357 YEARS AGO...?
YOU'RE LUCKY! HE TRANSFORMED ME INTO AN INCOMPLETE STATUE. I HAD TO WAIT 113 YEARS STUCK ON A CLIFF BEFORE THEY FINISHED ME!
OH, RIGHT! SORRY!
HEY! I'M GOING?!
YEAH, BUT YOU'LL BE BACK, LITTLE GUY. AND WE'LL BE WAITING! YOU STILL HAVE SO MUCH LEFT TO ACCOMPLISH...

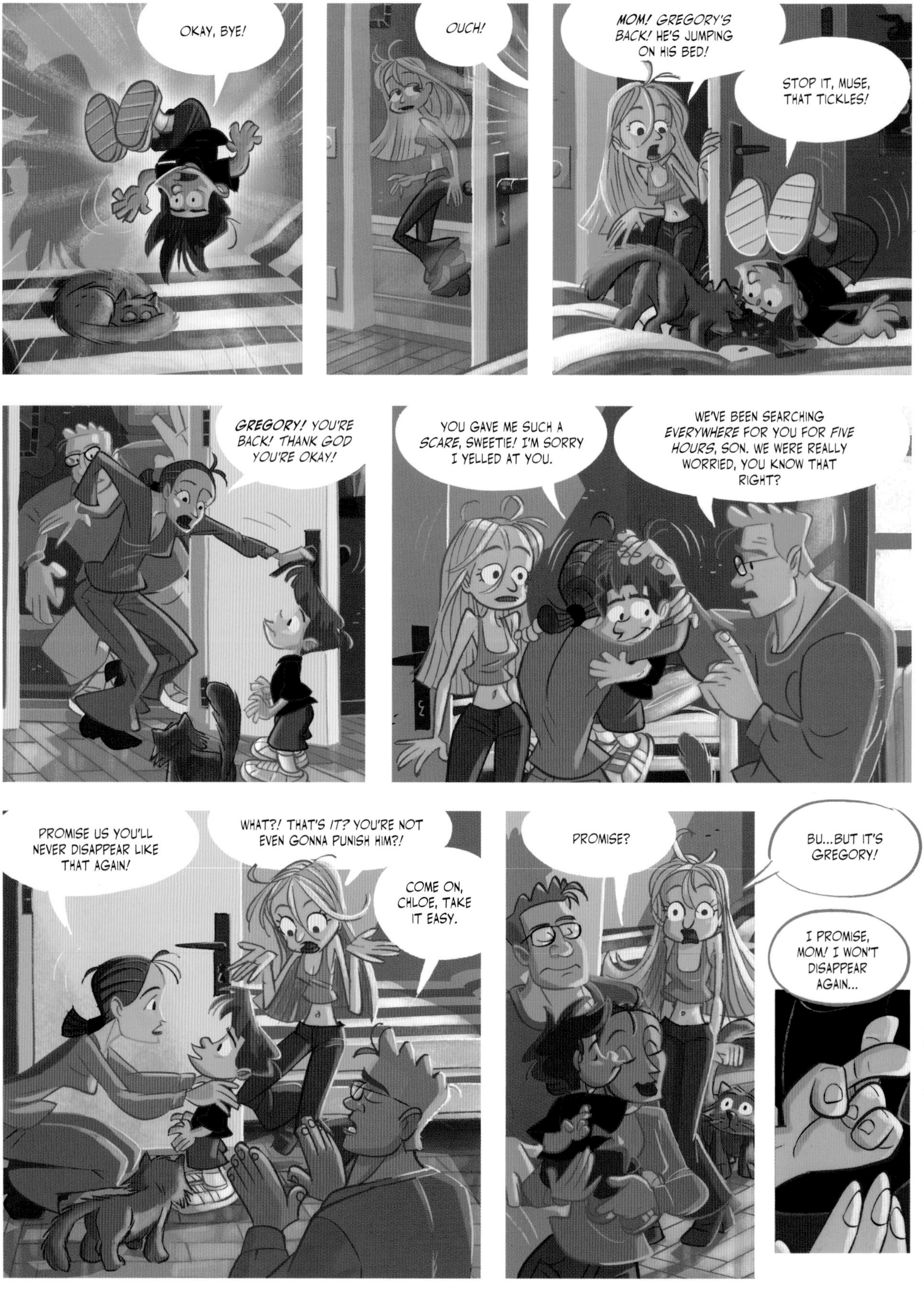
OKAY, BYE!
OUCH!
MOM! GREGORY'S BACK! HE'S JUMPING ON HIS BED!
STOP IT, MUSE, THAT TICKLES!
GREGORY! YOU'RE BACK! THANK GOD YOU'RE OKAY!
YOU GAVE ME SUCH A SCARE, SWEETIE! I'M SORRY I YELLED AT YOU.
WE'VE BEEN SEARCHING EVERYWHERE FOR YOU FOR FIVE HOURS, SON. WE WERE REALLY WORRIED, YOU KNOW THAT RIGHT?
PROMISE US YOU'LL NEVER DISAPPEAR LIKE THAT AGAIN!
WHAT?! THAT'S IT? YOU'RE NOT EVEN GONNA PUNISH HIM?!
COME ON, CHLOE, TAKE IT EASY.
PROMISE?
BU...BUT IT'S GREGORY!
I PROMISE, MOM! I WON'T DISAPPEAR AGAIN...

THE ADVENTURE WRAPS UP IN
GREGORY AND THE GARGOYLES BOOK 3!

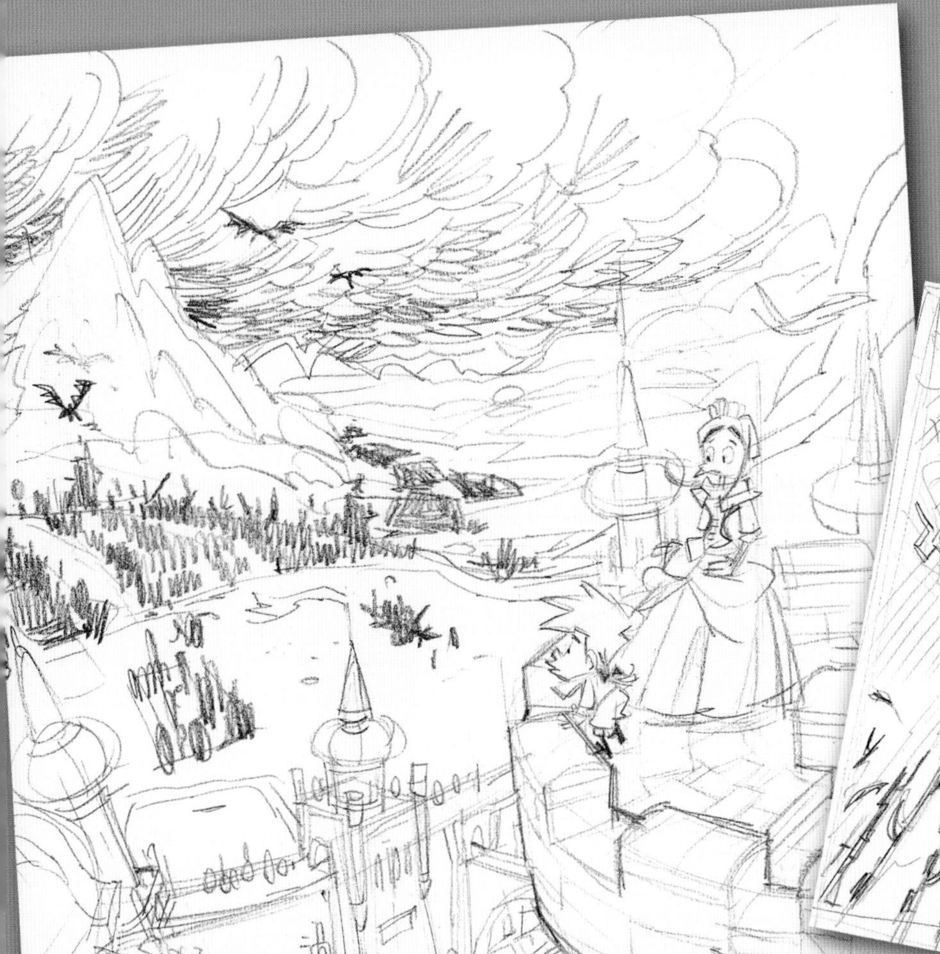

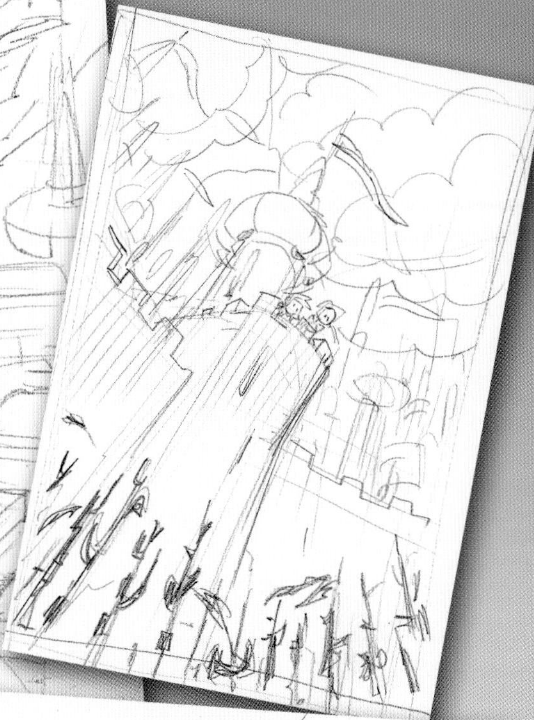

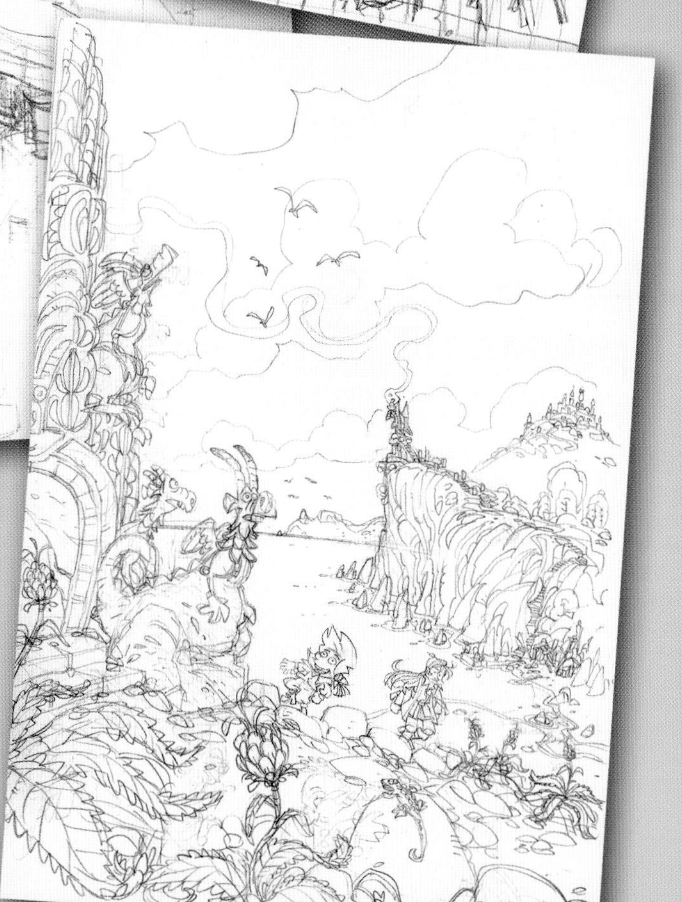

SILVIO CAMBONI'S ORIGINAL DESIGNS
FOR THE COVERS OF VOLUMES 3 & 4
OF THE FRENCH EDITIONS.

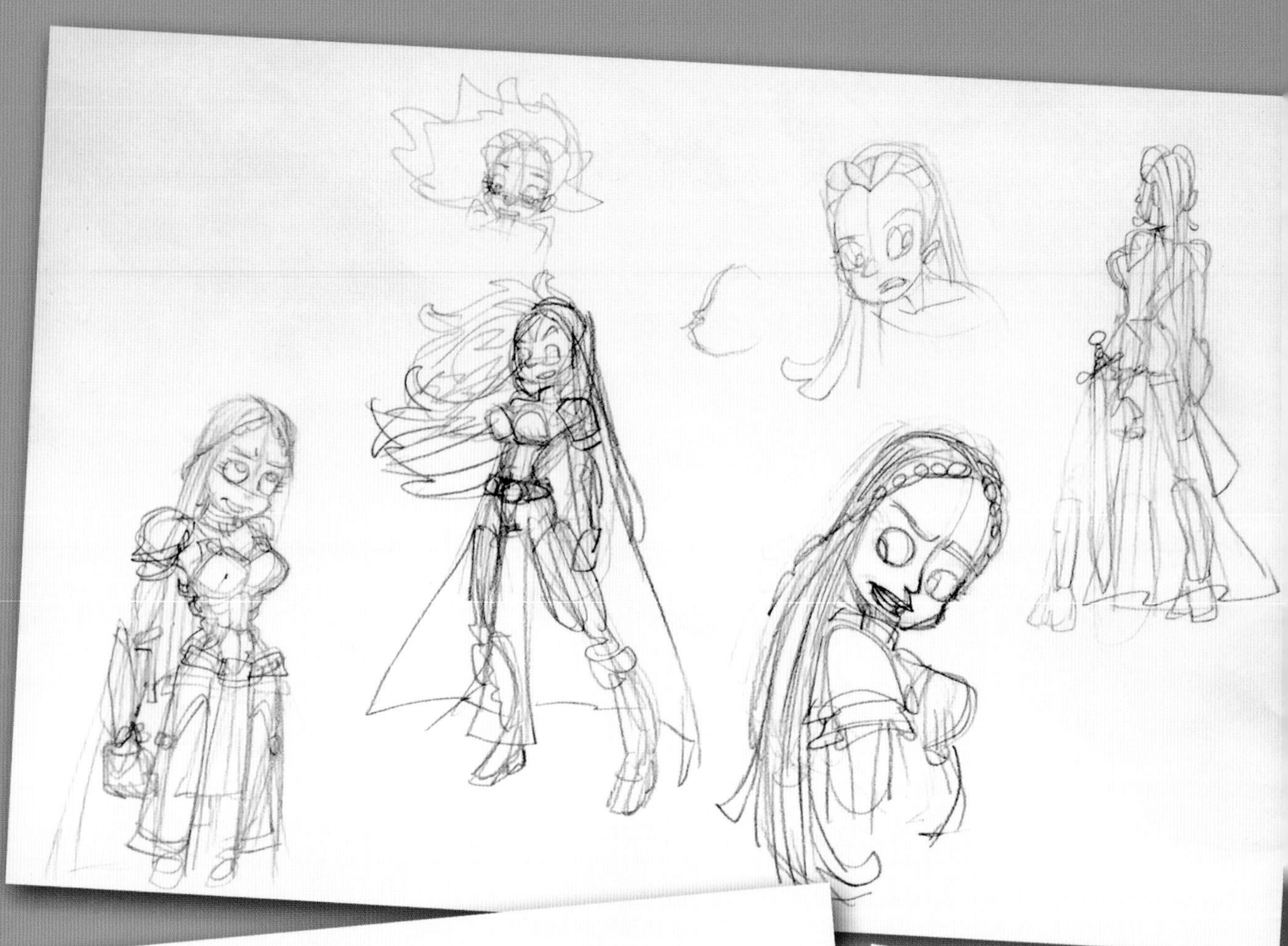

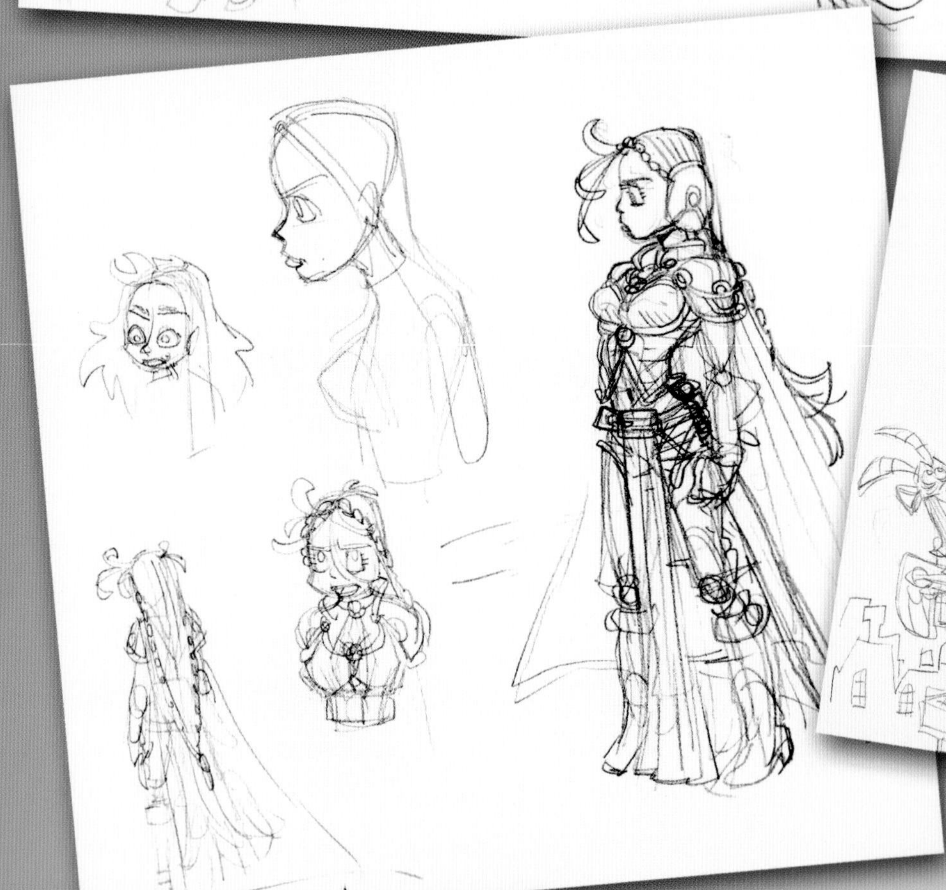

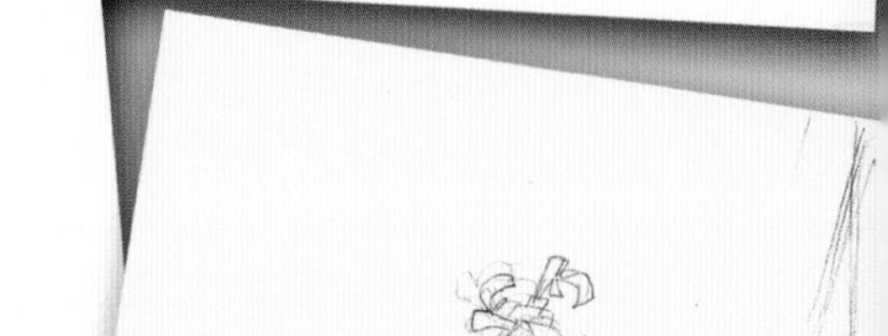

TOP AND LEFT: CHARACTER DESIGNS FOR THE OLDER EDNA.

ABOVE: SKETCH FOR TITLE PAGE.